Jase

Rebel Wayfarers MC
Book #4

MariaLisa deMora

Edited by Hot Tree Editing

Melissa Gill @ MGBookcovers and Designs

Shannon Williams Photography

First Published 2015

ISBN 13: 978-0-9904473-6-8

DEDICATION

You miss 100% of the shots you never take. – Wayne Gretzky

For my Rebels: This is the beginning of anything you want.

Contents

ACKNOWLEDGMENTS

This book feels like the perfect marriage of so many things I love: music, hockey, hot men, justice, and good friends. From the first word written about him in *Mica*, book #1 of the Rebel Wayfarers MC, I believed my favorite comedian/athlete needed his own book. Of course, that was back when Jase was supposed to be book #2. Then Mason would have been book #3, more hockey guys for #4, and finally Daniel's brothers for book #5. Best laid plans, right?

As these stories began to play out—when I finally put them onto the page as words, strung together into constructs of sentences and paragraphs—I knew I needed to develop the world of the Rebels more before bringing Jase into the mix. It is important that readers be able to understand how attractive the life could be for someone like our much-loved hockey guy. How seductive finding a sometimes elusive sense of belonging would become. So, here we are, book #4, and it is the perfect spot for Jase to tell you his story.

A big thank you goes out to both Elliot Weber, the beautiful man you see on the cover, and Shannon Williams, a super talented photographer. From the instant I saw Elliot rocking out onstage as the front guy for *Letters From The Fire*, a brilliant rock band, I knew he was my Jase. Cutely cocky without being at all obnoxious, he's hilarious and smart, totally good looking and immensely cool, and Elliot patiently submitted to the questions from this bizarre and weird lady while still happily signing CDs and posters for fans at the merch table. A couple months later, we found a possible slot in his tour schedule and booked with Shannon in Columbus. Elliot gamely came to the studio for the shoot, which was wedged in between load-in and going onstage for their show in town that night. He even busted out pushups to foster the look I wanted. And me? Well, I could not be happier with the outcome. Did you see the cover? Seriously? Close the book and look at it again...go ahead, I'll wait. Come on! Shannon Williams is a freakin' genius, and the discerning eye behind the lens for that stunning image.

From the beginning of this series, I've found friendships in odd and wonderful places. Musicians, authors, readers, athletes, bouncers, bartenders, bikers, photographers, graphic artists, business people, editors, exotic dancers, military veterans—no matter the walk of life, the most important thing you have in common is your willingness to give of yourselves, and I appreciate every stolen moment you've provided, along with your insight and expertise.

Within the professional hockey world, there have been a number of athletes who provided input on the mindset for Jase and the other players in my books. They helped guide my interpretation of pre- and post-game rituals and the process of training, transferring teams, preparing for games, pranking, dealing with nerves, and losing the game. Not just *a* game, but *the* game, which in many cases has defined their lives from childhood to adulthood. Whether that loss comes from injury, age, upward pressure, downward pressure—it matters to them that it be presented in a realistic way, and I truly hope I've done that. Thank you to Mike, Pavel, Bobby, Marko, Danny, and Lajii for helping me understand. Any mistakes are my own, because they tried extremely hard to educate me!

Thanks to Doc Matt for helping me understand that pure research is never a substitute to interviewing someone who has the hands-on experience of explaining bad news to professional athletes.

My friends and family, thank you. You have been tolerant and supportive, answering questions and providing feedback in an extremely patient way.

My wonderful critique partners—Hollie, Kristen, Kay, LeeAnn, and Brittney—each of you helped make this story better, and I thank you.

To my favorite guys in the world, the men of the Texas, Indiana, and Ohio MC clubs who have encouraged and ridiculed me by equal measures—thank you. Keeps my feet firmly on the ground to be called a stupid bitch at least once a week by someone in the life! For my pet VOL, Ditzy—babe, this is my promise that you and your old man will always be welcome in my home.

The loudest and proudest thank you, as always, is reserved for you, holding this book or reading on your device. *Yeah, you.* Every book you purchase, every post you read, every review or comment you leave, it all matters. Thank you and *enjoy!*

~ML

1 - Before

"Is this Mrs. Moser? Mrs. Martin Moser?" The voice on the phone was unfamiliar and the number unknown, not in her contacts. Understanding there was always the potential for threat through her husband's association with a motorcycle club, DeeDee chose her words with care.

"May I ask who's calling?" was her response, and she waited for the caller to continue speaking.

"This is Officer Hardwick, with the Indiana State Police, badge number nine eight four—"

She interrupted him, realizing something had to be wrong. "Yes, this is DeeDee Moser." *This is bad*, she thought. *Really bad.*

"Mrs. Moser, there's been an accident involving Martin and Lockee Moser. Documentation in the vehicle identifies you as the emergency contact. Martin and Lockee Moser are currently being prepared for transport to Lutheran Hospital. Ma'am, you're going to want to come down as soon as you can. May I arrange a ride for you? Is there someone I can call for you, to meet you there?" Officer Friendly—*no, his name was Hardwick*—sounded firmly helpful, but hadn't given her any real information.

"Are they okay? Are my husband and daughter okay?" She held her breath, her stomach rolling as she waited for his answer.

"Mrs. Moser, you're going to need to get to Lutheran as soon as you can. Would you like me to send a car to pick you up, ma'am? Is there anyone I can call for you?" Still calmly helpful, she found his insistence on getting support in place while avoiding the key question particularly alarming.

Trying to match his composed tone, she said, "No, I'll leave now. I'm about twenty minutes out. Can you tell me what's happened? Please, are they okay?" She shoved her sock feet into her boots then bent over at the waist to lace them up, holding the phone between her shoulder and ear.

"Their vehicle was involved in a two-car accident on I-69, Mrs. Moser." With his answer, she stopped moving, frozen in place as she thought, *Can this be for real?* Over the phone, she heard a mechanical staccato noise grow dramatically in volume then rapidly subside, and realized it was a helicopter. "The medical flight just left the scene; they should be at Lutheran hospital within a few minutes." He was carefully not saying how hurt they were, but to have a LifeFlight pick them up, it had to be bad.

"I'm on my way." She forced herself into motion again and didn't give him a chance to say anything else, hanging up the phone to grab her jacket and snap her 'possibles' bag with her wallet and identification onto her belt. Picking up her helmet, she slid her phone in her jeans pocket and walked out of the house, straddling her bike and starting it less than three minutes after the phone had first rung.

Pulling into the hospital parking lot, she looked around at the number of motorcycles, shocked. *There are bikes everywhere*, she thought, guessing there must be seventy or eighty bikes in the lot. She recognized a few of them, and that only increased her nervousness; this did not feel right. The combination of the call, LifeFlight, and seeing so many motorcycles at the hospital brought the sick feeling from earlier back in full force, making her hands shake.

Quickly parking the bike, she carried her helmet into the hospital with her, following the arrows and signs towards the emergency room. Rounding a corner, she entered a long corridor and halted abruptly, recognizing the man standing at the far end. All of a sudden, there was no air in the space surrounding her; her lungs could find zero oxygen...there was absolutely nothing to breathe. The man was joined by others, and as a group, they moved quickly towards her. Dimly, she heard a clatter, and she glanced down to see her helmet roll to one side, bumping into the wall as it tottered to a stop. Her knees unhinged and she was falling to the floor, when several sets of strong arms wrapped around her, lifting and supporting her.

***

Hoss stepped up beside Bingo just as DeeDee rounded a corner at the other end of the hallway, and he saw her come to a staggering halt, looking up at them with wide, frightened eyes. As Hoss, Bingo, and a dozen other brothers walked towards her, the helmet in her hands dropped to the floor, and she looked down to see it roll across the linoleum, coming to rest against one wall.

He picked up his pace as he saw the color leave her face in a wave. Watching her sway in place, he moved even faster, hearing the shuffling of leather soles behind him receding as he outpaced his brothers. Reaching out, he wrapped his arms around DeeDee tenderly, holding her upright just as Bingo and Gypsy did the same.

He pulled her out of their arms, pressing her into his chest, cupping the back of her head in one large hand. Feeling her go slack, he knew she couldn't hear him, but he still whispered, "I got you, pretty lady. I got you."

2 - Jase

"Yeah, yeah," he said into the phone, "I'll be there, one o'clock. Count me in." Jason Spencer threw the phone onto the couch beside him, retrieving the game controller. He glanced at the clock on the front of the DVR, checking the time. It was only ten; he had a couple hours before he had to get ready to go. Settling his headset back into place, he yelled into the microphone, "Invite me back to the game. I'm back. No longer AFK, so it's time to kick some ass! Woohoooo!"

His phone rang again, and he looked at the clock, realizing he had gotten lost in the video game. It was now several hours past when he was supposed to have been at the gym. Scowling, he threw his head back and shouted, *"Fuck,"* as he tore off the headset. Throwing the controller onto the couch, he reached over to punch the off button on the game console and picked up the phone.

"Jase," he heard when he answered. "Where the hell were you? Today's workout was not optional. What are you up to, man? What excuse is it this time?" The words weren't shouted, but said in a much more ominous, even tone, and he closed his eyes.

"Daniel...Cap'n," he groaned, running a tense hand through his dark hair. "I fucked up. I lost track of time. I'm sorry."

He heard Daniel Rupert, owner and captain of the Chicago Mallets professional ice hockey team, blow out a breath in a long sigh, sounding frustrated and tired. Jase, a key forward of the Mallets, was expected to show up to things like...say...mandatory workouts. You didn't blow Daniel's orders off, not and assume you would remain a team member for long, even if you were good friends. Chuck in the fact their team had just made the final round of playoffs and they needed to stay in top physical form, and in a single day, he tallied up an infraction of epic proportions. Then go ahead and pile on the knowledge Daniel was stressed, because he had recently broken up with his girlfriend, after which she retreated all the way to Texas...and it looked like this blowup could achieve nuclear capacity. *Fuck*.

"Jase, meet me down at the rink. Now. We'll do some drills. You can do two-a-days for the rest of the week in the gym." Daniel's ruling was lenient, and Jase knew it.

"Thanks, Cap'n," he said. "I'm on my way."

Laced up and on the ice within an hour, he was soundly regretting missing the team workout earlier in the day. It would have been far easier than what he was doing now: skating up and down the sheet, chasing pucks on legs that were shaky with exhaustion. Daniel seemed to have endless energy when it came to torturing him, and continued pushing him hard for the next forty-five minutes, smiling grimly every time he heard Jase out of breath.

"Again!" He heard the shout from across the ice and spun around, barely in time to deflect a puck shooting towards his knees.

"Goddammit," he muttered, using the blade of his stick to slap the puck hard towards the net, eschewing accuracy for velocity.

"Again!" came the shout, and he skated backwards into position, crossing over to snag the next puck and snap a shot at the empty goal.

He huffed, "Fuck," and kept his eyes trained on his friend leaning against the short wall in the bench area, watching yet another bucket of pucks make an appearance. They worked without speaking for the next thirty minutes, Jase skating up and down the neutral ice area, staying between the blue lines while setting up to take shot after shot. After completing that bucket, the third of their session, he slowly skated over towards Daniel, unsure of his reception.

"Stretch it out." The order was barked at him, and he dropped to the ice, gently stretching muscles and tendons hard used in their fast-paced drills. As he stretched, there was an annoying twinge of pain in his groin, tender since the last game. Using the blade of his skates for leverage, he got to his knees and pushed over backwards, gingerly stretching out.

As he stretched, he watched Daniel skate around with his stick, gathering all the loose pucks into a pile inside the goal net. Moving the net, the man used his bare hands to pick up the icy pucks, scooping them into the buckets. By the time he had finished stretching, Daniel was headed back. He was carrying two buckets and gently kicking a third across the ice in front of him, the handle of his stick trapped between his body and one bicep.

"Multitasking today?" Jase asked, laughing and reaching for two of the buckets.

Frowning at him, Daniel adjusted his grip on the remaining items, skating past Jase without a word, to clomp onto the rubber mats, angrily stalking down the hallway towards the locker room. Jase followed his lead, placing the buckets inside the equipment room along the way. Settling on the bench in front of his locker, he focused on getting his skates off and stripped the practice jersey over his head, leaving his torso in just his pads and undershirt. He tugged his arm pads down and held them in his hands, trying to decide how best to apologize again and make things right.

Looking up, he saw Daniel was sitting, elbows on knees, staring at the floor between the toes of his skates, not having moved since he sat down. "Cap'n," Jase said and watched him stir, straightening up and putting his hands flat on his thighs. "I fucked up this morning. Won't happen again. I'm down for the two-a-days, man. I'm sorry."

Nodding, Daniel looked through him with a distant gaze, eyes bloodshot and haunted. "Sounds okay, Jase." He paused then sighed heavily. "Mason came and talked to me a few days ago," he said.

"About?" Jase questioned, waiting.

"Said he's going to Texas to bring her back." There could be no question to which 'her' Daniel referred. It had to be Mica Scott, the girlfriend...ex-girlfriend. Davis Mason—now he was harder to classify. He was a local businessman, president of a biker club, a friend of Daniel's, and apparently Mica's best friend. "He told me if I didn't want her, he would be making a play." He shook his head. "I didn't know what to say to him. She's already left me, voted with her feet. So what was his gain in talking to me?"

He turned his head, looking at Jase. "Did you know her ex-boyfriend from her rodeo days hunted her down? Made threats against her? From years ago, he hunted her down. That's why she walked away. At least, that's what Mason said. Why wouldn't she just talk to me? Why did she run like she did? He said she was trying to keep me safe."

He pressed the heels of his hands to his temples. "She fucking broke me, man. I've never been like this over a woman. If she does come back to Chicago, do you think she's going to want to see me? See me like this? At all? Jase, man—I don't know. When I was with her in Houston a couple weeks ago, I thought there might still be something there, but I kept remembering that she *broke me*. I love her, but I can't set myself up for that again."

Jase moved over to sit beside his friend. He didn't exactly know what to say. Daniel was clearly hurting, and that was a position he had never been in. But, Jase knew from hearing other people talk that simply having someone to vent to could help with the pain of a relationship breakup. Not that he knew from personal experience. He had always been more of a love ‘em and leave ‘em kinda guy, but he could try to listen at least.

Daniel reached over his head, grasping the collar and pulling his jersey off roughly, dropping it into his lap where his fingers picked at the seams and folds nervously. “Am I wrong?” He threw the fabric into the locker, bending over to unlace his skates, jerking them off with hard, angry movements.

Jase shook his head. “I dunno, man. Do you think you still want her? Are you still in love with her?”

Daniel froze in place, a startled look on his face as if he hadn’t just been asking the same question. “I am. I feel it. God, I should have told him. I can still tell him. I love her.” Standing, he grabbed his phone from the top shelf of the locker, dialing a number and waiting, sock-covered foot tapping a brisk beat against the mats. “Yeah, is Mason around?” There was a pause, and he said, “Slate, it’s Daniel. Is Mason around?”

Jase frowned. Slate was Mason’s go-to guy. If he was answering the phone, it probably meant Mason was already traveling to get Mica.

Daniel’s face fell, and he responded, “I see. When will they be back?” Yeah, from that exchange, it was clear Mason was probably on his way to Texas.

There was a longer pause, and Daniel closed his eyes. “You sure he’ll want me there, man? I would hate to show up if he’s not expecting me.” A deep sigh, and then he grunted, “Huh. Okay, see you there.” Stabbing the phone with a fingertip, he disconnected the call. “Fuck,” he breathed, “I have a meeting.”

"What's going on?" Jase asked, not at all sure what he heard on the one-sided phone call, but assuming it didn't mean good things for his friend.

"Mason and Mica are already on their way back. I guess he bought a bike in Texas, so they're riding back on that. Slate's putting together a party tomorrow, a kind of 'welcome home' thing for Mica. He wants us all there, all the Mallets. Said Mason left specific instructions for me to 'show the fuck up', and Slate intended to call me today. I have a lunch meeting with sponsors tomorrow, so I guess I'll be heading over to the party after."

He looked gut-punched, and Jase was sorry for the guy. If his girl was gonna be riding on the back of some other dude's bike for hundreds of miles, her long legs wrapped around his hips, titties snuggled up to said dude's back, he thought he might look gut-punched too. "Okay, I'll call Gary and get the rest of the guys notified. You need anything else, Cap'n?" He didn't know what he could do to help, but he at least wanted to offer.

"No." Daniel sighed then said, "Yeah, why don't we go get something to eat?"

He nodded, turning for the showers, happy to be able to offer his friend support, if not understanding.

***

Jase called their friends and teammates Gary Millson and Dierk Hammond, a Mallets defenseman and their rookie goaltender, to meet them at Jackson's. It was a local bar owned by Mason and, for the most part, ran by the Rebel Wayfarers motorcycle club members. It might seem a masochistic selection on Daniel's part, but months ago, the Mallets had made it their unofficial bar for the team. Over the past season, the players had become regulars and logged many hours sitting in booths or at the bar debating game calls and plays with the club members.

Now, though, after suffering through his teammates harassment over him missing the workout this morning, he was having second thoughts about inviting them. Especially since he now had to listen to them dissect a couple of nights not long ago, when he met someone he could have liked, but who hadn't been interested in him like that. At all. Ego-killing disinterest on her part.

"I think I was sitting right here when I saw you with that biker chick," Gary laughed, pointing at Jase. "You threw out all your best moves, man, and she just batted them out of the air. Kinda like our slick-ass goalie here does with pucks. 'Hey, baby, you come here often?' *BAM*. 'Sweetie, you look good in leather, but you'd look better under me.' *WHAM*. 'Darlin', you look a lot like my next girlfriend.' *SLAM*. 'Do you have a jersey? Because I need your name and number.' *SMACK*. Right outta the air."

"It wasn't like that." Jase leaned over and punched him in the shoulder, hard.

"Oww, fucker," Gary complained, rubbing his arm. "You know I'm right. She wasn't having any of even your finest moves. She shut you down, even before puck drop. Close da door."

Dierk chimed in, "No, Gary, you missed it. You weren't here the last night she was in town. There were some dirty dancing moves going down out on the floor. Based on the body language, I would wager she was as much into Jase as he was her. I think our man here just failed to seal the deal."

Daniel opened his mouth, but seemed to reconsider his choice of topics when he saw the slant of Jase's jaw. "Knock it off, guys," he said instead. "Talk to me about the Fort Wayne team. We're in their house Friday for game five. Give me your thoughts."

Hockey dominated the conversation from there forward, and it wasn't until a couple hours later, as they were leaving the bar, that

Daniel reached out and stopped Jase with a hand on his arm. "Jase," he finally asked his question, "what biker chick were they talking about?"

Jase's gaze flicked down to the sidewalk. "DeeDee."

"DeeDee have a last name?" Daniel laughed.

"Yeah, Moser. DeeDee Moser. She's from Fort Wayne and, God, you should see her—she's beautiful, Cap'n. Smart and funny...and hot as hell. And she can dance circles around me." He looked up and knew he had a silly grin on his face, but didn't care.

"If she's a biker chick, doesn't it imply an old man in the club?" Daniel frowned at him, a puzzled look on his face.

Shaking his head, Jase told him, "Not any longer, she's single. She was up here helping out while Mason was..." His voice trailed off.

"While Mason was in Texas with Mica the first time." Daniel blew out a breath. "I get the picture."

"Yeah, anyway, she's fun to talk to. Handed cheek and sass right back to me as good as she got. Fearless, man. She's something else." His grin faded as he remembered how unlikely it was he would ever see her again.

"Okay. I was wondering, 'cause you hadn't mentioned meeting anyone. You need a ride home?" Daniel dug in his pocket for his keys, jingling them impatiently once he had them in hand.

"Nah, I can grab a cab. I'm going to head back inside for a minute. I need to ask Slate about something, and then I'll be heading home." He gave a wave, turning back towards the door of the bar with a laugh. "See you tomorrow. I got two-a-days to deal with, because I'm a jack and my captain is easy."

***

"You really think Road Runner's gonna want to sell his scoot?" Jase used the mug's handle to twist his beer back and forth in the small puddle of condensation on the bar top. "It's not the first time you've told me you found me a ride, man. Not to question you, just—questioning you." He laughed, looking up at Slate.

As Mason's second in command here in Chicago, Slate was in charge of a variety of things, and tonight, one of those things happened to be the bar at Jackson's. Since Jase met DeeDee a few weeks ago, Slate had been helping him look for a bike. He didn't want to admit she was the only reason he had become interested in riding, but since she had her own bike, if...when he saw her again, it would give them something in common—if he had one, that was.

"Yeah, I talked to him about it again a couple nights ago. His custom Bobber will be ready within a couple of weeks and he's looking to turn and burn his old one for the cash. You got what he's asking?" Slate wiped the bar top down, lifting Jase's mug and frowning while he cleaned away the puddle.

"Yeah, yeah. Cash on the barrelhead and all that." He trapped the tip of his tongue between his front teeth and cut his eyes over towards Slate. "Now, I just need to line up a trainer."

"Trainer?" Slate had turned to straighten the bottles on the back bar, and he looked up into the mirror to catch Jase's eyes. "You don't fucking know how to ride a bike? You're going to spend twenty grand on a ride you can't ride? Did you fucking think it was a good idea when you woke up this morning? Goddamn shit, man. My daddy had a saying that would fit you: 'More money than sense'." The thought had him laughing so hard he had to lean on the countertop, the motion setting the bottles in the liquor well shaking and clinking together.

"Shut the fuck up," was all Jase had to answer with, because he knew everything Slate said was true. It was stupid to plan to buy a bike without knowing if you would even be able to use it. But with the motorcycle, he knew it would be a built-in topic with DeeDee the next time he saw her. *Never let it be said I can't plan and plot.* He smiled, thinking about that.

Slate shouted across the bar, "Birdy, get your ass over here." A big man stood from one of the tables, sauntering over. Jase had seen him before; he was a recent addition to the Rebel club, coming to them from Utah or somewhere like that.

Slate indicated Jase with a jerk of his head. "Dude needs a tutor; he's buying Road's Bobber. You got time if I can line up a burner?"

The man grunted and turned to look at Jase. He frowned and cut his gaze back to Slate. "A waxer? We going into the babysitting business next? What the fuck, man?"

"Shut the fuck up," Slate said tersely, his tone hard and flat. "Dude is a friend of Mica's, friend of mine."

Grunting, Birdy looked at him again before he turned back to Slate. He nodded and said, "Lemme know when." Then he turned and walked away without ever speaking to Jase.

Blowing out a breath he hadn't realized he was holding, Jase said, "Dude doesn't seem to like me much. What's a 'waxer'?"

Slate barked a laugh. "Someone who doesn't actually ride, just gets his bike out and parks it in the driveway so he can shine it up."

Jase wrinkled his nose. "Slate, dude. That doesn't even compare to what I'm going to do. I got plans, man. I got riding plans. Gonna ride. Ride my ass off, once I learn how." Slate grinned at him and they both laughed.

3 - DeeDee

She focused, but muted noise was all she could hear; sounds came through as soft, wavering tones, and even loud noises were subdued, seeming to echo from far away. Her knees and breasts were cold. Her skin raised in goose bumps, nipples peaked and hard, but it didn't matter. Having this swaddling insulation against the world was far more important right now. She needed to remain exactly as she was—just like this—in this moment, this instant, for as long as she could. Her chest tightened and hitched, but she forced herself to remain silent and motionless, pushing to a place of peace and calmness. Fifteen slow ticks of the clock later, the demands of her body for breath overcame the longing to remain submerged in the water and she surfaced, gasping for air and wiping her dripping hair back from her forehead with a flattened palm.

Stretching her legs out the length of the bathtub, she wet a washcloth and draped it across her breasts, protecting them from the chill in the room. The water was warm, but Fort Wayne's late spring had been unseasonably cold and difficult to predict. It wasn't worth it to heat the big room just for a bath, knowing tomorrow might bring mild temperatures.

With a shiver, she reached out her foot and, using her toes, turned on the hot water faucet. Dropping her head back to the edge of the tub as the warm water swirled around her legs, she slowly relaxed. *Thank God for huge hot water tanks,* she thought, dipping the cloth back into the water and draping it across her chest again. That was one thing the clubhouse had going for it. Since they were nearly always catering to large groups of residents and visitors, everything in the building that needed to be shared was super-sized.

This bathroom was one of the common areas, and since she had been in here for a while, she expected one of the members to roust her out any minute. There was a party happening tonight in Chicago, and all the men of the club were getting ready to go. She, on the other hand, intended to hole up in her suite with a bottle of wine and a book. Even though she had lived in the Rebel Wayfarers' clubhouse for the past two years, she stopped attending any club functions that weren't absolutely required. After her last trip, it would take a serious demand for the club to get her back to Chicago. That town had become dangerous for her, with some temptations difficult to deny.

Thump. Thump. Thump. "DeeDee, honey, you okay in there?" That was Bingo, the club's Fort Wayne chapter president. She briefly contemplated not responding, but knew it would have him using his master key to open the door. Then he would be flustered, because she was naked, and she didn't have the patience to deal with that right now.

"Yeah, Bingo. I'll be out in a minute. You need in here?" She pitched her voice to carry through the door, leaning up to turn off the water and open the drain. Standing and shivering in the chill, she reached for a towel laid across the nearby rack, roughly using it to rub dripping water from her long hair, and then wrapped it around herself.

"I need to talk to you when you come out. Come find me. Okay, honey?" His voice sounded like he had scrunched up his face, which was his telltale that the topic wouldn't be comfortable. *Shit,* she thought, *what did I do now?*

Taking a deep breath, she forced a brightness she didn't feel into her voice, and responded, "Okie dokie, Bingo. See you in a couple of minutes."

Standing at the mirror, she stared at her obscured silhouette for a long moment before reaching out to swipe at the surface, leaving it streaked. A woman showed in fragmented images in the mirror, and she regarded the small pieces individually, studying them as if they were foreign to her. The reflection on the glass looked as broken as she felt inside.

Dark red hair, made darker than usual from the water. Deep blue eyes, almost violet, they were nearly black when she became emotional. Freckles scattered across her cheeks, demonstrating a foreshadowing of her penchant for burning instead of tanning. She had always been fine-featured, but she knew her face now looked gaunt more than anything else. She reached out one hand and dragged her fingers slowly across the reflection of cheekbone and chin, filled with memories of touching a face that looked remarkably like her own.

Smiling sadly, she drew a heart in the condensation on the mirror with a fingertip, tracing the letters MM on one side and DM on the other. Careful not to cross lines, she drew LM in the center of the heart. The smile slowly fled her face as she stared at the drawn figures for a minute, and then lowered her head, going about the business of drying off and getting dressed. When finished, she cleaned up after herself by wiping down the bathtub and hanging up her towel.

Giving the mirror a final glance, she opened the door and walked out, leaving the heart and its captured initials on the glass. They stood for Martin Moser, her husband and old man; Lockee Moser, her daughter and heart's love; and DeeDee Moser, widow and grieving mother.

***

Presenting herself at Bingo's open office door, she knocked softly on the doorframe, waiting for acknowledgment before entering. He stared solemnly at her for a minute, then sighed heavily and glanced down at his hands, fingers laced together in his lap. "Got a favor to ask, DeeDee," he said, frowning. "You know how you still ride Winger's bike?"

Puzzled, she nodded. "Yeah, I start it every week and take it out for a turn at least once a month to keep everything working. You know...so I can check it out periodically." Winger had been Martin's road name, the only name he answered to after joining his first club and being awarded the moniker. He had risen through the ranks of that original small club to president, the top officer's position. Eventually, he opted to fold that club into the Rebels in order to provide solidarity and stability for the members, the men he called his brothers.

"Okay, here's the thing. I need you to come to Chicago, ride up with the boys. You know about the party for Mica. Mason specifically asked you attend and ride Winger's bike, if you wouldn't mind." He looked up at her and waited, apparently expecting an argument.

She shook her head. "Bingo, I just spent several weeks in Chicago helping out at the bars. I'm ready to stay home for a while, if that's okay." *Shit, shit, shit*, she thought. She did not want to go back up there anytime soon.

"It's actually not a request, hon. You're gonna need to go." He tipped his chin down then looked up, pinning her with his gaze. "I know it'll be hard to see everyone, but it's been going on three years now, DeeDee. You've got to put things behind you and move forward."

"It's only been two years," she whispered, feeling herself beginning to tremble all over, eyes welling with tears.

They stared at each other for a long time, her husband's best friend and his best friend's widow, silently acknowledging the loss each still felt. "I loved them too, Dee. He was my brother." Bingo's voice broke, and she dropped her eyes, cutting the connection between them.

"Okay." She clenched her jaw, viciously digging her fingernails into her palms, slowly managing to regain control. "Will we be staying at the clubhouse?"

"Not you, hon. I wouldn't ask that of you. Winger would've had my balls." He smiled sadly. "Road Runner got the club some rooms at the hotel where he works, and Myron will have the info when we get there. The party is at Mason's house, not the clubhouse, so you'll have to find Myron after we roll in."

"All right. I'll head over to the storage and get the bike, take it to the garage, and change the oil. What time is everyone heading out?" She had already begun to run through a list of things in her head she would need to handle now, since she would be away for several days. "I'll let Melanie know. She'll be okay staying in the suite here, right? Like before?"

She and Winger had always wanted a big family, and after trying for years with heartbreaking results, they finally had been blessed with Lockee, their daughter. Melanie Davidson had met Lockee in kindergarten, and the two girls had fallen quickly into friendship. Over the years, the girl had spent so much time at their house she had practically grown up in the Moser household. Her home life hadn't been easy, but she managed to turn out a gentle soul and had found a special place in both Winger and DeeDee's hearts. Melanie might not be her daughter by birth, but it was only a technicality as far as she was concerned. Having the girl around made life better, and after coming through their tragedy together, that was truer today than ever before.

"Of course, hon," he reassured her. "It's her suite, and this is her family. Nothing will happen to Melanie here. We got her, DeeDee."

Nodding, she turned to leave, pulling her phone from her jeans pocket and punching in numbers. The call went unanswered, and she left a message. “Mel, baby girl, I’m going on the run with the boys this weekend up to Chicago. Not sure when I’ll be back, but Bingo knows you’re staying here. Be good, girl. The club will watch out for you. Love you.”

Winger and Lockee had been killed more than two years ago in a car accident. Distracted by an incoming text, an inexperienced driver’s careless swerve had forced their truck off the road where it flipped end-over-end multiple times. None had survived extraction from the mangled vehicles, and DeeDee had gotten the call.

Like an extended family, the club had rallied around her, offering her love and care in a loss they all shared. Someone had been with her constantly as she moved in shock through those first days following the accident. Even though she had been part of a club for more than two-thirds of her life and knew how close the men all were, the outpouring of support and love had still stunned her. There had been more than three hundred members riding in the procession from the church to the cemetery, and because Winger was ex-military, there was another whole group of Patriot Riders. Melanie had been beside her every step of the way, at times physically holding her up when overwhelming grief would crash over her.

The club knew she would have to sell their small house, so without even being asked, they had shown up a week later with boxes and a truck and moved her into a suite in the clubhouse. It had two bedrooms with a sitting room and half-bath, and they handed her the keys with no questions asked. She lived here since then, rent free, and the club placed no demands on her, but she voluntarily helped by keeping the clubhouse tidy, trying to make sure things ran smoothly.

Even with that, her status within the club felt tenuous, because with Winger gone, she wasn’t an old lady anymore, the typical place granted women. Winger had been a well-respected member, so she used the men’s memories of him, as well as any other advantage she had, to keep herself and Melanie housed, clothed, and safe.

That included doing things with the club. Like this weekend, when she would be going to a party she didn't want to attend, just because her presence had been requested. Davis Mason was the national president for the Rebels, and she respected him, was proud of the man he had grown into. With his role in the club, when he said jump, you didn't ask how high; you just hopped like crazy hoping you would hit the mark...even if you had known him all his life. So now, since he asked for her personally, she would by God show, even if it pained her to do so.

Mason had been in Texas recently and was riding back now with Mica Scott, a young woman not much older than Melanie. Mica had a unique status in the club. In a brotherhood where women were denied membership, she was named Princess. The ins-and-outs of the title and role were still muddy to DeeDee, but it sounded like she was granted the club's protection without any demands or strings. *Kind of like how things are with me right now*, she mused, shaking her head.

She heard rumors Mason was somewhat stuck on the woman, so who knew how long the gal's independent status would last. With men like Mason, once they set their sights on something, it was seldom they failed to acquire it. There were damned few exceptions, not even if that something happened to be a woman.

In the suite, she paused as she was packing her small bag, clothes clasped loosely in her hand. *I wonder if Jase will be there*, she pondered. Shaking her head and smiling, she told herself aloud, "Doesn't matter, old lady. He was fun to play with and pretty to look at, but you should not go there. Just decide now to set temptation aside."

Jase Spencer was a young hockey player who had pretended interest in her. Because he was a nice guy who noticed she was lonely, he set out to entertain her for a couple of evenings. She hadn't seen or heard from him since returning home, but to be fair, she hadn't left him her number and certainly hadn't expected anything. Snorting in amusement at the idea of her with Jase, she finished packing.

Downstairs in the main room of the clubhouse, she looked at the men scattered around the room, her gaze glancing across the scantily-dressed women seated with many of them. She sighed as she sized-up her options for a ride to the storage unit where she kept the bike parked. One of the visiting Chicago members waved her over, and wrapping an arm tenderly around her shoulders, greeted her with a squeeze. He had his long, white hair tied back with a bandana and nuzzled the side of her head with one of his most striking features, a dark, full mustache. "Tugboat," she greeted him fondly, sliding an arm underneath his leather cut to return his hug.

"DeeDee. You are looking lovely as ever, my lady. What a beauty." He smiled at her, bringing his hand up to softly pat her face. "You take my breath away."

"Goofball," she joked. "Hey, Mason wants me in Chicago on Winger's bike. Can you give me a lift over to storage?"

"You betcha, pretty lady. I could be ready now if you are, or you can let me know when. I place myself at your service. Anything you need." He smiled and winked, flirting as natural to him as breathing, but as always, she knew he didn't mean anything by it. He was a good-looking man and well respected in the club. No way would he be interested in her when he could have any young thing he wanted.

"Now is good. If that works for you." She lifted her bag to show him. "I'm all packed and ready. I want to get the bike to the shop and check it out quick. That way I can be back here in time to pull out with you guys. I don't want to ride up there on my own."

He frowned and looked at her through squinted eyes. "I'll follow you to the shop and stay until you're ready to come back. That way you're never alone, pretty lady." Reaching out, he took her bag from her hand. "Let me."

***

Hoss watched DeeDee leave the clubhouse with Tugboat, jealousy slicing through him. He saw the indecision on her face as she walked down the stairs and thought for a minute she was coming to him, but then Tug had waved her over. He knew Tug would be headed back to Chicago with them today, and wondered if this exit was him leaving early. But why would he take DeeDee with him?

Picking up his beer, he walked to the open door of Bingo's office behind the bar. The Fort Wayne chapter was structured differently than others, as they only had a few officers. The main ones were President, which was Bingo; their Treasurer, Torres, who was also manager at Down Range, one of the club's businesses; Road Captain, a position currently filled by PBJ; and Gunny, an ex-Marine, was Sargent-at-Arms. No Veep, no Lieutenant. That meant there wasn't anyone to run interference for Bingo when members wanted to see him, which worked in Hoss' favor right now.

Knocking as he walked in, he pulled one of the metal chairs back from the desk and sat, staring at Bingo steadily. "Where's DeeDee going with Tug?" Might as well get the question out there. He hadn't made any secret about his interest in the woman over the past year or so, which would make it more of an issue if Tug were making a play for her.

Bingo stared back at him for a minute, then said, "He's probably taking her over to get Winger's bike. Mason wants her at the party."

"Why would he want that? She hasn't been going to barbecues or anything with the club. She might live in our house, but she hides from club business. Why force her into something like this?" Hoss held up his hand. "Not that I'm questioning Mason. But why DeeDee?"

"Something to do with Mica, no doubt." Bingo shrugged. "Why you askin', brother?"

"Did you send her to Tug?" Bingo shook his head and Hoss nodded. "Okay then. Do you know if he's makin' a play?"

"Doubtful," Bingo laughed. "He's hoping she gets busy with that hockey guy she flirted with last time she was in Chicago. Said if he got a chance, he was going to spin her Spencer's way."

"What the fuck?" Hoss growled. "Jase Spencer? You want a citizen for Winger's old lady?"

"She ain't Winger's old lady anymore." He shrugged. "I want her happy. She's holding so tight onto what was that she ain't looking for what could be. Woman's fucking mired in the past, and we ain't done her any favors by keeping her close."

"Keeping her close helps keep her safe, brother." Hoss settled back into the chair. "And what could be is sitting right here in the fucking room. You and Tug both know I've been biding my time, letting her grieve and move past all that shit. I want her in my bed...want to keep her in the club. Hell, I've made a study of DeeDee; I can tell you anything you want to know about that woman."

"Anything except what she wants for herself, I wager." Bingo leaned back, propping his heels on the edge of the desk. "If you know that, then you know more than she does."

"I know what I want—"

Bingo interrupted him, "You want to fuck her. She needs more than that. She needs to be someone's sweetheart, needs a real bed in a real house, and needs someone who can accept Melanie as she is. What she doesn't need is a brother as mired in the past as she is, making a play because he's tired of being alone."

"Fuck you," Hoss said, folding his arms across his chest. "It isn't like that, Bingo."

"Tell me what it is, then. Because from where I sit, having someone like Jase Spencer sweep in and cover her shit is a good thing." Bingo frowned at him. “She needs someone who’ll focus on her, someone who sees her sweet for what it is, not what it could be for the club.”

“So you’d be okay letting her go?” Hoss was confused. He had come in here expecting to get a green light, and now it sounded like Bingo would back the citizen’s play before his.

“If it’s what is best for her, hell yeah, I’m okay with that. I want to see her back to herself. Want to see her looking with bright eyes towards the future. I want to write love poems about her life, and I want that life to be amazing. I loved Winger like a brother, independent of the club. How can I want anything less for his widow?” Bingo stood and stretched. “You think about what you want, and why, man. Ride beside her, keep an eye on her, and keep her covered. But while you do that, you consider what’s best for her.”

***

At the storage yard, Tug waited astraddle of his bike while she pushed Winger’s out of the bay, gliding it to a stop and putting down the kickstand. Walking back, she tugged hard on the overhead door, struggling to close and lock it. She turned to get on the bike and saw Tug looking at her with an odd expression on his face.

“What?” she asked, swinging her leg over the seat, tiptoeing up towards the tank to where she had enough leverage to balance the big bike. Sitting for a minute while she pulled on her helmet, he shrugged and silently made a motion for her to precede him out of the lot.

At the garage, she idled the bike into an empty service bay, heeling the kickstand down and settling it before she dismounted. She was taking off her helmet when she heard a sharp whistle and turned to see several men walking towards Tug as he sauntered in from outside where he parked. “Check out Winger’s bike, change the oil, and make sure everything’s right for a Chicago run. Mine’s outside; key is in it. Just top it off, check it out.” He was speaking to one of the men in the garage who gave him a chin lift and then looked up at DeeDee with a smile and an easy nod.

"No." She shook her head. "It's okay, Tug. I got it. I always do this myself. I don't mind, and I hate to be a bother." She moved towards the tool cabinets, pulling out her keys. "I still have Winger's wrench key, so I don't even have to bug anyone." Before she could reach her destination, however, a pair of firm hands gripped her elbows, pulling her to a stop.

"Let the boys do this for you, Dee. We all know how you hate to accept help, don't want to admit when you need it...but let them do this for you." Tug's voice was near her ear. The low tone coupled with the brush of his mustache against her neck made her shiver, and he chuckled at her reaction. "Come sit with me a minute, keep an old man company." He used a wheedling tone and she couldn't help smiling up at him.

"Old man, ha. More like in your prime, mister." Unsure, she hesitated, watching as the member looked at her then back at him, waiting for a decision. "Okay, Tugboat." Turning, she waved at the other members clustered around Winger's bike, quietly calling, "Guys, thank you." She received brief waves and a couple of chin lifts in response and turned to walk with Tug towards the office area.

"You want some coffee or tea?" he asked and looked at her closer. "Water, maybe?"

"Water's good, but I can get it, Tug." She demonstrated by opening the refrigerator and pulling out two bottles, holding one out to him.

They sat in companionable silence for a few minutes, watching out the window as Winger's bike was serviced, one of the men wheeling Tug's bike into the shop to begin the same process with it. She lifted the cold bottle of water to her lips, nearly spitting out the drink she had just taken when Tug startled her by asking, "You get laid in Chicago, woman?"

"No," she laughed. "Hell no." She shook her head.

"Why not? Jase was into you." Tug said this flatly, as if he was commenting on the chance of cloud cover for the day.

"Because I'm Winger's old lady," she retorted with a short laugh, twisting the top back onto the bottle with some force.

"Nuh-uh," he spoke gently, but the words hurt nonetheless. "Winger's dead. So, why didn't you sleep with Spencer?"

She turned, drawing on her fifty-two years of experience to form a look of disdain and contempt so withering two of the men in the garage stepped backwards when they glanced through the window and caught sight of her face. "I didn't sleep with him because I am Winger's old lady," she repeated, enunciating clearly.

"Bullshit," he shot back, tilting his water up and draining the bottle. "What are you afraid of, woman?"

"I'm not scared of anything," she told him, her anger still bubbling over his denial of how she felt, but she had a sharp pull of fear too. It was as if he were trying to strip her of the limited status she still had within the club, and she couldn't let that happen. Without them, she would lose the last pieces of Winger she still had. *I can't let it happen.* "I didn't want to fuck him," she said crudely.

"Bullshit again," he said. "I saw you dancing with him in Jackson's, and you were as into him as he was you. What happened to derail that love train?"

"I just—couldn't. It's disrespectful; at least, it feels that way." She dipped her chin, looking down at the bottle in her hands. "Plus, he's just a kid. A really pretty kid, but just a kid. Jase would be way more appropriate for Melanie than me."

"And there it is," Tug scowled. "I knew we'd get to the meat of the matter sooner or later. Who cares about the difference in age? What is it, anyway? A dozen years?"

"Twenty-two years," she whispered, licking her lips and repeating it even more softly. "Twenty-two."

"So? Who gives a fuck? I'm what, twelve years older than you? If I went after a pretty young thing of forty-two, would you say the age difference was too much?" He wiggled his eyebrows at her, pulling a lecherous face and making her laugh.

"Of course not. But you're...that's diff-er-ent," she stuttered over the last word, already anticipating his argument.

"No, it's not. It isn't different. Too much is too much, no matter if it's two or twenty-two—it all depends on the people involved. Honey, you know in this case it's *not* too much. Not for either of us. And it wouldn't be for any man out there in the shop, if you so desired. Hell, about any Rebel member, regardless of age, would be honored if you smiled their way. Whether you realize it or not, you're only alone because you want to be." He motioned to the window as he barked out a laugh. "So, you're saying it'd be okay for me, but not for you? I think you're sexist, which surprises me for an enlightened woman such as yourself. Why are you thinking like that, Dee? Do you care so much what people say? What they think?" He watched her steadily, waiting for her response.

"Don't do that. It's different for men in the club and you know it," she shot back.

"Nope. I'm not buying it. You're sexist. And that's a bullshit reason to deny yourself something sweet you want. It would be good for you. And darlin', Spencer's not a kid; he's a fully-grown man who has a pretty good idea of his own mind. He's also a decent guy, one of Daniel's best friends. You could do worse, DeeDee. Hell, you'd do worse by not doing him." He sighed. "Beautiful lady, you've mourned a long time. Let yourself have some good again. Take a chance on the sweet."

A rap at the office door broke the tension holding her in place and she stood, walking towards the shop. “I’m not having this conversation, Tug.” She threw the last over her shoulder and was shocked when he was right behind her, pulling her to a stop, hands again on her elbows. His mustache brushed against the side of her neck like before, the breath of his whisper bringing goose bumps to her skin, pebbling her nipples into hard peaks she knew showed clearly through her lightweight clothing.

“You need to move on, beautiful. Your husband died, but do you think he wanted you to die with him?” His question was harsh, but his tone was so soft and tender she nearly couldn’t respond. “Answer me, woman,” he pressed, and she shook her head. She listened for a moment to the song playing on the shop’s sound system, her mouth tightening as she heard the plaintive tones of The Weepies singing *Love Doesn’t Last Too Long*.

“Damn straight he wouldn’t have wanted you dying there on the side of the road with him.” Tug’s cheek rubbed her neck and he kissed the side of her head. The warmth of him at her back was so good. “That means he would want you to live. So you fucking honor him by living. That means loving yourself enough to live, not wasting away, pretty lady. It means letting yourself be loved.”

His hands moved, sliding up her arms, the backs of his fingers brushing against the outer curve of her breasts and her breath stuttered in her chest. *God*. She hadn’t been touched in so long. “Be open to love,” he whispered, slipping his hands back down slowly, leisurely…unknowingly caressing her. Her chin tipped up and she gasped softly, shivering. “That’s all I’m asking, Dee. Be open to love.”

He stepped back, releasing her, and she drew a deep breath. Without turning around, she nodded once and walked towards the bike.

***

Five hours later, their group of nearly sixty bikes pulled into the alley separating Mason's and Mica's homes. DeeDee followed the lead of the rider in front of her, backing into the first available parking space. She got the kickstand down just in time; her legs were threatening to collapse on her as she struggled to balance the top-heavy bike. She sat for a moment, black leather boots resting on the foot pegs as she straddled the bike. Smiling, she fell into memories about this bike, Winger's prize possession, one made specifically for him by Bear, the genius behind the club's custom motorcycle business.

Winger had been one of the first members to receive one of Bear's bikes after the Rebels and Baugh brothers had partnered together. He had been puffed-up, proud to show it off and explain the modifications, usually stroking the paint job on the tank while he did so. She reached down and patted the tank, smiling. Same as the patch sewn onto the back of the leather cut he had worn everywhere, the tank's paint job incorporated the club's emblem. The difference was here it was imposed on top of a background of stars and constellations, telling everyone the club was his world. There were tiny letters running around the edges of the painted patch replica. She traced Lockee's and her names, along with the names of the men Winger had counted as his most trusted brothers, like Bingo and Tugboat.

She remembered how excited he was to ride it home from Chicago. Melanie rode with him, while Lockee was pillion behind Bear. The girls had talked about that trip for months. Lockee had been thrilled her dad had trusted someone enough to let her ride with them, and speechless it was an older man as good-looking as Bear. DeeDee laughed quietly to herself. She had accidentally seen him in all his naked glory one morning, much to Winger's chagrin. He had named the man that day, saying he was as big as a bear, and the club name had stuck.

Still trembling from the strain of the long ride and wanting to rest another few minutes, she pulled her legs up, crossing them to balance on top of the seat. She sat, looking out at the chaos that was a biker party in near-full swing. Frowning at the many faces she didn't recognize, there were suits in the crowd, along with a lot of citizens. To compound things further, she saw there were patches she didn't know, indicating multiple clubs were present. *Oh, hell*, she thought in a rising panic, *I didn't even bring my 'Property of' rag.*

In her rush to leave, she had forgotten her leather vest at home with the patch and rocker that said 'Property of Winger'. Usually, she would wear it at all club functions, but since she hadn't been going to any events or worn the vest in so long, it slipped her mind when she was packing. The oversight now meant she would be dependent on the Rebel members who knew her to keep her safe, since she wouldn't be wearing any outward declaration of her affiliation. *Shit, shit, shit.*

She saw there were a few women already here, which made her feel a little better, but she might very well just stay on this bike all night. Few men would approach her here, assuming she would be sitting on her old man's bike. *Which I am*, she thought sadly.

She jumped, nearly falling off the motorcycle, when a large, warm hand settled at the small of her back. "Pretty lady," she heard and turned to find Tug standing beside her. "Time to rise and shine, beautiful." He smiled at her, warmth in his eyes and love evident on his face, his hand urging her to get off the bike, steadying her as she stood. "I've got you, DeeDee. Ain't nobody gonna mess with you."

He reached up, taking her chin in hand and turning her face so she could see the circle of men surrounding them. "We've all got you, pretty lady. Ain't nobody gonna bother you unless you welcome that botheration." She was surrounded by men dressed in jeans and patch-covered black leather, and plain henleys or tees with crude sayings under their cuts. She saw bearded faces and ones that were clean shaven, hands covered in silver rings or fingerless gloves. On each of the faces turned towards her, she also saw the same look of love that Tug wore, lips curling up at the corners, eyes crinkling, cheeks creasing in good-natured smiles. For her. They were all here...for her.

She smiled, overwhelmed with emotion, and he must have recognized this, because he leaned in, gently kissing her cheek, that damn mustache tickling her skin and making her laugh a little. Music played nearby, and she barely had time to recognize Sugarland's *Already Gone* before Tug gave her a little push then grabbed her hand, pulling and twirling her back in towards him, holding and swaying with her for a moment.

Before she knew what was happening, he had passed her hand off to another member, who whirled her around a time or two then gave her willingly to someone else. She knew all these men, trusted each of them with her life, and so now, she confidently gave herself over to their dance. Taking as much as they were prepared to give, she moved from hand to hand around and across the circle with a smile, spinning from embrace to embrace. She ended the dance laughing, bent backwards into a deep dip in Bingo's arms. He dropped his head, gently kissing the tip of her nose as he echoed what Tug had said to her. "We got you."

4 - Together

It would be another couple of hours before Mason and Mica would pull in, and even though a lot of people had already shown up, she knew there were still more to come. While they all waited for the guest of honor to arrive, everyone milled around, getting drinks from the kegs and food from the grill, using the time to catch up and visit with old friends. She saw Kathy, one of the girls who hung around the Chicago clubhouse, and walked over to chat.

Kathy was here with Digger, one of the Chicago Rebels, and it was cute the way the girl blushed when she talked about him. DeeDee's throat tightened at the now-familiar sense of loss that swept over her. It happened every time she encountered a facet of life Lockee would never be able to experience. Lockee never had a boyfriend. Not like this. Not like Kathy, sweetly coloring at Digger's name, her eyes and mouth softening into a loving expression.

Her daughter had frequently dated, but Winger was hard on the boys. Too hard, and few of them came back for a second round of his brand of inquisition. Kathy's sweet smile was good to see, and when her tall, fit biker walked up, wrapping his arms around her, she leaned into him trustingly, tipping her lips up for a kiss. He acknowledged DeeDee with a smile and a wink, ducking his head shyly to nuzzle into Kathy's hair.

Strolling away from the young couple, she spotted another Chicago member nearby at the grill and walked over to give the big man a hug. "Hey, Road Runner," she said, tiptoeing up to kiss the cheek of one of her favorites. "How're you doing?"

He held her with one arm, studiously attending to the ribs on the grill with the other before pulling the lid closed and turning to her. His attention to the food didn't surprise her; he was a Cordon Bleu-trained chef, working in the five-star restaurant at the hotel where she would be spending the next couple of nights. She laughed aloud when he wrapped both arms around her, picking her up off the ground in a rambunctious hug.

"Damn woman, you feel good. Love you, girl," he said as he sat her back on her feet and then his brows drew down into a scowl. "Except you're skin and fucking bones. That just isn't acceptable. Damn it, am I gonna have to move to the Fort to feed you?"

She shook her head and smiled, deftly sidestepping his comment about her appearance. It was one she was getting tired of hearing. "It's good to see you, big guy. Thanks for getting the rooms. I was glad to hear I wouldn't be staying at the clubhouse tonight."

"Aww, hell naw," he said. "No way in hell you need to be there. You know how crazy things can get." He gave a jerk of his head, saying, "Myron has the info. He was up on Mica's back porch last time I saw him." She smiled, reaching up to cup his face in her palm, tiptoeing again to kiss him goodbye on the cheek.

She made her way slowly across the backyard, frequently stopping to greet friends, as was her nature, more often with kisses and hugs than handshakes. Smiling, she eventually mounted the steps to the porch, finding Tug standing there with Slate and Myron. Pulling Slate into a hard hug, she nestled her face into his chest for a minute, feeling his laughter as a vibration through her body. She was glad to see the man here; he always made her feel safe. He had been patched into the Chicago chapter for more than a decade and had turned into one of her favorite members.

Reaching out, she tousled Myron's hair, asking with laughter in her voice, "Hey, Myron. Did GeeMa get you set-up yet? I heard she keeps finding beautiful girls for you back in Wyoming." It was a running joke that Slate's grandmother liked Myron, the club's Treasurer, but she wanted him to settle down. And by 'settle down', she meant in her hometown out west with a young woman of whom she approved, so whether at church or bingo, she was always on the lookout for potential matches.

He moved his head out from under her hand, but grinned as he reached into his back pocket, pulling out two room keys. Ignoring her question, he told her, "You're in a nice suite at The Admiral, DeeDee. Room seven-twelve. I want you to order room service at least twice a day while you're here. Don't go skimping, okay? Road Runner said he expects to see you for his lunch shift, but make sure you eat, sweetie. You're too thin. There's bike parking in the garage near the elevator, and they've got good security, so you shouldn't have to worry about anything."

She accepted the keys from him with a raised eyebrow. "Okay, thanks. But, two keys?"

He shrugged. "It's what they gave me. We have a few more rooms reserved, but they're scattered on different floors, so you won't be close to anyone you'll know. If you have any trouble, call someone. You have my number. Be sure to call me if you need me, okay?"

Nodding, she slipped an arm around his waist, hugging him tight and dropping a kiss on his cheek. "Okie dokie. Thanks."

Tug reached out, pulling on the waistband of her chaps, reminding her she hadn't yet taken time to remove her leathers. Stepping backwards into his hold, she relaxed, leaning into him. "You're sure hugging and kissing on a whole lot of men, DeeDee," he murmured.

"They're my boys," she laughed with a broad smile. "I love my boys; they are all such nice guys."

Cryptically, he said, "I don't think he likes it much. And I know for sure he doesn't like this." He patted her hip, sliding his hand around and possessively spreading his palm across her stomach for a moment. She tensed. His fingers were warm and the pressure comfortable, nearly stretching down far enough to reach...

With his other hand, he reached up, taking her chin with his fingers as he had earlier and directed her gaze to the crowd near Mason's garage, where a group of Daniel's friends had gathered around his two brothers. Her throat closed, trapping her breath in her chest for a moment as her eyes met smoldering, dark brown ones. Jase was staring across the crowd at her.

He looked furious; she wasn't sure why for a moment until Tug stepped back, dropping his arms from around her. The strain on Jase's face eased slightly and he padded across the space between them, dodging around individuals and couples without seeming to notice them, eyes only for her.

"There you go," she distantly heard Tug say and felt a little push on her ass, absently reaching back to swat the hand away. She couldn't take her eyes off Jase. Something about the look on his face held her captive.

There was a short laugh and then strong hands picked her up by the waist, lifting her over the railing and setting her on the ground next to the porch, bypassing the stairs. Jase didn't stop his advance until he was close enough to reach out and cup her face in his large, callused hands, leaning in without hesitation to cover her mouth softly with his own.

The noises around them fell away; it seemed as if she couldn't hear anything except her own pounding heartbeat and the sound his fingertips made when he stroked her jawline, rasping against her skin. She gave herself into the kiss entirely, reveling in the sensations of his lips against hers, the roughness of his short beard against her skin. He glided his tongue across her bottom lip and then dipped it into her mouth to tangle with her own, the unabashed sensuality of the kiss stealing her breath.

Too soon, his lips drew away, the heat of his hands still blazing against her cheeks. When DeeDee's eyes slowly opened, she saw he had a look on his face difficult to categorize, but if pressed, she might have said it was satisfaction. When she was in town previously, they had never gone past chaste kisses on the cheek, or a friendly arm draped around shoulders or waist. They certainly never kissed like this, with the toe-curling passion she just experienced. Short of breath, she smiled uncertainly up at him, her lips trembling. He was so handsome, with deep brown soulful eyes, and sensuous lips framed with a soft beard.

"Hey, DeeDee," he said, still looking down at her, thumbs stroking across her cheekbones. His eyes roamed from her eyes to her lips, down to her breasts and back to her lips, his tongue darting out to tap against his top one, finally smiling as she gasped. "I missed you."

He looked up, over her head, and gave a chin lift. "Tug." Tipping his face to the side slightly, he said, "Slate."

She heard Tug call her name and turned as he said, "I got you, pretty lady. You need me, let me know. I got you." Nodding, she stumbled when Jase tugged on her hand, pulling her towards him. Putting her hands on his chest to halt her fall, she drew up hard at the look that crossed his face when she touched him. Hunger and desire warred there, raw and shocking.

He closed his eyes and drew in a deep breath, obviously composing himself before he opened them to stare at her again. "Let's walk," he suggested, pulling her hand up and kissing across the backs of her knuckles.

"Okay," she agreed easily, swinging into place beside him, comfortably wrapping one arm around his waist as he laid his across her shoulders. She would often walk with Winger like this, and out of habit, she tucked her fingers into his back pocket.

As they moved into the crowd, she suddenly became conscious of eyes on them. Everywhere she looked, there were Rebel members watching, tracking their progress. Abruptly uncomfortable, she sidestepped a little, dislodging his arm from her shoulders and dropping hers from his waist as she moved away. Glancing backwards, she saw two Rebels were walking not five feet behind, pacing them stride-for-stride. *Oh, God,* she thought frantically, wondering, *what if they think I'm disrespectful to Winger's memory? What will they do?*

Jase reached out and reclaimed her hand, using it to pull her closer to his side. "What's wrong, DeeDee?" He asked her the question with a quizzical tilt of his head, looking sweet and charming. She smiled and shook her head, opening her mouth to answer him when she heard her name from the side.

"DeeDee, we got you, babe. You want this botheration?" This came from Hoss, one of her dancing partners from earlier in the evening. She was sure he had used Tug's words intentionally, the repetition reminding her of the previous conversation.

She turned to face him, and lifting her chin with confidence she didn't feel, she said, "It's all good, thanks." He and the Chicago Rebel standing with him nodded, moving another few feet away, but keeping a close watch on her in spite of her reassurances.

Jase set his back to a tree and pulled her closer, nestling her into his chest, her back to his front. He rested his chin on her shoulder, tilting his head to look back and forth between the several groups of Rebel members obviously keeping an eye on them both.

"Something I need to know, DeeDee?" His tone was questioning, but not concerned or afraid, and she snorted softly. If their roles were reversed and she had this many big, powerfully built bikers staring daggers at her, she would be petrified.

Taking a deep breath, she blew it out slowly, trying to choose her words carefully, but distracted by an acute awareness of his arms crossed over her chest, his hands curving around her sides. "No, nothing to worry about, Jase. They're just overprotective tonight. We have a bunch of members from different chapters here, plus a lot of other clubs as well. I forgot my rag at home, so they're all just making sure I'm safe."

As soon as the words were out of her mouth, she could have chewed her tongue bloody for speaking so freely. Now she knew she would have to turn away his questions about what a rag was, and why she might not be safe, and what the different clubs had to do with each other. All of which would be hard to explain without going into a lot of detail. She could claim club business, and that generic umbrella might deflect his inquiries. After all, he likely would never realize women were exempt from even knowing what was going on most of the time.

He surprised her, however, nodding slowly, rubbing his cheek against hers. Nuzzling the side of her neck, he dropped a series of hard, sucking kisses on the column of her throat, running his nose up behind her ear and earning a giggle from her. "There," he said proudly, pulling back to look at her neck. "Now everyone will know you're taken." He nuzzled her ear again, adding, "By me."

Oh, my God, did he just give me hickeys? She hadn't had a hickey since she was in her mid-twenties, and even back then, it was only funny for about five minutes. This was going to piss her off. He didn't miss the tension that flooded her body and snickered at the reaction. She twisted her head to look up at him and saw wry humor in his face. "No, I didn't," was all he said before laughing again. "But I had you worried and made you forget about the attentive audience for a half a minute."

"Jase," she scolded, laughing. She leaned her head against his shoulder, reveling in the feel of the warm body behind her and the strength of the arms wrapped around her. It was so good to be held again. She hadn't realized how much she missed this simple intimacy and interaction.

***

Hoss watched her all afternoon. He saw the fear that flashed across DeeDee's face as Tug forced her to abandon the island of safety Winger's bike presented. He watched her expression change again as she two-stepped and twirled between the group of Rebels, loving the bright smile that curved her lips just for him when she reached out for his hand. He watched her features soften as she thanked them with a hug and a kiss for each, her affection evident in her gaze.

He watched for the things she didn't want them to see, too. He saw her cataloging things that her dead daughter hadn't done, things she never got to experience. Saw her face close down when approached by a member of whom she wasn't certain, and saw that same face lighten and open for one she trusted.

He saw as she affectionately greeted groups of men, inviting herself to discussions with a kiss and a touch. Saw her mount the steps to the back porch of Mica's place, watching as first Slate and then Tug pulled her into a close embrace, feeling a possessive twist in his gut when Tug touched her with casual familiarity. Then he watched as Tug directed her gaze across the heads of the partygoers. Hoss saw the moment she transformed from the strikingly attractive woman he had known for years into an exquisite thing of beauty, the change driven by whatever it was she had seen.

She grew still, focused, taking in deep, rapid breaths through slightly parted lips. Her cheeks flushed hotly and her face held a look he had never seen before, not even when she was married to Winger. Anticipation, longing, desire, and fear all were a puzzle of emotions playing across her features as Tug caged her chin, keeping her face pointed towards whatever it was he wanted her to see.

Twisting half around, he saw a dark head moving amongst the crowd towards Mica's house, catching only fleeting glimpses of a man's face as he single-mindedly wove through the bodies in the crowd that stood between them. He turned back in time to see Slate lifting DeeDee over the railing of the porch, gently setting her on the ground. Taking a dozen steps her direction, he abruptly halted when he saw the dark head moving like a flung arrow towards DeeDee belonged to Spencer.

Too far away to get there in time to intervene, he was still close enough to witness the reverence with which Spencer touched her face, how he cupped her cheeks as if she were the most precious thing he had ever encountered. Then, when he covered her mouth with his own and kissed her like she was everything he ever wanted, as if she were already his, Hoss read her eager reaction. Her back arched instinctively, her body pressing closer to Spencer as the kiss slowed and they separated. Her face turned upward and Hoss saw her eyes flutter open, a look of such deep longing on her features that he felt that twist in his gut again.

He had long cherished her friendship and was proud of the way the club had supported her when Winger died. Then, for a long time, he had hoped for something more between them, but he knew he would never see *that loo*k directed at him. And, if he was honest, he had never ached for her as it appeared Spencer did. He now knew what Bingo meant, because having seen it, even as it was bittersweet, Hoss would be lying if he tried to say he didn't want that for her again. All of that.

Now he would just have to help convince her.

***

"Hey," Jase said softly, arms reaching out to capture her and pull her against him again, letting her lean against his side, smiling as she wrapped her arms around his waist. She kept leaving him to go talk to people. While she eventually circled back around, he missed her while she was gone and kept a close eye on her progress, anticipating having her in his arms again.

He said, "I have a feeling this party is winding down. Mason walked by a minute ago and told people to keep the noise down. It looks like Road Runner is packing up his grilling kit, too. You want anything else before it's all gone?"

She shook her head, hair rustling against his shoulder. Her breath fluttered feather-light against his neck; she had curved into him as if she were exhausted. He realized she probably was, because she had been up since early morning and had ridden for hours to get here, and then spent her time here at the party on her feet. "You tired?"

He heard a muffled sound of agreement and grinned, turning her to wrap his arms around her shoulders and belly, supporting her body and securing it against his own. Her hand rose to his arm and she patted gently before shifting and moving again, pulling away and standing on her own.

She turned to look at him and he stilled, taking in the full effect of her beauty from not two feet away, face shadowed in the uncertain light filtering through the trees. The sounds of the party muted, fading away as he focused on her. He saw fluffy bangs over eyes he knew to be a deep shade of blue. The bangs were a match in color to the dark red hair partially tamed into a side braid falling over one shoulder, the tail resting alongside one full, rounded breast.

He reached out a hand to cup her face and gave her a quick smile. Their conversation had been enjoyable, and even more than that, he had loved holding her, touching her all night, and wasn't ready for things to end yet. He found himself wanting more than these few hours with her, and impulsively told her, "You need to come home with me," not couching it as a question, but she still shook her head in response.

For the first time all night, there was no smile on her face or in her voice, and he thought she looked sad as she spoke. "I was assigned a hotel suite. They'll check to make sure I'm where I'm supposed to be...make sure I'm okay, so I need to go there tonight. Thanks, though, it's a...kind offer."

Kind offer, he thought with a snort. She wasn't getting away that easily. He knew he had affected her tonight; her responses to his kisses and touch were real, without artifice. She wanted...him. "Then I'll go with you," he countered, slipping his hand around the back of her head, pulling her towards him. "I'd like to spend the night with you, DeeDee. I want to be with you. Are you going to tell me I'm alone in this? Because I think I'll have to call you a liar if you try."

He moved closer, pausing briefly when his mouth was a fraction of an inch from hers, the heat of her breath gusting against his lips. "I want you," he said and kissed her. Slanting his mouth over hers, he saw her eyes flutter closed just before his did and drew in a harsh breath through their joined lips when her hand wove into his hair, tugging gently. The kiss waxed and waned, beginning again with every gasp and moan. "I want you," he repeated in a strained voice, breaking away to rest his forehead against hers, desperately trying to control his breathing. He didn't mean to make too big a fool out of himself if he had completely misread her reactions. "*God*, DeeDee. Let me be with you."

Her fingers dipped into his back pocket and he heard her whisper, "Admiral. Room seven-twelve, if you're interested." She stepped back, dropping her hands, and he immediately missed her touch, wanted his hands on her again. "Seven-twelve," she repeated, and he reached back with his hand, tracing and recognizing the rectangle shape in his pocket as a hotel door key.

"Try and keep me away," he told her hoarsely, his words drawing an uncertain look to her face. He watched as she smoothed it away, lifting her chin and reclaiming the confidence and courage that so intrigued him when he first met her. He had never seen a woman as willing to make her own way as this one seemed determined to do.

She walked away, slim hips swaying as her leather-clad thighs brushed and rubbed against each other, the sound of the soft caress of leather fading slowly into the night. Her departure was noted by a half-dozen men standing around, who, with various expressions of relief and disbelief, looked from him to her then back again. He pulled the room key out and flashed it at Hoss, one of the men from Fort Wayne, and the Rebel member gave him a brilliant grin accompanied by a thumbs-up. The rest of the men spread out behind her, not pursuing but escorting, ensuring she was safe as she made her way over to the bike.

Jase watched as she paused and spoke to dozens of people on her way, watching greedily as she greeted each with a smile and a touch, settling into a hug or rising on her toes to kiss a cheek. He would have liked to be able to walk beside her, shown them all she was with him, that she wasn't walking away from him. It wasn't what it looked like. Hoss came over to him, hand out for a forearm grip. "Spencer. You should park in the hotel garage; she'll put the bike up near the elevator. Maybe you can meet her there, keep her from getting cold feet?" He wasn't sure he heard correctly at first, but then it dawned on him this tryst had just been officially approved.

"Okay. Will do," he said, nodding at the big man. He made to release his grip on Hoss' arm, but the man tightened down painfully, holding on and staring Jase in the face with a hard look.

"Do *not* fuck her over," he growled, scowling. "She deserves to be treated like a lady, deserves to see sweet coming her way. Do not fuck her over, man."

"No way," Jase was quick to respond, shaking his head. "No way, Hoss. She's something special." Hoss tightened his grip again, nodding before finally releasing his hold. Jase looked up to see Birdy watching them, a guarded look on his face. He nodded at the biker and Hoss twisted to see who he was interacting with, then frowned as he turned back to Jase.

"He's not one you wanna piss off. Might want to walk softly there." Clapping a hand on Jase's shoulder, he said, "Don't forget she's ours, man. Treat her right, and there'll be no problem." Watching him walk away, he saw Hoss jerk his head at Birdy, and the men faded into the darkness at the edges of the yard.

***

At the hotel, he stood near the elevator, shifting impatiently from foot to foot. *Why isn't she here yet?* Remembering what happened to her husband, he had a sudden, near paralyzing fear that something had occurred along the way. Then he heard a muted roar quickly increasing in volume, and recognized it as the sound of bikes approaching. Bikes, plural...as in more than one. He frowned and then caught his breath as DeeDee rode into view around a corner of the parking garage. She sat the big bike with confidence and skill, hands and feet working in coordination to control the machine. *God, she looks amazing*, he thought.

She pulled in near him, walking the idling bike backwards into a parking space before she put down the kickstand and killed the engine. Three other bikes pulled up, but only one moved to park beside her. A couple rode that one, and the women hugged tightly before separating, promises of dinner passing between them. Standing beside the bike, DeeDee turned to him with a quizzical look. He said, "Hey. Hi. Thought we could walk up together." Feeling unexpectedly insecure, he stood there looking at her, watching as she retrieved a small bag from the bike, cinching the saddlebags tightly closed.

The other bikers offered him the signature chin lift so many used in place of a verbal greeting, and then took off, pipes roaring as they headed to the exit. He found the sudden stillness in their absence as startling as the initial noise had been. She was quiet as he reached to push the button for the elevator, then silent for their solitary ride to the seventh floor. The door of her room opened into a plush suite complete with a living area and a separate bedroom and bath. He stood awkwardly in the middle of the room, thumbs in his pockets, looking around. “Nice digs, DeeDee,” he said.

She dropped her jacket in a chair and carried her small bag into the bedroom, beginning to unnerve him with her silence. She had held his hand in the elevator, had readily submitted to his arm around her shoulders, but hadn’t spoken to him since giving him the room information at the party. Was she regretting the invitation? What if she was too tired, but was being polite and not turning him out? He eyed the big bed, deciding he would be okay if that were the case, as long as he got to spoon with her. Hold her. Soak up how good she felt in his arms.

As she came out of the bedroom in a t-shirt and jeans, he saw she had removed her boots, socks, and leather chaps. Her bare feet were slim and petite, and her toenails were painted a shocking green. For some reason, the color made him laugh aloud and she looked up, asking, “What?” as she walked across the room to him. Slipping her arms around his waist, she leaned into his embrace and took a deep breath as they touched. *I think she wants this after all*, he thought.

The cuddle helped him begin to relax, and now that his hands were back on her, he was more confident. “Love the pedi,” he quipped, dipping his head down for a kiss. It was good…sensual, soft, and slow, her mouth moving under his, but she ended it too quickly and tucked her head underneath his chin, cheek resting on his chest.

"My daughter did it," she said quietly, amusement evident in her voice. "She liked the color and wanted to try it, but not on her own nails."

"Did she?" He didn't care, but now that she started, he wanted to keep her talking.

"Did she what?" She tilted her head up, meeting his eyes with her question.

"Did she like the color?" He traced her cheek with the tip of his nose, drawing her earlobe between his lips and nipping softly at it then pulling back to study her face.

She drew in a sigh, her lips tipping up into a smile. "Yeah, she liked it."

"Do you like this?" he asked, leaning in to nibble her earlobe again.

Her head moved and nodded as she said, "Yeah, I like this a lot."

"Mmmm," he hummed against the side of her head. "I like it a lot, too." He drew his nose along her jaw, softly kissing the side of her neck. "How about this? Do you like this?"

"Yeah, I like that, too." This was murmured into his shirt as her neck arched towards him, which had the effect of keeping her lips from his. That wasn't going to work for him, and he nibbled down and across her collarbone, whispering, "I want your lips."

She was turning her head when his phone rang and he groaned, recognizing the ringtone. It was Nathan deWalt, the team's manager. He pulled back, digging the phone out as he told her, "I gotta get this, hon. Gimme a minute."

"Yeah?" he answered, not bothering to disguise his irritation.

"One word, Spencer. Bus. I got two no-shows: you and Daniel. You want to play tomorrow? You want ice time?" Nate didn't bother with pleasantries. He knew Jase well enough to skip to what he needed to know.

"Shit, what time are you pulling out?" He rubbed his forehead between finger and thumb, feeling the beginnings of a headache. In his pursuit this evening, he had forgotten the team was heading down to Fort Wayne tonight to be rested for the game tomorrow. Looking up as DeeDee walked out of the room, he frowned. *Why did she leave?*

"We hit the Skyway ten minutes ago. I have your gear. If I trust you to drive down, will you actually show?" Nate spoke to someone in the background. "Hang on, I've got Daniel." There was silence for a minute and then the line crackled. "Daniel said to meet him at Mica's at nine in the morning, sharp. He'll drive you both down."

"Okay, Nate. It sounds like a solution to me. Enjoy the bus trip, old man. See you tomorrow." Jase grinned. He wasn't sad to be free of the sardine can that was the team bus, especially the night before a playoff game. The scent of anxiety would be almost as thick as the stench of sweat-soaked hockey equipment in the vehicle. He hung up and tossed the phone onto the countertop behind him, stalking through the suite until he found DeeDee standing in the bathroom. She was staring into the mirror, and he wasn't sure she noticed him until he pressed up behind her.

"That was the team manager; they're on their way to your town, because we are playing in Fort Wayne tomorrow night," he told her, kissing the side of her neck. "Any chance of you coming to the game? I can get you tickets to the team box, or seats on the glass if you'd rather sit there."

She shook her head. "I'll be here in Chicago for three nights. That's what I was told."

He frowned at her. “You don’t get a say in it? Can’t go back early if you wanted to?”

“There’s a reason for the request,” she assured him. “I simply don’t know everything yet. Is this your last game of the season? I’ve seen your team play a few times this year, when you guys came to the Fort to play the Tridents.”

She likes hockey? He hadn’t known that and now looked at her thoughtfully, saying, “Hopefully not the last game. If we keep winning, we keep going in the playoffs. You came to some of the games? Who’d you root for?”

She turned in his arms and tilted her head, grinning at him. “Sorry, handsome, I’m a hometown gal. Tridents got the cheers.”

He leaned into the small space separating them and slid his hands around her hips to her lower back. Pulling her tightly against him, he buried his face in her neck, breathing in her scent. “You think I’m handsome? Will I get to hear you cheer for me sometime?”

“Do you need to leave soon?” She dodged his questions and asked her own, even as she tilted her head, giving him greater access for the soft kisses he was pressing to her skin.

“Not until the morning,” he murmured against her. “I’ll set an alarm so I’m up in time to head back to Mica’s by nine; Daniel’s going to drive us down. But right now, I’m with you, absolutely not going anywhere.”

She hummed, turning her head to kiss him softly. Lips only, the contact between them was soft and gentle, tender and sensual. He shifted, guiding her backwards to the bedroom. “I’m with you. I’ve thought about you so much…so often, DeeDee. I was glad to see you at the party tonight.”

Standing beside the bed, her hands went to his waist, fingers working to unfasten his jeans, her quiet demands quickly removing his clothing. Smiling, he reached out and disassembled her outfit as well, swiftly discarding her shirt and bra before the sight of his hands on her breasts distracted him.

His broad, tanned hands covered the pale skin, rough fingertips teasing her nipples into rosy peaks before he cupped and lifted one to his mouth. Working the hard bud with lips and teeth, he soothed the sting of gentle bites with soft sucking and flicks of his tongue. He asked, "You like that?" Her quiet sighs encouraged him and her hands played in his hair, fingers threading and stroking through again and again, touching and tracing the sides of his face, over his cheekbones and up into his hair.

He decided her jeans covered too much skin and had to go, telling her so. "These are in my way, baby. You are just going to have to lose them." Dropping to one knee, he tugged the tight material down, taking black satin panties with them. Resting his head on her thigh, he watched his hands trace down her legs, drawing the material over her feet and pushing it aside as she stepped out of them. He trailed his fingers over that damn nail polish, chuckling quietly.

Sliding his hands back up her legs, he tipped his head to look at her, seeing her gazing down at him, watching him caress her. She had a surprising look on her face, nearly like wonder, as if she had received good news or a present she desperately wanted, but hadn't really expected. He cupped his palms around the inside of her thighs, gently pressing outward until she wordlessly widened her stance, resting her hands on his head.

Nuzzling up along her leg, his mouth matched the speed of his hands rising to where her legs joined the rest of her body, fingertips and lips caressing with the lightest of touches. Her scent was wonderfully musky, and there was a spicy rush when he separated her lips, dipping his fingers into the slickness there. Her mound was closely trimmed, but not bare, and he immediately decided this was his favorite grooming style ever. He drew a gasp from her with a gentle tug and smiled, thinking, *So much better than bare*.

He brought his fingers to his mouth, keeping his eyes on her face, pleased by her smile as she watched him enjoy tasting her. "Mmmm. So good. Knew you'd taste good." Watching a blush rise from her chest to her neck, he whispered softly, "Bet it's better straight from the source, yeah? Let's see, shall we?" Using his fingers to touch and tease, he rubbed his face against her, darting his tongue out to explore and gently lap and lick. Stroking with the flat of his tongue, he licked from core to clit several times, resting his thumbs alongside her stiffening clit to lift and squeeze it tightly, exposing it to his caresses. "Oh, yeah, so much better," he murmured, the movement of his lips against the soft skin just above her mound making her shudder.

Drawing the bundle of nerves into his mouth, he stroked small circles over it with the tip of his tongue while he slipped two fingers inside her pussy, pushing deep inside and drawing a gasp from her. He was so hard already; he was afraid he might not last through pleasing her, but wanted to give her this, all of this. Everything that made her moan or groan, the movements or touches that caused her to gasp out those little sighs and sounds...anything that pleased her. She was so quietly vocal, and he wanted to hear her say his name, couldn't wait to have her panting for breath. Wanted to leave her gasping and breathless in the wake of her passion.

Everything she was doing conspired to drag him nearer than he wanted towards his own climax. The soft noises, that gently demanding pull of her fingers in his hair, the taste of her lust and arousal on his tongue, and the feel of her body under his hands...everything that was her excited him. He shifted, spreading his knees farther apart, and tried to ignore how his hard, thick cock wagged in the air, his erection insistently bouncing against his belly.

Feeling her clench and ripple inside, he moved his hand faster, his wrist flexing and twisting as he powered his fingers in and out. The heel of his hand was bumping against his chin while his other palm wrapped around her hip, holding her tight against his mouth so he could actively eat at her. She was tightening around his fingers again, and underneath his other palm, the muscles in her ass were flexing and clenching, nearly quivering with strain and he knew she had to be close. Loving her reactions, he changed the angle of his fingers slightly, pressing harder on the front wall, sliding over and behind her pubic bone with an unrelenting, rhythmic pressure.

Her voice was so small he nearly missed it, but even quavering and shy, she let him know how well he was pleasuring her. "So good. Yeah. I can't…mmmm. Jase." *My name, yes.* Her murmuring continued as she assured him his efforts were appreciated, were driving her closer and closer to orgasm. He drew her clit between his lips again and scraped his teeth across the engorged bud. She went motionless under his hands and then gasped as she came hard, hips thrusting forward as her pussy clamped tightly around his fingers.

He looked up to find her eyes squeezed closed, face flushed and head tipped forward, the tail of her dark red braid curling around the pale skin of her breast. She was biting her lips, keeping her cries quiet, hiding them inside as her fingers tightened in his hair, deliciously painful, tugging and drawing him close. The muscles in her flank twitched and jerked as she struggled to remain still, and he knew what she wanted to do, what she tried to deny herself. So he ground his face into her pussy, licking and lapping quickly, thrusting his fingers deep and holding there. That dragged a soft "Oh" out of her, the orgasm peaking again, the motions of his assault gradually slowing and softening as she slowly relaxed, swaying on her feet.

He stood and picked her up, earning a soft complaining noise as he carried her to the bed. Spreading her on top of the comforter, he lay next to her, dragging a blanket up to wrap them in warmth. He typically was confident about the outcome of his sexcapades, but this was one time he knew without a doubt he had pleased and temporarily exhausted his partner. He was proud of the drowsy, love-drunk outcome evident on her features, face relaxed and dreamy with pleasure.

Lying beside her, one arm around her shoulders holding her still and tight against him, he closed his eyes and listened as her breathing began to slow. His other arm moved lazily, languidly, palm stroking up and down her spine, over her hip and back up.

She moved, face nuzzling against his chest, fingernails lightly scratching over his skin and traveling down over his abdominals to his lower belly. He held his breath and waited to see what she would do next as the back of her hand bumped against the underside of his hard cock, arching over his body. Drawing a deep breath at a second contact, he tried to temper his response, but felt the twitch and bob of his cock as it eagerly sought her teasing warmth. Little Jase had a mind of its own, not just its own head, seemed like. *More touching, yes, good...more contact,* it appeared to be saying.

She stretched, lifting her face towards his, and he met her halfway, pressing his lips against hers in a soft, gentle kiss. Her fingers wrapped around his cock and she took advantage of the gasp that parted his lips, slipping her tongue into his mouth and deepening the kiss. Her hand smoothly sliding over sensitive skin kept his attention, even as she stroked deep in his mouth, her tongue playing with his. Feeling her shift in the bed, he realized she was pressing her pussy against his thigh, seeking her own pleasure, rough hair rasping on his skin. *Cock, lips, leg...so many sensations to keep track of.* Befuddled, his hips jerked involuntarily.

She had pulled back and was whispering something. What was she saying? He focused and heard, "—condom, Jase?" This he could answer; he had protection in his wallet. He gritted out the information, again thrusting through the grip of her hand. Softly kissing him, she patted his chest with one hand while squeezing him tightly with the other.

"Be right back," she said and released him to lean out of the bed. He gripped her hips. *Wouldn't want her to fall out of bed now; no reason to let her get hurt. God, her ass is beautiful, round and soft,* he thought. Using his thumbs, he spread her cheeks to get a brief glimpse of the tight rosebud hiding there and the soft, pink petals of her pussy before she straightened, his wallet in hand.

She handed it to him and he retrieved the foil square, then thought better and took out a second one, waggling the two packets at her between his fingers, drawing a laugh from her lips. "Confident, are we?" she asked in a teasing tone, and he nodded.

"Hell yeah, baby, I'm confident. I watched you all night. Watched you walking out and talking to people...men. Good lookin' sons a bitches, some of them. Then you came back to be with me. So, yeah, I'm confident. Come to think of it, two might not be enough. Might have to call the concierge at this fancy hotel and have them run to the pharmacy. We'll have to specify the size though. Most people don't worry about it, but size is important." He was babbling, thinking to himself, *Shut up mouth. Shut up now*.

"Is size that important? I thought all guys stuck to the old saying of it's not the size of the stick, but how you shift with it?" She leaned in and was licking and kissing his neck, distracting him from their conversation. *God. What had she said? Oh, yeah, size matters.*

"In hockey, we say it's not the size of the dog in the fight, but the size of the fight in the dog. Baby, I have not only the size, but the fight going for me too." He twisted on the bed, rolling her underneath him. "Now, stop talking. You're sidetracking me from important work here."

She laughed, giggling into his chest. He liked that she wasn't afraid to laugh in bed. He liked her. A lot. She asked him, "Important work?"

"Incredibly important, it's the most important thing I've done in weeks. I need to memorize you, every inch. I don't want to miss anything. It's a good thing I'm a quick study, dontcha know?" *God, was that my Alberta drawl coming out? Now?* "It's a hands-on study, no holds barred, utterly in-depth. I'll have to touch everything, everywhere. I work best with my hands, eh?" *Again with the Canuck-speak?*

Rising on his elbows, he framed her face with his hands, tracing her features with his fingertips. Moving slowly, he softly kissed a line from her ear across her cheekbone and down to her lips, parted and waiting for him. "I'll know everything about you by night's end," he promised, whispering against her mouth. "Have you all memorized. Everything. I'm up for it." He thrust his hard cock against her hip to emphasize this fact. "No worries about that part. Ready for an all-nighter, baby."

Laughing, she reached up and plucked the condom wrappers from where he dropped them, sliding one underneath the pillow and bringing the other to her mouth, tearing it open with her teeth. She kicked the comforter off them and scooted up in bed, telling him, "Slide up a minute."

He complied, rolling to his back, and she kicked the covers the rest of the way off the bed, leaving them lying together on an expanse of soft cotton. Grasping his erection in one hand, she brought her mouth to him, surprising him by taking the swollen crown inside, rolling her tongue around the sensitive rim and teasing the tiny slit. His eyes slammed closed and his head tipped back against the pillows, mouth falling open with an audible moan. "Ah, God, baby."

Her fingers traced his lips teasingly and he drew them into his mouth, sucking hard and moaning again when he tasted the slick, spicy fluid covering them. *Oh, God, she put her fingers in...God.* The head of his cock bumped the back of her throat and it closed around him as she swallowed, then pulled back. *Inside...and is feeding it to me.* He lost her fingers as she withdrew them, chasing them for a moment with questing lips, then she touched his cock, wrapping her fingers firmly around him as she rolled the condom down his length. *She'll kill me if she keeps this up.*

He moved back down in the bed, determined to regain control, and firmly covered her body with his own. Gripping her hands, he threaded his fingers through hers and pressed them into the mattress at either side of her head. “You are a vixen,” he accused with a smile, pushing one knee between her thighs, forcing her legs open so he could slip between them, pressing pelvis to pelvis. “Distracting me again, this is my workplace, woman. Let me work.”

She hummed, tipping her head back as a look of sublime peace crossed her face. He thrust once, twice, rubbing the length of his cock between her lips and up over her clit, stealing another gasp from her with a kiss. “Ready for me, baby?” he asked softly, resting his forehead against hers, waiting for her response. When it failed to come, he continued, “I think you are. Ready for me, ready to take all of me. Do you like soft and slow, baby? Hard and fast?”

“I want everything with you.”

He breathed deliberately, controlled. “Are you…” he drew a breath, “…ready…” he breathed out slowly, “baby?”

Nodding, she kissed him, whispering against his lips, “Everything.”

He closed his eyes, smiling, and tipped his hips, effortlessly aligning his cock with her opening and slowly easing inside. With measured, even strokes, he teased his way, releasing one hand to reach down between their bodies and rub lightly on her clit. She was invitingly open and wet, and so tight once he was seated all the way inside. *God, so fucking tight and hot*. The drag and draw of his cock inside her was so good he nearly lost his rhythm for a moment, having to bite down hard on his bottom lip, forcing himself to focus on her responses.

He heard her take a rushed, indrawn breath, then she held it for the barest moment before allowing it to trickle out. His gaze scanned her face, watching the way she gripped her lips between her teeth, once again containing quiet cries. Her hands roamed restlessly across his body as if she had been long starved for the feeling of flesh under her fingers and now found herself seated at a buffet of sensation, unable to decide what to touch first.

"God, you are so soft. I could touch you for days." He delighted in the feeling of her inner thighs against the outside of his legs, her hips cradling him in heat. His fingers drew circles and lines on skin that was creamy and soft, and then she moved and shifted with him as he rocked deeper inside her. He tried to memorize everything that made her unique, all that made this singular and memorable, and in that instant, Jase knew he would never be able to get enough of her. *Never enough*, he thought, *so right*.

Her teeth gripped his shoulder as she bit sharply, and he thrust deep inside her in reaction to the sweet sting, his breath gasping in her ear, tongue teasing along her collarbone. "You like a little pain, baby? Little teeth? God," he gasped again. "Me, too."

Curling his body around hers, his hands slid underneath her, cupping her ass and lifting to a different angle so he could stroke deeper, entering her more fully. He increased the pace, ignoring a twinge of pain in his groin.

He whispered about her body, her touches. "God, you feel so good. Mmmm, yeah, move like that again. Oh, fuck me, baby. Everything you do feels good." He changed pace, circling his hips with each deep thrust. "Feel my cock inside you? How we fit? Feel that velvety slip and slide?" He tightened his hands, pulling her harder against him. "My favorite kind of ride, that slip and slide. So good." Brushing his lips across her cheek, he found her mouth and kissed her hard and desperate. "Touch me, baby. Your hands. God. So good, DeeDee. It feels like a trail of fire left behind by your hands, my skin on fire for you." Her palms flattened against his back, the heat of their breath mixing as they kissed, his tongue twisting and pushing into her mouth, tracing the inside of her teeth, teasing against her tongue. She reacted to his words, gasping and tightening around him until he didn't know if he could hold back much longer.

Pleased when she jerked under him, he stroked her sides as she arched her back, her hips pulling back and then moving forward against his plunging cock. There was an increased pressure around him as she found her release, her pussy clenching his cock tightly while she shuddered underneath him. Jase gasped, letting go the tenuous grip he retained and cresting the wave with her, calling her name, "DeeDee. Baby, now. Now. Oh, God." Pressing deep, he thrust hard, grinding the base of his cock into her clit. "So good, so fucking good." She was matching every pulse from him with a clench of her inner muscles, drawing out his orgasm.

Arms shaking, he slowly relaxed on top of her, his forehead pressed into the pillow next to her head, finally panting out a question when he thought he could speak coherently again. "Am I too heavy?" He knew he was, but couldn't move yet; nonetheless, it seemed polite at least to ask, acknowledging the imposition, as it were. She surprised him with her response, nose dragging along his chest so she could lick at his nipple. He thought it was probably the only thing she could reach with him crushing her like this.

"Not heavy. I like it," she said quietly, her hands slowly sliding up and down his sides.

"Gimme a minute to catch my breath. That was a great workout, good cardio," he joked, laboriously lifting and shifting onto his elbows, their bellies and hips still pressed together. Kissing her softly, he licked his sweat off the tip of her nose, telling her, "God, baby. That was good."

She smiled up at him, pulling her bottom lip between her teeth before agreeing softly, "Yeah, it was."

He was softening, so he reached down to hold the condom in place as he moved, sliding out of her with a groan. She made a complaining noise too, which made him smile. Now came the part he usually hated, the cleanup process, which was generally followed by awkward silences or stilted conversation. There was a light touch on his arm and he looked down; her hand was there, offering him a tissue. Surprised, he accepted it and wrapped up the condom, placing it on the bedside table for later disposal. He turned back in time to see her slipping out of the other side of the bed.

Looking at him, she tapped her fingers on the edge of the mattress for a minute and then nodded decisively. “I’m going to shower,” she said. “You’re welcome to join me, or not.” With that, she turned and, seeming unconscious of her nudity, walked across the room to the doorway, rummaging in her bag for a moment and coming up with what looked like a t-shirt and panties. She walked out of the room and left him gaping at the doorway. No demands for cuddle time, no pushy questions. Hot in bed, easy out of it—this might be his perfect woman. *But what if I wanted cuddle time?* he thought with a silent snort.

He lay back in bed for a moment, fingers questing in the crease of his hip, finding the troubling, but still tiny bulge there. Pressing on it, he hissed as the pain bloomed sharply then decreased just as quickly when he released the pressure. *I’m a fucking hockey player,* he thought. *I’ve played with broken ribs before. A little groin pull ain’t no big thang.*

Laughing at himself, he rolled out of bed to pursue her into the bathroom and opened the shower door with a loud, “Here you are. For a moment there, I thought you escaped me, eh? No escape for you, my lovely.” Closing the door behind him, he pulled her into an embrace, tilting her head up with two fingertips underneath her chin. “No rest for the wicked, either,” he said as he kissed her, hands roaming her body. “Oh, would ya look at that. You are a dirty, dirty girl. I can fix that. Let me help you.”

By the time he had to leave the next morning, they had used not only that second condom, but also an additional few that he left the suite to buy. She wouldn’t let him call room service for the purchase, and laughingly wrestled him for the phone before he acquiesced and pulled his jeans on commando in his haste to return quickly. She willingly used that same phone to order breakfast, however, getting a variety of pancakes, eggs, and meats they ate in bed. Some of which he might have eaten off her, the syrup providing too much of a lure to resist.

Their breakfast in bed led to another shower, where he slowly ate his fill of her, too. His fingers explored every fold and crease, firm pressure of his tongue on her clit bringing her higher and higher. He drew out and extended her orgasm until her legs failed and she slid down the tile wall to join him on the floor. Draping her body across his, he held her close as she dozed. They relaxed, the hot water splashing on his chest, ricocheting up into her face, dampening her hair and causing lickable beads of water to form on her lips.

Driving to Mica's house, he mentally reviewed the vision of what he unwillingly left behind. Sleeping on her stomach, she was draped sideways across the bed, pillows underneath her hips from him taking her from behind the last time, his fingerprints still visible in dark, red marks on her skin. Thinking, *My baby's too thin; she needs someone to take care of her*, he kissed the marks gently, hoping they wouldn't bruise. Then, fully dressed, he slipped into bed beside her.

Pushing her hair back so he could see her face, he traced a fingertip across the scattering of freckles on her nose and cheeks. Grinning as her eyes opened no more than halfway, he watched as a contented smile tipped up the corners of her oh-so kissable mouth. She said, "Hey," in an adorably sleepy voice and he laughed. *I could get used to that*, he thought.

"I gotta go, baby," he whispered, pressing his cheek against hers. "I left my number next to your phone. Call me." He waited for her response, drawing back when it wasn't forthcoming. "I'm serious. Call me, okay? I want to hear your voice."

"Okay," she whispered, and he was surprised to see what looked like sadness at him leaving, but there was no mistaking the emotion on her face.

"I'll be back in town tonight. You said you'll still be here. DeeDee, I want to see you. Tonight, okay?" He pushed her for a response, relieved when she nodded. "Okay. I'll see you tonight. Right here, promise. We'll have a chance to reenact some of our best stuff, eh? Good deal, baby. Wish me luck?"

"Luck," she said softly, responding sweetly to his kiss.

He left without another word, surprised to find a biker standing outside the door. He remembered seeing one at the end of the hallway last night too, but hadn't paid a lot of attention to it at the time. Nodding silently to the man, he moved past and to the elevator, his mind already speeding ahead to the game.

***

Returning to the suite after an intensely awkward lunch with Road Runner, DeeDee quickly grabbed her things and threw them into her small bag. How had she allowed herself to be maneuvered into this...whatever it had been? Road immediately came to mind, because today at lunch, he poked gentle fun at her about her evening's activities, more than once mentioning how good she looked leaning up against the 'hockey guy'.

She knew he didn't mean to make her feel self-conscious, but the effect was the same, because if Road had noted their interactions, then probably every Rebel on the property had noticed too, and that left her with too many questions. Were the members going to be okay with her being with someone who wasn't in the club? Or, would this circle back around to become a problem and bite her in the ass? Her worst fear was that the club would grow tired of her and Mel, leaving them to shift for themselves, and this might be all the reason they needed.

She couldn't stay in the hotel, wouldn't let herself still be here when Jase got back from Fort Wayne. Looking around, she checked the room one final time to ensure nothing would be left behind and her gaze settled on the small piece of paper sitting accusingly on the dresser. Within a single breath, she went from panic mode to stillness and reached out a hand to pick it up as she settled onto the edge of the bed.

Her stomach filled with butterflies as she thought about the time they spent together. Jase had been sweet and attentive, and today her body was aching in the most delicious way from the energetic antics they shared. She loved that from the moment he took possession of her at the party, allowing her to leave his side but never letting her out of his sight, right up through the morning, when he gently woke her to say goodbye before leaving for the game, he was entirely focused on her...her pleasure.

She smiled softly, thinking she was glad he wouldn't have to drive, because they certainly hadn't gotten enough sleep to make it safely. He had dozed for a time lying next to her, his hair falling across his beautiful face, soft lips parted with slow, even breaths.

It had been so long since she shared a bed with a man, and Jase was so solid and warm, so there, that when he fell asleep and the opportunity presented itself to touch him without boundaries, she hadn't been able to keep her fingers from wandering.

Trailing her fingertips up his arms, she traced the lines of his colorful tattoos, which matched the man's character. She smiled at the whimsical alien in his spaceship, snorting a little at the brazenly naked woman on his forearm. His other shoulder held a winged skull with violets that trailed onto his chest, where a fierce lion's head stared at her. To get as much well-done and detailed ink as he had, it must have taken a number of patient and painful sessions in the artist's chair, and that kind of persistence exactly fit with his personality.

Once they had reached the room and he kissed her, he had stolen her senses much as he had done at the party, insistently rousing her passions. He was patient with her, gently easing her into their encounter, even after she initially fled as soon as there was an opening. When he received the call from the team's manager, she took the chance and escaped into the bathroom, nearly hyperventilating as she realized Jase was here...right here, standing only feet away.

She had shamelessly listened in on his call and been by turns afraid he would have to leave immediately...but terrified he would be able to stay. When she heard him ending the call, she took a deep breath and stared at herself in the bathroom mirror.

What she had seen there was surprising. Unlike the woman from earlier that morning, this reflection had high, riotous color in her cheeks, bright eyes, and kiss-swollen lips. This was a woman aroused, a woman who wouldn't be afraid to seek her own satisfaction for a change. This woman had once been a constant companion, but she had been absent for a long time...too long, and DeeDee liked seeing her in the mirror again.

Seeing her reflection like that had given her a boost of needed courage, so when he maneuvered her into the bedroom and undressed her, she stood before him without shame, ready to accept what he offered.

Now, touching her lips with the tips of her fingers, she remembered how good they were together. Then she thought about the teasing comments from Road, meant to be harmless, but echoing and twisting through the thoughts in her head, uncovering the barely buried fears and uncertainty she had lived with since Winger died. Why would anyone want her? *Now is not a good time to get involved, woman*, she thought. Aloud, she said, "Like you told yourself before, he's pretty to look at, but not for you, old woman."

Shaking her head, she stood from the side of the bed and looked at the scrap of paper again then carefully folded it, tucking it away for safekeeping, wishing she could do the same thing with her heart.

5 - Off-season visit

"Goddamn lucky charm!" Jase shouted, sitting on top of Daniel on their hometown locker room floor, pushing handfuls of cereal into his mouth. They had won the series, won the cup—the Mallets were champions, and he was celebrating the only way he knew how, over the top.

After they won the game in Fort Wayne and returned to Chicago, his first stop had been the hotel suite. He found DeeDee had already checked out and the key he had kept no longer worked. He remained standing in the hotel hallway for a long time, trying to figure out what had gone wrong. When he left only twenty hours before, he would have put money down they had connected in a very real way, but then she disappeared. She was just gone.

He made the rounds, looking everywhere for her, but the staff and regulars at Jackson's claimed not to know if she was still in town or had left to go home. There hadn't been much time to focus on how she bugged out; the team had been busy with promotional shit about the win that had brought the championship one game closer. With the series standing at three to two in their favor, all the local TV and radio stations wanted a chance to interview members of the team.

Even with splitting up the obligations, each of the principal players had wound up doing three or four interviews a day in the short interval before game six, the one they had just won. There hadn't been time to breathe, much less pursue a woman who had proven herself damn good at avoiding him.

His view of the world tilted and shifted, and he realized Daniel had taken advantage of his moment of inattention and flipped him, and was now holding him down while Gary approached, cardboard box in hand. Jase happily opened his mouth, chowing down on the symbolic winnings with a broad grin. After a couple of minutes, they were all three out of breath and exhausted, slumping in laughter. It had been a hard-won game and series, and all the players showed it.

Dragging himself off the floor, he sat on the bench in front of the lockers, phone in hand, thumbing through the well wishes of friends and family, some with attached pictures of his game-winning goal. Those made him smile, and he saved them to look through later. Flipping through the last few messages, he was about to put the phone down, when a new one came in from a number he didn't recognize. ***Congratz on the win, Jase! So proud of you. ~DD***

He read the text and was about to delete it when he received a media file from the same number. It was a picture of him right after a goal tonight, his stick raised high over his head in celebration. However, what captured his attention wasn't his own image; he focused on the reflection in the glass showing the photographer who had masses of dark red hair and a petite face, the figure wearing a jersey with his number on the sleeve. *She was in the arena tonight.*

He fired off a response, ***Holy cow, woman. You're here? At the game? Where are you?***

Nervously waiting for a reply, he stripped off his jersey and pants, tossing them into the locker behind him. Nothing yet from her, so he jumped in the shower and was finished in record time, picking up the phone and checking, but still nothing. He sent a second text, ***I'd like those gratz in person. Tell me where you are.***

Dressing in the suit he wore to the game, he sat again, waiting. Waving off invitations to after-parties, he was still sitting and holding his phone when Daniel walked into the locker room, followed by Mason. He jumped up, stepping in front of the biker. They were about the same height, but Mason always managed to make him feel as if he were looking up at the man. "Hey," he said and then paused; he didn't seem to know where to go from there.

Mason looked at him and sighed. "Hey what?"

"Do you know where DeeDee is staying?" He was crazy nervous asking this question. *Mason doesn't care who she sees, does he? Isn't like he's her big brother or anything, right?* He waited for a response and got an eyebrow quirk. Reading that as needing clarification, he rephrased. "Do you know where DeeDee is staying? Is she staying overnight here in Chicago? Or is she going back to the Fort right away?"

Mason dropped his chin. "Didn't know she was in town. No idea where she's staying, if she's staying, or if she was even here."

"Oh, she was here, she was. She sent me a picture." Mason's eyebrow quirked again and Jase handed over his phone, pointing. "See? Not the picture, that's me. Of course it is; you can see that. But lookie at the reflection in the glass. That's DeeDee. Right there, see that?"

Nodding, Mason pulled his phone out and compared the numbers. "It kinda looks like her in the picture, but wrong number. That's not DeeDee's phone, man. Sorry."

"But that's her reflection." He didn't even know why he was arguing. The man had already stepped around him, slapping his back on the way and telling him it was a good game. He was disagreeing with the air now. His joy at their win tempered with disappointment, he slowly slipped on his shoes, tying the thin laces with fumbling fingers.

Looking around the locker room, he realized he was the last team member to leave. Watching as the equipment managers slowly gathered up the worn and discarded jerseys, pads, and various pieces of equipment, he decided to get out of their way. Nothing to wait around for, she evidently wasn't going to respond to his texts. "Need to just chuck it in the fuck it bucket and move on," he said to one of the men, slapping him on the back and striding through the door.

Most of the players were at Jackson's, where they sat watching the highlights repeatedly play on the TV. He got some good ice time this year, averaging nearly thirty minutes per game, and skated more than fourteen hundred shifts in the forty-eight games played. Thirty-two goals, twenty-seven assists for a nice total of fifty-nine points. Regular season. He hadn't tallied up the playoff information yet.

Proudly, he thought to himself, *Those are damn good stats, no matter at what professional level you play.* He looked up, draining his beer as the screen filled with a video of him lifting his stick over his head, a broad smile on his face. Frustrated, he realized the angle was *just* wrong, he couldn't see the section from where the photo had been taken, couldn't see if she had actually been at the game.

Looking around the bar, he saw Slate standing across the room, doing his usual vulture thing, just waiting around for trouble to start so he could break it up. He got another beer from Merry, the bartender, and walked over to lean against the wall next to Slate. Receiving a silent chin lift in greeting, they stood there quietly for several minutes until Slate moved, standing up to his full height to stare down a couple of fans who had been baiting a player.

Drama over, settling back against the wall, Slate cut his eyes towards Jase. "I don't know where she is, man. Mason already asked."

"Well hell," he snarled, banging the back of his head against the wall, suddenly angry. "First, she wasn't here when I got back from Fort Wayne, and now she's in town, but just wants to tease me with a picture. Bet she's having a hell of a laugh right about now." He shut himself up by drinking deeply from the bottle, and then let his hand drop back next to his side.

Slate moved slightly, the leather of his vest creaking and sliding against the wall. "She's tender yet, man. I don't think you ever had a chance to meet Winger, but he was a hell of a good person. Good brother, a good member, and he seemed to be a good husband. Losing her old man and her daughter all at once like that...it's going to leave places that are hard to heal. The way she was at the party, she's interested. A woman doesn't act like that without being interested. You want my advice, I'm happy to give it, but a lot of things depend on what you're looking for."

"What I'm looking for?" he scoffed. "Hell, I'm not looking for anything. But, I want to get to know her better. Every time I've seen her, she blows me away with her wit, her intelligence, her attitude—everything about her is amazing. She's all that, man. I want to know her inside and out, figure out what makes her tick." That should satisfy him without pulling a kiss-and-tell rendition of their night together.

"Didja fuck her?" Slate's question caught him off guard and he laughed nervously. "*Fuck me*. Never mind, I can tell from your face. As I said, man, she's tender. You try to push or pull her, she's gonna spook and run. Did you say something to shut her down?"

"No," he said softly. "I left for Fort Wayne with full expectation that she'd be waiting for me that night."

"Then be patient. If she's interested, she'll reach out. Like she did tonight, letting you know she kept your number. She's smart like you said. She'll find you if she wants to." Slate straightened, walking quickly across to a table and grabbing a man by the collar. He shook the man back and forth, speaking to him with a raised voice and roughly slinging him back down into the chair.

From where he stood, Jase could see it was another biker, but wasn't a Rebel. The other two men at the table wore similar patches, and he watched as they slipped their hands behind their backs, faces tense with potential violence. The man Slate had been manhandling had a pistol shoved into the back waistband of his pants, and Jase could only assume the other two men were likewise armed. He took a half step away from the wall and Slate immediately brought his eyes up, giving him a small head shake, effectively waving him off.

Jase settled back against the wall, but intently watched the remaining interaction between the men. There was more talking, and then Slate reached out and slapped the back of the man's head, making everyone around the table laugh. He made his way back over to where Jase stood and resumed his posture of attentive waiting.

As if nothing had happened, he continued their conversation. "You'll just have to be patient, man. She's one of those women who would be worth it. She was a good old lady, respected her old man, respected the club, and she is respected by the club in her own right."

Changing the subject, Slate looked over at him with a grin. "I had the fucker handled, but thanks for the backup, man. Hey, be here next Friday. I've got a three-fifty rice-burner lined up for you to ride and wreck around the parking lot. Go buy your gear: helmet, jacket, pants, boots, and gloves. Be ready, man. Birdy'll get you trained up, and then by the time Road's willing to drop the hammer on the sale, you'll be prepared to ride."

Jase nodded enthusiastically. "Yeah, I'm ready. You betcha. I'll be here with bells on."

***

For the next few days, there was a cyclone of media events for the whole team to attend, but within a couple of weeks, things had eased off to what Jase termed offseason normal. He quickly settled down into a predictable routine. He hit the gym every day, met teammates at

Jackson's for beers and conversation, and video-chatted with his nephews in Canada at least once a week.

Birdy had proven a hard taskmaster, but more patient than Jase had anticipated. He went over things Jase hadn't expected to learn, explaining how to jumpstart a bike and what to look for when it wouldn't start. An example was showing Jase how to open the petcock to drain water from the fuel lines. That, along with a hundred other small details that were cool to hear about and try to absorb, but he was afraid he could never remember half of them.

When it came time to actually learn to ride the bike, he took Jase to an empty section of the parking lot at Jackson's. Setting up a series of barrels and cones, Birdy called out maneuvers and speeds Jase could barely hear over the pipes, and seemed to change his mind on a whim about the direction and gear Jase should have the bike in.

He offered the biker a drink after each practice session, with no success. Jase had finally counted it a win when after the third time he received a casual hand flip, instead of a gruff, "Fuck you," as the man walked away. One day while at Jackson's, he asked Slate what the story was on Birdy, but received a non-committal response and decided against pursuing it, suspecting it fell under the club business umbrella.

After four brutal practice sessions on the smaller bike, the pair of men deemed him road worthy, and he borrowed an old bike of Mason's to ride around town. Bear being out of town had held up the completion of Road Runner's new bike, but he would be ready to sell it within a couple more weeks, and Jase was determined to be prepared.

He hadn't mentioned DeeDee to any of the men again, and none of them broached the topic, which he took to mean she simply wasn't interested. *Oh, well,* he thought, shaking his head, striving for nonchalant. *Ya win some; ya lose some*. He didn't like the way it stung, and he laughed at himself for having such an ego he couldn't take one woman's rejection. *Situation normal*, he thought and frowned.

His days were generally solitary, typically starting early with a run, and then the gym. He headed home to cook lunch, and played video games for most of the evening. Daniel frequently called to check up on him, as he did with all the players he was planning on keeping on next season's roster. He liked to stay in touch and make sure nothing was going wrong in the offseason.

He was sitting down to a dinner one night, when an unknown number rang his phone. "Hello," he called out, tapping the speakerphone feature so he could continue serving himself.

"Jason Spencer?" a woman's voice came over the speaker, sounding unsure.

"Yep, that's me," he said loudly, looking around for his napkin. Flipping it extravagantly, he settled it across his legs, looking down at his meal of grilled chicken, broiled squash halves slathered with soft cheese, and pan-fried green beans. *I'm one hell of a cook*, he gloated, laughing silently. *Road Runner's got nothing on me*.

"This is Anita Patterson," she paused and took a breath, "Coach Patterson's daughter." She sounded more self-assured now, but there was a fragile tone threading through her voice.

"Nita, yeah. I remember you. You had a good slap shot. You hung out at practice and chased pucks." He smiled at the memory; she was about thirteen when he moved away, first to Quebec and then to Russia. Coach Patterson was his hometown coach before juniors, and had helped shape him both as a player and as a man. He held him in the highest regard and always made time to see Coach when he went home to visit.

"Jase, Daddy died. Yesterday. I'm sorry I've left the call so late, but I just found the paper where he had written stuff down, so I'm calling now. I'm sorry." Her voice cracked and broke on the last words as she sobbed softly over the phone.

His stomach clenched and he reached out to pick up the phone, turning off the speaker. This conversation required more intimacy than yelling across the table. “Anita, honey, I’m so sorry. What happened?”

“His heart,” she whispered and cleared her throat. “He had a heart attack. I found him when I went to pick him up for breakfast.”

“I’m so sorry, honey.” Jase didn’t know what else to say. He hadn’t much experience with sympathy, on either side of the fence, so he didn’t have ready platitudes to offer her. Both sets of his grandparents were still alive, and he never had attended a funeral that was personal.

“So I found this paper. And you can say no, I realize it is late notice and a long way to come, but he put you down as someone he wanted at his funeral. He put this pre-planning thing together, and I didn’t know about it until I found this paper. He’s got you down as eulogy and pallbearer. I know I don’t have a right to ask for it, but I’d be pleased if you could. He thought a lot of you, eh?” Her voice trailed off, and then she spoke again, “I’m sorry to bother you, Jase. I found the paper—”

He interrupted her, “When is the service?”

“Day after tomorrow, five in the evening,” she responded quickly.

“I’ll be there. Count me in.” He shivered; those words sounded familiar.

“Oh, Jase, thank you. Daddy thought a lot of you, eh?” It sounded as if she was wiping her nose.

“Is this a good number to reach you?”

She said it was, and from there they talked small details. Jase kept her on the phone until she laughed at least twice, then finished the conversation, hanging up with a promise to text her his flight details. He called his mother next, verifying he would be able to stay with his parents. He had been planning a trip up anyway, but sometimes she had his nephews over. When she did, there wasn't enough quiet or room in the house to suit him and he could make other arrangements.

Next day, he was standing in customs at the Calgary airport, waiting on the woman in front of him to finish flirting with the customs agent and move along. Once he was through, he texted his parents then picked up the reserved rental car and headed north. It was the early days of summer and the scenery this time of year was beautiful. Rolling green prairie to the west ran across a broad expanse of land up to the tree canopy pressed along and against the mountains in the distance. To the east was more prairie, broken only by scattered farms and homesteads.

The sun was slanting to the west when he pulled into Red Deer, and he hit up a Tim Horton's drive-thru, asking for his usual hometown order of a double-double and a box of Tim Bits. He finished his trip with a grin on his face, popping donut holes into his mouth one-by-one as he navigated the surface streets to his parents' neighborhood. Sitting in their driveway for a moment, he looked around smiling. Home was the one place in his life he could count on remaining exactly the same, with an unchanging neighborhood and unchanging people. Simply unchanging.

He exited the car, stretching and rolling the tension of driving for several hours out of his back and shoulders. He was about to pull his bag out of the trunk, when the front door of the house opened. "Jase," his mother called, walking towards him with arms stretched open wide. Jacqueline Spencer was an attractive woman, even at sixty-five. She was nearly as tall as he was, and he thought with a wry twist to his mouth that she would probably still be able to take him down. Shaking his head, he smiled and wrapped her up in his arms, hugging her tightly.

"Hi, Ma." Grabbing the bag, he turned to walk with her. "You're looking good. Where's Da?"

"He's inside. I'm about to put food on the table, eh? Come in and eat. I've made brown toast with the eggs; it's breakfast for dinner. Your Dad wanted white, but I'm making enough concessions with the frying, aren't I? You're looking good, fit and healthy. Healthy is good. We watched the games, saw you got a lotta ice time during playoffs, didn't ya? Congratulations, Jase! My boy's a cup winner. Oh, it's good to see you, son." She never slowed her chatter, just wrapped one arm around his waist and pulled him alongside her towards the house.

Entering his parents' home was like stepping into a time warp back to high school, the décor unaltered and the layout still the same; even the furniture placement hadn't changed. He craned his neck to look into a hallway to verify and saw that yes, in fact, the same pictures from high school of him and his older brothers were still hanging on the wall. He saw there was a single empty rectangle and sighed, shaking his head.

"Son," his father greeted him, standing at the head of the dining room table and gesturing him over. Ignoring the hand that Jase offered, Kenneth Spencer pulled his son in for a hug, thumping him heartily on the back as he released him. "Good to see you, Jase. Go ahead, pull up a chair and help yourself, son. You know how we do it here," he said, sitting back down and handing Jase a plate. "Looks like you made good time from Calgary."

"Good time, yeah. Was a shame, though. Traffic was a bit congested in Olds."

His parents both laughed at the old family joke, because while Olds was the largest town between Red Deer and Calgary, it was small enough it was unlikely to ever have a traffic jam.

Conversation continued back and forth during and after dinner, talking about his mother's charity work and his dad's staffing issues at the firm where he was a partner. Jase told them about the playoff series, reliving some of the critical moments with them. After dinner, one of his brothers showed, bringing his two oldest boys for a quick visit. Their favorite Unka Jase wrestled and played with the kids until they were exhausted and irritable, handing the boys back over to their dad with a wicked grin and a shrug.

Bedtime came and he was standing in the doorway of his childhood room, studying the furnishings with a sigh. This was one place he would have enjoyed seeing a change, but time had stopped in this room, too. *Oh, well,* he thought, *I slept my last two years under this roof with my big, cold feet sticking off the end of the bed. It won't hurt me to do it a couple more nights.*

The next morning, he dressed for a run and stepped outside, taking a deep breath and noting, not for the first time, that the air smelled so different here from Chicago. After stretching, he set off slowly, gradually building his speed as he crossed and re-crossed the river for which the city was named, settling into a moderately fast pace for the last half of his run.

***

Breathing hard, Jase paced back and forth in front of the coffee shop for a few minutes, trying to cool down a little before he went inside. It had been a good, hard run through the city he loved, but now he needed some caffeine before heading back to his parents' house.

Yesterday, he texted Anita when he got into town. He hadn't wanted to call and pull her away from anything important, but hoped to provide simple assurance that he made it into town and would be ready and prepared this afternoon as he promised. His mind was circling the coming events, trying to shove down his nervousness not only about speaking in front of a gathering of people, but about the funeral itself. He had never attended one as an adult and wasn't sure what to expect.

He headed inside and placed his order, then strolled down to the other end of the line to wait for his coffee. Glancing around the small shop, he was surprised to see Anita seated at one of the tables, her eyes on the laptop in front of her. Asking the girl behind the counter for another of whatever she was drinking, he bought the frothy cup of mocha-something and picked up both mugs.

Slipping into the seat opposite her, he grinned when without looking up, she told him, "Gimme a sec, I have to get this uploaded." He was surprised, because he didn't think she saw him come in, and when she finally glanced up from the computer, the shock on her face was nearly comical. She said, "You're not Bernadette."

He laughed, handing over the mug of coffee. "Nope, 'fraid not. Sorry to disappoint, Anita."

She wrinkled up her nose at him, half-standing and reaching across the table for a quick hug. "Jase Spencer, I didn't think I'd see you in here."

"Could say the same, Nita." He settled into his seat, sipping his coffee. "How are you holding up, hon?"

With that question, all the humor fled her face and her lips twisted down. It was as if for a moment she had been able to forget her father's death, and then his inquiry brought it crashing back down on her. "I'm so sorry," he said, reaching across awkwardly to cover her hand with his.

She shook her head, waving a hand at him and picking up her mug of coffee. "It's…thanks, Jase." She sighed, reaching with her other hand to close the laptop. "I can't believe he's gone, eh?" Seemingly impervious to the heat of the liquid, she took a large drink from the mug. "Thank you so much for coming on such short notice. He sure thought you hung the moon. He would be glad to see you back home."

Jase nodded. "It was a mutual admiration society, wasn't it? I wouldn't be where I am now if it weren't for Coach. He helped keep me focus on what was important, letting all the rest float past. I thought the world of him."

"And he knew it, Jase. You'd come home for a visit and he loved that you always made time for him. You always made a point of coming to see him at the icehouse, and it'd get the boys fired up for weeks, because the great Jase Spencer talked to them." She laughed, sipping more slowly at the coffee. "He milked those visits for a long time, would tell the boys you called to check up on one or the other of them. It worked to get everyone to dig a little deeper, work a little harder."

Jase laughed. "Yeah, but I did call."

She cocked her head to one side, a puzzled look on her face. "You called to check on the kids?"

"Well, yeah," he said as if it was the only reasonable thing to do. "They were good boys; some of them had talent out the wazoo. Like Coach taught me, it's never too early to evaluate the competition."

She gave him a brief smile, but it faded too quickly. "Were you out running?"

He nodded, sipping from his mug. "Wanted to get a good run in. It's offseason, but you never stop conditioning, eh?"

"How are Jacque and Kenny doing?" She smiled when she asked about his parents, and he remembered she had been friends with his little sister at one time.

"Good, real good. Da's busy with the firm."

He paused to take a sip, surprised when she said, "As usual."

"I keep forgetting you know them from before." Leaning forward, he tapped one finger on the laptop. "College?"

"Work, actually." She smiled. "I cover girls hockey and the local ice scene for a couple of papers."

"No way. You're a sports reporter? When did you have time to go to college?" He was astounded, because it seemed only a couple years ago she was racing around the rink, chasing down pucks that slipped past the practice lines.

"Silly, I graduated a while ago. Daddy wanted me to go into sports management, but I like the stories behind the players more than anything else. He finally let it go when The Advocate picked me up, then stopped talking about me going back to school at all when The Journal began running my stories." He was impressed, both the hometown Red Deer newspaper, as well as the Edmonton one, had hired her. Jase returned her smile when she glanced up at him and said, "I'll be headed to Sochi next year to cover the Olympics. Here's hoping Canada puts in a good showing, eh?"

He reached across and clicked the rim of his mug against hers. "Here's hoping."

They were quiet for a minute. Then she asked, "Where's Sharon these days?"

He sipped his coffee then shook his head. "Last we knew she was in Florida, some town with a lot of letters in its name. She doesn't call much."

"I haven't talked to her in a couple of years," she said, leaning back and leveling a gaze at him. "Before she got married, she called all the time, but now..." Shaking her head, she set her mug down. "I don't think her husband is right for her."

"Well, it isn't as if she asked permission to marry him, eh? We got a call that she was hitched, and then she emailed a picture to Ma." He twisted and waved, getting the attention of the counter girl who nodded when he pointed to their cups. "On paper, he seems an okay enough guy, but that picture..." He faked a shiver. "Toad-like."

Anita laughed, the first real laugh he heard from her since sitting down and he smiled. He could see the cute that lurked behind the sadness in her eyes, and couldn't help but draw comparisons between her and the last image he had seen of Sharon. There was sorrow, such as Anita wore like a dark cloak, the loss of her father bowing her shoulders, but that kind of sadness could be endured. Beyond sadness, there was devastation, the hopelessness of which had been present in his sister's eyes.

"Yeah, toad-like pretty much sums it up. Gave me the shivers, too." The smile slipped from her face and she glanced up at him. "She had a hard time in school. I'll never understand why kids are so cruel." They both pulled back from the table as the waitress approached, and Jase brought out his wallet. He opened it and laughed. "You want some American?"

Anita laughed, reaching for her purse and pulling out four toonies. "Keep the change, Bernie," she told the waitress, who accepted the coins with a laugh. Turning back to Jase, she said, "It's the least I can do after you flew all the way up here for Daddy." Shaking her head hard, she scrunched up her eyes. Apparently trying to control her emotions, she lifted a trembling hand to cover her mouth.

He softly said, "I'd do it twice over if it would help, Anita. As many times as you needed." Pressing his lips together tightly, he looked around the room, away from her struggle, trying to give her the illusion of privacy. "So Sharon kept up with you after she left town?" He could distract her with his family's disaster. "I haven't talked to her more than two or three times a year since she booked."

"Booked?" she asked, clearing her throat.

"Yeah, I was overseas when she left, but from what I heard, it wasn't planned. She just threw stuff in the Jeep and took off." He shook his head; he was angry with his sister for a long time, because she had stolen his chance to say goodbye. He had let go of that emotion a long time ago. "I'm glad she had a friend to talk to."

"Jase," she leaned in, putting her elbows on the table, "she didn't randomly leave. She had been talking about it for a long time. She planned and saved, had a list of places she was going to go." Shaking her head, she added, "Of course, that all changed, but it wasn't a sudden decision."

"She never said anything to me." He scowled at the bottom of his mug, raising his head and catching Bernie's attention again for a refill. "We talked a lot when I was in Russia."

"Sure, if you call once a month a lot," she scoffed, and he frowned at her.

"It was more often than that." He tapped his thumbs on the edge of the table; he was sorry now he offered Sharon as a topic. "We talked a lot after her accident."

"Not from her side of things." She shook her head. "She talked all the time about missing you." Anita took a deep breath. "Look, Jase, I know this isn't any business of mine, but Sharon was messed up before she left. She told me more than once that she thought you didn't want to talk to her anymore. Like you thought what happened was her fault."

Jase shook his head. "I never said that to—"

She interrupted him, "Not in so many words. But did you ever tell her it was okay? That it wasn't her fault?" Bernie came over with his refill, waving off his attempts to pay her, and he smiled his thanks.

He ran a hand across his jaw, feeling the coarse beard with his fingertips. "It wasn't her fault." After he had gone to Russia to play hockey in the KHL, Sharon had slipped sideways for a time. She made a lot of questionable choices, and started drinking and partying harder than anyone would admit to him for a long time. It wasn't until after he was home that his mother told him about the baby she lost.

"She got caught up in a slew of pressure, and people who didn't love her. I think she has to take responsibility for the choices she made." Even to himself, he sounded self-righteous, and he tried to tone it down. "And by that I mean the decisions to drink and party, not what happened when she was under the influence—because she couldn't make a decision at that point, eh?

"But she knew we loved her. Always, eh? Family sticks like glue, and the Spencers have always had each other's backs. I wish I could tell her, but if she thought about it for even a second, she would flat know." He finished his third cup of coffee and shifted. "Anita, honey, I'll see you in a couple hours, okay? I have to get home and out of this." He gestured to his sweat-soaked workout clothes.

Frowning, she moved to get up, and he motioned towards her laptop. "Big-time writer, make up some good stuff about me, okay?"

Leaning in, he gave her a hug, squeezing until she squeaked and told him, "All right."

Depositing his mug in the bin for dishes, he stepped outside and quickly stretched then set off on a slow jog towards his parents' home, turning his conversation with Anita over in his head. It was true. He had been caught up in the glitz of playing for an overseas league, but he and his sister had frequently talked. She never said anything to him about leaving as soon as school was over, making plans...lists of places to visit. She never said anything about the baby, either.

He frowned as he ran, remembering the harsh voices of his parents in the background of some calls. He wondered at what point his mother had known Sharon was going, or if they tried to stop her. Yeah, she was eighteen when she left, but the picture he had in his mind was of the fourteen-year-old kid he left in Red Deer.

He wanted...*needed* to know that she was okay. He decided to call the most recent PI he used. See if the man was willing to take another run at the job of locating her. The last he knew, she was in Florida, but it was a big state.

The empty frame on the hallway wall of his parents' house must have bothered him more than he thought, because he kept circling around it again and again. The Spencers had always been a tight family, good to each other. Just taking down a picture wouldn't remove her from their thoughts. Couldn't take her away from their love.

***

Back at the house, he showered and then looked for his mother, finding her on the back deck, tossing a ball for one of the neighbors' dogs. Sitting on the bench next to her, he watched as she threw the ball over and over, each time working hard to coax the dog close enough to surrender it again. "You have a lot more patience than I do, Ma," he laughed, startling the dog into stepping back.

"No doubt it comes from raising you and your brothers. You boys would try the patience of a saint, and a saint I ain't," she retorted sharply, then tilted her face at him and grinned.

His smile faded, and he looked at her, saying, "And my sister."

"Yes, I know." She tossed the ball again, eyes on the dog as it headed out away from them towards the creek that ran through the backyard. "Jesus Murphy, baby boy. Tell me about your love life," she unsubtly changed the subject, rolling her eyes at him in a warning to drop the topic.

"No time for love, Ma. Sorry to disappoint, but there's no time for love." He shifted uncomfortably on the bench and knew his mistake as soon as her eyes zeroed in on him.

"Liar," she accused. "Tell me what's going on. That's what a mother is for, to talk to. Well...and cook, take her boys to and from hockey practice, but mostly for talking." She shook her head, still looking at him.

"I met someone." He ran a hand through his hair nervously. "But it didn't work out. Turned out she wasn't as interested in me as I thought." He shrugged, hoping she would leave it at that.

"But you like her?" She pressed him, bumping his shoulder with hers. "You do. You liiiikkke her." Drawing out the word, she laughed, bumping him again.

"Yeah. I liked her. I mean, I like her. She's incredible. She doesn't seem afraid of anything, and she's smart. Smarter than me, most definitely." He laughed. "I've never met a woman as secure in just being herself."

"What happened?" His mother picked up the ball and tossed it again. They watched the dog run after it and come back, standing just out of reach with the ball, wagging its tail as it looked them over cautiously.

"I had to leave for game five and she was gone before I got back into town. No number, no nothing. As I said, she wasn't as interested as I thought." He sighed and reached out, grabbing the ball from where the dog had finally dropped it near her feet.

"Maybe she got too scared? What if she is interested, but got nervous? Handsome man, big-time hockey player...lots to make a woman nervous about." She took the ball from his hand and threw it again, then stood, looking down at him with a thoughtful expression on her face. "If you like her, and you want her, I expect you can find her, son. She can't have gone too far, eh?" She trapped his hand on his knee, threading her fingers through his and squeezing tightly.

Bending down, she put their faces close together, looking him in the eye. "Go after what you want. I've never seen you back down from anything, once you set your sights on it. Like Russia, eh? Scared me silly to think of you over there, playing in that league. Brutish, big men. But, you knew it would be good for you, teach you a different style of the game. It made you adapt, learn to adjust, and it moved your game forward in ways you could not have found here. You knew that's what you needed and you went after it. Fearless and bold.

"So just like then, you gotta figure out what you need to do and do it. No excuses. That dirty word has got no place in our house, and you know better, eh? If you want this woman, then go get her. Take the shot, boy. If not, then move on. Neutral ice has its own rules, right? Go after what you want. *Je t'aime*, Jase." She cupped the back of his head in her hand, drawing him close to press her lips to his forehead in a kiss.

He wrapped his arms around her, hugging her tightly. "Beauty. When you're right, you're right. I love you, too, Mama."

***

Jase had worked on a brief eulogy for Coach Patterson last night and was ready when the pastor motioned him and three other men forward. He nodded at Coach's widow and Anita, huddled together on the front row in the church. Straightening his jacket, he stepped to the podium, smoothing the paper on which he had written his notes, and spoke confidently to the people gathered in the church. With only good memories of his time under Patterson's expert hand, it had been easy to come up with anecdotes that highlighted the encouraging influence the man had been throughout much of his life.

Before long, it was time to take his place alongside the casket with the other pallbearers, carrying their burden to the waiting vehicle and following it across the road to reverse the process to the graveside. Speaking to the family afterward, he rolled out the patented condolences he knew were expected and then he took his leave, heading back to his parents' house.

Another night in the too-short childhood bed left him grumpy and ready to go home to his much larger and more comfortable bed in Chicago. He would miss his folks—he always did—and it had been good to see his family, but his life was stateside now. Daniel called while he was waiting in the terminal in his connecting city, and they talked through a few of the tentative player selects for the next year's team. It was still weeks before the draft, but it sounded like negotiations were moving forward as expected. If things worked out, it would be a good team for the next season, another chance at the cup.

On the flight to O'Hare, he sat in first class, staring out the window, earbuds in as he listened to his favorite music list. His mind kept dredging up his mother's words about how he had never been afraid to go after what he wanted and he just needed to decide what he wanted now and pursue it.

Leaning his head back against the seat, he remembered DeeDee's face at the party, when she first caught sight of him headed towards her. She had not even looked back as Slate lifted her by the waist and set her over the porch rail; she only had eyes for him. Those blue eyes had darkened to twilight violet by the time he pulled back from kissing her the first time, and she circled around him the rest of the evening. Wandering out to greet groups of friends, but always coming back to him, as if there was a gravitational pull that returned her to him.

Did he want DeeDee? They had proven more than a fit together in bed; that was for sure. He smiled and reached down, discretely adjusting his hardening cock at those memories. She eagerly met his every advance between the sheets and given him unrestrained passion in return. He thought they fit together out of bed too, if their time spent at Jackson's and the party were any indication.

Okay. So, let's say I want her, he thought. *Now what?* She was in Fort Wayne; he lived and worked in Chicago. He got down that way about four times a year, for a limited number of hours surrounding a game. *But, that's only if I stay in Chicago*, he mused, shaking his head at where his thoughts were taking him. Was he honestly thinking about moving, living in the Fort during the offseason? That was only about four months a year, less if you count conditioning camps or playoff runs.

By the time the plane landed in Chicago, he was no closer to a solution, and grabbed his bag to catch a cab back to his apartment. He checked in with Daniel via text message, letting him know he arrived home safely. While unpacking, he found an unexpected box in his bag and laughed. His mother was always doing this kind of thing, slipping gifts into cars or suitcases and then claiming no knowledge of the item.

He opened the box and sat there for a minute, stunned. Inside were two items, and both were surprising. One was the missing picture from the family portrait hallway, a high school senior picture of his sister, laid flat in the box and wrapped lovingly with tissue paper. No note, no letter, simply an image to keep safe. In his mind, the implication was he would keep her safe as well. He shook his head. God knew that was a tall order. The girl had been intent on self-destruction for as long as he could remember.

The second item was more puzzling. It was new, but looked exactly like the ball his mother had been using to play with the neighbor's dog. She had a good time throwing it out and waiting for the dog to consent to bring it back. Again and again, she had waited tolerantly until the dog decided it was ready to approach her with the toy; she had been waiting for the dog to trust her, patient with faith it would come.

He sat on the couch in his living room and tossed the ball against the opposite wall, catching it on the return bounce. After a dozen times, he was no longer seeing the ball as he threw and caught it, his mind returning again to the puzzle that was DeeDee and what he needed to do if he wanted her.

***

The next night, he showered after his run and dressed quickly, then climbed on the borrowed motorcycle and headed down to Jackson's.

Mason had told him as long as he rode the bike, he could park in the row closest to the building, in a spot usually reserved for Rebel members. This would ensure no one messed with Mason's property, and Jase certainly didn't mind the preferred parking space.

Straddling a stool at the bar, he raised an eyebrow at Merry. "Mason or Slate around?" He used the mirror to check behind him, making sure he hadn't missed them when he came inside. Looking around, he noted Birdy's absence, too.

"Nope," she said, vigorously shaking a mixer then using a strainer to pour the liquid inside into a smaller glass with a couple ice cubes. "Haven't seen Mason all day, but I think he was over at Tupelo's earlier." She referenced another bar in town that he owned, and Jase knew Slate had spent a lot of time over there in the past.

"Slate over there with him?" He picked up his beer and took a drink, seeing her put a draft on a tray along with the prepared glass.

"Nope," she repeated herself, sliding the tray over to him and setting his beer on it as well. "Haven't seen him in a couple of days. Daniel I've seen, though. He and Mica are in a booth to the left. Take them the drinks, then why don't you hang there for a little bit. You're harshing my mellow with all your questions, young man."

"No tray needed, lovely." He shook his head, leaning across the bar to loudly kiss her cheek before picking up the mugs, balancing the glass with his fingers. She laughed and pointed, then turned to walk down the bar, stopping to speak to a beautiful brunette near the end who looked familiar. Walking across the room, he saw a hand waving from a booth, rightly assuming it was his boss and the cute girlfriend. They had gotten back together the night of the party, and he had hardly seen Daniel without Mica at his side since.

He sat there with them for a couple hours, the two hockey players hashing and rehashing games, dissecting plays that worked and ones that didn't. Mica had sat quietly for a time, an indulgent smile on her face as they talked circles around her. She finally spoke up, lifting her hands in a timeout signal. “Guys, as engrossing as this conversation is, I’m going to go sit and talk to Molly and Merry for a bit.” Leaning over, she kissed Daniel on the cheek. “Come find me when you’re ready to take me home.”

She picked up her glass and walked over to the bar, taking a seat next to the brunette who Jase now assumed was Molly. Looking closer, he realized why she looked familiar; there was a strong resemblance between the two women. “Her baby sister,” Daniel said, answering the unasked question.

“She up here for long?” He knew Mica was from Texas, so the sister was probably visiting.

“A few months,” Daniel said, shaking his head. “She’s pregnant, and Mica’s trying to settle her here so we can help out as needed. I think Mason’s offered her a job, so we’ll see where that goes.”

“Oh, man, that sucks,” Jase spoke sympathetically, thinking of his own sister. He had never wanted kids, so he made sure to wrap things up securely every time. No excuses, no surprises, no eighteen-year commitments.

The outside door opened and he looked up to see Mason walking in. He lifted a hand in a casual wave and Mason changed direction, heading towards their booth. Pulling up a chair, he sat at the end of the table, looking between the men with a muttered, “Hey.” Lifting three fingers over his head, he gave a piercing whistle and held the pose until Merry yelled across the room, “I see ya, old man. I got ya.”

“How was Red Deer?” Mason asked, surprising Jase with his knowledge.

“Good. Sad, but good. I got to see the parents and some family while I was there. I’ll be headed back in a couple weeks, but this was a good pre-visit visit for that part at least. How’d you know I was out of town?”

He jumped when Merry appeared over his shoulder, noisily dropping three full beer mugs on the table and leaving without a word.

"Mica mentioned something," Mason said, taking a sip and looking over at Daniel. "I heard J.J. was back in here this morning. He's sniffin' around, man. He knows the situation with Molly?"

"Yeah, he knows. I'm not sure what he's doing, but that man has been gone from the garage more in the past two weeks than he has been for years. Maybe ever, since his accident. Do you think she's upset with his interest? I can talk to him if you think I need to." Daniel's brow furrowed. His older brother J.J. was a paraplegic, wheelchair-bound for years since he was injured in an accident at the trucking garage he still ran. In the years that Jase had known the man, he had never expressed interest in any woman, so for him to ditch work to come see one now was a big statement.

"Naw," Mason drawled. "She's not showing any favorites between him and the goalie; they're both sniffin' around. She's showing both of them her sweet side, but nothing more."

They sat in silence for a few minutes, and then Jase asked, "Slate around?"

"Nope," came Mason's response. "Had to send him to Fort Wayne on club business. Whatcha need, man?"

"How about Birdy?" he asked. "I'm determined to make that man like me."

"Fuck that, man. He doesn't like anyone I know of." Mason stared at him, repeating, "Whatcha need?"

"Was going to ask Slate something about DeeDee. I'll give him a call later; see if I can catch him." Jase blew out an irritated breath. He was hoping to find out what DeeDee's status with the club was without asking Mason. After going over every conversation with her in his head, some of the things she said made him uncomfortable. He hoped Slate might be willing to shed some light without judging him for asking in the first place.

"Whatcha want to know? I've known the woman since we were kids." Mason offered this calmly, picking up his beer and taking a drink.

"Since you were kids? I thought you moved here when you were barely a teen. She's originally from Chicago, then?" He was embarrassingly eager for any information about her, and nearly rolled his eyes at himself.

"Nope, she's never lived here, just visited from time to time. Whatcha want to know?" This final repeat of the question had Mason's mouth drawn tight. He had given away personal information, probably more than he intended. That made Jase want to analyze their conversation, but he had an opening and wouldn't waste it; he had to at least ask.

"At the party, I saw she was watched and escorted pretty carefully by your Rebels. I thought her old man was dead, so it kinda confused me. What's she still doing hanging around the club if she doesn't have anything holding her there anymore?" *Shit that came out wrong,* he thought. "I mean, it's not like she's a hostage or anything, but is everything okay?" *Fuck, that's no better. Remember, he's known her all her life, apparently.* "What I meant to say was it seemed odd, like she didn't have control over small things. She was even told how long she would be here and where to go. Why would you do that if she's not in the club?"

"Jesus, Jase. You ask the oddest shit." Mason shook his head with an amused expression. "You know about Winger, her old man." This was a statement, not a question, but Jase nodded anyway. "He was a lifer. He lived as a Rebel, and dead or alive, we honor him by caring for his family. As long as she wants or needs to be associated with the club in any capacity, she has a place. That means we keep her safe. I asked her to come up for the party…for a lot of reasons. But, that party had the potential to be a cluster with so many people there. We had a bunch of different clubs with lots of tension about how some things are going down, changes I'm putting into place. With some of them, we have…strained relations. So, we watched out for her; that's all. Kept her safe." Mason brushed aside his false starts at questioning, answering the real one hidden in the mix. "We keep her safe."

Jase nodded, then paused and shook his head. "I don't get it."

"Fuck. Okay, look at it this way. You have a family, right?" He waited for Jase's nod. "You'd protect them against anything. It's what we do as people. We come pre-programmed to protect the ones we love, right?" He waited for another nod before continuing, "Well, to us, she's family—and we take care of family. Give them a place to stay, a reason to wake up in the morning, protection from potential harm, purpose in life—we take care of family, no matter what." Tilting his head, he looked at Jase. "She decides it's time to walk her own line, we'll respect that, too. Give her space as needed, but she knows we'll always be here if she needs us. She's family."

6 - Road trip

"No, Daniel, I'm only going for a couple of days. I'm planning to ride Mason's bike down. Birdy recommended I get a taste for longer rides and see if I like road tripping. Slate's already in Fort Wayne. I'm gonna hunt him up and show off my skills." He laughed, dropping a shirt into his bag as he switched the phone to his other ear. "Motorcycle ridin' skills, I gots 'em."

Daniel snorted and said, "Okay, let me know if you need anything. You barely got back from a two-week trip to Alberta, make sure you're not too tired when you head out."

"Will do, Cap'n...or should I call you mom?" he joked, pausing for a minute to listen to the background noise coming from the phone. "What the hell is that racket?"

"Mica's stressing over the wedding. When she stresses, she needs to work it out." Away from the phone, Daniel yelled, "Beautiful, turn it down."

There was a dramatic reduction in the volume, and Mica said in the background, "Sorry. I'll finish vacuuming later."

"Dude, it's like midnight. What is she cleaning?" Jase was laughing; he didn't know why his friend felt the need to rush their wedding, but the man seemed determined to be hitched before the season started. The truncated timeline for the event gave them only a few more weeks to get things ironed out.

"Everything. It's just stress, as I said. She's gotta work it out. Hey, keep me updated with your location. I worry about you riding that bike. Don't fuck up and get hurt, man." Daniel had always been a worrier, but Jase laughed it off like he usually did, hanging up the phone.

The next morning, he was up early and on his way, making the trip to Fort Wayne in about five hours. He found a restaurant on the north side of town and pulled into the parking lot to rest, regroup, and feed his stomach, which had been growling for the last fifty miles. Sitting at the table, he looked down at his phone lying there innocently, taunting him. He used one finger to spin it slowly, first one way and then the other. Not particularly wanting to call Slate, because the man hadn't been terribly helpful the last time they spoke, he was trying to decide what to do. He heard through the grapevine Tug had come to town with Mason's kid, and if Tug was here, he might have the information needed to find DeeDee. He was a ton more approachable than Slate too, at least for this.

Now to figure out who might have Tug's number. The waitress brought his food and he dove in enthusiastically, eating with gusto. *Mica*, he thought, *she'll have Tug's number. Hell, she might even have DeeDee's*. Setting down his fork, he picked up the phone and dialed. She answered breathlessly, "Hello?"

"Hey, pretty woman," he teased, laughing when she sighed.

"Jase," she said evenly, "what do you need?"

Oh no, she sounded upset. "Mica, honey, I hate to bother you, but do you have Tug or DeeDee's phone numbers?" He cut right to the chase; he didn't want to irritate the team captain's soon-to-be wife.

"Let me look. I think I have Tug's, but I doubt I have DeeDee's. She's always in Fort Wayne, so we haven't had a lot of girlfriend time. Is everything okay?" Her voice sounded distracted; there was a rustling noise in the background, then Daniel's voice closer to the phone asking who it was. She responded to him, "It's Jase, give me a second," and then rattled off a number.

He entered the number she gave him into the phone, thanked her, and hung up before his boss could ask why he was calling. Saving it into his contacts, he dialed, surprised when Tug answered on the first ring with a brisk, "Whatcha need?"

"Hey, Tug. It's Jase. How you doing, man?" Small talk...yeah, that would save him. Sure.

Silence greeted him, then a terse repeat of the question, "Whatcha need?"

"Hey, I wondered if you knew where DeeDee was these days. I'm in town and wanted to see her. Say hello, that kind of thing. Just say hello. If you knew. Where she was, that is...was." Damn he was nervous and his mouth was running away from his common sense.

"She's at work right now," Tug spoke slowly, seeming to weigh both the words and the worthiness of the audience.

"Yeah? Working is hard. Good, but hard. It's good she's working. Wherever it is. I bet she's good. At working, yeah." He cleared his throat and took a breath, feeling like an idiot. "Where's she working?"

"She's taken over managing a strip club we own." Tug said this casually, as if that wasn't simultaneously the hottest thing Jase had ever heard and the most frightening. *If she was managing, did that mean she wasn't dancing? I hope she's not dancing. That would...what? What would that do to me? But, her watching other women dance? That is seriously hot. Damn. I needed to ask Tug something, but what?*

Oh, yeah. "That's cool. Where is it?" He needed a name or address so he could go find DeeDee and see how she was doing...what she was doing.

"North of town a bit, called Slinky's. It's a nice place, not sleazy. She'll be there for most of the day; she's getting everything whipped into shape after the previous manager fucked it all up." Tug's voice carried the slightest level of amusement, as if he could see Jase fidgeting to get off the phone now.

"Beauty. I'll look her up. Look it up, the business that is. Go in, have a good visit with DeeDee. I'll see ya, Tug. Thanks, man." He disconnected the call and dropped his forehead onto the tabletop, rolling his head back and forth. Shit, he sounded like an idiot. Tug would have to be stupid not to realize he had it bad for the woman. *Shit.*

Pulling into the parking lot of the club, he saw a couple dozen bikes already parked near the building, so he backed Mason's bike into the row at the end. Pocketing the key, he strolled towards the door, admiring the motorcycles as he went. The one beside the door made him pause and narrow his eyes. He knew this bike; it was the one DeeDee had been riding in Chicago. *Shit, she really is here.*

Opening the door, he stepped inside, letting it close behind him as his eyes adjusted and he took in the layout of the room. Moving to the bar, he hooked a stool over with one foot, propping his ass on one edge of the cushioned seat. The bartender looked up with a silent question, continuing to hand-wash the dishes in the sink.

"Crown and Coke, lots of Coke. Nah, change it up, forget the Coke, and just keep the Crown. Double, rocks." He said this with a smile and watched as she dried her hands on a bar towel, pushing hair out of her face with the back of one wrist.

"You got it," she told him pleasantly, turning to grab the liquor from the display as he laid a bill on the bar.

"Hey, Spencer," a voice called his name, and he turned his head to see Hoss walking over to him. Standing, he stuck out his hand and they clasped wrists, shaking twice while the man eyed him up and down, asking, "You in town for long, man?"

"Few days," he said. "Got back yesterday from a couple weeks back home in Canada, and wanted to try a small road trip. Birdy said this seemed a likely destination, seeing as I know people here. So, I decided to come see what you boys are up to in the Fort, eh?" *Shit, give a boy two weeks in Alberta and I sound like a Canuck again.*

Hoss pulled up a stool next to him, tilting his head to look Jase up and down again. "And it wouldn't have anything to do with a particular cute redhead, would it?" He laughed softly, looking at Jase with sympathy. "Tug called, man. Any cover you expected is blown with the club, but she doesn't know you're here yet. "

He blew out a heavy sigh, his words coming in fits and starts. "I just...she wasn't..." He sighed again. "I want to see for myself that she's okay. We had a...but, and then she was gone. Just gone. Then she came all the way to Chicago to a game. She came to a playoff game, but then wouldn't see me. Hoss, man...there's something about her. I can't get her out of my head. There's something there and I...I can't...I just wanna see she's okay, eh?"

"She's taken on a lot in the past few weeks. We needed her and she stepped up, man. Don't know if she's got time for a sometime thing." Hoss shrugged and shook his head dismissively.

Jase frowned at him. "What do you mean a sometime thing?"

"You know, a guy who trots into town when he wants some pussy, gets what he wants, and goes back home. She ain't gonna have time for that sometimes shit." He waved his hand at the bartender and she brought him a glass of iced amber liquid.

Jase sat quietly for a few moments, calming his anger at Hoss' description of what he might have with DeeDee. In a tense voice, he said, "It isn't like that." He took a deep breath, trying to understand where Hoss was coming from. *He just wants to protect her; he's being like this to see how sincere I am.* "What if it wasn't only that?" He mused aloud, for the first time saying what he had been thinking. "What if it was living here in the offseason and home during bye weeks? If I moved to Fort Wayne? Would she have time for that?"

"She might," Hoss allowed, taking a drink and grimacing. "It sounds more serious, more like what she needs. Delia, honey, pass me the sugar, would ya?" The bartender dropped a container and a spoon on the bar in front of him and Jase watched in amusement as he ladled spoonful after spoonful of the granulated sweetener into the glass.

"What the hell are you drinking?" he asked, finally.

"Tea, but these damn Yankees all think unsweet is as good as it gets. Fuck that shit. Give me Southern sweet tea any damn day." He stirred the tea, watching the clouds of sugar settle and swirl, dissolving into the liquid.

"You're from the south, eh?" Jase stuck the tip of his tongue between his front teeth and bit lightly. He wanted to stop with the stereotypical Canuck-speak.

"Yeah, sweet home Alabama. Birmingham, I got folks there still." Taking another sip from the glass, he smacked his lips in satisfaction. "Now that's some damn sweet tea." He took another drink, setting his forearms on the edge of the bar. "That might be good enough for now."

Puzzled, he frowned at the man again. "Excuse me? Good enough?"

"Yeah, sounds a lot more than sometimes. We could get behind that." Hoss met his eyes in the mirror. "She's always going to be ours, man," he spoke quietly. "You gotta understand."

"Yeah, she's family. I get it," he responded, his focus shifting away from the man. He stared at the mirror, drinking in the form that appeared as a silhouette in an open doorway behind him. His breath caught in his chest, and his throat was tight as he looked at her. "I gotta...I'll be back, man."

Standing, he walked across the room towards her, the lighting from the office shadowing her face and obscuring any reaction. He couldn't get a read on her, wasn't sure what she might be thinking. She stepped backwards, inviting him into the room with a small gesture and closed the door behind him, shutting everyone else out. In the sudden silence of the office, he could hear his own breaths rasping in and out of his chest. She was here...right here in front of him. Finally within reach. *Fuck*, he was so nervous his hands were sweaty.

"Hey," she breathed, and he saw her hands anxiously twisting around each other.

He responded, "Hey." Smiling at her, he said, "You wore my jersey."

She dipped her head, a small, shy smile breaking across her face. "I did. Wouldn't want to wear anyone else's."

Moving towards her, he reached out, pausing before he touched her, holding his unsteady hands only inches from her face. He didn't think he would be able to breathe right until her skin was under his fingers again, but he didn't want to assume or pressure her. "Can I...may I?"

Reaching up, she cupped her hands around his, bringing them to her face wordlessly. He sighed when he touched her skin, soaking up the warmth and softness underneath his fingertips. He slowly bent his arms, drawing her to him, bringing her face to meet his as he gently traced her cheekbones with his thumbs. "God, DeeDee, you're so beautiful you take my breath away. I want to kiss you," he whispered against her lips. She nodded and he grazed his mouth over hers, dragging slowly across, nipping gently at her bottom lip.

"I can't stop thinking about you." He trailed his mouth along her jaw, pressing soft kisses to her skin between every word. "I…can't…stop…wanting…you." Moving back to her lips, he kissed her passionately, capturing her quiet moans in his mouth. "I need you, baby. I haven't seen you…talked to you…touched you for weeks, and I need you. I need to have you again." He angled his head, taking her mouth fiercely, reveling in the feel of her.

Her hands remained on top of his, holding them against her face even as he realized she was trembling. His cock was hard and throbbing, but he was determined to ignore little Jase as best he could. This was her work, her job. They were standing in her office and he couldn't disrespect her like that. He slowed their kiss, trying to hold onto his control, but she pursued his mouth, opening hers and stroking the tip of her tongue along his lips, asking for entrance.

Ah, God. Groaning, he surrendered to her soft demands, their tongues twisting and battling, gasping as the need for breath made its presence known, then diving back into each other, teeth clashing. He pulled back abruptly and shifted his hold on her face, forcing her cheek against his chest, trying to control his breathing, his reactions. He groaned again at the throbbing in his cock, his hips surging forward involuntarily, seeking the heat of her body where it pressed against him. "Nothing in my life prepared me for you," he whispered.

Her breasts flattened against his chest, upper body rising and falling with out-of-control breathing that matched him gasp for gasp. One of her hands slipped up his wrist, stroking his forearm over and over, soothing herself and him. They stood there, holding each other for long minutes, as they slowly calmed, hearts moving from a rapidly pounding beat to a steady, fast thud. She ran her hand over his skin, fingertips trailing gently along his arm. Trembling, he slid his hand up and down her back, underneath her hair, everywhere he could reach. Jase found himself unable to stop touching her now that his hands were back in contact with the woman, now that she was again in his arms. She finally pulled in a deep breath, letting out a slow sigh before stepping back, seeming reluctant to break their embrace.

"Jase, why did you come here?" Her face was noncommittal, her features unemotional as she asked the question. This was the mask she used at the party when speaking to the Rebel members.

"I wanted to see you, baby," he responded. He thought he communicated that with the kiss, but evidently he missed the mark.

"At the strip club?" She seemed puzzled and he was feeling the same.

"Anywhere," he told her, reaching out and tugging her close with the waistband of her jeans.

Laughing, she swatted his hands away. "I meant why are you here at Slinky's?"

"Because this is where you are," he said, leaning down to drop a soft kiss on her lips.

There was a knock at the door and it opened part way, bumping into his back. A man's voice came through the narrow crack speaking loudly over the background noise. "DeeDee, we need you out here, hon."

"Okay. On my way, Gunny," she responded, stepping back and reaching out to pull Jase away from the door. "Jase, it sounds like I need to take care of whatever this is. Can you wait around for a bit?"

"Okay. Just...is it okay if I sit at the bar? If I wait for you there? Or should I stay in here?" He wasn't sure what protocol was in a situation like this. His erection was going away slowly, but it would probably come back if he thought about her too much. *Is it okay for me to look at the strippers, with her as their boss? Will she be pissed if I look? Normally, I'd be a big-time lookie-loo in a titty bar, but if it makes her mad—*

She interrupted his internal dialog with a quick response. "Yeah. It's fine if you sit at the bar. The girls are pretty good, but right now, I gotta take care of whatever this is, so give me a few."

He nodded and said, "Okay." *That seemed like permission to look. Unless it was a test. Maybe I shouldn't watch. No, it was permission. Clearly permission, she's not the kind of woman to say one thing and mean another.*

He let her precede him from the office and they saw the problem at the same time. One of the customers at a table near the stage had evidently gotten handsy with a dancer. It looked like her response was to trap him underneath a chair, the rungs across his neck and chest. The scarcely clad woman was kneeling on the chair and had one stiletto-heeled foot balanced on the man's crotch, threatening without words to impale his junk. Jase winced.

"DeeDee, it's him again. I'm not putting up with this asshole one more time." The woman's shrill voice cut through the background music like a blade. "It isn't enough he talks about what he's thinking the whole time he jerks off in his pants, but then he tries to touch my ass with his goddamned spunky fingers."

Her voice smooth and even, DeeDee walked over, looking down at the man on the floor as she spoke. "Brent. You're banned." He looked like he was going to answer her, but she cut him off. "Nuh-uh, nope. No talking. No mouth. You're a level of sleaze we got no need for." She looked up and glanced around at the attentive faces in the bar, then back down at him. "Do I need to recruit help to deal with you, or can I have Mercy let you up nice-like?"

"I'm sorry," the man ground out, wincing and yelling as the dancer applied more pressure with her heel. "I'm sorry. I'm sorry."

"Well...yeah, we're in agreement that you're a sorry asshole. But that doesn't matter, because you're still banned. You'll have to talk to Slate to get back in, so keep that in mind." She made a gesture to Mercy, who somewhat reluctantly moved off the chair, picking it up and placing it beside a nearby table. Sauntering back to the main stage, she turned, hiking her ass up onto the platform, performing a fluid twist and roll move that put her into position against the pole.

Jase watched as DeeDee escorted the man to the door, closing it behind him with a firm thud. None of the other men in the room had moved to help her, not even the big bouncer standing near the door, and he realized with a start he hadn't either. She was so confident in herself that everyone seemed to assume she knew what she was doing and could manage just fine.

He walked to the bar, seeing his drink still sitting where he left it, ice melting and watering the liquor down. The music rose in volume and he looked up to see Mercy gyrating around the pole, evidently picking up her routine from where she had been interrupted. DeeDee was coming towards him and he smiled at her. He said, "You're busy. I can see that. I know I dropped in out of the blue. Baby, I'm going to go line up a place to stay for a few days. Give me your number so I can call you. I'd like to take you to dinner tonight. Please?"

She dug into her front pocket, pulling out a small leather wallet. Retrieving a card from inside, she asked the bartender for a pen and wrote on the back. "Here," she said quietly, handing it to him. "Jase, dinner would be nice." The logo for the club was on the front, with her name listed as manager. He flipped it over, seeing she had written her first name and a ten-digit number.

He tucked it into his pocket and reached for her hand. Threading his fingers through hers, he lifted it to his mouth, softly kissing the backs of her knuckles. "I'll see you in a bit. Decide where you'd like to go eat, okay?" She nodded and he turned to walk towards the outside door. He pretended to forget to let go of her hand and drew a laugh from her when he spun in an exaggerated fashion, whirling back to press a quick, soft kiss on her lips. "See ya," he whispered, and left.

Three hours later, he was settled into a downtown hotel, showered and waiting anxiously. Before checking in, he first rode around the Coliseum arena where they played hockey, then past the Rebel clubhouse, making sure he would be able to find it again if needed. He texted her the room information, but hadn't gotten a response. It didn't worry him, because she was working. *Yet.* Didn't worry him yet.

Pacing the perimeter of the hotel room, he was checking his watch every few minutes, trying hard to wait until at least five o'clock to call DeeDee. He knew most people worked from eight to five, so waiting until five seemed to be the courteous thing to do. He checked the time again. *Another five minutes more, and I'll be hearing her voice again.*

There was a tentative knock at the door, a single light rap of knuckles on the wood, and he looked at it, an eager question in his mind. *What if she decided to just show up instead of responding to my text?* he thought.

A second knock had him moving, looking through the peephole to find one of the hotel's housekeeping staff standing there. Disappointed, he opened the door and she looked him down, then up, wordlessly holding out a piece of paper. He accepted it and she turned, walking quickly away, casting a smile and an appreciative glance over her shoulder at him.

Shaking his head at the odd encounter, he backed into his room, unfolding the paper as he kicked the door closed. In about two seconds, he wished he had kicked the door a hell of a lot harder. ***Can't make it, sorry. It was good to see you today. Be safe, ~DD***

"Fucking hell," he yelled, punching the door with a rattling force. He dug in his pocket for the card, pulled out his phone, and angrily punched in the numbers she willingly wrote down only a few hours ago. After only a single ring, the call went straight to what he assumed was DeeDee's voicemail, but was just a robotic voice repeating the phone number he had dialed. "Goddamn, mother*fucking,* cock*sucking*, son of a *bitch,*" he hissed, punching the door again as he disconnected.

He grabbed his jacket and hit the door at a run. Unwilling to wait for the elevator, he headed for the stairs, going down them two and three at a time in his haste. In the adjacent parking garage, he straddled the bike, roughly shoving in the key, twisting it, and hitting the start button firmly. Closing his eyes, he forced himself to sit for a minute, bringing his anger under control. *No way in fucking hell is she going to get out of seeing me tonight.*

He had been through this before when she agreed to wait for him and then bailed; she had cut and run before he could get back to her. When it happened at the end of hockey season, it had hurt, but he let it go due to circumstances on both sides. He knew her dealings with the Rebels and his obligations with the team had both conspired against them. But not tonight, it wasn't happening again. Not after how they connected today in her office. There was something between them, and he...needed her. He wouldn't let her run this time, not again...not ever again. *No fucking way.*

Pulling out of the garage, he headed north towards Slinky's, but when he rode into the club's lot, he wasn't surprised her bike was no longer there. Running inside for a minute, he found out from Gunny that she left not long after he had this afternoon. Remembering what Hoss had said at the party about her getting cold feet, he knew taking off early had only given her that much more time to let her nerves get the better of her. *Fuck me and my waiting until five o'clock; she was long gone by then.* Sitting for a minute, he cast his mind around what little he knew of Fort Wayne, deciding to take a turn past the Rebel clubhouse so he could see if her bike was there.

He slowed to a crawl when he rode past the building, but her distinctive bike was nowhere to be seen. He did recognize Birdy walking into the clubhouse, which surprised him. Circling the block, he headed back east on Main Street, deciding to return to the hotel to find the housekeeper and make sure it was DeeDee who had given her the note. He was mentally making plans when he saw both the bike and woman, *that frustrating woman*, going the other way. Making a U-turn, he quickly caught up to her, seeing her startled reflection in the mirrors as she watched him fall into formation to the side and slightly behind her bike.

When she turned into the clubhouse, he rode in behind her as if he had every right, ignoring the scrutiny from the man holding the gate open. She parked her bike and sat there for a minute, shaking her head as she took off her helmet. Glancing up at him, she offered a trembling smile, looking as if she was going to burst into tears any moment, her face ashen. He walked over, captured her chin in his palm, and tipped her head up so she faced him.

They stared at each other for a long time, and he sighed at the look on her face. Those dark blue eyes met his gaze, raw fear leaving her vulnerable and open. Her hair barely tamed into pigtails, there were loose tendrils trailing along her cheeks, dark red against the smooth, creamy skin. His memory painted the picture of her naked body beneath him, muscles shifting as she pulled at his shoulders, wanting to be even closer.

He broke the silence, quietly saying, "Don't be afraid of me. Never be afraid. I'm not pissed. I just want to talk, DeeDee. If dinner seems like too much, then we just talk. But I need you to tell me what's going on in your head, okay? We don't even have to go to my hotel. We can go to your place. Whatever you want, wherever you're comfortable, all right?" He shook his head. "You're in charge. I know it's been a long time since we were together in Chicago, but all I have to do is think of you and suddenly, it's harder to breathe. There's something between us I've never had, the potential for something here I'm not willing to walk away from." His voice hoarsened. "You tell me to walk away right now, and I don't even know if I can. But...if you want me to, I'll...try. You're in charge, baby, but I want to...need to talk this through."

She laughed on a sob, covering her mouth with one hand and gestured behind her at the building. "This *is* my place."

He looked around, shocked. "You live at the clubhouse?" He knew from listening to the men in Chicago how crazy things could be in the house on an average night; forget about parties and weekends. *Is this what she didn't want me finding out? Has she been forced into some weird arrangement?*

Nodding, she said, "When Winger died, they gave me a suite. My daughter Melanie and I live here."

He sighed, relieved his sudden fears were ungrounded. Now he felt stupid, because he knew from experience how protective the club members acted when she was around, and that alone should have told him the same thing. "Can we talk?"

Standing, she climbed off the bike, absently patting the fuel tank, and nodded at him. "Just talk."

***

The next morning, Jase stretched lazily in bed, running his palm up and down DeeDee's naked back, slowly stroking her skin. He tucked his body in alongside hers, rocking his hips to brush his erection against her thigh and ass, continuing to touch her softly with his hand. There was soft music playing from speakers on her dresser, and he pressed his lips against her shoulder with a smile. Humming, he found his place in the song and then softly sang a few lines of *Hey Darlin' Do You Gamble* along with Ben Nichols from Lucero.

She rolled and pulled away from him slightly. "You're good," she said, smiling. "You have a good voice." Leaning in to kiss the tip of his nose, she slid her hands over his arms, drawing herself closer again.

"Pfffftt." He blew air through his teeth in a dismissive noise. "Receptive and affectionate audiences make concessions and excuses to cover a lack of talent." He laughed, closing his eyes to better focus on the heat building inside him from her touch. "Or something like that. What the hell did I just say?"

"I don't know," she whispered, her lips against his neck. "I wasn't listening anymore."

He gasped when her fingers wrapped around his cock. She stroked slowly up and over the crown and gave her hand a twist before sliding back down to the base. Every time they came together, it seemed she knew more of what he liked...wanted. He shivered, feeling himself lengthen and thicken as every nerve ending in his body came alive under her attention. Eyes still closed, he groaned and jerked involuntarily when her other hand cupped his balls, lifting and rolling them gently in her fingers.

He murmured, "Tighter. God, please, tighter. I won't break." Feeling her grip firm, he arched into her hands, thrusting as muscles tensed over his entire body. "Baby," he said softly, encouraging her. "Yeah, just like that, baby. God, that feels good." He took a breath. "You've got three minutes to make me come, or I'm back inside you."

She chuckled and he peeled one eye open to look at her when she asked him, "Is that supposed to be a threat? Because if it is, I don't think threats mean the same thing to you and me."

"That's a promise, baby. Not a threat. A pleasure promise." He thrust in her hands again, feeling the climbing tingles up his spine. Reaching over, he pulled a condom from the bedside table and handed it to her. "I can't wait. Nope, cannot wait. Now, God—I want to be inside you now. I need to feel you around me again."

Eyes closed, he listened to the foil wrapper tear open, and then groaned when her hot mouth surrounded the head then began engulfing him. It nearly broke his control when she took him to the back of her throat, the flat of her tongue pressing and rubbing on the underside of his cock, teasing the frenulum. Pulling off him with an audible pop, with firm strokes of her hand, she slowly rolled the condom down over his length, the heat from her palm blazingly hot as she moved it along his shaft.

Rolling over, he settled himself between her thighs, cradled by her hips as he ground into her clit, drawing a quiet moan from her. "You're always so quiet, baby." He nuzzled his nose along her ear, kissing her cheek as his hips moved in slow circles, dropping the tip of his cock ever lower and closer to her entrance. "Is this good for you? You have to tell me; talk to me, baby."

"Mmmm hmm," she made a soft, agreeable noise, tilting her head backwards into the pillow. Her hips shifted and he was *there*, inch-by-inch, sliding inside her again, feeling her inner walls grip and pull at him. "Mmmm, Jase," she crooned alongside his ear, cheek-to-cheek as he slipped his arms underneath her, holding her to him tightly.

"God," he breathed. "I'll never get tired of this, baby. You feel so good. So right. Tight." He kissed her hard and demandingly, keeping his cock pushed deep inside her, holding still. "And hot." Kissing her again, he stroked his tongue against hers, groaning into her mouth, beginning to thrust slow and deep into her pussy. "And drenched. God, you're wet...so wet for me."

Moving steadily, he pushed deeper inside her with each stroke, making small, slow circles with his hips. His groin gave a twinge for the first time in days and he ignored it, changing the angle a little to rock into her with an upward push, pulling countless breathless gasps from her.

"I'm close, baby," he told her, rolling his hips as he kept the pace painfully deliberate, even as she was tightening around him, gripping his cock hard.

"Mmmm hmm," she made the same noise as before, and her hands slipped down his back, cupping his ass and tugging as she pressed up hard against him. She stiffened and tensed under him, muscles in her legs tightening around his hips. The movements of her hands became erratic and her breath came in quick pants as she moved closer to the edge of a climax. Undulating with a full-body shudder, she shattered, pulling him along with her. He buried himself inside her, calling out her name with a reverent tone while she hid her face in his neck, lips frantically pressing against his skin. They stayed like that for long minutes, with him occasionally pulling out partway to glide back inside, rocking against her slow and gentle, pleasing her…loving her.

"God, baby," he said when he had caught his breath somewhat. "You are incredible. Just incredible." He ground his pelvis into hers, laughing when his softening cock slipped out of her. "Aww. Look at it, baby; we made a mess. Let's go clean you off so I can dirty you up again."

"The bath is shared with the other suites on this floor. Give me a minute to grab a washcloth. I'll be right back," she said, slipping out of bed and pulling on a t-shirt. Back in a moment with a warm, wet cloth, she deftly removed the condom, cleaning his cock and groin before heading back into the half-bath. She busied herself in there for a minute; it was quiet for a time, and then he could hear water running and the distinct sound of brushing teeth.

Hopping out of bed, he found her standing in front of the small mirror, finishing what looked like her morning routine. Pressing up against her, he covered her back with his chest, wrapping his arms around her tightly. Nuzzling his nose into her hair, he sniffed deeply and sighed loudly, making her laugh with a whispered, "I like that you smell like me." That laugh cut off abruptly when he reached beneath her shirt, cupping one breast with his large palm, sliding his other hand down between her legs, covering her pussy possessively.

"Let me take you to breakfast," he said, intently watching her in the mirror.

She tensed and sighed, shaking her head. "There's been some club business over the last couple of days. I'll have to find out how things are today before I leave for work. I might be needed here."

"Then let me cook breakfast for you," he persisted, frowning as she again shook her head. Something was going on here that didn't make him happy.

"The kitchen is a common area and prospects do most of the cooking. It's probably not a good idea to invade their space." She shrugged, looking down at the countertop.

He pulled back, dropping his hands to his sides, releasing her and watching a sad, resigned look sweep over her face as she kept her gaze down. He took a breath then hazarded a guess. "You don't want them to see me with you."

"It's not like that," she said, still not looking at him, but now he was getting...not mad, but something like it, and he interrupted before she got any farther. This wasn't his DeeDee. She didn't hide her face, didn't hide from things. He needed to provoke her, draw her out, make her admit that what was going on was something they both wanted...both needed.

He said, "I'm gonna go out on a limb here, but I suspect you're not willing for them to see us, because you think they'll react badly." She opened her mouth and he held up a hand, silently asking her for patience. "In all my life, I've never felt as seriously under scrutiny as I have while chasing after you these past months. Even when scouts came to the games when I was playing in juniors, I didn't feel this watched. But, baby, you have to know the attention has been far from discouraging. If they had been after discouraging me, I suspect I'd be stuffed in a box somewhere."

He sighed, keeping his eyes on her face in the mirror. "When I think about everything that's happened with the club members, I know I'm right. From them telling me not to let you get cold feet weeks ago in

Chicago, to yesterday, being grilled about my long-term intentions, it feels like they're rooting for us. Hell, I'd say it's even a fair bet they know I'm here right now, since the bike I'm borrowing from Mason is parked right next to yours outside in the clubhouse lot. Baby, it hasn't escaped my notice that no one—in the hours I've been here with you—not one man has come up here to throw my ass out. That tells me something."

He turned her to face him, palms sliding up and down her arms. "Baby, I think you already know all this, and also know you're holding a bad hand when it comes to putting me off. So, if we take any difficulty about the Rebels off the table, what arguments are left? I have a couple of guesses. One is that, evidence aside, you simply don't want this thing between us, whatever it is. Do you want me to go? Want me to leave? Like I told you last night, you're in charge. You want me to go, I'll walk. At least, I'll try to if you truly want me to leave.

He took a breath. "Then my second guess is maybe you just want the physical and would rather I shut the hell up. Do you only want my fingers and mouth, my cock, but not the rest of me? Is there no chance of a relationship here? Which is it, DeeDee? Because you're pushing me away pretty hard, and have been since the beginning. I think there's something here, baby, and I'm willing to keep fighting if you just give me the slightest sign that this thing is mutual. What do you say?"

She closed her eyes as he was talking and now shook her head, sighing as she tipped her chin up to face him, her eyes opening wide. Inwardly, he was encouraged, because here again was the bravery he had grown accustomed to seeing from her. He watched her, waiting patiently.

"I don't know what 'this thing', as you call it, is. I don't know what to call it, much less what I'm expecting. Does it have to be defined and discussed right now? Today? Jase, I'm not afraid of the members seeing us together, but you have to understand this is not my house. I feel like I'm here on sufferance, and staying here definitely means all the rules are theirs. It's their house. I've been looking at an apartment, because I hate feeling...like I'll end up owing a favor. Not that they would ever do or say anything to make me feel that way, but...something for nothing isn't the way of the world. And, right about now, God...I wish I'd already taken that leap, because things between us this morning would be very different." She offered him a one-sided smile.

"Do you want me to go?" he asked.

She shook her head and he kept trying to reassure her with soft touches, stroking slowly up and down her arms while waiting for her response, keeping that constant contact between them.

"How long are you in town?" She asked the question and then bit her lip hard, looking as if it had slipped out by mistake.

"A few days. I told the hotel three nights, which leaves two now." He closed his eyes, leaning forward and rubbing his cheek against hers, smiling at the small gasp when his stubble stroked over her soft skin.

"Can I stay with you until you have to leave?" Whispering her question, she pulled back and looked down as if she expected rejection.

He smiled at her, reaching out to tip her chin up, bringing her gaze to meet his. "Sounds perfect, sweetheart. We'll roll around in the hotel bed for hours, me wrapped around you. Then do it again, you wrapped around me. What time do you get off?" He laughed and changed his question. "Off work. What time do you get off work? I know you'll get off as soon as I get my grubby hands on you." Dropping his head, he growled and playfully bit the side of her neck, drawing a laugh out of her.

"I'll call you when I'm leaving work," she said, sidestepping out of his arms with a smile.

***

“Did you see that little son of a bitch slipping out of the clubhouse this morning?” Hoss was pissed, because for the first time ever, there had been an overnight visitor in DeeDee’s suite. “What the fuck did he think he was doing, inviting himself here?”

Slate turned his head, looking over at Hoss with a crooked smile. “Yeah, saw Jase sneakin’ out a little bit ago. What’s got your ass in a twist? She seems to like him well enough, and you told me last night you were happy with what you got out of him at Slinky’s. Second thoughts, man?”

“Motherfucker parked in the lot all night.” Hoss didn’t know why he was so angry. He talked to Jase yesterday and had ended that conversation feeling like the man would be a good match for DeeDee. Seeing how gently he treated her had gone a long ways towards settling his mind, too. In ten minutes, he had drawn a half-dozen laughs out of a woman who seldom smiled anymore. Then, seeing the morning-after evidence climbing on his fucking bike in the lot, knowing they were together...had been together, made him irate.

“Hard to park outside the lot in this area. Besides, he’s borrowing Mason’s scoot. You heard the boss same as me; he’s evaluating Jase. Man’s a friend of the club, means he gets a welcome into the clubhouse as long as there’s no private business in motion.” Slate shrugged and turned to glance up the stairs. “Seen Ruby this morning? I was thinking of taking a run.”

“Not yet. PBJ said he found her sleeping in one of the unoccupied rooms last night, made sure she was covered up, locked the door behind him. What about DeeDee?” Hoss had lost the edge of anger from before, but needed guidance here. His decision not to pursue the woman wasn’t sitting right, and he kept worrying at it like a dog with a bone.

Slate lowered his chin. "You know my answer, brother. We've had this discussion. She's her own woman, and that makes it her own decision. She's ours, but we respect her choices."

"Yeah, I know. I got you, Prez. Breakfast is ready, so why don't you go get something to eat. Last night was a little tense with Machos in our house." He yawned.

Agreeing with a nod of his head, Slate walked towards the kitchen. Hoss' phone rang and he looked at the display, hissing, "Fuck," and then answered the call from a man he knew in the Detroit Highwaymen MC. After the conversation, he went to hunt Slate down again.

"Hey, Prez, Highwaymen reported some issues with non-patched assholes up north. You sure you don't want a couple brothers on your six?" Mentally, he was going through the list of vertical and awake brothers already at the clubhouse. If Slate wanted company, he could roll with him, along with PBJ and a couple of the prospects.

Shaking his head, Slate said, "Nah, we won't go far; I just want to get the cobwebs out of my head with some wind. There's been a lot of shit rolling around for days. Things are finally starting to settle down. Want to get it out of my head for a while, and I thought Ruby could use a break too."

Hoss nodded, and then asked, "You heard Manzino vacated?" Slate gave him a chin lift and looked a question at him. Shaking his head, Hoss said, "I don't trust it. It was too easy after all the shit we went through." Manzino was a drug dealer they had a fuckton of shit with while Bingo was president. The riffraff drug dealers had ranged closer and closer to the clubhouse and other businesses without any serious pushback from the club, setting a dangerous precedent.

When Slate had taken over as president in Fort Wayne, that pushback had been reengaged with a vengeance, and the club had eliminated threats within a broad boundary around all Rebel properties in town. Not surprisingly, Manzino had taken it personal, and in retaliation had sent dozens of his men to try to reclaim his territory, buzzing around the members like pissed off hornets. Now the man had dropped off the face of the earth, and Hoss didn't trust it at all.

Slate agreed, "I know; I'm not feelin' it either. We put a hurtin' on his business, though, so he has to relocate in order to make his bank back. It could be as simple as that. We'll sort that shit out over the next couple of weeks. Today, I want to take a run."

Hoss nodded and turned away.

7 - What is this?

DeeDee found herself humming quietly as she folded and packed clothes into their bags. Jase would return to Chicago today, and while this interlude had been beyond enjoyable, it was time for her to go back to the real world. It was early morning, and she should be tired, given she never made it to sleep last night, but found herself strangely energized instead. Jase was showering, pouting because he hadn't been able to tempt her into the shower with him…again. Shaking her head, she smiled, her hands pausing in their task for a moment.

Since she walked through the door two nights ago, they hadn't left the room except for one brief run on the bikes so she could show him the apartment she was considering renting. He wanted to see it for himself, had loftily informed her he had to see it, because not just any place would do. Fortunately, it was in a lovely complex on the north side of town, convenient for shopping and close to both Slinky's and her favorite bar, Checkerz.

He approved of the apartment. Then he shocked her by putting the deposit down right then and there, ignoring her very vocal protests. It was as if he didn't even hear her. Frustrated, she threw her hands in the air and walked away, giving up trying to stop him.

She had grown to realize over the last forty hours that it was nearly impossible to argue with Jase Spencer. The man was accustomed to getting his own way, but he wasn't a bully about it, merely convinced that his way was the right way. His arguments about the apartment had been conducted with a heaping measure of utmost respect, as well as a chaser of humor. It made for a potent cocktail and one that she found hard to resist.

Finishing folding the shirt in her hands, she placed it in his small duffle and patted it fondly. That shirt had been all she was wearing last night when he bent her over the edge of the bed. She had been trying to talk to him about the apartment again, and he derailed the conversation with his naked body. Pushing the shirt up gradually, he layered kiss after kiss on the skin of her back as he exposed it, nibbling on her ribs and shoulder blades as she laughed and wiggled to get away. The position had pressed his hardened cock against her ass and he rubbed it ruthlessly up and down, teasing against her anus with the head, giving her a thrill of tense anticipation.

Reaching around her body, he had groaned when his fingers found the slick wetness between her legs and arched his body, holding his cock in place as he slowly pushed into her. Wrapping his other hand around her hip, he pulled her back against him in an unbroken rhythm, his cock gliding deep inside her with every smooth thrust. He held the pace steady until she climaxed, coming with a clenching of every muscle, his words of praise and desire helping to ratchet up her reactions, pulling a little groan from her. He then followed her over the edge, losing his words and control within a few hard, erratic strokes. She sighed, thinking, *I'll figure out a way to repay him the money*. Now, she simply had to find the right counter-argument when he wasn't distracting her in what had quickly become a myriad of her favorite ways.

Sex between them had been explosively passionate every time. Around Jase, she was nearly out of control, constantly wanting him to touch her, cover her skin with his hands and body.

They discarded condoms on the first night after a conversation about sexual partners. She had only been intimate with one man before Winger, and none since his death. Jase told her his last sexual encounter had been months before at a drunken party on the road during the previous season. The team's regular physicals included testing, and he offered to provide her a copy of the paperwork. She believed him, not because she didn't think he got hit on, but because he didn't shy from her questioning. He also wasn't taking the opportunity to crow about what she assumed were the many conquests and encounters he could have had as an attractive, professional athlete who was a favorite with fans and press.

She shared with him that pregnancy wasn't an issue for her due to a hysterectomy right after Lockee was born. After having multiple miscarriages and two stillbirths as she and Winger tried for a child, when she finally had been able to carry a baby to term, her doctor had recommended the procedure. He explained to her that her body couldn't continue to take the abuse she was piling upon it. Told her some things weren't meant to be.

When she spoke of the surgery, glossing quickly over the agony of the pregnancies that wouldn't stick, wouldn't go to term, Jase had gently used the tip of one strong finger to stroke the tiny scars she carried. She had always been troubled that it had only taken three small, inch-long incisions to remove any possibility of ever becoming a mother again. While silently pressing kisses to those indelible reminders on her skin, he slipped between her legs and then trailed his mouth down her belly, not stopping until he brought her to climax with his fingers and tongue.

They talked. God, how they had talked through these hours together. She explained about Melanie, telling him how Lockee and the girl had bonded early and hard. How she had been there after the accident, helping DeeDee keep putting one foot in front of the other, day after day. Mel had stayed as close to her as a daughter, which was how she had come to think of her.

Jase had wanted to know about the accident, and about what happened to her the day Winger and Lockee died. She shared her emotions with him, feeling his arms tense around her as she talked about being alone when the call came in. He kissed the top of her head when she spoke about seeing Bingo in the hospital and knowing instinctively that it was bad…that her family was gone. But, even beyond those conversations about difficult topics, he was full of surprising questions about everything. He wanted to know how she took her coffee—black—what kind of socks she liked—ankle-high—her favorite color—yellow, and her favorite animal—bunny.

Even when deep inside her, he didn't stop asking questions, constantly murmuring into her ear. But those inquiries were about speed and depth, comfort and arousal, feeling good and coming hard. She had never met anyone who wanted to know her in that kind of intimate detail. It was flattering; hell, this whole thing was flattering, because he was both young and hot, and *still* seemed to want her with a fierceness that was startling.

He was so different from anyone she had met before. She thought back to something he said in an unguarded moment, how nothing in his life had prepared him for her. She felt much the same way, because all her expectations and reactions were programmed to match the man she spent decades married to, and Jase was…well, Jase. He was lighthearted and fun, gentle and sensual. He made her laugh a lot, and around him, she was confident in a way she hadn't been for a long time.

Not that Winger hadn't been fun; they had a lot of laughs over the years and had shared a deep and profound love. But he was sixty-six when he died. There was a big difference between how one acts at thirty and how one acts at sixty-six. She smiled, thinking that even at that age, she suspected Jase would keep anyone on their toes.

After Winger's death, she had done her best to come to terms with the idea of living the rest of her life alone—without companionship. She knew, by nature of being in the life, there were few opportunities to meet new people within the club. And while she loved every one of them, she couldn't see herself leaning on any of his friends for a real relationship of any kind, much less a physical one. She remained close friends with Bingo, and of course, loved Mason beyond belief.

She actually loved all the Rebels, because they were her boys...but she kept her guard up around most of the men. Many of them, like recent addition Birdy, made her somewhat wary, afraid of making a misstep and earning his judgment. There certainly wasn't anything romantic between her and any of them, nothing conducive to being more than friends. And now, after being with Jase for only a few days, having this little bit of a relationship, she couldn't imagine going back to her lonely life.

There was no warning. One minute, she was standing at the end of the bed, distractedly looking down into the bag she was packing, and the next, she was lying on her back in the middle of the bed with one very wet, very muscular, very aroused man on top of her. He shook his wet hair, flinging water droplets in every direction, leaning in to lick the water from her face as she giggled. He pressed full length against her, his wet body molding her shirt to her chest.

"You're wet," she protested, and he nodded, giving his hair a shake again.

"Yeah, but I've got great shower hair. See?" He shook his hair again, the ends of the slightly long, dark blond locks coming to rest against his cheeks. "Great shower hair. All I have to do is towel it and then shake and I am good to go."

"But now I'm wet," she complained, and he laughed.

"You are wet," he murmured, sliding his knee between her thighs and pressing against her core. "Your clothes are all wet. So wet." He trailed his tongue down her neck to the collar of her shirt, tugging it gently with his teeth before raising a hand to unbutton the garment.

"Drenched. We need to get the wet clothes off you," he spoke with his lips against her breast. "Can't have you getting sick on us, eh?"

That was something she found endearing, the way his accent slipped out of him at unguarded moments. Most often it was an 'eh', but she caught him in several 'doncha knows', and even one 'there okay', which until now, she thought was strictly Minnesotan. Laughing, she slipped her palms down his sides to his hips, fingers tracing the curves of his thoughtfully bare ass to pull him in closer.

***

Walking into the clubhouse, DeeDee looked around cautiously. The atmosphere was different; something in the club had shifted in her absence. Seeing Hoss standing near the bar, she walked over, smiling up at him. He had always been a brother and good friend of Winger's and had helped her navigate through many events since the accident, including the recent shift of leadership within the chapter when Bingo stepped down to focus on his sister's kids.

He smiled at her, motioning to the prospect for another mug of coffee. "DeeDee," he said in his deep voice by way of greeting.

"Hey, Hoss," she responded, thanking the man behind the counter for the coffee. "Anything I need to know before I head out to Slinky's?"

"Ruby call you?" he asked, and she was surprised he referred to Melanie by Slate's nickname for her.

"No, should she have?" This kind of questioning made her nervous, because she wasn't at all sure where he was going with it, so, as always, she answered carefully.

"Looking like she's Slate's old lady," he said bluntly, and she drew in a shaky breath.

"That so?" Casually, she wiped her sweating palms on her jeans. Propping her elbows on the bar, she opted to lace her fingers together, cradling her chin in her hands, leaving the mug sitting on the bar. She knew if she tried to pick up the coffee right now, her hands were trembling so badly she would spill most of it.

"Yeap," he said, picking up his mug and blowing across the hot liquid. "Couple days ago, they came back off a run and she was wrapped around him. They've been joined at the hip since. Looks like a good thing for our girl." He smiled and sipped his coffee.

She pulled in a breath, not allowing herself to feel relief yet, even if it sounded like it was Melanie's choice to be with Slate, the man who had quietly pursued her for months. He had given her a choice when he took over as chapter president, granting her wish for stability and status by flagging her as club princess, same as Mica was in Chicago. He had also given her a job around the clubhouse, and together the two things helped to raise her self-confidence immeasurably.

Not long after the accident, Melanie had been hard-used by a man, and she still bore the psychological scars from her time with Demon, the president of a Michigan club. For a long time, DeeDee had been hoping she would be able to put it behind her entirely, but until now, every time it looked like Mel was beginning to recover, something would happen to set her back.

But from the moment Slate showed up at the clubhouse, she knew...she believed he was the one who could help Mel. He was handsome and kind, and she knew her girl was attracted to him. DeeDee's expectations weren't just because he was a good man, but more because he had been in love with the girl almost since he laid eyes on her.

"So, where you been, hon?" Hoss sipped his coffee, gaze fixed on her in the mirror behind the bar.

"I was with Jase," she said, lifting her chin in an unconsciously defiant move.

She was so focused on Hoss the voice that came from her other side startled her. “About damn time, woman,” Tug said with a smile. She jerked, elbow hitting the mug, slopping coffee over the rim onto the bar top.

“He say anything to you about what he’s thinking?” Hoss asked the question casually, making her wonder exactly what the two men had been talking about at the strip club before she walked out of the office.

“What do you mean?” She asked this casually as she took a bar rag from the prospect’s hand, cleaning up her own mess. She always treaded cautiously when questioning club members, not wanting to seem demanding.

“I mean, did he tell you what he’s got planned where you are concerned?” Hoss was being overly patient with her, and she saw Tug’s mustache twitch as he tried to conceal a smile.

“It was just a nice weekend,” she said, and then stopped when both men laughed aloud at her statement. “It was,” she protested. “Nothing more.”

“Yeah, keep telling yourself that, hon.” Hoss pushed his mug back over to the prospect. “Fill 'em up, kid.”

Hearing the dismissal in his voice, she excused herself and went upstairs to the suite, finding Melanie in the middle of packing some of her clothes into a cardboard box. “Hey, sweetie,” she said, turning the girl around for a quick hug. Finding a bright smile on her face, she looked into her clear green eyes and let go of a little more of the worry she had been carrying around.

“You’re happy?” She asked the question casually as she picked up a shirt, her mind going back to her morning with Jase as she folded Melanie’s clothes.

"Yeah, I am," Melanie said shyly. "He makes me feel safe. He doesn't rush me or push me." For someone as broken as Mel, that feeling of safety would be critical for her trust to grow.

A comfortable silence fell between the two women, and it was several minutes before Melanie spoke again. "He says things to me and I believe him. Said he loves me." She took a breath, looking up at her. "He said it's forever. 'For-fucking-ever'." She smiled and gave a one-shoulder shrug. "I believe him."

She folded and refolded the shirt, waiting because she knew Melanie wasn't finished talking. "He calls me Ruby and I like it. A ruby is precious, and that's how he makes me feel. DeeDee, I think I've loved him for a while. I'm his Ruby."

"I'm glad, baby. No one deserves a happily ever after more than you do. Slate's a good man. He's honorable, and he'll protect you if needed, sweetie. I believe right along with you, because if he said it to you, then it's true." She hugged Melanie, softly kissing the top of her head. "Slate's Ruby, I like the sound of that."

She helped Ruby move most of her things into Slate's room, and there was the smallest pang of guilt at not giving up the suite for them. But this had been her space since she moved into the clubhouse, and even though she knew she would depart the clubhouse herself in a few weeks, she hated to leave what had become comfortable. The apartment manager had texted that morning to let her know she could take possession at the first of the month. She had already begun cataloging her belongings in her head, trying to remember all the things packed into boxes in storage, pushing away thoughts of anything that could complicate matters.

***

Several days went by and she kept careful watch, seeing Ruby's demeanor change, lightening and easing. Her smile made a much more frequent appearance as the young woman relaxed into the new belief that Slate loved and wanted her. DeeDee was thrilled to watch her open up to Slate, but knew that left to her own devices, Ruby would avoid the topic of Demon for as long as possible.

Demon. DeeDee shuddered at the name.

He was the dark shadow in Ruby's past, and while it was an ugly story, it was one Slate needed to know. She had seen Ruby withdraw into herself before from just a chance question or phrase, and she knew their shared bed would hold even more possibilities of terror. Slate had to know what had gone on before in order to understand Ruby. It was the only way to assure he wouldn't misread her responses, and hopefully they could avoid a catastrophe triggered by a bad reaction.

Pulling all her courage together, DeeDee took a seat in Slate's office and told him everything. The devastation Melanie suffered after the accident that took her best friend and surrogate father. How she thought she found something worth exploring with a visiting member of the Devil's Sins, Demon. Talking about Ruby going to Michigan willingly...and then betrayed, kept as a prisoner, brought DeeDee to tears, but that wasn't the worst of it. *Demon*.

Demon had isolated Ruby once he had her in Michigan, restrained and terrified her for months, abusing her daily...until she lost value in his game and he finally released her, pregnant. But even that hadn't been enough for the man, and as a final blow, he had caused her to miscarry the baby while she waited alone for rescue.

From the Rebel members, over the years, DeeDee had overheard stories about the harder side of Slate, but she never truly understood how frightening he could be until that morning. During their conversation, she saw for herself the truth behind the rumors. He was furious at the treatment Ruby suffered, and even though she knew his anger wasn't directed at her, it was still a terrifying thing to see. He made it clear Ruby was his first priority, but she was certain Demon would be paying for his evil before long.

At the end of their conversation, she braced herself, and using the last of her courage, told him about the apartment, asking what he thought about her moving out of the clubhouse. More than anything, he seemed pleased she wanted to stay on, managing the strip club. When he said they were glad to keep her on, an enormous weight lifted off her shoulders. Until that moment, she hadn't realized how deep the fear ran that the club would think she wasn't grateful for everything they had done for her, but he put those fears to rest. As she told Slate, it was just time to begin moving on.

***

For the next couple of weeks, every night before bed, she and Jase talked on the phone. She was growing accustomed to laughing and joking with him as he told her about his day and found herself looking forward to the sound of her ringing phone. He had finally bought Road Runner's bike and was excited about riding it down at the first opportunity so they could take a short run together. It would be a while before he could, because things were beginning to ramp up for his upcoming hockey season. Regular games ran from early October into the middle of April, and the team would be playing two or three games a week, sometimes more. In an effort to soothe him, she reminded him that between the cold and the weather, the time of year wasn't usually conducive to rides anyway.

His descriptions of the team's conditioning camp workouts sounded brutal. He sometimes called her while he cooked dinner for himself, and she smiled as she responded to his running commentary, hearing the exhaustion in his voice, but also hearing the determination that so personified him. Lying in bed or on the couch, he fell asleep more than once while they talked. When he did, she stayed on the phone, listening to him breathe for a long time. Remembering the first time he slept beside her would bring a smile to her face before she called his name to wake him, laughing at his sleepy voice as they hung up.

Everything was chaotic with work and in the clubhouse, and there was so much to do that she nearly had given up trying to plan things out, just taking them day-by-day as they came. Frazzled, her nerves kept her on edge, because it was down to less than a week before she moved, and she still wasn't entirely ready. She began going to the storage building after she got off the phone with Jase in the evening. Exhausted, she would sort through boxes by flashlight until she couldn't keep her eyes open any longer. Finally, she had all the necessities moved to the front, where it would be easy to grab them when moving day came.

Even trying to reserve a rental truck for the move was a disaster. When Hoss overheard her making arrangements, he reached out and plucked the phone from her hand, telling the agent that their services were unneeded. Then he scolded her, "DeeDee, hon. You're family. We got you, babe. Slate and I already talked about this."

Aggravated, she rolled her eyes at him and snapped, "I'm capable of organizing the move myself. Getting me out of the clubhouse is not your responsibility, Hoss. Not yours and not the club's."

"Capable don't matter. Hon, you aren't leaving the family, merely relocating your living space. Now, would you stop giving me shit?" He reached out, cupping the sides of her face with his palms. "Let us. You matter to us. Let us do this." Leaning in, he kissed her forehead, pressing and holding his lips there for several seconds, the gentle act infused with such love and patience it took her breath away.

"Okay." With tears in her eyes, she nodded when he pulled back, looking down into her face. She let him see her gratitude for so much more than help with the move, rewarded when his face softened in recognition. Swallowing hard and smiling up at him, she said, "Okay. Thank you."

Slate and Ruby had moved out of the clubhouse two weeks earlier, and on her moving day, they were both at the apartment bright and early. Ruby boldly directed the members as they trooped in and out, carrying boxes and furniture brought from both the suite at the clubhouse and the storage unit.

DeeDee was standing in the kitchen when she felt an electric charge in the air and instinctively turned, finding Jase standing in the doorway behind her. "Hey," he said, smiling crookedly, "heard you could use a strong back today."

"Hey yourself," she answered him, closing the distance between them quickly and wrapping her arms around his waist. She burrowed her face into his chest as his arms folded around her, holding her securely. Her pleasure at seeing him and being in his arms surprised her. "I didn't know you were coming. What a lovely surprise."

"DeeDee, where do you want—" Ruby abruptly stopped talking as she entered the room, her feet dragging to a halt when she saw Jase holding DeeDee.

Turning in his arms, she smiled at the young woman. "Ruby, this is Jase Spencer. Jase, this is Melanie Davidson, my daughter. She's Slate's Ruby."

One arm still around her waist, he thrust out a hand and Ruby looked at it distrustfully, wrinkling her nose before drifting slowly over and offering her own for a quick handshake. Jase said, "I'm glad to meet you, Ruby. I've heard so many good things about you from DeeDee."

She silently nodded at him and took a step back as Slate walked into the room, coming up behind her and cradling her into his side. "Jase," he nodded as he spoke, and Jase offered him a chin lift and a gruff, "Hey."

"Ruby, baby, where are we putting the desk?" Slate kissed the side of her head and smiled over at DeeDee, winking. He could have simply asked her, but Ruby had put herself in charge of the move and he was always looking for ways to build her self-confidence, even with such small things as furniture arrangement.

Ruby shrugged and Slate pulled her into the other room telling her, "Show me." DeeDee smiled. He was patient and good with Ruby, and his adoration became more apparent every day.

She laughed as Jase's arms tightened around her, going quiet when he asked, "What am I?"

"What do you mean?" she asked carefully, not sure what the question meant, but suddenly...intensely afraid of getting it wrong.

"You introduced us and told me Ruby was your daughter. But what am I to you?" He didn't seem upset, only curious. "If you had to label me, what would I be?"

"I—Jase, what do you want to be?" This was dangerous ground, the footing treacherous, and this entire topic made her nervous. Realistically, she knew they had only been together a handful of times over two weekends. And even though they frequently spoke on the phone in the interim, she had studiously ignored any desire to dissect their relationship, not wanting to clarify or qualify things. Foolishly thinking she could skate along for a while yet, she hadn't anticipated him showing up today, hadn't thought she would have to introduce him to her family.

"I'm a little old to be a boyfriend." He mused, "I could be your lover, but that might be awkward in some settings. Plus, it just doesn't have the relationship validation I'm looking for. What about calling me your man?"

"If you're my man, does that make me your woman? Nuh-uh, I don't think I like that, oh, caveman," she teased him gently, hoping to steer him away from the language club members used for their significant others. He wouldn't understand that being someone's old lady was like being married.

"You *are* mine," he growled softly next to her ear. "My woman, my lover, my playmate, my sweetheart, my main squeeze. You're my girlfriend, my partner, my plus one, my steady...I got a million of 'em, baby. I can do this all night."

Laughing, she turned to face him, tipping her head to the side, joining in with his joking as she said, "My confidante, my companion, my beau. Any of those strike your man-fancy?"

Nuzzling her neck, he lowered his head to kiss her collarbone softly. "My cherished, my treasure, my fantasy come true. My darling, my one and only, *mon amour, ma belle, je t'aime*, DeeDee. *Je t'aime. Sais que je t'aime.*"

"I don't know what you just said," she rose up onto her toes to whisper in his ear. "But I'm drenched now. That is so sexy, Jase."

Laughing hard, he cupped her ass with his big palms, pulling her tightly into his groin, letting her feel the erection pressing against the seam of his jeans. "I can't wait to christen the bed with you, *ma belle*. Let's get the rest of this stuff moved in and we'll get you unpacked." He kissed her softly. "Then I get you."

***

Jase threw himself backwards onto the middle of the bed, bouncing on the mattress with arms outstretched. "And with the final box broken down and stacked for disposal, I pronounce that the move-in process is now officially *complete*. Woooo!" He punched his fists into the air, laughing. "Woooo, baby."

DeeDee laughed at him. She didn't know where he found the energy to be enthusiastic; she was exhausted. "I never asked when you have to be back in Chicago, Jase. You weren't planning on riding tonight, were you?" She looked at the alarm clock on the nightstand and saw it was nearly midnight. "I hope not. It's so late."

"Nope," he said, laughing. "We're on a four-day, good-weather weekend, baby. The newlyweds wanted to spend time together before the season starts, so I came here to spend that time with you."

Smiling, she said, "Good. Stay." Standing close, she reached out and stroked her fingertips on his thigh, asking, "What did you think of Ruby?"

"She's a sweet kid, loves you a lot," he said, rolling his head back and forth on the comforter, winding his hand around hers. "You should join me down here, baby. I'm comfy, but I'd be comfier if you were lying on top of me. Come comfy me. Please?"

Curling her hand around his, she smiled at his coaxing tone, but shook her head. "I need to go grocery shopping before I let myself relax too much."

He raised his head, looking at her with a puzzled expression on his face. "Why? What do we need at midnight that can't wait for the morning?"

"Well, coffee for one. Something for breakfast for another—" she said, and he interrupted, laughing.

"You didn't see PBJ and Hurley when they came in, did you?" he asked, mentioning a club member and prospect as he rolled off the bed. "PBJ said Hoss organized the grocery run. Come look, they hooked us up. Let me show you."

She reached out, letting him take her hand as he led her into the kitchen. She watched as he opened the pantry door and then the cabinet next to it. To her surprise, both were filled with food, canned and boxed goods. There were containers of pasta sitting alongside mix packets for gravy and one-skillet meals. He opened the small cabinet over the coffeemaker and pointed wordlessly to the tub of coffee sitting on the shelf. Shaking her head, she opened the refrigerator to find it stocked with milk, juice, fresh vegetables, and fruit, along with lots of other things. Hoss had thought of everything, it seemed.

"*Now* will you come comfy me?" He wrapped himself around her and bent his knees to gain leverage, pressing their torsos together and lifting her effortlessly. He walked towards the bedroom as her feet dangled around his shins, swaying back and forth with his strides. "No funny business. I know you're tired, baby. I just want to lie beside you in the bed. I'm comfier with you. Wrap yourself around me and comfy me."

DeeDee twined her arms around his neck, resting her head against his shoulder. "I'd be happy to," she murmured, taking a deep breath. Once in the bedroom, he quickly disposed of his clothing then slowly removed hers, lovingly kissing her as he did so, his hands stroking the revealed skin until she moaned into his mouth.

Leaning down to pull back the comforter, he tilted his head and looked at her with a soft expression on his face. "Mmmm. Looky what I found under all those clothes. A nakie DeeDee, my favorite kind. Come on, comfy me," he said, lying down and tugging on her hand until she yielded and tried to snuggle into the bed alongside him. "Aww naw, not a chance, baby. I don't get you often enough, so I want to feel you all over me. Comfy me, baby. You're on me all night long." He shifted until he pulled her partially onto his chest, reaching down to drag her knee up and across his hips.

Wrapping one arm around her waist and cradling her head into his neck with the other, he hummed softly as she relaxed into him. "Yeah, baby, sleep. We'll bum around in the morning, settle the last few bits into place. Make it entirely yours. *Je t'aime,* DeeDee. Night, baby."

***

She woke by slow stages the next morning, becoming aware she was still spread out over Jase's chest, his arms firmly holding her in place. Sighing, she flexed and stretched her feet and ankles. Feeling his chest shaking, she picked up her head to look at him through her bangs. His eyes were open and gazing back at her, a look of mirth on his face. "Are you laughing at me?" she asked, frowning.

"What are you doing with your feet, baby?" he laughed, releasing his hold on her for a moment while he stretched his arms towards the ceiling before wrapping them even more tightly around her.

"Stretching them," she said, asking "why?"

"You made cute, little, baby dinosaur noises. Rawwrrah. Rawwaarrrah." He kissed her nose. "Cutest thing I've heard in my life, eh? First thing in the morning, she's cute. This woman's gonna be the death of me." He rolled his eyes towards the ceiling, laughing. "Baby dinosaur noises. Heaven help me."

She leaned in and kissed him softly, feeling his chest expand as he took a deep breath when their lips made contact. Bringing up one hand, she slowly stroked her thumb across his cheek. "I need to use the bathroom and stuff, but I'll be right back." He grinned lazily and his arm around her waist tightened.

"What if I won't let you go?" he asked, and she stroked his cheek again.

"I'm pretty sure you'll have to let go eventually," she whispered and watched his expression change, becoming darker, his features tensing with desire.

"No. I'm pretty sure you're wrong." He took a breath and she squeaked as he rolled to the edge of the bed with her, pulling her up and into his arms. "See? I can completely do this constant contact thing."

When they returned to the bedroom, he laid her gently on the bed, stretching out alongside her. Propping his head up on one hand, his other idly caressed and stroked her breasts, his thumb slowly circling her nipple. He watched his fingers on her skin, traveling back and forth between the two objects of his attention, and his light touch caused her to shiver with anticipation.

Without a word, he reached down and pulled the comforter up to her waist then tilted his head and pushed it down to her hips. Glancing up at her face, he grinned and pushed it down mid-thigh, trailing his fingers up the inside of her leg before he cupped her pussy. "I'll warm you up, but I don't want to miss a thing," he said softly.

He leaned down and covered her mouth with his and she tasted toothpaste and Jase, sighing as he slanted his lips across hers. His fingers parted the folds of her pussy, one thick finger trailing up and down before pushing inside. Tongue teasing across the seam of her lips, he thrust slowly with his fingers as his tongue assaulted her mouth, twisting with her own.

With a sigh, she spread her legs farther apart, giving him full access to her core, and he responded with a groan, his hips pressing his hard erection against her hip. Murmuring against her lips, he said, "Want to be inside you, baby." She nodded and he moved to lie between her thighs, hips cradled together.

She reached down between them, taking his cock in her hand and stroking him slowly, root to tip, rolling her thumb across the head. Teasing the slit, she spread the silky liquid across the crown of his cock and he hissed, thrusting through her fingers before stilling. "Baby," he whispered, "put me inside you. Let me in." She smiled, her lips against his shoulder and complied, easing the head of his cock to the entrance of her pussy. She took a deep breath as she rocked her hips up and he began to enter her, then he paused before going more than a couple of inches inside.

He groaned and twisted his head to press his mouth to hers. "God, DeeDee. I'll never get enough of you. I hate not being here for you. With you." He thrust deeper and she rocked her hips again, matching his movements. "With you. In you. Here, now," he muttered, slipping an arm down underneath her back, "all the time." Hand cupping her ass, he tilted her hips a little farther and sank to the root, her pussy clenching hard around him as he seated deep inside her. He froze in place, the only movement his fingers clutching her asscheek, the only sound his desperate breathing. She flexed her internal muscles again, gasping as his cock twitched in response.

"Fuck," he ground out, and with a lunge he moved again, hard and fast, his hips pistoning against her. "Baby, I can't," he whispered on a groan, and she smiled, loving that she could make him lose control.

"I'm there," she whispered back, and she was. All it took was a touch of his teeth on her shoulder in a gentle bite and she was rising up to meet him, back arching off the sheets as she came.

Jase reared up over her, his gaze steady on her face, watching without slowing as she shuddered underneath him. Thrusting harder, he was pounding into her, and she recognized the slap of the headboard against the wall, the loud sound punctuating every movement. Their gazes remained locked together as his mouth opened in a silent cry, hips pushing his cock in deep and holding there, his stomach muscles jerking as he came. There was a softness to his expression, even as every muscle tensed, and she let herself soak it up, feeling cherished and loved, hoping her features reflected the emotion back at him.

***

By the time he headed home two days later, they had settled the apartment and she moved a few of the extra things back to storage. Living in the clubhouse had her accustomed to minimal clutter, and she found she now preferred less over more.

Kissing him goodbye, she smiled against his lips when he whispered, *"Je t'aime et je te verrai bientôt,* baby."

"What does that mean?" She raised an eyebrow as she questioned him. He had been saying it a lot over the past couple of days, and while it sounded sexy as hell, she hadn't taken time to wonder about the meaning behind the words until now.

"I'll see you soon," he said, pressing a kiss against the corner of her mouth.

She frowned. "*Je t'aime* means I'll see you soon?" He said that phrase most frequently, and the use didn't match the meaning.

Laughing softly, he kissed the other corner of her mouth. "No, that's *je te verrai bientôt*, baby."

"Then what does *je t'aime* mean?" she pressed for an answer.

"Something you aren't yet ready to hear," he murmured, kissing her with tautly controlled passion. "I gotta go, baby. See you soon."

"*Je te verrai bientôt*," she mangled the phrase, smiling up at him, and he chuckled against her lips as he kissed her goodbye.

8 - Traded

"I'm serious, Cap'n," Jase said from his deceptively casual pose in the chair facing Daniel's desk. "This is what I want. Bring me any deal, as long as it gets me where I want to go." He might not look it, but he was nervous as hell about this conversation, because it was going to dramatically change the direction of his career and life.

"But why?" Daniel's face screwed up into a frown and he tented his fingers, propping his elbows on the desk. "In another year, I'll be retiring, which would leave you the leading franchise player in the forward position. More money, more time flying up and down the sheet. If you do this, you're going to be starting from mid-rung again. Not bottom, because you're too damn good and have enough experience to carry nearly any line. But mid-rung for sure."

"You've said you're retiring every year for the past four, and yet here you are, stitched and iced from last night's game." Jase laughed, because while Daniel was nearly at the upper age range for a hockey player, he didn't think the guy had ever actually considered retiring until he married Mica. She hated the physical side of the game with almost as much passion as she loved Daniel, and you could see her give a full-body flinch every time he took a hit or checked someone.

"And I'm okay with mid-rung. There's less pressure to convert, less expectation to perform, but still plenty of ice. You know me, I'll work my way up, Cap'n." Jase needed Daniel to understand and get behind what he was requesting. "I need to be there. I thought about setting up an apartment for offseason and when we're not playing, but that's not enough. There's no way that would be enough."

Leaning forward, he settled his forearms on his knees and looked at Daniel earnestly. "Six months out of a year total isn't enough. I need to be there all the time I can be. I understand I'll take a salary hit, but I'm still solid from my days in Europe. I'm not worried about that." He rushed to say, "That's not saying you can tell them that. I want the best deal. But...I want a deal. I need to move to Fort Wayne. I'll hate like hell playing across the circle from you, but I gotta go. I've considered all angles, looked at other possibilities, and I've made up my mind."

"You love her," Daniel said wonderingly, and Jase nodded.

"Yeah, I do." That heartfelt statement seemed to convince Daniel.

"You tell her yet?" Daniel asked.

"Not in so many words," Jase said with a small smile, thinking of his secret phrase. "I wanted to make sure I could pull this off before I said anything."

"Okay," Daniel said, rubbing his face with both palms. "Okay. I'll give Tridents' management a call tomorrow, see what I can scare up. Jesus, I hate losing you, Jase. We make a hell of a team. You talk to any of the guys yet?"

"Nope, wanted to hash it out with you first. You know, make sure we were on the same page." Jase dropped his gaze, looking at the floor between his feet. "I'll miss playing with you, man. I'm glad you recruited me when you did. Coming back from Russia was tough, but you helped stabilize things...me. Forever grateful, my friend. You *are* my lucky charm in a lotta ways."

Jase's thoughts turned to his time spent in the KHL. "I was such a kid when I went over to the league. Everything was an adventure. Hell, even getting paid was an adventure sometimes. The money was good, but now and then I wonder where I could have gone if I hadn't spent those years there."

Getting off the plane in Moscow, he was lost from the start. He knew he had a connecting flight to Penza, but the boarding pass printed in Edmonton was in English and French, while most of the signs in the airport here were in Cyrillic. He tried stopping a man in a business suit to ask if the man spoke English, but was brusquely pushed aside as the man kept walking.

"Spencer." A voice called his name and he turned, seeing a group of men standing near a desk. They all looked like him in nearly every way, meaning they had broad shoulders, were physically fit, and had hockey gear bags. Walking over, he lifted a hand in a half-hearted wave.

"Yeah, Jase Spencer," he introduced himself, shaking a hand offered by one of the men.

"Milton Carmichael, d-line," the man said, and Jase nodded. He knew the name if not the face.

There were introductions from the other men, and Jase asked, "The plane for Penza board here?"

Laughter erupted around him and he grinned, not in on the joke, but knowing that something was going on. Carmichael said, "Plane is canceled; we're waiting for one more guy and then we get in a truck and drive for ten hours. We'll get in about four a.m., and practice starts at six."

"Peachy," was all Jase said, leaning a hip against the wall. They chatted as they waited and he found that most of the players were Canadian or Swede, but there were two Americans and a Fin. The language differences between their varied nationalities and the native

Russian players would make chatter difficult, but he wasn't worried. He knew the physicality of the sport was universal.

By the end of that open-sided truck ride, the players' relationships had begun to gel; then the camaraderie from their hard-skating practices flowed naturally into flawless games. A few of the men were unable to deal with the culture change and bailed, but he found a solid core of players that remained on the team for game after game, season after season. Jase was one of those players; he had found a comfortable niche on the team and planned to fill it for the foreseeable future. The money was good, creature comforts were accessible, and hot chicks with zero relationship expectations and little knowledge of English or French were easy to find.

He had been playing in Russia for nearly three years the night he received a phone call from his mother. Having gone home only a few weeks earlier during the offseason, he was somewhat surprised to hear her voice over the crackling and hissing line, and Jase felt a shiver of fear, immediately knowing the call was bad news.

"Jase, it's Mom," she said, and his breath caught in his throat at the stress in her speech.

"Ma," he said. "What's wrong?"

"Son, it's Sharon. She's in the hospital. I wanted to call you before you heard from anyone else. She's going to be okay, but she's at Royal Alexandrea in Edmonton." His mother sounded exhausted, about ready to collapse.

"What happened? Where's Da?" He was full of questions, but these were enough to begin.

"Dad's in with her right now, son. I stepped out to call you." She took a deep breath, blowing it out slowly. "She was in a car accident. She's going to be all right, but she's knocked around pretty good."

"I'll get the first flight home, Ma. I'm so glad you called." His body sagged against the wall, leaning on the flat surface for support.

"No, Jase. She'll be out of the hospital before you could even get here," she argued. "Stay and play, we'll schedule some phone calls. I know she'll be right glad to talk to you, but I don't want you throwing your season away by leaving. You know what they'll do."

He did know; he had seen it in action several times as players had family emergencies. They would leave for a couple weeks, but by the time they could return, the slot in the team was full. Negotiations here were different from back home, and he had not seen a player successfully lobby for their position back after missing more than two games.

"Tell me about the accident." He sidestepped the conversation about going home, deciding to play that more by ear based on what he could get out of her in the next three minutes.

"She was leaving work and had just gotten out on the highway at Blackfalds, and some pickup bashed into her car. They hit pretty hard and she lost control, wrapping around an electric pole. The car impacted on the passenger side and her seatbelt saved her. Thank God she was wearing it." She paused for a second. "Jase, she was OUI." She didn't elaborate, just put it out there and let it rest between them. Oh, God, not again, *he thought, taking several deep breaths.*

"Was she drunk or stoned?" He asked the question in a flat tone as if the answer didn't matter.

"Both, actually, eh?" She sighed.

"Jesus Murphy, what was she thinking?" He tipped his head back against the wall in frustration. "You sure you don't want me home for this, Ma?"

"I'm sure, Jase. We have things under control for now and she's okay. She will be okay. I'll call you again tomorrow, give you a bit of an update, eh?" She took a long, shaky breath.

"Yeah. Give the old man a hug and tell my Sharona I'll talk to her soonish. Love you, Ma." He rolled his neck and shoulders, working out the stress and tightness.

"Je t'aime, Jase." She disconnected the call and he stood holding the handset for a few minutes.

Giving himself a shake, he brought his attention back to Daniel's office, realizing he missed a question. "I asked do you want me to do the whole thing or pull an agent in for you?"

"I trust you to do the honors," he said with a smile.

"Yeah, you just don't want to give up the twenty to an agent." Daniel was joking with him, but there was a seed of truth to the words.

"Twenty percent is a lot to some of us, man," Jase said, standing to leave. "Thanks again, Daniel. This means the world."

***

Sitting in the locker room unlacing his skates, Jase found it hard to believe it had only been a month since he first approached Daniel about leaving the Mallets. Things had moved quickly once Fort Wayne understood he was serious about the trade. Tonight was his last time skating on the Chicago home ice, his last time wearing the green and black colors of the team he had been a part of since returning from Russia at twenty-two, over eight years ago.

The silence of the room caught his attention, and he looked up to see team members with phones in hand, their faces turned his way as the word of his departure swept through the locker room. He wanted to wait until the last minute to tell everyone, so he didn't screw up the dynamics of the team for this series. Daniel had managed to get the Fort

Wayne and league management to agree to hold the announcement until after tonight's game was over. He was certain they would have published something by now, and the Mallets fans had probably already picked it up and were retweeting and reposting like mad.

Half of the team was looking at him, but the other half were staring over at Daniel, apparently assessing his mood. Some of them were probably wondering what had happened between the two men, because their tight friendship had long been a stable foundation for the entire team's game play. They were trying to analyze the situation, because while evidently he was traded and had known about it beforehand, he and Daniel together had skated some of their best shifts of the season tonight, and he had been awarded one of the team's highest honors just before the game.

Slapping the trademark smirk on his face, crooked and full of playful adventure, he slipped off his skates and stood, facing his teammates. "Aww, naw. Come on, none of that, guys. This was my request. I'm ready to move on; you boys just aren't challenging enough any longer." His attempt at a joke fell flat and he grimaced.

"I'm kidding. About your skills, 'cause you got 'em in spades. But, it's my request. I need a change. And if things work out the way I want, then everything will be worth it. Like Gretzky said, 'You miss one hundred percent of the shots you never take', and I'm taking this shot, eh? So, there you go. I'll need you to wish me luck, tell me to break a leg, chuck a puck, whatever.

"It's been an absolute honor to share ice with you guys, and I'm proud as hell to have worn the Mallets colors for so many games. We won the fucking playoffs last year, and that's a memory to hold to, yeah?"

He stepped up on the bench behind him, clutching Gary's shoulder to steady himself. The man looked furious, and probably had a right to be, since he had been kept in the dark along with the rest of the team.

The only people he told other than Daniel and Nate had been his parents.

"So tonight let's go to Jackson's and celebrate, eh? Get our celly on. Fucking win column for my last game here. Couldn't have asked for a better way to go out, eh? You gotta keep this going too; don't want Coach here to lose his job." Laughter scattered across the group and he saw a loosening of tension in jaws and necks as his teammates realized this had been his request, that it wasn't a trade forced on him by someone supposed to be his friend.

He threw his head back and yelled, "WOOOO! Fuckin' win column, baby! Let's shower and get the hell outta here, so we get our celly on." Hopping down from the bench, he accepted the handshakes and back-pounding hugs from his friends and teammates. Catching Daniel's eyes from across the room, he nodded at him in thanks, fingering the co-captain patch that had been sewn to his jersey for tonight's game. Daniel nodded back and then dropped his head, busying himself with his own post-game rituals.

***

Mason stared at him from across the bar, a look of incredulity on his face. "You're doing what, motherfucker?"

"Moving to Fort Wayne. Starting in two days, I'll be playing for the Fort Wayne Tridents. Got a condo lined up, furniture rented, eighty-inch flat screen already in place. It's a fucking palace." Jase took a drink from his beer, cautiously watching Mason's face across the rim.

Turning to look at Daniel, Mason narrowed his eyes. "You on board with this, man?" He asked the question casually, but his posture belied that with the muscles in his arms tensing, the side of his jaw ticking with pressure as his teeth gritted together.

"Yeah. The man made a convincing argument. I could have forced him to stay and play out his contract, but he's found something worth fighting for. Seems like he's willing to make a hell of a sacrifice to see where things go. Kinda reminds me of someone." Daniel smiled at Mason.

"She knows you're coming?" He directed this question back at Jase, who shook his head.

"We're talking tonight. I plan on telling her then. She wanted me down for the weekend," he laughed. "This will just extend the stay indefinitely. I'm not invading her neighborhood; the new condo is a ten-minute drive from her apartment, but it's close enough to be convenient. I figured I'd touch base with Slate as soon as I get into town, see if he can hook me up with someone to keep my riding skills in shape."

"I'll let Slate know so he's expecting you. Birdy's moving down there, too, so you'll know a couple of the boys. DeeDee though, that's all you, man. Respect, Jase. Turning your life upside down for a woman that don't even know you're coming is crazy. I hope it works out the way you want." Here, he leaned closer to Jase, lowering his voice. "But if it doesn't, then you will leave her the fuck alone. You get in her space unwanted and I *will* fuck you up, friends or not. You fuck her over? I will fuck you *up*. Stay out of club business, keep your goddamn nose clean, don't fucking shit on her, and we'll be all fine and dandy. Stray from that path, and we got us a goddamn fucking problem. You get me, Jase Spencer?"

Jase felt a kick of fear while Mason was speaking to him. Mason on a rant was frightening, but Mason like this, quietly delivering a threatening promise, was downright terrifying. His balls were trying to escape back up into his belly and his skin rose in goose flesh all over his body. All he could hear was Mason, all he could see was Mason, and he knew that his friend meant every word. While it might bother him to do it, he would deliver on every promise if Jase fucked up. Davis Mason was a dangerous man, and it was never smart to lose sight of that fact. Jase had faced and fought some of the fiercest enforcers in both the

KHL and AHL, but this man was scary at an entirely different level. He swallowed, his suddenly dry throat clicking as with a serious tone and a steady, slow nod, he responded, "I got you, Mason. I understand, man."

"Well, all right," Mason said. His shoulders and arms relaxed as he leaned back, and with that, the air around them lightened, the noise of the bar rushing back into the vacuum, click and clack of pool balls and murmur of conversation audible again. "Have a couple of rounds on me, man. Will be strange not seeing your sorry ass around here anymore."

Setting up several shot glasses on the bar, Mason splashed liquor into the glasses and spoke to Daniel. "Good game tonight, caught the last frame on the box. How does Jase leaving change things for you?"

Daniel launched into an explanation of how Rodney Dahl, a sophomore forward, would be stepping up. Jase watched as other members of the team drifted up, listening while their captain laid out the strategy for the next few games. He already felt a separation from them, knowing that they would be the ones executing Daniel's plans, while he would be on the ice in another town with a pack of strangers, their only commonality a love of the game. Even with these guys, playing alongside some of them for several seasons, he knew that few would make the effort to stay in touch. Their careers were too transient to maintain long-lasting connections.

Small fingers slipped into the back pocket of his jeans and he whipped his arm back, grabbing the hand tightly as he turned around. Shouting with laughter, he wrapped the petite blonde in his arms, picking her up off the floor in a tight hug. Gripping her waist, he lifted her to the bar, setting her beside where Mason was still working on the drinks. "Jessica Nalan, I hoped I'd see you tonight." He grinned at her, laughing as her blue eyes narrowed with a frown.

"Help me down, you Neanderthal," she scolded him and then grinned, reaching out to playfully slap his face. "I haven't seen you in too long, Jase. How's a girl supposed to get her cockblock on if she can't find a cock to block? Hmmmm?"

Next to Mason, Jess was Mica's best friend, and the girls had worked together since the two of them graduated college. Together, they made up the backbone of Mica's company, MishMash Development. Jess was a talented programmer, and Jase had watched her when she was working on the team's revamped website last year, marveling at how quickly she pulled the various components together while fielding outrageous requests from management and players.

"She bothering you, mister?" He heard the question and recognized the voice, so without looking, he reached out to wrap his arm around the shoulders of the dark-skinned woman beside him.

"Hey, Brandy. I'm gonna miss all of your delectable deliciousness, darling." Grinning, he looked down at her. Brandy Still was Jess' girlfriend and the owner of a local bakery. "You gonna miss me, sweetie?"

Jess piped up from her perch on the bar, "How can we miss you if you won't go away?" Reaching over, she picked up a shot glass and smelled it, smiling at Mason and saying, "Oh. Lemondrops. Yum!"

Daniel looked up, asking her, "Mica come with you?"

Nodding, Jess said, "She's sitting in the car. Something went wrong with a project, so she's got folks on the phone. She'll be coming in a minute." She sipped the drink and turned to Jase, asking, "Why would we miss you, chunk of hunk?"

"It's my last night in Chicago," he said, watching her face slowly lose the laughter as she realized he was serious. "I'm trading to Fort Wayne."

Without taking her eyes off him, she yelled, "Daniel!" pulling everyone's gaze to her. Turning to look at her best friend's husband, she continued shouting. "What the fuck are you thinking? Did you seriously trade Jason? *My* Jase?" She put her feet on a wobbly stool and carelessly stood while Jase wrapped his arm around her legs to keep her from falling. "Dude. You, Jase, and Gary are the magic line. You are the fucking mystical shift. You can't do this to me. Daniel, please." She held out her hands. "How can I like you if you trade Jase? And then, how can I stay friends with Mica if I don't like her husband? Don't take my best friend away, Daniel." Her voice turned pleading. "Be reasonable. Give me Jase back. Let me keep Mica."

Laughing, Daniel reached up and helped Jess down from the stool. "He didn't give me much of a choice. Talk to him; he's the one who demanded the trade."

Whirling around, she poked Jase in the chest repeatedly and painfully with a stiff finger. "You *wanted* to leave us? I'm wounded…devastated. Why would you want to leave? These people are your friends. *I'm* your friend."

Nodding, he grabbed her finger with his hand, pulling her into another hug. "True love," he whispered into her ear, and she stilled against him in reaction.

Pulling back, she looked up into his face as she blindly reached behind her. Brandy seemed to know what she needed and grasped her hand, threading their fingers together. She stared at him for a long minute, then sighed and thumped her forehead against his chest, mumbling, "Well then, okay. Now *that* I can understand."

***

"What do you mean you're moving to Fort Wayne?" The disbelief was thick in DeeDee's voice; the giveaway was that carefully modulated tone she used when trying to clarify something without seeming to question you. He noticed she used it a lot with the Rebel members, less frequently with him, but when she did, it meant something.

"I'm traded to the Tridents, baby," he said, waiting for a reaction.

"You'll be playing for the Fort Wayne team? Why would Daniel do that? When did this happen, Jase?" She sounded affronted on his behalf, which he found cute as hell.

"Daniel worked out a deal for me," he told her. "Tonight was my last game as a Mallet. Tomorrow, I move down there. There's a condo all set- up and waiting. Furniture should be delivered while I'm driving my truck down in the morning. Practice is the day after tomorrow, and the first game is Saturday." He paused, waiting for her to respond, and when she didn't, he said, "I was hoping you'd be pleased, DeeDee."

An additional beat of silence passed and he sighed, smiling, ready to give her an out, take the pressure off. "I know it's a lot to take in, baby. Let me know when you're ready to talk about it. Tell me about your day. Did Mercy behave herself?"

Anxiously, he waited to see if she would take the opening, holding his breath and then letting it out in a silent rush when she responded, "Yeah, she's kept her heels off customer crotches for nearly two weeks now. For a while there, I was afraid we had to register her shoes as deadly weapons." Laughing, he asked more questions about managing the club, giving her a chance to establish their customary, comfortable back-and-forth repartee.

They had been talking for about thirty minutes when she received another call. She told him to hang on and placed their call on hold. Almost immediately, he received a text from Mason, and then one from Hoss, and then another from Mason. Putting the call on speaker for when she came back, he flipped over to the messages, and as he read them, his stomach dropped, fear rushing in. Ruby, DeeDee's daughter and Slate's woman, had been abducted.

Staggered, he texted DeeDee to call him back as soon as she could and hung up, dialing Mason as instructed. "What can I do?" he asked by way of greeting.

“Get your ass down there. DeeDee’s gonna need you, even if nothing else happens tonight, and especially even if she doesn’t think so right now,” Mason growled. “I’m hanging tight here until things are resolved. Then I’ll be in the wind myself. Mother*fuckers* don’t know what they stirred up with this shit. They do not fucking understand how it is. We will coat the motherfucking streets with red. Get to the Fort; someone will text you with DeeDee’s location. She’s being moved right now to make sure she’s safe.”

“I’m on my way, Mason. Keep her safe for me,” he pleaded, not knowing if she was in danger, but wanting Mason’s reassurance.

“We will, brother. She’s family. We got her, man. Ratchet it in and get in the wind.” Mason disconnected the call and Jase leaned back on his couch for a moment. Straightening and unfolding to his feet, he looked around the apartment, glad he already packed the truck with everything except what he had on his back. As the door pulled closed behind him, he focused on what was ahead of him, easily setting aside what was behind.

9 - Learning the ice

"I want a hard around dump and chase." The coach was yelling from the bench area, calling a multi-player skills practice routine and Jase lifted a tired hand, indicating understanding. This was the second week as a Trident, and he was pushing himself harder every day, learning new drills and trying to anticipate the offensive needs of the team. They won three of the four games in which he played, but things still weren't clicking with his line.

Since nothing was instinctive yet, he couldn't relax and flow with the play. He thought he understood now why Daniel was so tired after playing, because that man was constantly analyzing games, even when they were going on around him. That was how Jase had to skate right now, reading things on the fly and then matching the way the line was skating to a mental index card of plays.

He knew it would come with time, but he wanted very much to make this work quickly, since he requested the trade. There was a deep need to prove his worth to the organization, even if none of the players were aware of the circumstances. In fact, as far as anyone on either team knew, this was an ordinary trade, something management had worked out. Daniel had gotten a good backup goaltender in the deal, which was key for the Mallets, because while Dierk was talented, it was important to have a strong second in the wings.

"Good," the coach yelled, "that's good. Bring it in, Spencer."

Skating over to the bench, he stepped off the ice and onto the mats, grabbing a water bottle and shooting a long stream of water into his mouth. He pushed his unfastened helmet on top of his head, took a towel from one of the equipment guys with a thankful nod, and wiped the stinging sweat from his eyes.

"Looking good, Jase," Leeland Dugger, the Tridents' long-time team captain, told him as he slid to a stop against the boards beside the bench.

"Thanks, Cap'n," Jase responded, feeling a twinge of disloyalty. Daniel had been his captain for a long time, but that was part of what was behind him. From what he saw so far, this man was well deserving of the honorific, working to develop a good rapport with all the team members and encouraging everyone during practice and game play.

He wasn't one to take shit from opposing, though, and had earned the nickname Duke It Out Dugger. Jase had watched some promo reels of the man's fights. He was good on his feet and with his fists, hammering on his opponents with both finesse and power.

Finally, he thought, *practice is over*. The rest of the team was leaving the ice. Not wanting to seem eager to unlace, Jase stepped back onto the ice and skated to the far boards. He worked through an agility routine he learned in Russia, skating through neutral ice, pushing his legs hard as he moved forward and backwards across the rink, then repeated it to come to a stop against the far wall. Turning, he saw Coach and Dugger were both watching him and was afraid he had held them up, thinking maybe they didn't leave the ice until everyone else was off.

Skating back across to them, he nodded as he stepped onto the mats, pleased when the coach said, "Good initiative, Spencer."

***

In the parking lot outside the practice arena, he straddled his bike, pulling on his gloves. His helmet balanced on the tank in front of him and he was staring blankly at it, straightening the seams on the fingers of the gloves when he heard a bike enter the lot. Looking up, he recognized Slate's bike and lifted a hand, watching as the man rode over to him.

"Hey," he offered as a greeting, continuing to fiddle with his gloves. With away games last weekend, it had been a week since he had seen DeeDee, and it had been nearly as long since he talked to her. All his calls went unanswered, except by an occasional, brief text. After Ruby had been located and rescued, she had spent several days in the hospital, and during her stay, DeeDee was understandably busy, spending a lot of time with her as the girl recovered from her ordeal. The few details Jase knew were sketchy, but it had sounded seriously scary for a while.

He had gotten a text from Mason earlier today, thanking him for looking out for DeeDee. Responding with a brief ***No problem***, he hadn't thought anything else of it until now. Seeing the look on Slate's face, he had an idea that Mason's communication and Slate's visit were connected somehow, and strongly suspected he wasn't going to like it.

"Jase." Slate reached out a hand and they gripped wrists, shaking firmly. "How's Road's old ride treating you?"

"Good, man. Loving the bike," he responded, settling back onto the seat and tapping his fingers against the sides of the helmet. "What brings you out this way? How's Ruby doing?"

"She's doing really good. Everything is beginning to settle back down like it was before that shit all happened. Doing good. Still needs some help, but we have plenty of that around the apartment these days." He took a deep breath. "Kinda on that topic, DeeDee wanted me to let you know she's going to be busy for a while. What with helping Ruby and still managing Slinky's, she's got a lot on her plate right now." Slate had the good grace to look bashful as he delivered the message. If his heart hadn't been clenching in his chest right now, Jase might feel sorry for the man.

"She couldn't tell me herself?" Every breath he sucked in brought pain, as if he were breathing ground-up glass. He was breaking apart inside, and his chest hitched when he locked his eyes on Slate. "She had to send someone? She afraid I'm going to go off on her if she dumps me? That's what this is, right? She's dumping me?"

"Dude, I don't know what this is, honestly. She's been with Ruby so much, her and Bear's mom, and I don't know if she's tired, or scared, or yeah...dumping you. No fucking idea, man. I got nothing." Slate shrugged at him. His face twisted as he said, "Mason told me to remind you there was an understanding."

"All right." He closed his mouth resolutely, locking the rest of the words in his throat. After a minute, he swallowed and nodded, saying, "All right. If she wants me, she's got my number. I'm aware of Mason's words to me before I came down here, and I...I won't bother her." He swallowed again, shook his head, and said sarcastically, "Beauty. Just fucking beauty."

Slate looked at him for a long minute, then without another word, kicked his bike to life, pulling away and out of the lot. Pain in his chest at the thought of losing DeeDee, Jase watched him leave, sitting on the bike, his shoulders rounding with exhaustion. He tipped his head and pulled on the helmet. Turning the key to start the bike, he turned towards home, wondering what he had done to make her draw away again.

***

She stood in Ruby's kitchen waiting, hands twisting in the hem of her shirt. Slate had just gotten home and she wanted to ask him if he had a chance to talk to Jase. He stalked into the room and threw her a disgusted look, then glanced around. "She's napping," she said quietly, knowing he was looking for Ruby.

"Woman," he took a step closer to her, his voice low and harsh. "If you didn't matter so much to my Ruby, I'd be kicking your ass right about now." The venom in his tone surprised her, but she kept her face expressionless, waiting. "Man was devastated. I don't know what kind of fucking game you've been playing with him, but this shit stops right the fuck here. You don't want him, well then that's just fucking fine. You just stay the fuck away from him."

She balled up her fists, and then consciously relaxed them. "How did he look?"

"Nope, you don't get to ask that kind of fucking question. The man's as close to a brother as an unpatched friend of the club can be, and I am not going to be goddamn well sucked into your game. This is the last time I fucking play messenger boy for you." Angrily he stripped off his jacket and shrugged out of his cut. "I'm going to go lay with my woman. I'm going to lay with her, because I fucking love her, and I ain't afraid to tell her, so she knows where I stand. She don't play no fucking games, so I know where she stands, too. You need to get your shit straight, DeeDee. You're family, but part of being family means I get to call you on your shit, and this is shit."

He turned to walk up the stairs and paused, his foot on the first step. He lifted the cut in his hand and looked at the patch, then glanced over at her before looking back down. Head bowed, he stood there a moment, and then told her, "He said if you want him, you got his number. Man said he won't bother you." Slate turned his head, looking at her with hard eyes, reminding her of that scary side she had seen once before. "Mason told him if he fucked this up, he was a dead man. Did he fuck this up, DeeDee? I need to worry about putting him to ground for fucking you over?"

Her breath caught in her chest and she shook her head, terror making tears gather in the corners of her eyes. She infused all her certainty in her voice when she said, "No, Slate. This is all on me."

"Good to fucking know." Heavily, he walked up the stairs, and in a moment, she heard the murmur of his voice and Ruby's.

Their easy intimacy brought Winger to mind, and she leaned her elbows on the countertop, face in her palms. He had always been so proud of her, proud to have her ride tail on his bike, proud to have her wear his patch, her rag, proud to have her on his arm. They owned each other, and he made sure everyone that saw them knew it.

She listened to his flattering talk about her more than once, sometimes even when she was present and sitting on his lap. He always called her a 'pretty, young thing' and crowed loudly about their age difference, because he had been sixteen years older. The brothers would rib him about keeping up, and he would puff up and grin, pulling her in for a hug and a squeeze. It was important to him, added to his machismo.

When she and Jase first were seeing each other, she brought up their age difference a couple of times and he laughed it off, saying it didn't matter. Maybe it didn't matter to him like it had Winger, at least not now, but she feared it would eventually. *But what if I made the wrong decision?* she thought.

Standing, she pushed back from the counter. No, this was the right thing to do; she just needed to push past the pain. Winger had been so proud of having his pretty, young thing, and she wanted Jase to have that in his life, too. He deserved to have the opportunity to find love...but with someone his own age. Scoffing, she asked herself, "Did you finally admit to loving him, old lady?"

***

The next morning, Jase was an hour early for the team's gym session, already deep into a strenuous leg workout, when Leeland Dugger walked in. He walked over to where Jase was lunge walking with a heavily weighted barbell across his shoulders, and stood watching, arms folded across his chest. Jase grunted, "Dugger," and continued his workout; he was in the middle of the rep count and didn't want to lose concentration.

Dugger warmed up, keeping his attention on Jase, even as he pulled and stretched his muscles. Finally finished, Jase straight-armed the weights up and then down his front to chest level, controlling the drop and placing the equipment quietly on the rack. He stumbled a bit backing up, deciding it was easier to ride the fall out and landed on the mats on his ass. Once down, he reached out for his bottle of water now conveniently within his grasp, as if he intended the move all along.

Dugger snorted, laughing and said, "Never seen a guy so intent on punishing himself as you are this morning. Care to share what the hell you've done to deserve this kind of treatment?"

Breathing hard, Jase swigged from his water again, draining the bottle. He looked at it for a moment, then crushed it and twisted the cap back on, tossing it into a nearby trashcan. Looking up, he huffed, "Nothing. Really. Couldn't sleep, so might as well work out. I'm just tryin' to keep up with the Duke, man."

"Fuck you." This was said without rancor, and Jase nodded, paused, and then sadly shook his head.

"Nope, not my type, Cap'n. Sorry." He smiled tightly as his response drew a laugh from the man.

"Just call me Lee, dude. You're making me dizzy with the name changes every time we talk," he said, finishing with his warm-up stretches and moving to the leg press machine. "Lunch when we're finished. We'll meet a couple of the guys at a local rib joint and feed the machine."

He nodded. "Sounds good. What time does the bus leave this afternoon for Kalamazoo?" They had a three-game series in Michigan and would be staying in a hotel for two nights.

"Two o'clock, I think," Lee grunted, continuing his leg workout. "You're rooming with me."

Surprised, Jase glanced up. Normally, the captain would have his pick of roomies. While Daniel always selected the guys who needed the most babysitting, he knew he shouldn't assume that's what Lee was doing. He stood, walking over to pick up the barbell again, ready to continue his workout.

"Don't look like that," Lee said, letting the weights down with a clang. "I'm tired of rooming with kids. I always have to sleep with one eye open, once they get over the fear of the captain. Last year," he picked up a bottle of water and took a drink, "I woke up with a shaving cream beard. Another night, they carried all the furniture out of the room and into the hallway of the hotel."

"Rookie moves," Jase scoffed, breathing hard as he lifted. "Last year, I got our new goalie three times with the same prank. I bet the boy will check his skates' blades for tape for the rest of his life. His crush was at the game every single time. To this day, she's convinced he can't skate, because he falls down so much."

Lee laughed, throwing his empty bottle away. "The year before I earned captain, I got our goalie with a water bottle at four games." Holding up four fingers, he made a face to emphasize his success and then pantomimed tipping a bottle up and squeezing it, then being covered with liquid. "Booosh. Classic."

Jase finished the set as several of their teammates strolled into the gym. He and Lee shared a glance then they both looked pointedly at the clock, noting the scheduled session should have begun thirty minutes ago. Jase stepped back, leaning his elbow on the weight rack. "Go ahead, Cap'n. This should be good."

***

They won all three games in the series in Kalamazoo, but tonight it had been by the skin of their teeth. Hanging onto their one goal lead for the entire last period had seemed impossible, but their lines had skated hard and aggressively to pull off the win. Now, they were in Cincinnati for a game tomorrow night. They hadn't even stopped in Fort Wayne long enough to grab clean clothes.

"Jesus Murphy." Jase threw himself backwards onto the hotel bed, dropping his duffle to the floor. "Those motherfuckers had a hard-on for you, Lee. I was only collateral damage, and I'm beat to shit and back, eh? What the hell did you do to that Biannac guy, sleep with his mother?"

Lee smiled grimly and tossed his bag against the wall with force, watching as it fell to the floor. "His sister, actually."

Jase picked up his head in disbelief, looking at his roommate with wide eyes and an open mouth. "Tell me you're kidding, man. Hell, I have a sister. That would cross a line. I wouldn't want you sleeping with her, and I *like* you."

"She and I went to Boston at the same time. I didn't know her brother played, but it probably wouldn't have mattered if I did. What are the chances that we would be facing off across the circle?" Lee shook his head. "The hell with it. I don't care if it is a half-hour after midnight curfew; I'm headed to the bar for a drink. After that game, I need one. About the only perk of being team captain is I can break curfew when I decide to and there's no one to give me shit. Why don't you come down with me, Jase? I could use the company."

Jase let his head fall back on the bed again, plugging in one earbud. "Nuh-uh, man. No way. Have you met our captain? He's a ball-buster from way back. I'm staying right here. Might not move again. Ever. Jesus Murphy, man, you're a line crosser. Stay the hell away from my sister." His breathing slowed and just before he fell asleep, he heard the click of the door as it closed behind Lee. Lucero was up next on the playlist, and Ben Nichols was singing about drinking, explaining how hard it was to get back up in *I'll Just Fall*. Twisting his head back and forth, he murmured, "She would be bad for you, man."

He woke up in the middle of the night to breathless giggles coming from the other bed and groaned, pulling his pillow over his head and rolling onto his stomach. He hoped the position would keep him from the attention of wandering hands, but knew it wasn't a sure thing, especially if the girl was a puck bunny, out to fuck as many players as she could boast about.

"Jason Spencer." Lee said his name in response to a whispered question, and he groaned again when the girl's voice rose in excitement.

"Spencer from Chicago? Seriously? He won the championship last year." More giggles and then the sound of rocking, swaying bedsprings began, and with the images the noises evoked, Jase felt his cock start to harden, swelling and lengthening until it was uncomfortable. Shifting his hips, he reached down to stroke himself slowly as he listened to the gasps and sighs filling the room, hearing the bedding-muffled slap of flesh-on-flesh as Lee fucked her harder. *I do not want to jack off to this*, he thought, removing his hand, disgusted with himself.

He thought about the hotel in Chicago and DeeDee, seeing her red hair spread out over the pillows as he made love to her slowly, but that didn't help deflate his hard-on at all. Fisting his hand in the sheets, he tried to derail those memories by reciting the Prime Ministers. *Macdonald, Mackenzie, Macdonald again, Abbott, Thompson, Bowell. Laurier, Borden twice, Meighen, King, Meighen again, King again, Bennett, King me three*. He realized the sounds had faded away and turning to look, he saw Lee spread-eagled, seemingly asleep. There was a slim brunette standing between the beds looking down at Jase.

"Hi," she said, biting her bottom lip.

"Not happening," he responded, turning his head away. Feeling fingers trailing across his shoulders, he sat up in the middle of the bed, moving away from her. "I said *not happening*, sweetheart. You should get your clothes back on and head out."

She pouted prettily, sitting on the edge of his bed, perky breasts pushed up and out at him. "I could blow you." She smiled. "I'd like to do that for you." She shrugged. "Or we could fuck. He kinda passed out. He didn't...you know."

Running his hand tiredly through his hair, Jase asked her, "What's your name, sweetheart?"

"Kimmie," she said brightly, taking his question as interest and easing towards him on the bed.

Holding up his hand to stop her advance, Jase said, "Kim, it's time for you to go. I have a game tonight, and if I don't get some rest...well, I could get hurt. You wouldn't want me to get hurt, would you?" She shook her head, eyes wide. "I appreciate the offer, Kim, but I need to sleep. So it's time for you to get your clothes on and head out, eh?"

When the door finally swung closed behind her, he breathed a heavy sigh of relief. Looking down at Lee still flat on his back in the bed, he said, "You owe me, fucker." Yawning, he scooted back into his spot on the bed and slipped into dreamless sleep.

***

"Holy shit," Lee ground out, wrapping his hands around his head tightly. "Sledgehammer. Has to be what you used to beat me up."

"Not a sledgehammer, and you didn't gain the headache by my hands. If I had to guess, I'd say Jack and Coke. Just a guess by the smell, mind you." Jase sprawled on one of the chairs by the window. Reaching up, he slowly and deliberately drew on the pull-cord for the curtains, gradually flooding the room with brilliant sunshine.

"You motherfucker," Lee said with a groan, pressing the heels of his hands against his eyes. "Close those, man. You're killing me."

"Nope, not a chance, *Cap'n*." He used the title, emphasizing it. "You're supposed to be an example, an inspiration. Someone we want to be, not someone we have to clean up after."

Tilting his head, Lee squinted a single eye open, glaring at him, "What are you talking about?"

"Kimmie sends her regards." Jase held his gaze steadily.

"Who the hell is Kimmie?" Lee asked, shifting. Evidently, he sensed something wasn't right, because he reached down and must have encountered the dried remains of his evening's activities. "Oh, hell no," he said in shock, squeezing both eyes closed tightly again. "Please, tell me I didn't bring some chick back to the room."

"I'd like to tell you that. You have no idea how much I would like to be able to say those words to you." He paused, taking a deep breath. "But, nope. I cannot tell you that you didn't bring some chick back to the room. Because, in fact, you did. You brought Kimmie home with you."

Lee dropped his head back into his hands. "Was she at least pretty?"

"Dude." Jase sat forward on the chair, elbows on his knees. "A puck bunny? You? Doesn't match what I've heard about you. Yeah, she was hot, but I'd be more worried about the lack of trash if I were you. Unless she packed it out with her, I'd say you didn't wrap it up last night. What the hell happened in the bar, man?"

"Oh, hell," Lee looked at him, "I haven't done anything like that in years. God, I feel like shit."

"Need some hair of the dog?" Jase tossed him a small flask, nodding as Lee unscrewed the lid and took a sip. "Slow and easy, Cap'n. If it's any consolation, Kimmie said, and I quote, 'He didn't...you know'. So I think you might be safe from a paternity suit in three months."

Swinging bleary eyes towards him, Lee squinted against the light streaming in from the window. "You've made your point, Jase. Close the curtains; I'm begging you." He tossed the flask back to Jase and staggered to his feet, hand out to the wall to maintain his balance.

"Gonna share what started the Jack-valanche?" Jase manipulated the pull-cord again, dragging the curtains closed.

"Talking about Ree, Biannac's sister, Mareena. She's the one who got away, ya know?" This last was called through the open entrance of the bathroom as the door closed, effectively shutting down the conversation.

Headed back to Fort Wayne after the game, Jase tried to take advantage of the quiet on the bus, stretching his legs into the stairwell next to the front row and closing his eyes with a sigh. He was ready to get some sleep, but hated the stuffy bunks in the back of the bus. Hearing a body fall into the seat next to him, without opening his eyes, he said, "Go away."

"Nope," Lee's voice said from beside him.

"Yeah. Go away," he repeated. After the wake-up call the previous night, then the pounding he took in the game tonight, he desperately wanted to sleep for a while. They would be back in the Fort by three a.m. and he would be in his bed by three-thirty, but they had a game that night at home. "Cap'n, if I don't sleep, I'm gonna be shit tonight," he said, cracking one eye to look over at Lee.

"I wanted to apologize again for last night," Lee said.

Recognizing the signs of a conversation that couldn't be derailed, Jase scooted around until he was sitting sideways in the seat. Leaning tiredly against the window, he said quietly, "Tell me about Ree."

"She was a year ahead of me at Boston, a triple threat. Stop-the-presses pretty, off-the-charts smart, and shut-the-door funny. My scholarship didn't cover much, so I was working at the coffee shop on campus. Between rink time and classes, I didn't have a lot of time to socialize, and working cut into that pretty hard. She came into the shop and ordered the same thing every day. Every day, she would take her coffee, sit at the same table, and open her books to study." Lee leaned his head back and smiled.

"After a couple of weeks, I found out we were taking a couple of the same classes, but on different days. We exchanged names and numbers and she became my study buddy. She was serious about her grades, and kept us on track most of the time, but *damn* if she didn't have the prettiest smile. After I got to know her, all I wanted to do was make her smile. I'd turn the entire shop upside down if I could get her to smile. She was nervous around me at first, because I had a bad reputation in school up to that point; Boston is where the Duke thing started, you know?" Jase nodded.

"It got pretty serious, at least as serious as college kids get. By the time spring rolled around, she was spending more time in my room than her own. At break, I went home with her, met the family—with the exception of her brother, who was up in Canada in the juniors."

"Things were good before that visit, but after we had got back on campus, she pulled away. There were lots of excuses about class and studying, helping out a friend...that sort of thing. Then one night, she showed up at my room beat up and bloody. She wouldn't talk to me, and when she passed out in my arms, I freaked out. I called her parents and they came down, took her home. I know they believed me when I said I didn't have anything to do with it, but she wouldn't tell any of us what happened."

He sighed. "She withdrew from school. Wouldn't return my calls. Her dad finally told me to stop phoning, that she didn't want to talk to me. Biannac never said, but I know he thinks I hit her. I'd never do that, man. She meant everything to me, and what happened swept that away. It pulled the rug out from under my feet."

Rubbing his hands over his face, he leaned forward in the seat, looking out the windshield at the limited world illuminated by the headlights of the bus. "Ree was gone out of my life. The one who got away."

"Did you ever find out what really happened?" Jase asked, thinking he already knew the answer.

"Yeah. It was a local boy. She had been tutoring him and he was coming on to her. I think he…raped her, then held that over her to make her spend time with him. I never knew what was happening. We didn't sleep together except the one time after we got back from spring break. Looking back, I should have known something, should have seen what was going on, but we were finishing up the season and everything was crazy, and I let her push me away. I found out afterwards and took care of him."

Jase nodded. "Did you tell her dad?"

"Yeah, I told him she didn't have to worry, that I took care of it. He thanked me and hung up." Lee turned his head to look at Jase. "I loved her."

"Loved or love?" Jase questioned him.

"Love, man. Present tense."

"Wise woman told me not long ago that excuses aren't allowed. If you love her, then find her and tell her. Take a fucking chance, man." Jase sat up straighter in the seat. "Don't let circumstances rob you of that. Take the shot."

10 - Broken things

Home ice is the best, Jase thought as he skated around the rink holding his stick high in the air after their win. He had been in Fort Wayne for nearly two months now, and looking into the arena stands, he saw several jerseys with his number. That was good, seeing the folks who had spent their money on a jersey and then chose to have his name and number put on it, and he made sure to wave to the fans. All night long, he felt eyes on him, and if he were gaining in popularity here, that would make sense.

Ready to head home after changing, he was joking with Lee and another player as they walked through the tunnel and out the door into the parking lot. They planned to head for a local sports bar where members often gathered, but he wanted to go home for some veg-time in front of the flat screen. There were several fans staking out the area with autograph requests, so Jase moved aside, letting his teammates take the lead. Stepping around the cluster of bodies, he was surprised to hear his name called and turned back to see a tall, leggy blonde walking towards him.

Just his height in her heels, she reached out a casual hand and tousled his hair as if she thought they were friends. Without smiling, he reached up and pulled her hand off him, because he had no desire for company tonight. *Or ever,* he thought, *unless it's DeeDee.* Clasping her hand in both of his, he shook it quickly, saying, "Thanks for your support. Means a lot for the new guy from out of town."

She swayed closer and he bit back a groan, realizing that she wasn't going to be dissuaded as quickly as that. "Jason," she purred, pressing into his side as he turned his body to avoid the full frontal assault at least.

"Yeap, that's my name." He laughed and stepped backwards, finding himself up against the outer wall of the building. "Did you have something for me to sign?" Perhaps he could get her on her way by being obtuse. He rolled his eyes, thinking, *She probably doesn't know what obtuse means.*

"Skating around on that ice all night looks like hard work, and ice is cold." She leaned close again, whispering into his ear, "I could warm you up, give you a massage, take the edge off."

"Sweetie, no offense, but I'm not up for company tonight." Direct and to the point was the way to go with this one, and he waited for her to move away. When she didn't, he continued, "My teammates might have other ideas, but I'm not on the block, honey."

Something brushed against the front of his suit pants, and he looked down to watch as her hand first cupped his groin, and then gripped his hardening cock through the fabric. "This tells a different story, Jason," she said.

"Yeah, well, little Jase doesn't get his way very often, so don't listen to what he's telling you." He twisted sideways, reaching down to grab her wrist firmly, pulling her hand away. Seeing a flash of movement out of the corner of his eye, he turned his head to see someone rapidly retreating. Recognizing the sway of those hips and that head of red hair, he groaned.

There was a protesting, "Hey!" from behind him as he pushed the blonde away, taking off across the lot after DeeDee.

"DeeDee, wait," he called as he ran to catch up with her, settling into a fast walk beside her as they moved across the lot towards fan parking in the front. "Wait," he said again, reaching out a hand to touch her arm. She stopped so suddenly he stumbled and had to turn around, having passed her with his long, hurried strides.

"Hey," he said softly. Looking into her face, he saw the glint of tears on her lashes and his heart clenched. Blinking furiously, she swallowed and lifted her chin, meeting his gaze straight on.

"Hi, Jase," she said cheerfully, as if she hadn't just been about to cry.

He took a long look, drinking his fill of her. He hadn't seen her in six weeks. Six long weeks, and Jase saw she had lost back the little bit of weight she gained when they were together. He thought she looked too skinny again, beginning to lose the soft curves he loved. Arms crossed over her chest, she had her fingers tightly wrapped around her biceps, the tension in her hands giving lie to the smile on her face. He lifted a hand to stroke her cheek and she stepped back, out of reach, her reaction twisting his heart in his chest again. *What? She can't even stand my hands on her now?*

"You came to the game?" He didn't know what else to say, what to ask. He knew what he wanted: he wanted her to come home with him, let him wrap her up…let him love her. His mouth was full of those words, his tongue frozen with fear. *God*, just having her this close was good, and he didn't want to do anything to send her running again.

"Yeah, the radio station gave me some tickets for advertising the club." Smiling politely, she took another step back and to the side, trying to shift around him but he moved with her.

"Oh, promo tickets. Nice. Were they decent seats?" *Doesn't she know I'd get her tickets to every game if she wanted?* He should do that anyway, have them at the ticket office for every home game. That way he would know by looking if she was in the arena.

"Yeah, on the glass behind home net. You played a lot." The first hint of a real smile crossed her face. "You look good."

"The team seems to suit me," he agreed. "You look good too, baby." *Crap,* he thought when he saw her flinch as if slapped when the endearment slipped out. *Don't do that again, man.*

"It's good to see you, Jase," she said, stepping back again. Clearly preparing to leave, she shifted further around him and he turned to track her movements.

"DeeDee," he was frantic now to keep her talking, keep her here...keep *her*. Casting around for a topic, he latched onto the most recent thing he knew had happened in her life. "How's Ruby?" *There, look at that; her real smile is back.* He relaxed minutely. *I picked a good topic.*

"She's good. Seems recovered from everything. Things could have gone a different way, so we're all glad she's better." Her gaze dipped then rose again, "Slate loves her."

"Yeah, he does, eh?" He smiled, thinking about how crazy Slate was for Ruby. "It's still a good thing between them, eh?"

She laughed, and his breath caught in his throat at the sound, bright, clear, and mirthful, so...her. "Well, Ruby's happy, and that's all I care about. I love seeing her smile again. You don't know what she was like before the accident, but this is as close to that as she's been for years." She looked wistful, and Jase was thrown off balance that he hadn't been with her to see all of this as it happened. He would love to be there every day. His heart twisted again and he frowned, thinking, *I do still love her. I love her.*

"So, how's work?" *Yeah, you're officially floundering for conversation starters now*. Next would be the weather. He groaned silently.

"Work is about the same." She flashed him a grin. "Mercy asks about you sometimes. Said you were the shyest guy she had ever seen in a strip club. I have a new girl auditioning in a couple of weeks; she's coming up from Florida. It's nice. Really nice, because, for a change, everything is running smoothly, which kinda makes me want to find some wood to knock on so I don't jinx myself."

"Mercy's a jackass," he grumbled, grinning. Leaning over, he offered his head. "Here's my thick head; you can knock on that. It's as good as wooden." He held the pose, looking down to watch her legs and feet, and he saw them angle as she leaned forward a second before her hand settled on his head. Her fingers delicately threaded through his hair to the back of his neck, tracing the skin there softly. Then he lost the heat of her hand as she made a fist and gently rapped her knuckles on top of his head.

Straightening slowly, he caught a look of pain on her face before she smoothed it away, plastering that damn fake smile back on. "There you go," he said softly. "Crisis averted. You are officially un-jinxed." Her smile faded, and an uncertain look took its place, making her look open and vulnerable. She opened her mouth to say something, when the loud clicking of heels came from across the lot behind him. Her eyes darted over his shoulder, and with a slam he could almost hear, the shutters drew across her features again.

"I have to go. It was good to see you, Jase." She turned on her heel and walked away.

"DeeDee," he called, taking two steps to follow her, when a hand wrapped itself around his arm, pulling him to a stop.

"You left me." The blonde pouted, and he nearly shouted with frustration.

"Like I told you back there, I'm not interested. Go find another player to bag, honey." He twisted back around and scanned the lot, but DeeDee had disappeared. Groaning, he turned from the blonde and stalked over to his truck, jumping up inside and locking the doors before the bimbo could think to open them. He pounded the steering wheel for a moment, roaring out his disappointment and pain.

***

A month later, and he still hadn't seen DeeDee again. Not for lack of trying on his part—Mason be damned—but she wouldn't take his calls, wouldn't open her door to his knocking, and Gunny, the bouncer at Slinky's, would no longer let him inside the club. He called Slate to tell him about the tickets at the box office, begging him to let her know they would be there waiting every game, and Slate promised to tell her. It was no use. While there had been Rebel members in the seats at each game since then, he was disappointed DeeDee hadn't come to even one. Not one game.

Frustrated, he was taking his anger out on the ice and, as a result, was skating one of the best seasons of his career. His tally of goals and assists grew with every game, and he had seen more than thirty minutes ice time in each of the last ten games. Tonight was no different, and the Tridents entered the third period ahead by three.

Jase and Lee skated past their goalie, tapping his shin pads with their sticks as they made their way to center ice for the puck drop. In his assigned position, Jase sculled for advantage against his opponent, scooping his stick to the front time after time, waiting for the drop and trying to anticipate the upcoming action. Totally focused on the puck, when the Tridents won the faceoff, he reacted swiftly, scooping up the loose puck and slapping it across the ice to Lee, watching as he passed it to the other forward on their line.

Skating hard to get in position behind the net, Jase was waiting when the puck came rocketing down ice towards him. He moved out to meet it, deking around an opposing player, and effortlessly tapped it into the goal. Skimming it cleanly between the padded legs of the goaltender, he had only a moment to recognize his success and begin to lift his hands in celebration, when he was slammed hard from behind.

Falling forward on his knees and elbows, Jase screamed when agony bloomed in his groin, growing and peaking at an impossible level while he stayed still, frozen, unable to move or breathe. Yelling wordlessly, he bit hard on his mouth guard and arched his head back, trying to get away from the pain. Spitting the useless plastic out of his mouth and onto the ice, he yelled again, "Fucking shit."

There were voices nearby and then hands under his arms preparing to lift him, so he dropped his stick and gloves. Clutching his legs at the knee, he tried to keep them from moving apart as his teammates stood him up on his skates. Slowly unfolding, only partially upright, he became aware of the silence in the arena as it was gradually broken with clapping and cheers. Guided back to the bench by teammates, he balanced unsteadily on his right skate, his left lifted off the ice. "I can't pick up my feet," he gritted out when they got to the access door and hands lifted under his elbows, raising him enough to get him over the threshold and onto the mats.

Falling towards the bench, he caught himself with his arms, twisting his torso with a groan to sit. He was clutching tightly at the edges of the seat as he leaned his head back, eyes clenched in pain. "Jase, what's going on? Talk to me." The calm voice of the team's doctor, Adam, came through over the noise of the arena, and through closed teeth, Jase said, "Left groin."

He grunted, feeling hands fumbling with the ties of his hockey pants, unlacing the girdle and tugging it down and open. Gasping as the cold hands found the source of the pain, the sudden pressure caused the ache to bloom unbelievably large again.

Tipping his head back again, he ground his teeth together as those relentless fingers applied even greater pressure, and he yelled hoarsely, "*Fuucck.*"

"Ice pack," Adam said just before freezing cold descended into his groin, pressed firmly into place as he dropped his chin to his chest. "Fuck," he said more quietly and took a shallow breath, then another, shaking his head back and forth with the pain. "How bad?" he asked, already knowing the answer.

"Feels like a middling groin pull, Jase. Sorry, man." Adam reached over for another ice pack, sliding this one up the leg of his hockey pants and strapping it into place high on his thigh. "We'll know for sure after we MRI you. For now, I want to get ice on it, see if we can keep the swelling from happening."

Deftly unlacing and removing the skate from that leg, Adam carefully assessed the rest of him. Jase tried ignoring him, attempting to push the pain to the back of his mind, watching the game as both teams raced hard down to the conclusion. They were still four goals up and had one minute left to go in regulation. Lee skated towards the boards in front of the bench and caught his eye. Shaking his head at the unspoken question, Jase saw his friend's face fall before he offered his gloved knuckles. Forcing a stoic look, he bumped his knuckles to Lee's, telling him, "Kick ass for me."

Looking down at Adam still crouched at his feet, Jase asked the question, dreading the answer, "How long on IR?"

"Won't know until we see how things shake out over the next couple of days." The doc patted his other thigh reassuringly. "Don't worry about injured reserve, Jase. I still think it's middling, definitely won't need my skilled hands in surgery. If we keep the swelling down, then you're probably looking at five days to begin rehab, then probably three weeks to skate, five or six total to play. Less if you're good and follow orders."

"Jesus Murphy," Jase said. "And if it's worse?"

"Don't borrow trouble. Let's wait for the win, and then while the stands empty, we'll get you moved back to exam. I have them setting up everything we need. I'll have you home before you know it." Looking up at him, Adam asked, "You have someone who can help you out for a few days?"

Before he could answer, a voice came from over their heads, causing them both to look up. Slate was leaning head and shoulders over the six-foot glass behind the bench, teetering with his feet on the seat arms below and behind him. "We got him. He'll have help," he said, and Jase looked up at him in bemused wonder.

"Where the hell did you come from?" he asked, staring at the incongruous sight of the black-leather-clad biker in the hockey arena.

"Wyoming, you asshat," Slate joked and stood upright, jumping down from his perch and turning to thank the woman who'd moved so he could use her seat as a stepladder. He pointed at Jase and then towards the tunnel, and Adam mouthed something at him. Slate gave a single nod and then was striding up the narrow cement stairs, disappearing into the crowd at the top of the section as the game-ending siren sounded.

After a more complete exam, Adam was still convinced the groin pull needed ice and rest, in that order, but wouldn't require surgery to repair, which was exceptional news. Jase was now wrapped and strapped, and under strict orders to ice for fifteen minutes every two hours for the next twenty-four. He would be at the hospital Monday for the MRI, and then meeting the team's trainers in their office two days after that so they could evaluate and plot out his recovery. If the pain became worse or the swelling was unbearable, he was supposed to call, but otherwise, he would be lying on his ass for a few days.

Jase looked with loathing at the crutches Adam tried to hand him, pulling his hands back in repugnance. "Are you fucking kidding me?"

"Hey, man, if you think you can bear weight on that leg, show me." Adam stepped back, sweeping one hand in front of him in a go-ahead gesture, and Jase snorted.

"Fuck you, doc," he said mildly as he reached out for the crutches, shaking his head in disgusted resignation.

"Hey, Prince Charming," a voice said, and he looked up, seeing Slate and Bear coming towards him.

"Hey, man." He held out his hand, gripping each man's forearm in turn, nodding in greeting. "It's okay, Slate. I can manage." He held up the crutches. "They got me sticks. I can use them to walk, pull things closer, close doors. These are all-purpose sticks. I can even rub them together to start a fire. I'm good."

"Naw," Slate said, slapping him on the shoulder. "We've got enough brothers to help you out for a couple days. Not gonna be as pretty as some of your little ice chippies, but we can keep you off your feet for two days like they want."

"Ice chippies, puck bunnies—whatever, their primary purpose is out of my reach for a few weeks, so it's just as well." Jase laughed humorlessly, feeling the pain medication Adam had given him beginning to loosen the stranglehold the pain had on his groin and inside thigh.

With Slate driving his truck, in just a few minutes, they were pulling into the driveway of his condo, and through the open door, he was surprised to see there were already a half-dozen Rebel members inside. He turned and frowned at Slate. "Did you jackasses find a key under the doormat I didn't know was there?" he asked without irritation, his head tipping to one side inquisitively.

"Naw, got one from a friend of yours," Slate said, coming around the front of the truck and handing him the crutches.

He maneuvered them underneath his arms and tried to stand, overbalancing and tipping backwards against the side of the truck, groaning as the sudden jarring movement woke the pain. "Fuck," he muttered, catching his balance with some effort. "I got no friends."

"Yeah, you do, asshat." Slate snorted and grabbed one arm. Bear, walking from where he parked behind Jase's truck, gripped his other one.

"Now, how the hell am I supposed to make the sticks work, when you're holding my arms, eh? Fuck, it hurts. I think my dick's broken, eh? Serves me right for not using it for so long; poor thing feels neglected. Little Jase misses her, too, eh? Not as much as big me, but still." He couldn't make the crutches work and held them out, dangling them from his fingers and laughing.

"What the hell'd they give him?" Bear asked the question, and Slate mumbled something back to him, but Jase couldn't make it out.

He snorted. "Can't hear you. You're inaudible. That's a funny word. In-aud-i-ble. Inaudible. Unaudible. Nonaudible. Illaudible. Laudanum." Putting on a British accent, he said, "May I have some laudanum?"

Laughing, Bear shoved the crutches back under his arms. "Work the sticks, man. Crutch your ass up to the door."

Once installed on the couch with the TV remote in hand, legs stretched out along the cushions, the pain was not as bad. He arranged the ice packs with care, making sure to cover where the swelling was beginning to make an appearance. His head seemed too heavy for his neck, so he leaned back against the arm of the couch, looking up at the ceiling.

Slate's face came into view upside down, and Jase saw his mouth moving. "Inaudible," he croaked, turning away.

There was a tap on his shoulder and he looked back up at Slate, this time hearing him ask, "How's the pain?"

"My fucking dick's broke. How do you think the pain is?" he asked querulously and jerked his head to look around as a familiar, feminine laugh filled the room. Seeing a dark-haired woman standing near the kitchen door, he frowned, confused, because he didn't know her. "Who's you?"

She came forward and he lifted his arm, reaching out to take her hand, but letting her do all the work when they shook. Still frowning and trying to figure out how that laugh came out of her mouth, he asked fussily, "Who are you?"

"I'm Eddie. I'm with Bear," she said, and he blew a big breath out between pursed lips.

"Well, thank God you aren't here for my dick," he said earnestly, widening his eyes for emphasis as she smiled. He stage whispered, "It's broke."

"I heard," she said, nodding and laughing a different laugh. Different tone, different sound, not nearly as beautiful. That laugh sure wouldn't make him hard, even when his dick wasn't broke.

"I liked your other laugh better. I miss that laugh. I miss the woman that made that laugh. Miss her all the fuckin' time." He sighed, and his head lolled sideways. He worked to bring it back to face her with some effort. "But now, I think I'm gonna sleep," he mumbled, the room growing dark and then light again by turns. After a few cycles, he realized the light changing was caused by him blinking his eyes and smiled, chortling to himself, "Ohhhh, pretty. Light show."

***

Hoss looked over, frowning as he called, "He's out, babe."

Okay, woman, you can do this, DeeDee thought as she walked across the room, pulling a chair up beside the couch, her entire focus on the man lying in front of her. She knew the men weren't happy with her being here, but she had to know he was okay, and the only way to do that was to see for herself. Look him over, sit with him, and touch him—even if he never knew she was there.

When she saw him go down on the ice and realized he wasn't getting up, that he was hurt, her heart had leapt into her throat, choking the breath from her body. The sight of him being assisted off the ice had been hard to take. Her focus left him only long enough to read a text from Slate telling her about the injury and letting her know the club would be helping him out for the next couple of days.

Slate didn't know she was there to see it first hand, didn't know she was sitting across the arena so she could see the players' faces where they sat on the bench. No one knew she went to the games, that she couldn't stay away, even though she knew she had to for his sake. She bought a Tridents jersey after the first game, wearing his number to all the games she attended, both home and away.

She had taken a gamble one night, following other fans around the outside of the arena to where the players parked, thinking if she could only glimpse him from a distance, it would be enough. Then, she saw him walking out of the hallway into the parking lot, and without clear thought, had begun moving towards him. She realized she was still as drawn to him as she had been all those months ago at Mica's party. Her advance abruptly halted when she saw him step to the side with a beautiful young woman. That was another moment when her breath was stolen, but that time by pain as his friend fondled him unashamedly, barely blocking the view with her body.

It was what she wanted for him. But...*God,* it hurt so badly to see.

Eyes welling with tears, DeeDee had turned on her heel to flee, nearly panicking when his voice called her name, because she stupidly had gotten too close and he clocked her. Of course he had, because there was no way the universe would let her slink away in quiet humiliation. That was too much to ask, apparently.

She knew Jase was coming after her, his footsteps fast and loud in the parking lot behind her. It seemed like she was moving through molasses, each step away from him a struggle. Then he touched her, and she froze in place, looking up into his eyes. The smile on his face had brought more tears to her eyes, because he looked well and happy, so even if she was miserable, it looked like she made the right decision. Brazening it out, she stood and chatted with him as if she wasn't tearing in two. He teasingly invited a caress and she had been unable to hold back, reaching out to touch him gently, lovingly, as if she still had a right to do so. Now she closed her eyes, remembering the feel of his hair between her fingers, the unguarded look on his face as he straightened.

Then his friend was stalking across the lot towards them, and from the stormy look on her face, DeeDee thought he might be paying for his actions for a long while. She knew if it had been her, he would have had hell to pay for first chasing, and then having a private conversation with another woman, especially one with whom he shared a history.

She quickly said goodbye, fleeing like a coward, leaving him standing there alone to explain things to his woman. She didn't want to stick around and hear him fumble for words to address what they had once been...what they now weren't to each other...not after they teased each other so lovingly about labels and titles. She didn't want to see the pity in the woman's face either. It would be a knowing look, acknowledging without speaking how much it hurt to lose all that was Jase, how much it distressed her to see him under another woman's hands.

That didn't stop her from going to the games, though. Slate told her Jase was leaving tickets at the box office for each game. Declining to use them, she told him to make sure other club members did, so the tickets wouldn't go to waste, implying she wouldn't be attending. Buying her own tickets online, she selected her seat with care. Far enough away from the glass to prevent a chance meeting of eyes, but not so far away she couldn't see his face.

Now, sitting beside the couch as he slept, she bowed her head, tracing his features with her gaze, reaching out to push his hair back off his face. From across the ice, across a parking lot, or across these few inches separating them, however it happened, she loved looking at him. His features were normally so expressive, but now, in a drug-induced sleep, the muscles were slack, relaxed, which held a beauty all its own. Her fingers continued to slide through his hair then around his face to cup his jaw possessively. He stirred under her touch and she froze, but he turned his face into her hand, burrowing into her palm and sighing deeply as a smile curled the corners of his mouth up and he murmured something.

The weight of a presence loomed behind her and she knew what was coming. Looking up, she stared into Slate's eyes as he scowled down at her. Mutely, she asked him...what...she didn't even know what she was asking, just something. For him to give her this, a few minutes Jase would never have to know about. A salve for her heart and emotions. Something to hold close, bring out in the night when she was alone and lonely. She might not be able to have him in her life, but she would by God fight Slate for these few moments. Her chin quivered, lips trembling as she pressed them tightly together, and he closed his eyes, shaking his head. "Fuck me," he muttered and turned, stomping back to the kitchen as she hiccupped a sob. Looking back down at the man she loved, she ran her fingers tenderly through his long hair.

***

Hoss stood in the kitchen, watching through the open archway as DeeDee sat next to the couch, one of her hands constantly in contact with some part of Jase. There was a slow easing in his chest, a loosening in the tightness that had started building when he found out DeeDee had closed the door on Jase again. He remembered the blinding beauty on her face he had seen only once before, having caught a glimpse of it again tonight when she first approached where Jase lay. He turned to Slate and nodded. "I get it, Prez. I totally get it. I was wrong, man."

"Come again?" Slate asked, cocking a hip to lean against the countertop.

"What you and Bingo've been telling me. I like DeeDee, always have, but I don't love her. I don't have that kind of connection with her. Did you see the man's face when she laughed? He knew she was here, even if he couldn't see her. Doped to the gills, he still knew she was here, and it eased something inside him." He looked down at the tips of his boots. "I wanted to keep her in the club, because...hell, I don't know all the reasons. Mostly because keeping her in the club meant we kept part of Winger. That man was a good fucking friend, a good brother."

"Yeah, he was."

"Jase is a good friend, and he's good for DeeDee. They're good together." He made a face. "I don't want to fucking lose her, too."

Sighing, Slate leaned over and looked around him, one corner of his lips lifting in a slow smile. "I'm pretty sure we get to keep her, man. Jase is one of us, but for the patch. Now, she just needs to pull her head out of her own ass, see what you've seen."

***

Sitting in Adam's office two weeks later, Jase was ready for some good news. "Come on, hit me," he joked, turning his shoulder towards the doctor. "See how ready I am? Come on."

Shaking his head, Adam said, "Funny, Jase. It wasn't your arm that got hurt, was it? Maybe your head? I bet that's it. You hit your head when you fell down?"

"No, really," he nodded, "I'm ready to get back to two-a-days in the gym."

"From what I hear, you already are," Adam said dryly, laughing as Jase winced.

"Eh, not so much. I'm doing a few extra reps of the exercises and stretches you've prescribed. Nothing wild and crazy, just ready to get back to life." Jase ran his hands through his hair, leaving one palm pressed against the back of his neck, rubbing as the muscles tensed. "Skating is my life, man. I'm ready."

"All right," Adam said, turning to his desk and making a note.

"All right?" Jase questioned, not believing his ears.

"Yeah, all right." Adam shrugged. "You're working hard at getting healthy, and as a result, you're healing fast, about five days ahead of what I expected. But, I don't want you to overdo it. Five mile light runs, no more than two-a-days in the gym, and no exercises other than what's on your sheet. Keep the weight to what we've discussed, and I'll see you on the ice this time next week."

"Yes, sir." Jase snapped off a faux salute, standing with a smile.

As he was climbing into the truck, his phone rang. He switched it to Bluetooth and answered, "Hello?"

Daniel's voice echoed in the truck and Jase smiled. "Hey, Jase, how's it hanging, man?"

"Hanging quite fine, thank you very much," he responded. "What's up, Cap'n?"

"Just calling to check up on you. How did the appointment go today? They release you to skate yet?" Daniel asked seriously.

"Next week, I'm back on ice. This week, I get to sweat my balls off in the gym." Jase grimaced as he started the truck, pulling into traffic.

"Ouch. At least you're off the couch, right?"

"Yeah. That's something, at least. Fucking IR, hate the list. Hate it. I've got too much time on my hands. Hell, Daniel, I've been reading. Who the hell do we know that reads?" Jase turned the truck towards the gym.

"What the hell are you reading?" Daniel was laughing now, and there was something in the background of the call.

"Is that Mica? Tell her hi from me," he said. "Bear's gal left a book at the house, some kind of submissive stuff. Not much in the way of dialog, but it's descriptive with the cock and pussy action; I'll give it that. Leather and silk, swings and benches, and lots of other things I've never heard of."

Mica's voice asked in disbelief, "Mommy porn? You're reading mommy porn? Jeeze-oh-PETE, Jase!"

"Why the hell don't you warn people when you put 'em on speaker, Daniel? You know I'm not the kind of person you can have on speaker, man. What the hell?" He laughed, then said, "Hey, Mica?"

He waited for an acknowledgment from her and continued, chuckling, "You should come visit me. I've been reading for days. You might even call it studying. I've learned a lot from my studies, I mean...reading. Plus, my dick's not broke no more. Little Jase is working just fine."

It sounded as if there was a scuffle in the background, and then Daniel's voice came back on the phone. "Talk to you later."

Jase said, "Laters," and hung up the phone, laughing.

11 - All I see

"Whoooo! Win column. Champion City, coming to a theater near you." Jase was crowing, standing on the bench in the locker room. "Way to go, boys. Smash those—who were the losers we were playing again? I already forgot! Whoooo!"

Laughter filled the room and Jase looked around at his teammates. Nodding, he stepped down from the bench and made his way over to Lee, standing near Coach. "Good team, Cap'n," he said. "We are right and tight. Ready to keep winning, man."

Lee made a face, cutting his eyes over to Jase. "You know who the next set of games is against, right?"

Jase blew a disappointed raspberry. "Yeah, Mallets. Daniel accused me of getting hurt so I didn't have to play them the last series. He's gonna pay for that comment Friday, *wham*." He slammed a closed fist into his palm with a broad grin.

This would be the first time Jase played against his former team. The Tridents and Mallets had met for four games during the five weeks he was injured, but he hadn't been able to go watch, much less play. The teams had split that series, which hadn't hurt Jase's feelings. He knew it would be tough to play against his old teammates, but he would figure it out. *Them's the breaks*, he thought, leaning down to unlace his skates.

Hardly anything had worked out as he intended when he asked for the trade, but this had still been a good move for him, both as a player and as a person. He might not be with DeeDee, but things everywhere else were good, and he hadn't given up hope on her yet, either.

The next morning, he had barely walked in from his run and was standing in the kitchen, sweating and drinking water, when his phone rang. Pressing speaker where it lay on the countertop, he answered without looking at the caller information. "Hello?"

"Jase, how you doin'?" Mason's voice came through the phone and Jase cocked his head, looking at the phone as if it could tell him what the man wanted. There could be no good reason for Mason to be calling him. That man was seriously scary.

"I'm good. What'd I do?" Jase asked and winced. *And, once again, your mouth leads with stupid*, he thought.

"You didn't do anything, fucker." Mason laughed. "Calling to see if you wanted to go on a run Sunday before the game. A few of us are coming down and we'll be taking part in the first charity ride of the year; thought you might want to get in on it."

"Sure, count me in. You coming to the game then?" He wondered if the charity or the game was the real reason for Mason's presence in Fort Wayne.

"Hell yeah, wouldn't miss it. The monster match-up of the century is how they're playing this up in Chicago. Prodigal son Jase Spencer pitted against Daniel Rupert and crew." Mason snorted. "If they only knew, right?"

"Yeah, yeah. If only," he said quietly. *If they only knew how stupid I was.* "Hey," he paused, clearing his suddenly constricted throat, "will DeeDee be on the ride?"

"Naw, she's got other crap to do. She's helping Ruby plan her wedding long distance. Slate's been out of town and finally got tired of being alone, and he called for Ruby to come out west last week, asked her to marry him as soon as she got off the plane. They'll be back in a few days, but not before the game. Did you know she's pregnant?" Mason asked, curiosity evident in his voice.

Jase's throat closed and he couldn't breathe. *She lied?* His next thought was full of joy, because she had wanted a child so badly. *Did I give her that?* "DeeDee said she couldn't get pregnant."

"I dunno about that shit, but that girl is definitely preggers." Mason laughed.

"The girl...you mean Ruby is pregnant?" Jase drew in a ragged breath of relief...and sadness. "Not DeeDee?"

Mason's tone sobered. "No, not DeeDee. You're right; she had the one chick and no chance of others. She wanted a baseball team at one point, right after her and Winger got together. They worked out the names and preferred batting order. Not in the cards, man." He was silent for a minute, then said, "Ruby's baby is due not long after Mica and Daniel's son."

"A wedding and a baby. Slate's turning into quite the family man, eh?" Jase grinned, knowing Mason couldn't see him. "Things are changing fast, Mason. Bear working on adopting a passel of kids, he's got four, right? Plus, Mica's expecting soon. And I heard Molly's little boy Tomas is a cutie. You should buy a daycare, man. You'll make a killing off just the people you know."

"Maybe I should. I'll take that under advisement, man. Thanks for the business recommendation," Mason laughed. "I'll text you the details for the charity run; it's for the kids' hospital there in the Fort. They do cancer research, and we're trying to raise about twenty grand to donate. Why don't you hit up the team owners, see if you can get anything out of them."

"Will do. I'll see you Sunday." He tapped the disconnect button and drained the bottle of water. "Ruby's pregnant," he mused aloud. "Good swimmers, Slate. Way to go, man."

***

Never having taken part in an event like this before, Jase wasn't sure what to expect, but he figured Mason wouldn't steer him wrong. It was scheduled to be a fifty-mile ride with five stops. There was something called a fifty/fifty at one of them, with a tattoo contest and auction at another. *At least I know what a tattoo is,* he thought with a smile, flexing his arms in his coat.

He looked around at the crowd, seeing what must be about a hundred bikes parked in the lots at Checkerz. They were beginning and ending at this bar north of Fort Wayne, with three stops in between. There would be live music later, plus the contests for tattoos, longest beards, and other fun things. He glanced down, twisting the armband he got at registration. He had an entry card too, tucked into the inside pocket of his plain, black leather vest.

The Tridents management had pledged to donate a hundred dollars for every participant who completed all five stops and had put up a two-thousand dollar prize for the winner. That gave the Rebels more than half the amount they wanted to raise right off the bat. Mason had slapped Jase on the back when he brought them the news last night at the Fort Wayne Rebel clubhouse.

"Jase." A voice called his name and he turned his head, seeing Tug walking his way. Straddling his bike, he held out his hand for a shake and was pulled into a back-thumping hug. "Damn, man, I wasn't sure we would see you here today. You looked a little green last night when we were talking about the fun we have on runs."

"It's for a charity, right? So, it's well worth the time," Jase said. "I didn't see you last night. You should have come over and said hello."

"I had to leave, had shit to take care of." Tug spoke curtly, and Jase dropped it. He had learned that particular tone meant it was all club business and none of his. He looked around, seeing several other faces he knew and raised a hand to wave at Pinto and Pops, two members who spent time with him when he first moved to town.

By the end of the run, Jase had drawn absolute trash cards with no chance of winning the poker hand, but he had a blast riding with his friends. Returning to where they began, he was ready for something to eat, and a chance to sit on a stool for a while. As they were pulling in, he recognized one of the bikes parked next to the building, and his driving became erratic, resulting in him nearly running into Tug in front of him. It was DeeDee's bike; he had seen it often enough over the past year to know it. *Maybe she's inside. She has to be inside, right?* As he clumsily parked in his haste to get off the bike and into the bar, he thought, *She wouldn't just park it here and leave*.

"Tug," he called and pointed to the bike. Getting only a chin lift in response, he was frustrated, thinking, *What the hell does that mean?* Finally dismounting his bike, he walked quickly to the bar's door, looking back when a hand gripped his arm just as he reached for the handle.

"She isn't in there, man," Tug told him with a shake of his head. "She donated the bike. The auction's in about thirty minutes; that's why the bike's here. She ain't in the bar."

"Her bike? She's giving her bike away. What the hell for? Why would she do that?" Jase asked questions frantically, running a hand through his hair, fingers tangling in the wind-snarled, too-long ends.

"It's her old man's bike. Yeah, she rode Winger's scoot sometimes, but it's honestly too big for her. She's got her own ride, lighter and lower, easier for her to handle." Tug scrubbed his hand along his jaw, smoothing his mustache over his chin. "Some brothers wanted to buy the bike, but she wouldn't choose between them. Said this way it was up to the highest bidder, and has the added benefit of leaving her in the clear. Can't say she's wrong about that. Some of the brothers were from other chapters. With them not knowing her like we do, they could have taken it wrong if she didn't lean the way they hoped."

"Anyone I know?" Jase asked, looking around the lot again.

"Birdy wanted the bike in the worst way, but he lowballed his offer," Tug laughed. "I told her I'd pay her twice what he offered, but she decided to go the auction route."

"And she's okay giving Winger's bike away? I guess I knew it was his, but she looked at home on it. She always patted the tank when she got off like it was a puppy or something." Jase shook his head, reaching for the door handle again. A thought was beginning to churn in his head, and the more he considered it, the better it sounded. "Can anyone bid?" He turned to Tug as he asked the question, getting a startled, wary look in response.

"Anyone with the money to back it up." He nodded, and then shook his head. "If you're gonna do it, make sure to register for the auction at the top bar. Talk to pretty Dixie, the bar manager, she'll take care of you. There're other things up for auction: some leathers, saddle bags, and I think there're a couple more bikes on the list, too."

"What do you think it will go for?" Jase asked, striding over to where an attractive, dark-haired bartender was taking down names, using paperclips to attach IDs to notecards.

"Less than it should," Tug responded, slipping behind the bar and hugging Dixie from behind, tickling her neck with his mustache until she giggled uncontrollably. "Pretty lady, how you been?"

Half an hour later, Jase sat at one of the high-top tables near the stage. The auctioneer was working his way through the things up for bid, and DeeDee's bike was apparently expected to be the big-ticket item, last on the list. He registered and signed an agreement, and now he had to outwait and outbid any other interested parties.

He wasn't sure yet what he would do with a second bike, but the thought of that motorcycle—*her* bike—going to some faceless stranger pissed him off. He had ridden beside her for quite a few miles and didn't want to see anyone else straddling the seat; it was as simple as that.

***

"*Fucking* overtime shootout rules!" Jase yelled and punched the boards as he bounced off them. "Goddammit." The buzzer had sounded for the end of the five-minute overtime period and the Tridents and Mallets were still tied up, three all. If this had been a playoff game, they would move into another overtime, but because it was still regular season, the game would be decided by a shootout.

He looked over at the visitors' bench, shaking his head. If he knew the Mallets, Dahl would shoot first, then Gary, with Daniel last. *We'll have to get ahead of it*, he thought, skating over to his home bench and looking at Lee, who nodded at him. He knew they were on the same page with this as Lee turned to talk to Coach.

Coming into this third game of the series, they had lost two games, with the Mallets having swept them so far. Jase had run the numbers in his head a dozen times, looking at the fancy AHL website to confirm what he already knew. Even with the point from overtime, if they didn't win this game tonight, it would take an unlikely turn of events for them to be in the playoffs. Essentially, Cincinnati and Kalamazoo would both have to lose four games in a row, and the Tridents would have to *win* their next four games for them to make the first round of the playoffs. Might as well say toads had to fall from the sky too, because it was as unlikely to happen.

Lee waved him over, and as Jase approached, he caught the middle of his conversation with Coach, "...flaws. He's bigger this year. No more five hole on this kid." Jase nodded, saying, "Dierk put on thirty pounds of muscle over the offseason. Pair that with the fact he's always been a demon on lofted pucks and you pretty much gotta catch him out of position or skim one under his pads. We just gotta put the biscuit in the basket, eh? Light the lamp."

Nodding, Coach pointed to Pavelza, a forward who skated second shift, then Jase, saying, "One, two," pointing to Lee, "three."

Dahl and Pavelza's shots were both denied, leaving the shootout zero all. Gary skated next and he slapped a pretty top shelf shot around the Tridents' goalie and into upper right-hand corner. He looked as comfortable as if he were at home pegging pucks at a freezer in the back of the family garage.

Jase's gut tightened as he stepped out and skated up ice to his goalie, gliding past and tapping the kid's pads with the blade of his stick in encouragement.

The puck was waiting for him at center ice and he approached slowly, hearing Dierk chirping and catcalling from the crease at the other end of the rink. *Focus*, he told himself, pushing everything else out of his mind. The sounds of the arena faded as everything not in front of him moved away, becoming unimportant.

He watched the young goalie's body language, noting what appeared to be a favoring towards the right side of the net. Picking up the puck on the blade of his stick, he skated down ice slowly, legs moving on muscle memory from side to side, hands loose and comfortable on the stick. *Tape to net*. The thought passed swiftly through his mind. *Light the lamp*.

Feinting right, as if he was going for the fake favor, he dragged the puck behind him, and then tapped it between his own legs. He gave it a quick toe drag to the side before he slapped it towards the goalie, deftly avoiding the quick poke check Dierk attempted.

He saw the puck pass straight between Dierk's legs, the goalie's dropping to the ice too slow to block the shot. Jase smiled in triumph as the red light lit up behind the net, indicating he had been successful in scoring a goal.

Dierk reached around the edge of the net as Jase skated from behind and tapped him with his stick, saying, "Pretty one, old man."

"Yeah, you've slowed up since you lost me, kid," he responded, and they grinned at each other.

Exiting the ice to the accolades of his teammates, he looked across to see Daniel stepping onto the sheet, intent eyes focused on their hometown goalie. "Poor kid," Jase murmured. "He's fucked."

Within ten seconds, Daniel had scored and was skating back to his bench, bumping fists with the team as he glided past the bench to the access door. Shaking his head, Jase watched Lee as he skated towards the puck at center ice, trying to read the goalie waiting in the net at the end of the rink. "Come on, Cap'n," he muttered, his fists pounding the top of the short wall in front of him. "Come on, Lee. Get it on net."

The team watched as the shot left the stick and saw it batted out of the air by the glove Dierk wore on his off hand. That was it, game over. Mallets won, four to three. The rest of the Tridents team turned to walk up the alley towards their locker room, but Jase stayed in the bench area, waiting for Lee and their goalie. Punching them in the shoulder, he said, "Good game, boys. Left it all on the ice, didn't we, eh?"

He turned to follow them to the locker room and a voice called his name. Looking up, he saw Mason standing at the wall above the alley, looking down at him. "Hey, man," he called with a wave of his glove.

“We’re going to Marie’s. I want you to meet us there.” With a chin lift, Mason turned and stalked up the steps towards the main concourse. With a snort and a shrug, Jase walked down the tunnel. He guessed he would be going to Marie’s, since the man hadn’t given him a chance to say no.

He sat on the bench in front of his locker, looking around at the somber and quiet team. Everyone had probably done the same calculations he had, and now they were probably tallying up the money they wouldn’t earn if they didn’t make the playoffs. Elbows on his knees, he dropped his head into his hands for a minute, trying and failing to find his usual, clownish, locker room persona.

“Hey, listen up,” Lee said from across the room, and he looked up. Coach was standing behind him and they motioned for Jase to stand. Slowly, he did so, looking around at the rest of the team. “I’ve never seen anyone work as hard to come back from a debilitating injury as this guy has, and he did so with one hell of a positive attitude.” He reached behind him, taking something off the shelf in his locker, and walked over to Jase.

“No one deserves this more than you do, Jase,” he said, putting a ‘C’ patch in Jase’s hand.

He looked up, stunned, and frantically tried to hand it back. “No, no. Nuh-uh. I’m not no captain. No, no. That’s your job, man.” Frustrated, because Lee wouldn’t accept the patch, he looked over at Coach, only to find an amused smile on the man’s face.

“Seriously, I’m not captain material, eh? I’m the comedian; I know what I am. That’s my job, to keep the spirits up, eh? Not lead and inspire, that’s your job, Lee. Your name even fits, Lee…lead, see? Not me. No, no, no.” He was nearly panicking, trying to get the man to take the patch out of his hand.

"*Co*-Captain," Lee said, clapping a hand on Jase's shoulder. "My new Co-Captain. You'll be okay. You thinking you don't deserve it only reinforces my belief that you do."

Jase stood still, looking down at the patch in his hand. Next game, it would be sewn to his jersey and he would have a slightly different position to fill, still encouraging his teammates, but with less humor, a more serious role. Nodding, he lifted his eyes to look around the room, seeing the smiles on the faces of his team, hearing the tapping of their stick butts and palms against the floor mats and walls. His team. *When did the Tridents become my team?* he wondered with a grin. "You fuckers don't know what you've unleashed upon the world. Giant lizard stompin' on a city got nothing on Jase Spencer, Co-Captain." He made roaring noises, flapping his arms around, and the room erupted into laughter.

Lee slapped him on the back again and the room filled with chatter about the game, dissecting the plays that had garnered them goals, as well as the ones that stole them. His team.

***

"Too bad, man," Mason said, turning to put his elbows on the bar behind him. "You played a hell of a game, though. That was a nice shot you put in during the shootout."

"Too little, too late. Was a good, tight game," he said, taking a sip of his beer. "Hard loss. That probably killed playoffs for us."

"Ouch." Mason winced. "That sting a little? Coming off the win last year?"

"Hell yeah, it stings," he acknowledged. "This move's been good for me, though. I wouldn't change it up. I've done all right here, and they're a talented team; we took too long to gel earlier in the season. If I play for them next year, I think we'll do well." In the mirror, he saw Daniel and Gary walking up behind him. “There’s no shame in losing to the defending champions, even if Daniel Rupert is their captain.”

“Hey, watch it,” Daniel said, slapping Jase’s shoulder.

“Oh, hey, Daniel. Didn’t see you standing there,” he deadpanned and then laughed. “Good win, man. Your team is tight as ever.”

“Tridents aren’t pushovers. You made us work for every goal.” Daniel ordered a beer with a flick of his fingers. “Was a good game.”

Jase looked around. “I don’t see your lovely wife. Did she come with?”

“Naw, she wanted to stay closer to home. She’s only got a couple more weeks before she’s due, and travel is hard on her, even for short distances.” He smiled, and in that simple expression, Jase could clearly see the man’s love for Mica. Cutting his eyes over to Mason, he was surprised to see happiness on his face, too, as he watched and listened to Daniel. He never understood the dynamic in that kind of triad relationship, where two men loved the same woman, but one willingly stepped aside.

Shaking his head, he looked over at Daniel with a grin. “Guess what you’re looking at?”

With a snort, Daniel tipped his head back. “No idea, idiot. With you, so many different answers immediately come to mind. Why don’t you tell me what I’m looking at?”

“Tridents’ new co-captain, that’s what,” he said proudly, and was gratified to see both Daniel and Mason smile. “It’s about time someone appreciated me,” he laughed.

“Congrats, Jase.” Daniel shook his hand. “That’s awesome. Lee’s a good guy; you can learn a lot from him.”

Later, standing at the bar, he was watching Mason sitting across the room. The man had been in his element all night, chatting with all the Rebels in the house as well as fielding conversations with members of other clubs who approached him. Jase saw at least three other patches in the bar, and he admired Mason's natural confidence when confronted by someone who could well be a rival.

Catching his eye, Mason stood and walked over to him, motioning to the barkeep for another beer. They stood in companionable silence for a few minutes, watching the ebb and flow of the crowd around the tables and bar. Mason said abruptly, "You bought Winger's bike."

Not quite a question, but it deserved a response, so Jase said, "Yeah. Didn't seem right letting it go to a stranger."

"You didn't know Winger though, did you?" Mason looked at him, taking a long drink from his beer.

"No. To me, it's DeeDee's bike, man." He sighed.

Mason nodded, his lips thinning at something. "I can see that. Can see why it would bother you, too." He set his beer down, crossing his arms over his chest. "What happened there? I thought y'all were good."

"I did too," he responded, sipping from his mug. "I don't know what happened, to be honest. When everything went down with Ruby, she was leaning on me, and it seemed like she needed me. We fit. Then it was as if she dropped a brick wall down between us. I had a three-day road trip for away games, and by the time I got back, she had fallen off the face of the earth. A week later, she sent Slate to tell me to stop trying to contact her."

He looked over at Mason. "She came to one game, but then bolted before we could do much more than say hello. As I said, I don't…I don't know what happened."

Mason sighed, uncrossing and re-crossing his arms. “I think I do, but I’ll have to talk to Maggie, Bear’s mom, to know for sure.” He looked at Jase, shaking his head. “You still sure she’s what you want, man?”

“She’s all I see, Mason,” he answered simply, and Mason nodded his head once, decisively.

***

“Jase,” Slate’s voice came through the phone, “you have plans tonight?”

“Nope, not as far as I know right now,” he responded, stirring the corn chowder simmering on the stovetop. It had been an easy week; he only had one game, so he’d been able to do some shopping today and finally had supplies to cook with again. “Planned to head to Chicago tomorrow and see Daniel’s baby, but that’s not set in stone. Whatcha need?”

“You still have your truck, right?” Slate’s question was clear, but there was so much noise in the background he wasn’t sure the man could hear him.

“Yeah, still have the truck. Whatcha need?” Repeating his question, he reached into the cabinets, pulling down a bowl and ladling out a measure of the chowder for his dinner.

“DeeDee is moving. I’d like your help to get things shifted over to her new condo.”

Before Slate could even finish speaking, Jase was talking over him, agreeing. “You betcha. Tell me where. I’ll be there.” He took a shaky breath, turning off the stovetop and moving the pot to one side. “I’ll be there, man. Thanks.”

“Meet us at her apartment in twenty. She’s over at the new place right now. We can get a load ready and haul it over.” He paused and said, “Jase, man, she doesn’t know about this.”

“Okay. It's all right,” he babbled. “Apartment, got it. Best behavior, on it. I'll be there,” he repeated and grinned. “I'm all over this, Slate. I'm on it.” Hanging up, he left the bowl and pot cooling on the stovetop and walked briskly to his bedroom, dressed in record time, and headed into the parking lot. He jumped into his truck and sat for a moment, trying to gather his wits before seeing her.

12 - New beginnings

Moving slowly, she turned in a circle, admiring the pristine walls of her new condo. No more renting for her, she had finally made the leap and bought a home. A couple of hours ago, the local store had delivered the brand new furniture she purchased. None of it was fancy, but she was proud of what she had accomplished.

She finished putting linens on the new bed and had walked to the living area to consider placement of the couch and chair, when the apartment filled with the chatter of voices as her front door opened. DeeDee turned to face her helpers with a smile that quickly faded when she saw the man walking through the door behind them. Jase Spencer was trailing behind Slate, carrying a box labeled 'Bedroom'.

A roundly pregnant Ruby walked up to her with a commiserating look on her face, and without speaking, patted DeeDee on the shoulder as she passed through into the kitchen. Slate had the good sense not to look at her as he carried his own carton, following Ruby.

Jase paused in the living room and stared at her. She couldn't tell anything from the expression he wore; his face was uncharacteristically hard to read. His gaze drifted down then paused with a slight frown, and she realized she was reflexively wringing her hands in the hem of her shirt.

She hadn't seen him up close since the night of his injury. Every day, she missed him so terribly, and seeing him here now...in her new home, it was unreal. Taking a deep breath and trying to pull together her fleeing composure, she dropped her hands to her sides and lifted her chin, giving him a wide, genuine smile. "Jase," she said, unable to keep the pleasure from her voice, "it's good to see you." Moving forward, she held out her hands. "I can take that. Thank you for bringing it inside."

He shifted sideways, keeping the box out of reach. "I got it, DeeDee. Just show me where to set it. I have another half-dozen in the truck labeled the same." He gave her that half-smile she loved, crooked and rueful. "It's good to see you, too. Really good. You look good. And it's good...to see you. Off the charts—"

Snapping his mouth shut, he first looked at her and then down the hallway towards the bedrooms. Swallowing hard, he flashed that damn smile again and asked, "Show me?"

Walking up the hallway, she was acutely aware of Jase behind her. It was as if there were a scalding heat rolling off the man, winding its way around her, slipping underneath her clothes to cover her skin. It nearly felt as if he were touching her, caressing her...stealing her breath. She opened the master bedroom door and stepped inside, mutely pointing across the room to the far wall.

When he walked around her, she caught a hint of the woodsy scent from his body wash mixed with pure, raw male. He always smelled so good. When they were together and he stayed over, he left his scent on her pillows. Then, even when he had to go out of town, she would sleep better for days, surrounded by the smell of him in her bed.

"Hey," he said, jerking her from her daydream, and she realized she had been in a daze, staring at him. Had to have been, because he put the box where she directed and was now standing in front of her. Sad lines framed his eyes and she dropped her gaze, not wanting to see that look on his face.

Reaching out, he tipped her chin up with his fingertips and ran his thumb gently across her lips. “Hey,” he repeated quietly, and she watched as his mouth quirked up into that half-smile again. Slipping his fingers along her jawline, he traced the edges until he cupped her face.

Squeezing her eyes shut, she turned her head and pressed her cheek into the palm of his hand, unable to stop herself from seeking the warmth and feel of his caress. She missed that so much, the way he never had been able to keep his hands off her, the way he could make her feel with just a touch.

The tip of his thumb dragged her bottom lip down, and her lips pursed with a breathless gasp. He moved and she opened her eyes to find him leaning closer, lips slightly parted, his expression begging permission.

Closing her eyes again, she met him halfway, rising on her toes and pressing her lips against his in a questing, exploring kiss. They remained like that for seconds, neither of them asking or demanding more, just their lips working gently together. He pulled away, capturing her bottom lip between his and she opened her mouth, the tip of her tongue sweeping along his lips as he released her.

Reaching up, she cupped her hand over his where it still rested on her face and tilted her head, silently encouraging him to kiss her again. When he didn’t, she opened her eyes to find his dark gaze slowly scanning her face, his expression remote and shuttered. *Oh*, she thought sadly, sighing and settling back onto the heels of her feet. *He gets it. He finally gets why I’m wrong for him. All it took was him seeing me again for it to sink in.*

She moved to step away and his eyes flared wide, his hand moving to cup the back of her neck, holding her in place. He groaned then, pulling her into him even as he pushed her against the wall, his mouth crashing onto hers as he flattened her against the hard surface. She fisted her hands, trying to deny the need for contact. She couldn't touch him; it would only make things more difficult when he pulled away, because she knew once she started touching him, she wouldn't be able to stop.

The kiss went on for a long time, his hands roaming everywhere, as if he were relearning the feel of her. They would break apart, panting for breath, and then dive back into each other, tongues sliding and dueling. His hands were restlessly seeking and stroking her body, lifting and caressing her breasts, stroking down and over her ass. He buried his fingers in her hair, tugging to tilt her head for better access. She allowed every touch, shifting, unresisting as his hands moved her, his body pressing against her, and she welcomed the burning heat he brought to her skin.

He finally pulled away, propping his arm on the wall beside her head and resting his forehead against his wrist. Breathlessly, he said her name. His other hand wrapped around her waist, palm cupping the curve of her hip, pressing against her skin where he slipped his fingers into the top edge of her jeans.

DeeDee stood still, framed between the heat of his body and the cool plaster of the wall. She kept her eyes closed, not wanting to see if there was disappointment and regret on his face. She had been afraid all along that when he realized how things were—when they were finally over, with no hope of reunion—it would hurt, and she had been right.

He didn't move or speak, and tears slowly slipped from underneath her lashes, trailing down her cheeks as she bit back a sob. It was happening now, here. This was it. This was when he listened to her and ceased his hopeless pursuit. This was the moment when she accepted he was well and truly no longer hers—and she knew, had known all along this would destroy her. Like the night in the parking lot after the game, the pain rested heavily on her chest.

"Look at me," he whispered, and she physically rejected the notion, jerking her head side-to-side. She couldn't do this...didn't want to see. "Baby," he said, his hand clenching on her hip. "Look at me, please." The feather light touch of a kiss fell on one corner of her mouth and she was suddenly confused. *This doesn't feel like goodbye,* she thought. *Why is he kissing me again?* Another kiss, followed by a repeat of the plea, "Baby, please look at me. Open your eyes and *see* me."

Clamping her lips together to still the trembling, she opened her eyes, looking at him through her tear-spiked lashes, her hands pressing flat against the wall behind her, holding her steady. "DeeDee," he breathed her name. "Baby, tell me you want me."

Startled, she stood silently, watching while he leaned closer, kissing her gently with eyes wide open, looking at her. "Tell me I'm not alone," he whispered against her lips. "Don't leave me alone," he pleaded, kissing her again. "Touch me, baby. God, *please* touch me. Show me you still want me...us."

Curling her hands around his hips, she ran her hands up his back slowly, reverently brushing her palms against the shirt as it molded to his ribs. "Jase, of course, I still want you," she said, and he pulled back, moving slightly away.

"There's no 'of course' here, baby," he said, looking down into her face. "You walked away from me, from this...from what we were building. Am I the only one feeling like I'm ripped wide open? You walked away, and now I don't know what's going on in that pretty head of yours, but I'm scared...I'm lost. You turned us off, walked away. There's no 'of course' here."

"I didn't turn anything off," she protested, frowning. "I couldn't. I still care for you...still want you. But, Jase, sometimes things just aren't meant to be." She closed her eyes and then opened them again, swallowing as tears streamed down her cheeks, looking at him.

He shook his head. “I don’t understand. If you still care...want us...then why would you walk away?”

“It’s difficult to explain,” she lied, cutting her eyes down to avoid looking into his face.

He threaded his fingers through hers and stepped backwards, pulling her with him to the bed. “Come here.” Tugging her close, he sat her on his lap, letting her lean against his chest. She snuggled her face into the crook of his neck and breathed him in deep. His voice was echoing, her ear on his chest picking up the vibrations as he said, “Talk to me, baby. Help me understand.”

“You have to let me talk,” she said, holding her breath as he nodded. If he argued with her, she would never be able to tell him, and he deserved to understand how this was better for him.

“I spent—” She paused, that wasn’t right.

Beginning again, she said, “There were some days—”

She paused once more, then shrugging, said, “When you find—”

Pressing her face against his chest, she sighed in frustration. “I had this all worked out in my head. For weeks, I’ve had this conversation in my head and everything made sense. Now you’re holding me, and nothing makes sense. Nothing seems like a good enough reason, Jase. I don’t know how to say what I need to.”

“Start at the beginning,” he whispered. “Tell me what happened between me rolling out of your bed for a road trip, and three days later when you wouldn’t take my calls. Help me understand.”

“Twenty-two years. That happened. That’s the difference in our ages. You’re thirty, and I’m fifty-two, Jase. I realized it’s more than I thought.” She wrapped one hand around his wrist, where he held her waist.

"Baby, it's always been twenty-two, and you know it's never been an issue. We talked about this. What happened? What made you change your thinking?" He was tense as he asked the questions.

"I was talking to Maggie, Bear's mom. She laughed and talked about him still being like a kid, and one day, I realized he's older than you are, while she and I are nearly the same age." She shrugged.

"Hold on. She's not much behind Tug; Maggie has to be several years older than you are. What exactly did she say that put you on edge?" He sounded frustrated and she didn't blame him. He had reassured her repeatedly that age was only a number, and not once had he made her feel like the difference in years was the problem for him it clearly was for her.

"It wasn't anything she meant to say. We were sitting in the hospital with Ruby, and someone started a round of 'where were you when', just reminiscing. We went through significant dates like the Oklahoma City bombing in '95, 9/11, things like that. Then she asked where I was in 1976, the bi-centennial. I was fourteen and still lived at home in Kentucky. Turns out, that's the year Bear was born."

"Then someone mentioned that Mica was born in '84 and I realized you two were the same age. Once I started doing the math, I couldn't stop. I moved to Fort Wayne in '78, so Winger and I had already been together for six years when you were born. I literally could be your mother. Hell, Mason is ten years younger than I am. I remember when he was born. I wiped that man's snotty nose, and he was twelve when you were born."

"Jase, baby, watching Bear and Eddie, I realized you should be with someone you can discover life with, not someone who's already been there, done that. Someone you can build a life alongside, without worrying about having to take care of them in twenty or thirty years." Her shoulders hitched with an unvoiced sob.

"You deserve to be with someone who can give you a family, someone you can be proud to take home and introduce to your parents, your brothers, and your friends. You deserve so much more than I can offer. I knew you wouldn't listen, so I made you a way out, a chance to discover someone better suited." Her body shook with the strain of holding back her tears.

"Are you done?" he asked quietly after they sat through a long, silent pause. He had been tightening underneath her as she spoke, and was now nearly vibrating with some emotion she couldn't define. She nodded, feeling the heat of his chest on her cheek.

"Okay." He paused, taking a deep breath. "First off, I didn't want a way out. I never asked for a way out. I've been trying for months to find a way back in. I want back in, baby."

His thighs tensed underneath her legs and his arms contracted around her, his body reacting to what he was saying. "Second, and I've told you this before, but it must not be sinking in. I don't want kids. I never have. I don't have any kind of pull to have baby Jases running around. My brothers have had plenty of offspring to carry on the family name, but I have no desire to follow along. I like kids, love 'em. Don't mind being around 'em. I like teaching them, being a mentor, but I don't need to have my own.

"Third, it would be my great pleasure to take care of you for the rest of my life. Not a worry, not a bother, never a burden—an honor. It would be my privilege, baby." She shifted slightly and his arms tightened again. "Shhhh. Just listen, please.

"Fourth, I *am* proud of you. I'd love nothing more than to take you to Red Deer right now, tonight, so I can introduce you to my folks. Anywhere, everywhere…I am *proud* to have you on my arm, standing beside me…proud for people to see me with you. I want you, and I don't care who knows it, eh?

"Fifth, the age difference does not matter to me at all. I get that it is a big deal for you, something I've tried to understand, but it's hard, because it's not even on my radar. DeeDee, months ago, when you finally let me in, I didn't communicate well enough how I feel about you. I think I was afraid of pushing you away, but that happened anyway, and I never got the chance to tell you."

He kissed the top of her head, then her temple, wrapping himself around her as she balanced on his lap. "I think about you all the time. I wake up from dreams of you—of us. I've never dreamed of anyone before you. I need you, baby. You are all I need, just you."

He kissed her again, his hand trailing up her side from where it had been resting on her hip. "Everything about you thrills me, makes me excited. Top of the mountain. *Je t'aime*, baby. *I love you.*" She stopped breathing at those words.

"More than I can say, more than I can explain. You are it for me. Everything, baby, you are everything. I let you walk away twice now, but you never left my heart. I've loved you nearly since I met you, and every time we're together, it grows deeper and stronger. I want you. I love you. I need your light in my days, and I can't let you go, baby. I can't. Not and keep breathing. You belong with me. Let me stay where I belong."

They sat there in silence for a long time after he finished speaking, listening as Ruby and Slate moved around in the other rooms of the condo. He had been so eloquent; she didn't know what to say in response after he so effortlessly negated her argument. His pain had been communicated in tone and words, and she hated that she hurt them both in what seemed now like a misguided effort to do right by him.

She had a thousand questions. What would his parents honestly think about him dating a woman twenty-two years his senior? Would his friends think her a monster, someone taking advantage of him? A cougar? What would his brothers and sister think? Could she face them? *Okay, looks more like five questions.*

As her thoughts calmed, winding down, she realized her fears were all about the opinions of his family and friends, which for her were the unknown pieces of the equation. If he was confident, then she needed to trust that he would be okay with their reactions. She already knew everyone important in her life was okay with this relationship. Actually, they were not only okay with it, but had actively encouraged things. Just look at what Slate and Ruby had done today.

None of her family or friends believed the age difference was a barrier; none of them saw anything other than two people who loved each other. *I love him*, she suddenly thought, smiling against his chest. She registered movement under her hands, realizing that while she was thinking, he had begun to shudder irregularly.

Looking up, she saw tear tracks on his face, his eyes clenched tightly closed. He licked his lips and told her in a raspy voice thick with emotion, "Just give me a minute. I'll let you go. One minute more, okay?"

"Don't let me go," she said, pulling his head down to kiss him as his eyes flew open wide. "I've been a fool. Jase, you're not alone. I love you."

***

DeeDee smiled to herself as she ran her fingertips across her still swollen lips, remembering how this morning Jase had come back again and again for a series of goodbye kisses before he finally left for practice. He couldn't seem to get enough of her kisses and body, and she reveled in the attention and love he showered on her.

Yesterday, it had been hours before they had surfaced from the bedroom to find Slate and Ruby had finished the move and left them alone. The only boxes remaining to be unpacked were labeled 'bedroom' and stood neatly stacked in the hallway outside her door. Jase's truck was locked in the driveway, and the keys laid on the dining room table.

In the kitchen, DeeDee had made a plate of food while Jase distracted her, hugging her from behind and dropping butterfly-soft kisses on her neck and shoulders. Laughing, he grabbed bottles of water and followed her back into the bedroom, where they shared kisses while feeding each other, nibbling on fingertips and lips.

When they finally slept, his arm stayed wrapped possessively around her waist; even in his sleep, he tugged her back against his side every time she moved. She had woken this morning to his fingers stroking her slowly while he eased her into the day with a sensual touch, bringing her to a shuddering, lingering orgasm in minutes. Lying close beside her, he dragged his fingertips across her ribs and belly, caressing her breasts as she shivered, drifting back down from the heights to which he had driven her.

Once she was coherent again, he leaned in and kissed her deeply, moving to lie between her thighs, her hips cradling him. "DeeDee," he said, reaching between them to line himself up with her opening. He paused on the brink of entering her and she opened her eyes, looking up at him. "I love you." Sliding deeply into her with one long, slow stroke, his eyes held hers and she felt incredibly desired, wanted…cherished by him as they made love.

***

"So what did you guys finally decide to name the rugrat?" Jase balanced the phone on his shoulder as he threw clothes into a bag. Tridents had a short out-and-back road trip to Wheeling, so he would be packing light. On the phone, he heard a short, sharp cry that sounded like a very pissed-off cat, followed by noises in the background. "You didn't go with Jason Mason, did you? Mason was right, that really does sound like a serial killer's name."

"No, we didn't name him after you. We decided we loved him too much to do that to him." Daniel's voice sounded tired, he thought, listening to his friend talk about his son, born just yesterday. "Jonathan Mason Rupert," pride swelled in his tone and brought a smile to Jase's face. "He's so perfect, I can't get over how it makes me feel. I was a basket case, but Mica was so strong, so brave."

"So everyone's healthy, wealthy, and wise?" Carrying the bag to the bathroom, he stood for a minute and looked around, noting for the first time the differences between his apartment and DeeDee's. After only a couple of days, she had personal things everywhere. Touches that made it feel like a home. He stuck his head back into the bedroom and scanned the walls, furniture, shaking his head. Rented everything, no pictures on the walls, nothing of *him* on display. This was how he had lived since he left his parents' home for juniors. Never settled, nothing that couldn't be packed into a couple of bags.

"Yeah, probably take them both home tomorrow," Daniel said, and there were more noises in the background. "Hang on," he heard, then away from the phone, "Road Runner, you're spoiling her." Light laughter sounded, then a rumbling voice saying, "She's worth spoiling, Danny Boy."

Jase laughed, and then asked, "What did he bring her?"

Daniel relayed the question, and Jase heard the response from the biker cum chef, "Boneless, skinless chicken rubbed with mustard and parsley, roasted and served with a peppercorn-brandy sauce. Tasty for the pretty Mama, but bland enough that it won't bother the bitty boy's tummy."

"You still have a full house of black leather?" he asked Daniel. Jase had heard how the Rebels had descended on the hospital when Mica went into labor, and he had heard something else. After Daniel grunted in acknowledgement, he asked, "Was Mason really in the labor room with you two?"

"Yeah, she wasn't going anywhere without him," Daniel said in a tolerant tone and Jase shook his head. *Odd ducks, all of them*, he thought.

"Give her a hug and a kiss from me," he said, and then laughed. "I can't wait to see little Jon. Congratulations, man. Daddy Daniel and Mommy Mica, you guys make a good pair." His phone buzzed as he was hanging up, and he looked to see a text canceling the road trip due to bad ice.

Pleased, because he had been dreading leaving DeeDee for even a single night, he texted back an acknowledgement, then looked around the apartment again. "No reason to spend any time fixing this place up," he said aloud, "it isn't where I want to be."

***

The next few days flowed past in a blur between rekindling her relationship with Jase and tying up the final details for Ruby and Slate's wedding this weekend. He came to her condo straight from practice every night, and wherever he found her, he swept her into a tight embrace, standing for a long minute with his arms wrapped around her. Slate and Ruby came over for dinner one evening, and the four of them had talked and laughed late into the night. She had been in the kitchen when Ruby approached her, glancing nervously over her shoulder to check on the men.

"DeeDee," she said and paused, taking in a deep breath. "You can't tell Slate."

"Tell him what, sweetie?" she asked, rinsing a plate before placing it in the dishwasher.

Ruby whispered breathily, "—ins."

"Hmmm?" DeeDee asked distractedly, her mind already moving ahead to tonight. Jase needed to get to bed earlier than they had been managing. He had a game tomorrow evening, and she would be ferrying the first loads of supplies for the wedding up to Pokagon.

Ruby reached out and grabbed her shoulders, turning them face-to-face and pushing her forehead against DeeDee's. Stilling, because the girl had gained her complete and undivided attention, she listened as Ruby repeated herself in a whisper, "Twins."

Pulling in a breath to shout her happiness, DeeDee found her mouth covered by Ruby's strong, tiny hand. "Shhhh. Don't tell Slate."

Shaking off her hand, DeeDee asked, "Why, baby? This is good news, surely?"

"He's going to be so freaked out if he knows ahead of time. I want things to be easy for a couple of weeks. I'll tell him when it's time—" Ruby's whisper trailed off as she quickly glanced to where Slate sat talking to Jase.

"Ruby," DeeDee said on a sigh. "That man loves you more than he wants to breathe. You can do no wrong in his eyes. What possible reason could you have for keeping this close?"

Ruby's eyes dipped then she raised them back up. "Just...don't tell him. He'll know soon enough."

"Baby, there are different risks with twins. You'll likely go early, for instance. You're due in just over eight weeks, and in two days, you're leaving for the honeymoon. If he doesn't know, how can he care for all of you like he needs to? If he doesn't have all the facts, he's likely to make the wrong decision." She was frustrated with the girl, but knew she would never do anything to endanger her baby—babies, because she wanted them so badly. "How have *you* even kept this from him?"

"He was out west when I had the sonogram, and I told him what he wanted to hear, that our peanut was healthy. He didn't ask anything else." She shrugged, reaching a hand down and rubbing her rounded stomach.

DeeDee pulled Ruby into her arms, whispering into her ear, "Baby girl, if you have these babies in Georgia, I'm gonna be so pissed." Stepping back, she smiled and asked, "Do you know what you're having?" Grinning widely, Ruby nodded. "Well? Tell me."

Grin still in place, Ruby shook her head and DeeDee groaned.

***

"I want to treat you, take you out. Dinner? Movie? What sounds good?" Sitting on the couch next to her, Jase cocked his head to the side, watching DeeDee's reaction.

She yawned and stretched. "Honestly? I'm so tired, Jase. I want to just stay home with you."

His face went still and she wondered what she said. They got back yesterday morning from Ruby and Slate's wedding at Pokagon State Park. It had turned out beautifully, but she was exhausted. With Ruby pregnant, she had taken on most of the planning, and the whole wedding had been a whirlwind of effort, even after asking Maggie and Eddie to help as much as they could stand. Jase was probably bored, because with all the planning, they had been staying home every night the Tridents didn't have a game.

"Never mind, Jase. Give me a minute to get ready and we can go wherever you want," she said. She had begun to stand when his hand landed on her hip, pulling her back to his side.

"You're tired. We stay here," he said, nuzzling the side of her neck with his nose.

Sighing, she pulled away and moved to face him. "Jase, just give me a minute. Pick a movie and surprise me."

Laughing, he gripped her wrists, pushing her body down onto the couch by stretching her arms over her head. Wedging her between his body and the back of the sofa, he gently kissed the tip of her nose. "Do you even know what you said?" he asked.

"Guess not," she bantered, loving the feel of his weight against her. "Since I don't know what's going on now."

"You called this our home." He nuzzled the side of her neck again, nipping and kissing his way up to her earlobe. "*Our* home," he repeated, gently kissing her lips, sliding a palm down the inside of one arm, trailing fingertips down to cup her breast. "As in *my* home, with you." He moved to cover her, looking down at her with a soft smile. "*Je t'aime*, DeeDee."

***

The next morning, she was standing in front of the coffeemaker, waiting for enough of the life-affirming liquid to trickle through the grounds and filter to make it worth her while to steal a cup. Eyes closed, she had leaned one hip against the countertop, making mental lists of things to do that day, when an arm slipped around her waist, tugging her back into a hard, male body. She put her hands back to cup his ass and amended that thought to a hard, *naked*, male body.

"Jase," she said, leaning her head back for a kiss. "Good morning."

"Mmmm," he said, covering her mouth with his, pulling back to murmur a good morning against the side of her head before asking, "What's on your agenda for today?"

"Clubhouse, make sure someone's got the place cleaned up. Head over to Slinky's; close out the month-end books. Go to the grocery store; pick up something for dinner." She ticked off her list items on her fingers, laughing when he pulled her hand to his mouth, kissing her fingertips.

"Sounds busy," he complained. "Too busy for easy. We both know I'm easy, so that means you're too busy for me. In fact, there's no me in there anywhere, and that's just wrong. I'd like to amend your agenda to include me at some point. Slot me in, baby. My tab in your slot." He nuzzled along the side of her neck, slipping one hand up to cup her breast beneath the light shirt she slipped on earlier.

Laughing, she turned in his arms, eyeing the coffeepot wistfully. "What did you have in mind, crazy man?" Pushing backwards off his chest, she levered herself far enough away to grab the mug waiting on the countertop, twisting to pull the pot out and pour coffee into the cup. Bringing it to her lips, she blew softly across the top of the liquid while keeping her gaze on his.

"Lunch. I have food on the brain now that I'm awake from the smell of that coffee. Let's have lunch. How does Maples sound?" He mentioned one of her favorite places to eat, a swanky place downtown.

She frowned up at him, blowing the steam from her mug again, waiting another few seconds for her first sip. "It sounds too good to be true. Kinda like a bribe. Whatcha got goin' on?"

"Baby, I'm wounded you'd think that way, that I'd bribe you somehow with fancy food. Me using your favorite place in order to manipulate things in my favor?" He sighed dramatically. "No, you're right; that totally sounds like something I'd do." With a hangdog look, he tipped his head to the side, and she burst out laughing. He smiled at her, running his nose along her cheek. "I have a favor to ask."

"Ask away." She nestled into his chest, reaching out to set the still un-tasted coffee mug down.

"My lease won't be up for another few months, but I found someone to sublet the condo." He said this proudly.

She was glad he couldn't see her face, because she didn't know where he was going with this, but it sounded like... *Stop jumping to conclusions, woman*, she thought fiercely. Keeping her cheek against his chest, she said, "Mmm hmm, good for you. There are another few weeks of games and then done, right? What are your plans?"

"I thought I could move in here now, rather than wait." He had stilled, frozen in place underneath her palms, but she could feel his pounding heart through the wall of his chest, and she smiled, because he was clearly nervous about asking. That gave her a warm feeling and she leaned back, looking up into his face, carefully keeping her smile at bay.

"That's not a favor." She watched his eyes dart from her lips to her eyes, back to her mouth.

His tongue slipped out, wetting his bottom lip. "It's not?"

"Nope. Not a favor." Holding steady, she waited for his response.

"What is it then?"

"It's a gift." Stretching up on her toes, she slid her lips over his with a grazing touch. "When can we move you?"

13 - Family

Jase counted his steps as he paced around the kitchen, six steps up one side, four across, six back, and so on. He was having a hard time believing what DeeDee had told him not fifteen minutes ago, standing in their bedroom, looking at a ten-year-old picture. He believed, but it was hard to allow himself the hope that his family's long nightmare could be over. *Sharon*, he thought, shaking his head. After practice today, he had a couple voicemails from DeeDee, the first telling him they would have a houseguest for the near future, then another letting him know that Gunny, the bouncer from the club, would be staying with them, too.

How was it possible that Sharon could be working for the club, could be working for DeeDee, and he didn't know it? Here in Fort Wayne, only a few miles from where he laid his head last night, her ex-husband Elkins had been brutalizing her. Jase had looked for her for so long...so many years...it seemed like a dream to find her, but like this...a nightmare.

DeeDee was in talking to Gunny now; the man had evidently saved Sharon from being hurt worse than she already was. Even before he knew who the woman in their guest room was, his blood had run cold as Goose related the extent of her injuries. Now, he knew it was his baby sister, and he couldn't imagine what he would do if left alone in a room with the animal that had done this to her. *Motherfucker doesn't deserve to still be walking around and drawing breath*, he thought angrily, wondering what measures the club would take against the man once they found him again.

Pulling out his phone with jerky motions, he called Slate, hearing the tension in his friend's voice when he answered the phone. "I don't know anything yet, Jase. We're doing a sweep for him, and we will pick him up. Gunny fucked him up bad enough he probably found a hole to crawl into so he can lick his wounds. It's a matter of finding who knows where his hole might be. We'll find him and bring that motherfucker to light. We're going to bring him in; I promise you."

"I want him when you do." Breathing hard, Jase spoke in a low, brutal tone. "I want him. I want that motherfucker to pay. His ass is mine. You get it?"

"Yeah, I get that." Slate blew out a frustrated breath. "Brother, I got another call coming in. I'll text you when we come up with something."

He angrily punched the disconnect button on the screen, trying to rein in his rage.

From what Goose had said, her ex-husband hadn't been content with beating her head-to-toe; he also violated her with something other than his dick. With a wordless roar, he turned and leaned against the wall, fists pressing to either side of his head. He wanted to smash something, tear something to pieces. If the man were within reach right now, Jase wouldn't be responsible for what happened. His family, his sister...he needed to protect her, to keep Elkins from ever touching her again. He would kill him, Jase decided, taking a deep breath. *If the Rebels hand him over, I will kill the man without a second thought.*

He heard a noise and looked up, seeing DeeDee walking up the hallway towards him. The muscles in her face and neck were tense, and he could see her jaw working as she gritted her teeth. She was taking this hard, seemed to have a misplaced sense of guilt for not being able to protect someone who worked for her. Even someone like his sister, who had sought out danger her entire life. He opened his arms and she walked into them, wrapping hers around him tightly. "How is she?" he asked, tentative now at the evidence of her distress.

"It's bad, Jase. Really bad." She sighed. "And Gunny, I don't know what's going on there." Pulling back, she leaned against his arms and looked up into his face. "Like Goose told you, tread lightly. I don't know if this has triggered a PTSD episode or what, but he's protecting her with every fiber of his body. He's like a coiled spring, though, so be careful."

He nodded and released her, heading up the hallway to see his sister for the first time in years.

***

Standing in the doorway, in the low light, he could barely see his sister's face in profile, her features smooth and calm as she slept securely cradled in the curve of Gunny's arm. After months of not knowing if she was still alive, seeing her like this seemed surreal. He heard whispered words on the air of the room and realized they had come from him. "My Sharona."

Crawling up into the bed, he settled in near Gunny, looking down at Sharon's face. Wincing at the bruising on her temple, he jumped when the big man spoke to him. "If that shit turns your stomach, you sure don't want to look at the rest of her, man."

Jase leaned back against the headboard, not nearly as comfortable as he wanted to seem to be, lying in bed next to his sister. Make that his estranged, nearly naked sister, who was snuggled into the side of one of the scariest—and also nearly naked—bikers he ever met. He didn't know Gunny well at all, but from talking to Slate, he understood that the ex-Marine was hardcore when it came to the club, having been a member since he got out of the military more than a decade ago.

Speaking softly so he wouldn't wake her, he asked, "How bad is it?"

Gunny grunted and shook his head. "Bad. Real bad. Bad enough Goose doped her like a fucking racehorse so she would pass right the fuck out."

Jase drew in a hard breath at his words. "DeeDee tell you she's my sis?"

"You and I are going to have words about that, man. What kind of man doesn't protect his fucking sister from shit like this?" The scowl Gunny gave him could have flayed skin from bones, but Jase understood.

"It's hard to protect her when I can't find her." Stretching out his hand, he softly stroked her hair away from her face, taking care to avoid touching the man who held her. "She graduated high school while I was in Russia, and she was gone from home before the season ended. I haven't seen her for more than eight years. That's a lifetime. The few times she called and talked to Mom or me, we would try to talk her into coming home, even just for a visit, but it was a no-go, eh? The most info we ever got was when she got married, but that was nothing more than a last name, nothing else to go on. Nothing any of the PIs could use to find her."

Gunny grunted again, shifting slightly on the bed and pulling her against him. "You hired folks?"

"Yeah, every time we got a call. I would put together everything we learned from those conversations and kick off with an investigator. Handing that over to strangers to try and find her was hard, but I figured it would be worth reliving everything if they could only find her." He swallowed, sweeping the pad of his thumb across her eyebrow, no longer as worried about the man holding her.

The bed shifted and he lifted his eyes to see DeeDee perching on the corner of the mattress. She smiled at him then turned her eyes on

Gunny. “Food?” One word was all she asked, and when the man nodded, she smiled again and stood to leave the room. “Okay, I’ll make something simple so you can one-hand it.”

“How much do you know about what she’s been doing?” Gunny turned his piercing blue gaze on Jase, a scowl on his face.

“Not anything, really. We haven’t heard from her in months. She got married six years ago to a guy named Elkins; she called to tell me she said he was the ‘love of her life’. Goose said earlier she had been beaten up. Is Elkins the one who hit her?” He rested his elbow on the bed, scooting down so he could lay his head nearer to hers.

“Elkins was the name of the man who fucked her up, yeah. We had a discussion with the man, but that was before I saw how bad shit was for her. Boys are picking him back up; they’ll hold him for me to deal with.” He sighed and shifted again, tightening his arm around her. “He fucking beat her everywhere it would be hidden by clothes. Not the first time she’s endured this level of abuse, either. She’s got fucking scars all over her goddamned body.

“She walked into Slinky’s to talk to DeeDee with her head high though, and didn’t want to cop to the shit either. Had to convince her to unload. She’s one tough fucking bitch, man.” There was a tone of admiration in his voice, and Jase twisted to look up at him. He saw Gunny was gazing down at Sharon’s face with a pained look, and Jase watched the muscles in his jaw bulge as he clenched it tightly.

Gunny took a ragged breath and raised his gaze to him. “Took care of that piece of shit and got her stuff back. Got her money back. Went inside to tell ‘em we could leave, and she’s hurt so fucking bad she can’t even sit up, man. I picked her up and she latched onto me. Grabbed ahold of me as if I was a fucking life jacket, like I was saving her. Wrapped her fingers around my shirt and wouldn’t let go. Latched on like I was the last knot in her rope.

"I held her in the van and she cried with every bump, but she wouldn't let go. Got here, she still wouldn't let go, and you know what? I didn't want her to. By the time we got in here, I was the one holding on, the one that couldn't let go. Couldn't put her down. Made Goose triage her in my lap, man. Couldn't let go. Been holding her for hours, and still can't let go.

"I don't know what the fuck's wrong with me. I laid her down like I knew she needed to be and I couldn't breathe. Couldn't fucking breathe until I was touching her again. He fucked her up, Jase. Seeing her laid out like that for Goose to do his thing about made me sick. All I can think of is watching her walk into the club with her chin in the air, trying to convince us everything was o-fucking-kay, when she's beat to shit and back. So fucking strong." He drew in a long breath and lowered his head, resting his forehead against hers for a moment. She stirred and he moved back as she twisted her neck, tilting her head towards Jase.

Her eyes flickered, opening and closing erratically. The corners of her mouth tipped up, her lips parting in a contented smile as they finally obeyed her wishes, staying open.

"Hey there, you." Jase saw recognition in her eyes as he whispered the words.

"Hey there, you," she slurred as she repeated them back to him and then twisted her head the other way, looking up at Gunny. "Safe," she said, struggling to pull her hand out from the covers. He helped her free herself, and then it looked like he held his breath as she touched him, cupping his jaw in her palm, whispering, "Thank you."

Closing her eyes again, she snuggled her cheek against his chest, pulling her hand down to tuck it underneath her head. Barely audible, she said, "Ace and Gunny. Safe."

***

"It doesn't seem real that Sharon is less than twenty feet down the hall," Jase said, kissing the top of DeeDee's head as she lay in his arms. He stayed in the room with Gunny and Sharon for hours, the two men quietly watching her sleep and speaking only about things that didn't matter, saving their harder discussions for tomorrow. Gunny had finally kicked him out, saying he needed to sleep. Jase called his parents, listening as his mother cried when he described Sharon's injuries. She wanted to jump on the first available flight, but he talked them into waiting, giving Sharon time to heal, giving him a chance to speak to her.

Now he laid in bed with DeeDee, his head spinning. "Life is weird," he blurted and laughed nervously.

"It can be," DeeDee said, her fingertips were tracing the lines of his sleeve tattoo where stars, aliens, and planets decorated his arm. "What do you find weird today?"

"It's the 'what if' factor, you know? What if Daniel hadn't met Mica? That's the first bit of chaos in this whole trip. My best friend met the woman he would fall in love with and marry, but along with the woman came Mason. Mason's an officer in the club—"

DeeDee interrupted, correcting him, her fingers continuing to stroke across his forearm, "National president."

"Yeah, Mason's the national president in the club, and you're part of the club. Chaos bits two and three. I meet you and we have chemistry," he said, kissing the side of her head and tightening his arms around her. "Chaos four. You manage the club, where Sharon now works. Chaos five and six. Do you see how tenuous this thread is? One change in the middle, and I wouldn't have my sister sleeping down the hall. One single change, and I'd still be wondering every day if she's alive, well, warm, fed, loved...harmed." He took a deep breath. "Chain effect in action."

"Isn't the entirety of life like that, though?" She shifted in his arms, tilting her head up to look into his face. "If Winger had been five minutes early or late that morning, everything would be different. If I hadn't hooked up with Winger in the first place, Mason might still be in Kentucky. Baby, that 'what if' factor can make you crazy. What if Sharon hadn't run off when she did? What if one of the investigators had found her? Or, looking into the darkness, what if Gunny hadn't had his eye on her today?"

Reaching up a hand, she smoothed her fingertips across his forehead. "Fate's a fickle mistress, Jase. Let the bitch have her secrets or she gets pissed off. If I've learned one thing, it's that we just have to take what she gives us; the happy is entirely up to us. I could never be glad I lost my husband and daughter, but now I can't imagine my life without you."

Tipping his head down, he kissed her, lips pulling and nibbling at her mouth, laying a trail of soft kisses along her jaw and down her neck. She arched to give him better access, and he took everything she offered, loving her.

14 - Time to train

"Yeah, I know I'm healed, but that's not the point." Jase was talking quietly on the phone and DeeDee tilted her head, listening. "I've been thinking about everything you said and you're right. I need to get a plan together. Lee has been talking about the business school here in Fort Wayne. It sounds like they have a flexible program for working professionals." He paused and turned to look at her, blowing her a kiss.

"Yeah, sounds good, eh? Email that to me and I'll fill it out. We have a few games left, but I'd like to have things lined out." Nodding, he listened to whoever was on the phone. "Yeah, yeah, sounds good. Thanks, Daniel." He reached out and turned up the sound system a little, but not enough to bother their houseguests. She cocked her head, smiling as Lynam's *Rise Up* began to play.

Walking across the kitchen to where she stood, he stopped in front of her and looked down into her face, wearing a curious expression. "I'm nearly afraid to say anything," he said and shook his head.

"Spit it out," she said, laughing at his unexpected reticence.

Hooking his fingers through the belt loops at her waist, he tugged her into his body, holding her close for a minute. “How would you feel about me going back to school?”

She looked into his face, puzzled at the true concern there. “I think that’s great, if it’s what you want to do.”

He offered her a one-shouldered shrug. “I know you didn’t see me when I got hurt, but it made me stop and think—” He interrupted himself, raising one eyebrow at the face she was sure she was making. “What?”

“Well, I kinda did see you.” She tipped her chin down, resting her forehead against the center of his chest, trying not to laugh.

“I think I’d remember it, baby.” He ran his nose along the side of her head, dropping kisses on her neck, raising goose bumps and causing a shiver to run up her spine.

Pressing her lips together, she tried to hold the laughter in, but lost the battle. His voice sounded hurt when he asked, “Are you laughing at me?”

“Don’t be mad,” she whispered, wrapping her arms around his neck and lifting her face to steal a kiss. “I was there, Jase. I…” she sighed. “I didn’t use the tickets you left at the box office, but I had a ticket to every game. I couldn’t stay away.”

Keeping his arms around her waist, he pulled back, looking down at her with a frown. “You came to the games?”

“Yeah, home games,” she said, smiling. “Almost every one of them. Some of the away games, too. I was there when you threw down the gloves against that goon from Michigan. I saw the high stick that cost you eight stitches. And, I was at the game the night you got hurt.” She paused and took a deep breath. “Slate was there that evening. He texted me as soon as he talked to the doctor and knew what was going on. Thank God he did. I was hyperventilating in my seat with fear from not knowing what had happened. I knew you were hurt and down on the ice for a long time, but then you sat on the bench instead of going to the locker room."

He kissed her hard, hands moving up to cup her face tenderly, pulling her into him. His mouth covered hers, tongue stroking hard and deep as he ate her moans. Slowing, he pulled away, resting his forehead against hers, eyes closed and breathing hard. Pleased surprise evident in his tone, he said, "You came to see the games." Kissing her again, he lifted his head, asking, "Where did you sit?"

"Center ice, next to the visitors' bench, about five rows back from the glass," she told him. "I wanted to be able to watch you, on and off the ice." She shrugged. "That seat gave me a great view without putting me so close to the glass you could see me by chance."

He pulled in a breath. "That close? God, you were that close, DeeDee?" Pulling away, he turned to face the window, fingers of one hand pushing on his bottom lip. "Right there in front of me every game and I didn't see you?"

"I hate that I hurt you," she whispered.

"No, baby," he responded, catching her gaze in the reflection of the glass. "We're past that. I just didn't know you had…I knew the one game, but you were at…" He took a breath. "And I didn't see you. Didn't know."

She moved to him, putting a hand between his shoulder blades, feeling the tension in his muscles. "I didn't want you to see me, Jase. But, I just couldn't stay away."

"So that night, what did you do after Slate sent you the message?" He was curious, turning to face her and tilting his head with the question, the heat from his fingers sinking into her upper arms where he held her.

"I went to your condo," she said quietly, and he shook his head.

"Pretty sure I'd remember *that*, baby," he said again.

"Oh, I was there." She bit her bottom lip for a moment and then in a passable imitation of his voice, she grinned and said, "'Beauty. My dick's broke. Hope nobody's got no ideas about my dick, 'cause my dick is full-on broke, eh?'"

Stunned for a second, he roared with laughter, grabbing her around the waist and swinging her around, holding her close against his body. "God, I love you." She smiled up at him as he let her slide down to rest her feet on the floor. "You came to see me when I was hurt? Why didn't anyone tell me?"

"Threats of death," she said, a wry smile twisting her lips. "I didn't want you to know I was there. I had a hard time staying away, and...I wouldn't...I told them not to tell you. I needed to see for myself that you were okay." The music changed, and Tove Lo sang about how it felt when you *Got Love*, DeeDee smiled and reached up to softly cup his face.

"Baby," he said, leaning down to kiss her.

"I love you," she whispered against his lips.

***

Mason leaned back in the chair behind the desk as Slate entered his office, feeling as comfortable in his suit as he always did in jeans and his leather cut. It had been a hard-won ease for a backwoods Kentucky boy, but over the years, he had found enough reason to court the citizen side of things to make it work.

He continued talking into the phone, holding up one hand to Slate, finger extended indicating he would only be a minute. Distractedly, he listened as the first strains of Wye Oak's *Civilian* rang through the office.

Slate reached back and pulled the door closed behind him, turning up the music, but still listening to Mason's side of the conversation.

"I want to know the asking price. Get that for me, and I'll take it from there." He paused, listening to Myron arguing against the purchase, and he laughed, saying, "I know, but I like the idea of buying that venue. It's Ohio, which is a known state for us, and we have support clubs in Toledo, Findlay, and Lima. So get the price and text me." He paused. "Get another message to Donny Baugh; tell him I want Bear to fucking call me."

He hung up, tilting his head to look at Slate. The two friends were silent for a minute, and Slate shook his head, pulling a chair over to sit down. "What are we buying now, Prez?"

"Concert venue and bar in Ohio. It looks like a good investment, and it'll give us another business that could run a fuckton of cash through the till. I'm merely looking ahead, brother." Mason tucked a finger into the knot of his tie, loosening it around his neck. He leaned the leather chair backwards, pulling out a drawer on which to prop his legs, getting comfortable for a conversation with one of his most trusted brothers. "The manager has good connections. I think if we keep him, we can play those connections off to book more bands into Marie's, too. Win, win."

He looked at the door quizzically as it remained shut. "You look good. Georgia must have agreed with you. It's been a pain in the ass couple of weeks here with Bear taking off like he did. I thought you were bringing Jase with you, man. What happened?"

"Shit, you haven't heard? Hoss said he talked to you." Slate leaned forward, elbows on knees, and scrubbed his face with his hands. "Our dancer at Slinky's, the one whose ex-husband beat her all to hell? She's Jase's sister."

Mason's breath caught in his chest. It hadn't been characterized as a beating when the news was relayed to him a few days ago. "I knew we had a dancer get smacked around—" he started speaking, but Slate interrupted him.

"Beat her all to hell," he clarified, emphasizing every word. "Goose said it was the worst he had ever seen, man or woman. When I first called you about the problem, I didn't know how bad it was, or that it was our man's sister. Hell, no one knew until later that night, when Jase identified her. She was using her married name, and our background check only covered her time in the US. We didn't go far enough back to pick up the Canadian connection."

Beat all to hell? Why didn't anyone bother to fucking mention that detail to me? he thought. They didn't even have her ex contained anymore; he had somehow gotten away from the clubhouse, with the entire member roster on alert. Mason set his feet on the floor and stood abruptly, ripping the tie from around his neck, shrugging out of the jacket and tossing it onto a nearby chair. Turning to face Slate, he was trembling with barely contained rage and his lip curled up into a snarl. "What the *fuck* are you doing here in Chicago then, Slate? *Brother*. Shouldn't you be home taking care of your chapter's garbage?" *Civilian* swelled in the background, the tense qualities of the song feeding his nerves.

Slate pulled the back of his neck with one hand, the other still slowly rubbing his forehead. "Gunny was supposed to have taken care of it, same day. I'm on the beach, got the call, and was told he cleared the trash, that he got the gal's shit back, and warned the asshole off with significant emphasis." He shrugged. "But then, once he saw how bad it was with the gal, he changed his mind, wanted us to scoop the ex-husband back up. We did, and then held the bastage for a few days, waiting on Gunny to get back to the clubhouse to finalize what he wanted to do."

Slate cut his gaze up at him, narrowing his eyes cautiously as he finally realized what kept Mason quiet was an overwhelming anger. "I told you this part already, Prez. Pie wasn't paying attention; he got sloppy, because the guy, Elkins, was hurt. He hadn't been moving around much for a couple of days, so Pie moved his watch post inside the room. Elkins knocked him cold with a chair and managed to make it out of the clubhouse without anyone seeing him. Birdy found Pie unconscious in the room, raised an alarm, but the motherfucker was long gone. I was on the way home, but didn't get back until the day after. Now, here it is, the day after that, and I'm in Chicago by your orders."

Mason ground his teeth together in frustration, stalking around the desk to lean against the front edge. Piebald was a long-term prospect, recently bounced from Chicago to Fort Wayne in the hopes a new sponsor would make a difference, but the man just kept fucking up. With this most recent round of fuckupism, Mason would personally make sure he wouldn't be patched in anytime soon, if ever.

"Gunny's still with the gal. They are bunked up over at DeeDee's, which is how we found out she's Jase's sister. Small fucking world, yeah?" Slate leaned back, throwing an elbow across the back of the chair next to him. "Pie fucked up; he's on prospect probation and knows it. This Elkins guy, her ex, he isn't the sharpest crayon in the box, Prez. We'll scoop the guy again."

Mason found he still couldn't speak, but Slate seemed comfortable enough that he didn't feel the need to fill the silence, so he sat there looking up at him. The music of Wye Oak had changed over to The Veer Union, Crispin Earl's voice soaring over the swell of Ryan Ramsdell's riffs and the pounding drums and bass on *The Antagonist*. Clearly clueless about Mason's growing rage, with warring emotions on his face, Slate finally asked, "What are you thinking, Prez?"

Mason's anger exploded. He found himself leaning forward, threateningly invading Slate's space as he shouted, "I'm *thinking* that woman was an employee of ours, under our fucking protection, and someone let her goddamn ex get close enough to her to fuck her up. You need to thank *fuck* Gunny was on the fucking ball enough to see what was going down when she got to the club, or who the hell knows what would have happened? She works for us, then *she's ours*, motherfucker. We always protect our own.

"Now, here you sit in fucking Chicago, while our own is fucking at risk from that mother*fucker* being in the wind. After escaping from *your* fucking clubhouse, while being watched by one of *your* goddamn prospects. That's what I'm thinking, *brother*. I want to know what you put into play to keep the rest of the girls safe. What about Ruby, DeeDee, Eddie...*fuck*, what about *Willa*? You got a watch on our women, brother?"

Slate had flinched back in surprise when he first began to yell. Now his tone was contemptuous enough to cause angry color to rise in Slate's cheeks, as he called the man's motivation, loyalty, and dedication into question in a way he would never accept.

Mason's resolve wavered, seeing the pain on his brother's face, but before he could say anything else, Slate stood abruptly, shoving the chair, pushing it aside when it crashed noisily backwards onto the floor. The two men were inches apart, close enough Mason could feel the heat boiling off Slate's skin in his rage.

"Ruby is my old lady, my wife, the woman carrying my child in her belly. Yeah, I got fucking eyes on her, *brother*. Gunny's got DeeDee, along with the gal, and when he doesn't, then Hoss does. Birdy has Eddie in hand and, goddamnit, Tug is on Willa as well as Maggie, Mason. He's pulling in other brothers as needed. So, yes, I have my shit in order. *Yes*, I thought about all this fucking shit long before I slung a leg across my goddamn fucking bike to come up here and talk to you by *your damn order*. I even covered the fucking prospect you shoved down my fucking throat, so he would know how bad he fucked up."

He raised a clenched fist, crashing it down on the desktop. "Don't you *ever* question my loyalty to the club. You fucking know better, Prez. And my woman? *Fuck you*, Davis Mason. She's my whole fucking world;

you know that. I'll take no motherfucking chances with her after what happened. Demon took her right from my fucking side...right from beside me. You think I want a repeat of that goddamned hell?"

Mason set the heels of his hands against the sides of his head, pressing hard as he wheeled, shouting wordlessly and kicking his chair out of the way as he stalked across the room. *Fuck*. He overreacted. He knew he overreacted, but even now was still having trouble controlling himself. *Willa. It could have been Willa*. His Willa, best friends of Eddie; woman was a little kooky and he liked her that way. *Willa*. Her face flashed before his eyes like a warning, and he imagined it bloodied and bruised, marks from another man's hands on her skin, letting loose another growling roar.

"Goddammit. I knew this was going to fuck me up. Knew she would." He turned back to Slate, thumping his fist against his heart, speaking with anguished emotion in his voice. "I know you hold the club first, keep your brothers safe, have our backs. You are my brother, and that's no fucking joke, Slate. I was out of line just now."

Nodding, Slate glared at him, snarling, "Goddamn right you were out of line. What the fuck is going on? Something has your ass twisted tighter than I've ever seen it, even with Mica." A small measure of the tension left his voice, "Talk to me, brother."

"You think lightning ever strikes twice?" This cryptic question had Slate frowning, and Mason laughed humorlessly at the look on his face. "I remember the day I first met Mica. She was moving into the house next to mine, and with a single look at her across that alley, the woman took my breath away. Then I got close enough to really see her...and she knocked me for a fucking loop. It took me years to get my feet back underneath me. Now, we've finally settled into a friendship that I treasure, like I still treasure the woman, but it's with the knowledge that she will never be mine. I will always love her, but I know...have always known she's better off with Daniel. And now she's had Jon, her family is complete."

"Yeah, I know all that shit. Kinda lived through a lot of that hell with ya, Prez," Slate said, sarcasm thick in his voice.

"I know you did, brother. More than most, you know the toll my obsession for that woman took on me. Took on you, hell...took on our entire fucking club. You know, even understanding the cost...you know I'd pay it twice over to get her to the point where she is today. But there was a hell of a price for us all." He paused, waiting until Slate nodded.

Reaching out to grab the back of the chair, he rolled it back over towards the desk, sitting slowly as Slate bent over, righted his own chair, and sat back down. He refused to look at his friend as he confessed, "Willa is everything, Slate. From then to now, I can't get her out of my mind. Lightning struck again that night at the River Rider's clubhouse, the first time I saw her. You weren't there, but I couldn't get over to her fast enough. She drew me in, was all I could see. She owned me, man. Still does, owns me body and soul."

He rubbed his hand across his scalp, unbuttoning his shirt slowly. "The thought of someone getting his hands on her pushes me beyond reason. You saying our stripper was 'beat all to hell' flew all over me, because suddenly all I could see was Willa's face, brother. Snap, crackle, pop, there's that fucking lightning again. Owned."

They both took a deep breath as the energy between them began to bleed off, dissipate. They had been friends too long, been through too much together for an argument to have any lasting effect. Slate traced the inside of his front teeth with his tongue, and then deliberately changed the subject by asking, "What's with the monkey suit today, Prez?"

"Had a City Council meeting this morning. There's talk about rezoning some of the wards. I'm trying to slow things down until I can get a read on what that would mean for us." Mason rolled his head side-to-side, stretching out his neck. "They won't be hard to stall; those political motherfuckers are all about the talking without the doing."

He removed his cufflinks, rolling up his shirtsleeves, exposing the phoenix tattoo that rose from his left hand up the arm, feathers and flames wrapping around his forearm in striking reds and yellows. Blended into the tail feathers were words in a script so elaborate it was difficult to separate from the flowing lines of the rest of the tattoo. *I choose to become.*

"It still boggles the mind that you got roped into this. Do they know much about you, past the business owner façade you put on for these meetings?" Slate snorted a sharp laugh, leaning back and resting his heels on the edge of Mason's desk. "It's a good smokescreen; I'll give you that," he said, flicking a glance at the suit jacket. "You clean up nice, Prez."

"Naw, it ain't no big thing. When McDaniel's wife got sick, he came to me and asked me if I'd accept the remainder of his term. He's been a good friend to the club, and it's not a tough gig. We've now got better and deeper ins with the city than we ever did before, which is good for us." Mason gestured towards his clothing. "They don't look past the surface much, so they don't see the man, only the suit." He shrugged. "Even if they did, we've worked hard to build a club that we can all be proud of. The public face of the Rebels is one of power and authority; they don't need to see beyond that."

His phone buzzed with an incoming text and he pulled it out of his pocket, looking at the display. "Red said he's got news for us on the Jase front. Reach back and open that door, would ya? Let's hear what he found out about our man."

***

"Jase," the cautious voice came over the line. "How're you doin'?" Trying to place the voice's owner, he was coming up blank until the man spoke again. "This is Red from Chicago. Mason asked me to call."

"Hey, Red," he responded pleasantly. Along with Birdy, the man had helped teach Jase to ride, and he had seen him around Jackson's often enough before moving to Fort Wayne. "It's good. Everything is lots better. What can I do for you?"

"Mason said you were interested in going back to school for a business degree. Is that right?" The man didn't beat around the bush, asking his question straight out.

"Yeah, talked to a couple of guys on the team who went that route, and DeeDee agrees it seems the smart thing to do. I know I won't be able to play forever, and right now, I don't have anything lined out for after. Why...what can I do for you?" He restated his previous question, still unsure of the reason for the call.

"We've got a proposition for you, if you'd be interested in hearing it." He was hedging now. It sounded as if he chose his words with care.

"What's the proposition?" Jase asked.

"Why don't you come to Chicago, sit down, and talk to Mason? He can explain it better, but it will definitely be a benefit to all of us if things work out." Red said something unintelligible away from the phone then came back. "Team schedule shows you up here next week for a game. Can we book some time with ya then?

"Sure," he said slowly. "I can drive up and stay an extra day that way. We play here Friday, and the Chicago game is on Saturday, so let's plan on chatting Sunday?"

"Sounds good. Someone will text you details. Thanks, man," Red said, and then the call disconnected.

He turned, looking across the room at where DeeDee was on the couch reading. "Weirdest phone call ever, baby," he said, picking up bottles of water for both of them and walking over to sit beside her.

"Hmmm?" She made a quizzical noise, shifting to snuggle into his side, resting her head on his shoulder.

"Red called from Chicago. Seems Mason wants to talk to me about—" He stopped speaking, because DeeDee had straightened, turning to him with what looked like fear on her face.

"What does he want? Nothing has happened that I know of." Her face had gone white and she was nearly babbling. He reached up a hand and gently covered her mouth.

"Mason has a proposition for me that Red said would be mutually beneficial. I don't think it's bad, baby. Breathe. It's okay." He soothed her with his words, reaching out to do the same with his hands and laughing when she shivered at his touch. "They *were* extremely cold water bottles. Icy even. I'm sorry, baby. Here," he whispered, trailing kisses along the edge of her jaw, murmuring against her lips, "let me warm you right up."

***

"How's she feeling today?" Jase directed the question at Gunny, watching as the man poured himself a cup of coffee.

"No more blood in her piss, which is good. Goose said the acute pain is nearly gone, and now she's gonna have to work out the soreness, but I fucking hate to see her move. Every fucking thing hurts; you can just tell. Fucking Goose doesn't have to listen to her hold her fucking breath so she doesn't whimper, man." He opened a cabinet door then closed it. "Where the fuck is the cereal?"

Wordlessly, Jase pointed over to the pantry door, watching as the big man strolled over. He was an impressive sight today, the tattoo and bulging muscle on his arms and shoulders in clear view since he had no shirt on, but his pale feet sticking out from under the soft sweatpants were in stark contrast. "Let me know what you need. I'll make a run to the grocery store today."

"Ain't gonna be here much longer. Soon as Shar can be moved, I'm taking her to my house." He said this without turning around, dumping frosted wheat cereal into a bowl.

"Is that what she wants?" Jase asked without thinking, then stilled when he saw Gunny's head swing around, the weight of the man's gaze palpable as it landed on him.

"Think I'd force her? After the shit she's been through? Yeah, she's on board with the idea, motherfucker. What the fuck you thinking? You even seen us together the last few days? This thing goes both ways here, Jase." Gunny's voice was tight with anger.

"I didn't mean it that way. I see how she is with you." He smiled. "I get that she likes you. What I was trying to ask before my mouth got in my way was if she was ready to move out. She...and you...can stay as long as you want. I love having her here, knowing she's only a few feet away." He held Gunny's gaze with his own steady one.

"I don't think you get how this is for me, Gunny. Not since I was about fourteen have I gotten to see Sharon every single day. See her at the breakfast table," he gestured at the bowls the two men had, "and if I've missed that, she might have too. Stay as long as she wants." Without another word, he turned and walked up the hallway to the guest bedroom.

Pausing in the doorway, he watched Sharon for a few moments. She was standing near the window to soak up the heat of the sun, her body swaying stiffly to the music in her earbuds. He could hear only the tiniest, scratchy sounds, nothing to correlate with her efforts, so to him, it looked as if, even with the pain, she were dancing for the pure joy of movement. At least, if he didn't pay attention to the green and yellow bruises that covered nearly every inch of her body.

Watching closely, he saw what Gunny had been talking about. You could see the pain in the way she held her body, in the way her arms were kept close. Deliberately, she stretched her hands, and then rubbed one forearm with a wince. Returning to the movement, she continued extending her hands, rotating the joints and slowly pushing her arms straight over her head, reaching full extension after several slow seconds.

Her head tipped back and she dropped one hand to rub at the column of her throat, fingertips stroking gently along the muscles and tendons in the back of her neck. She brought her other hand to meet its mate in her hair, and he saw her arms tense and tighten as she rubbed with firm fingers up the back of her head, shoulders rotating as she tried to loosen the knots in her stiff muscles.

"Hey, you," he called quietly, and she twisted her head to the side, smiling at him.

"Hey, you," she responded.

"Got a minute?" he asked.

"For you, I got two," she said with a fake pout, and he laughed.

Moving to the bed, he sat on the edge, continuing to watch as she stretched and pulled her muscles, twisting her torso. She was moving so slowly it was hard to decide if there were places that hurt worse than others. If there were, she ignored the sore spots, pushing through to methodically stretch and work everything on her body.

"I'm not wanting a play-by-play, but I've missed so much. Gunny said you are moving out soon, and I want to know everything. I want to know you aren't going to drop out of sight again." He startled when a voice came from behind him, then saw the soft look on Sharon's face as she listened to the big ex-Marine.

"She ain't going anywhere without me." Gunny sat in a chair he had brought into the room. "You don't have to do a heart-to-heart, thinking this is the last time you'll see her. She's gonna be around."

“I hope so,” Jase said fervently, pulling Sharon’s eyes back to him. Abandoning her stretching, she walked over and sat on the bed beside him, reaching out for his hand and threading their fingers together.

“I never meant to go away like I did. The Spencer pride cost us both quite a bit, didn’t it?” She wasn’t looking at him, and he let her have that bit of isolation, hoping it would keep her talking.

“Mom and Dad didn’t know what to do with me, ya know? After having their boys, and all of you stayed so focused on the goals lined out for you, they had me, and I didn’t like anything they suggested. I didn’t have anything to work towards. After school, and then everything that happened, my eighteen-year-old stupidity said it was the best thing for everyone if I left. I’d sacrifice myself for the greater good or something like that.” She laughed, the sound harsh in the room, and Gunny shifted restlessly in the chair.

“I drifted for a while, job-to-job, place-to-place. Made friends, but left them behind when I’d move on, not setting up anything lasting. Met Derek and it felt less temporary. We settled in Florida, got jobs, and became contributing citizens.” She laughed again, and it sounded sad. “And shit happened.”

He sighed, tugging at their joined hands to bring her eyes to meet his. “I love you, Sharon.”

A smile lit up her face at his words and he jumped, because he never heard Gunny move, just saw him appear as he settled on the other side of her, pulling her back against his chest, his face pressed into the side of her head. “Fucking love that smile, babe,” he muttered, and the fine hairs on Jase’s arms stood straight up. The adoration in the man’s tone was so real and true it gave him goose bumps. “My fucking smile.”

She laughed again, but this one was light and full of joy. “Yeah, big guy. Your smile.” She wrapped her other hand around Gunny’s arm where it banded across her chest, slowly stroking his skin. “So shit happened, and I was too stubborn to go home. I kept thinking I could get a handle on things. All I did was run; I see that now. Every time he would find me again, I'd run." She leaned her head back, bringing her lips to meet Gunny's in a slow, soft kiss.

"Until this guy wouldn't let me." Sighing, she nuzzled the side of her face against his chest. Without looking up, she said, "I missed you every day, Ace. Missed Mom and Dad, everybody. Thanks for showing me the pictures of the boys. It's hard to believe I have nephews."

"Everyone wants to see you; you know that." He grinned. "I've been successful in foisting Ma off so far, but that won't last. She's gonna come down sooner or later."

"I'll deal with that when it happens," she said. "I know they are disappointed in me, so I'd rather it be later than sooner, if you know what I mean."

He nodded and stood. "Love you." Waiting for her response, he raised his gaze, meeting Gunny's. "You have a good man now, Sharon. Keep him safe, okay? He seems a decent sort."

She laughed as Gunny lifted her, placing her on the bed and stretching out beside her. "I'm on it, Ace."

15 - The offer

"Jeeze, Mason. That's an awful generous offer," Jase said with a frown.

"Then what's got your face all scrunched up like you just heard latex snap behind you?" Mason's laughter rolled through the room, echoed by a chuckle from Slate.

"I'm trying to find the catch, man. In my experience, there's always a catch when the offer seems too good to be true. Which, no offense intended, this slots directly into that better than expected category, eh?" Shifting in his seat, Jase propped one elbow on the arm of the chair, hand suspended in the air. He flicked one finger up. "One, it's a hell of an expense for the club to take on. No matter how you slice it, getting a degree is expensive." The second finger flicked up. "Two, there's no clear payoff for you. I don't have influence, no wealthy relatives in my closets whose connections you can leverage." A third finger flicked up, followed quickly by a fourth. "Third, and maybe even fourth, you aren't putting any clauses on the offer. No time limit, no early termination, nothing. If I took this to my old man, he would smack my head for even considering it, because again, in my experience…there's always a catch."

Mason nodded, pressing his lips together in irritation; he wanted to talk Jase into at least thinking about this offer. “I hear ya, but there’s no catch, man. Seriously. The club will foot the expense of your schooling, and in return, you agree to consider managing the Fort Wayne businesses. If it works out, we’ll make it back fast; I know that for sure. Myron has more than he can handle with Chicago, and now he’s had to layer St. Louis and Memphis on top of that.”

He eyed Jase, evaluating his reactions and attitude. Jase still looked unsure, holding his four fingers up in argument. “DeeDee has taken over a lot of the business side of things for our shit in the Fort, but that spreads her too thin for my comfort. Hell, she pretty much has her hands full with Slinky’s; forget all the extra shit. She wants to open a private gentlemen’s club, but unless we can cut her free from some of what she’s doing now, that won’t happen. That’d be one of the payoffs.” Mason held up four fingers and wiggled them at Jase, then folded them all down against his palm, bringing his hand down to his knee. “There’s no downside here, man. I see benefits all around. No strings...no catch. If you decide it’s not for you, then that’s okay. Way I see it, in any case, your degree will benefit DeeDee, and she’s family.”

“What if I decide to play for another five years after I finish the degree? Would you be willing to wait that long? Somehow, I don’t think that would play into your favored scenario. I’m not saying I plan on it, or even could, but look at Daniel, eh? He’s got nearly fifteen years on me and he’s still playing. Every year, he says it’s the last, but then come late summer, he’s out there conditioning. I know there are no guarantees in this game, but it doesn’t seem a fair payoff for you unless we set some terms to the deal.” Jase shook his head, reaching up to tug at his earlobe. “I can’t believe I’m telling you to lock things down. My old man would have my ass.” He laughed.

As one corner of his mouth lifted in a wry grin, Mason placed his hands palm-down on the desktop. “See, that’s one of the best reasons right there. Honest to a fault, loyal as the day is long. And you don’t mind working hard for what you want.” He snorted. “Hell, look at

DeeDee. You gave up thousands of dollars a year in salary, set your career back by a half a decade, all in order to get the girl. Let me do this, Jase. It's the right thing...for both of us." He shifted back into his seat, propping his elbows on the desk. "Tell you what, why don't you take some time to think about it, go ahead and talk to DeeDee. Let's say a month from today you give me or Slate an answer, yeah?"

"I can do that, man." Jase nodded.

"Alrighty then, business out of the way. How's my cousin treating you? You're looking pretty good." Mason smiled at him.

He watched as Jase's face split with the widest grin he had ever seen on the man, his happiness shining through his expression like a blinding light. He was one happy man, and apparently, life with DeeDee suited him. Some of the joy left Mason though, and he stopped listening to Jase, because his mind was wandering back to the woman in Fort Wayne who had held his interest for months now. Willa Grace Shipman. They spoke on the phone a couple days a week since he took her to Slate's wedding, but she was under his skin now, winding herself into his thoughts throughout the day, becoming necessary. *Hell, a few days ago, I nearly took off Slate's head over an imagined threat to her.* Slate, *my brother in every sense but blood.*

"—move out. I think he's tired of us chaperoning." Jase laughed.

Mason furrowed his brow, trying to catch back up. Slate took one look at him and laughed, then took pity on him, saying, "Gunny's gonna move the gal to his place. He's sayin' she's his old lady now."

Surprised, Mason frowned. "Gunny? That mean motherfucker took an old lady?"

Seeing Jase shift in his seat, Mason patiently clarified, "No disrespect for your sister intended, man. You know us calling a woman an old lady is a title of respect. It's like being married, but bigger, more. Loyalty from the club includes his woman, and she becomes family for us all.

Any Rebel would die for her now. I'm surprised, because Gunny wasn't ever in the market for a steady hookup. He's a good man, good brother, rock-solid member, but never even fucked around with club pussy. It's one of the reasons he was a good fit for the strip joint, because he wasn't tempted to dip into the girls."

Jase's eyes darted up, gaze catching on Mason's. He opened his mouth and closed it, then opened again. Slowly, he spoke, "He told me something that's stuck with me. He said when they were taking her to the house that by the time they got there, he wasn't able to let her go. The whole time they've been staying with us, I don't think she's been more than an arm's length from him more than two or three times. The look on his face when he watches her...it looks like how I feel about DeeDee." He cut his eyes over to Slate. "How you feel about Ruby."

Mason rubbed a hand over his scalp, feeling the bristle of hair against his palm. "Sometimes, when you know, you just know. Out of the blue, like lightning, yeah?"

The two men nodded along with him, all in agreement that the ways of love were mysterious.

***

"Jesus Murphy, man." Jase gasped for air, bending over, hands on his waist. "Are you trying to kill me, Dugger?"

Lee laughed at Jase, continuing to jog in place. "Where's that famous Spencer stamina? Come on, we've only covered seven miles. Three more to go before we can even call this a real run."

Shaking his head, Jase stepped back onto the path, beginning to jog onward at a slower pace. Side-by-side, they ran in companionable silence for a few minutes. Lee pressed him again, gradually increasing their speed until they were once more at a fast run, but not quite a sprint. Looking sideways at Jase, he asked, "You healed?"

Nodding, Jase pounded out a few more paces before he responded, dragging in air between phrases. "Yeah, Adam says one-hundred-percent. Feels good, too. That groin had been tweaked for a couple months before it finally went. Being on IR forced me to give it real time to heal."

"I heard you had an interesting meeting in Chicago a few days ago." He was looking straight ahead, and even though it wasn't couched as a question, Jase couldn't miss the tight, interrogative tone in the man's voice.

"Not sure interesting is the right word. I just met with some friends from my Chicago days." Jase was having to work hard to control his breathing; the pace Lee set was faster than his usual run. "Why? What's up?"

"Nothing," Lee said quickly.

"Lotta something for nothing," he said in return.

"It was mentioned at a league meeting." Lee looked sidelong at him again, apparently gauging his reaction.

Jase pulled to an abrupt stop, his chest rising and falling with his hard pants for breath. "A league meeting? What the hell does the league care who I hang out with in an away city where I used to live?"

Lee had circled back around and now stood in front of him. "It's mostly back up the chain to NHL, but when you're the co-captain and burgeoning franchise player, they care. They don't want any clouds to stain their idea of what a team leader should be. Malinowski questioned me pretty hard about your association with a known criminal figure."

"Known criminal figure?" Jase's voice held a tone of frank disbelief. "You talking about Davis Mason?"

Lee nodded, pulling up the tail of his shirt to wipe the sweat from his face. "That's the name they were most interested in, yeah."

Barking a disbelieving laugh, Jase said, "Did you know he's on the Chicago City Council? He owns at least a dozen businesses in Chicago, and another near dozen here in Fort Wayne. He's also my girlfriend's cousin, and my friend. You and Malinowski can back the fuck off, man." He shook his head in disgust. "Was this the reason for the invite this morning? Thought you'd grill me while we ran? Fuck this. I'm going home."

"Jase," Lee said, but stopped when Jase turned and nailed him with a glance.

"No, man. I give a hundred-fifty-percent on the ice every single game. I do the extra assignments along with the rest of the team, show up ready to go at practices, gladly lead, even during loss slumps. My commitment and dedication to the team are above reproach. But that's where the team ends, where the game ends. My life is my own, and if they don't like it...well, they can cut me. Put me on fucking waiver." He turned and jogged across the park towards the parking lot.

"Jase." Lee chased after him. "It's not like that."

"No? That's funny, because it sure sounds like that from here. They gonna dictate what color boxers I wear, too? How about what flavor condoms I use? Have at me, then. But wanna know what I think? Wanna know where I think we're going with this? Judgmental *asshole*. Cut me." Jase made a dismissive gesture, sweeping Lee's unspoken words aside. "Fuck. This."

He continued jogging towards the lot, taking a moment to plug his earbuds in, turning the music up loud. He laughed aloud when Like A Storm's song *Love The Way You Hate Me* began to play. *Definitely fitting*, he thought, listening as the words reminded him it was worth it to stay true to what he knew was right, and being associated with people like Mason was right. He knew that...no doubts.

The Rebels were people who... *What had they done that suits would have knowledge of and consider a crime?* Was it because they had supported his girlfriend and sister unconditionally? That they stood beside a grieving woman for years, selflessly giving so she had time to heal? That they spent tirelessly of themselves to make life better for so many people? No, the Rebels dared to live their own lives without worrying about fitting into society's normal categories. That was their crime. *Fuck the suits*, he thought.

He climbed up into his truck and listened to the song again, looking across the lot at the man standing there, someone he thought was his friend. A man who had just judged him based not on his own values and qualities, but on some kind of jumped-up, unwarranted, biased bullshit he heard from fucking suits who lived a world away. Men who would never know the value of a friendship like he shared with the Rebels. *I'm the only one who has to live in my own head*, he thought. *I'm the only one who knows what's right here*. Reaching out and viciously twisting the key, he started the truck and drove home.

16 - Could be more

"Now *these* are the kinds of events I don't mind getting roped into," Jase spoke to Lee from his position nearby, both men leaning casually against the wall. He felt the distance that had begun dividing their friendship over the past week and realized he missed joking around with his friend.

"Yeah," Lee said, "the kids are awesome. The setting, not so much." Jase nodded in agreement. "I wanted to apologize, Jase," he told Jase quietly. "I was out of line. I checked things out after what you said and you were on target. While there might be some shadows there, the man is not what the league painted him to be."

Looking at him, Jase saw the sincere regret on his face and nodded. "I appreciate it, but you don't have to worry about it, man. I just don't care what the league thinks about my friends." He shrugged. "Mason's solid, and he's been a very good friend to me. You have to meet him to understand. He put together a charity drive with the club that raised more than seventy-thousand dollars for this wing of the hospital. That's only part of the stuff they do. There is a holiday toy collection and a couple of events throughout the year for veterans. It's a club, not a gang, and they are all good men."

Lee nodded and shrugged. "Yeah, I get that I was wrong. I'm sorry."

They looked around at the open-plan room, painted in vibrant, cheerful colors. Filled with clusters of chairs and sofas, the room was also dotted with wagons laden with precious cargo. The team had several community outreach activities every year, many of them children-related. Last month, they had gone to local schools and read to classrooms full of bored third and fourth graders in order to promote literacy. Today, the visit was to the local children's hospital, hanging out and chatting with the kids in the cancer ward.

Jase stiffened, his gaze focusing on a man across the way. Seated in an armchair next to a boy who looked about fourteen years old, he was dressed in jeans and a long-sleeved shirt. The grey-bearded man was also sporting a black leather vest with familiar patches sewn onto the back. Jase knew the man, as well as the kid, and he was abruptly sick with fear, because he knew what them being in this room had to mean.

Jase strolled across the waiting room, coming up behind the man. The boy glanced up, and recognizing their visitor, crowed, "Jase, hey there. Good to see you."

"Tyler, how you doin'?" Jase stepped over to him, reaching to grip his shoulder, leaning down to touch his forehead to the boy. He stepped back, turning to look into Bingo's face, seeing what looked like sullen resignation on his features. He had lost a lot of weight and didn't look good. In fact, he looked under a great deal of strain. "Bingo, man, haven't seen you in a while." He reached down a hand, surprised when Bingo stood, pulling him into a firm, one-armed clench. His back was thumped three, four, five times, and then he was shoved roughly back.

"Jase," he muttered, sitting abruptly, his motions somehow disconnected. "How're things, man?"

"Good, good. Game is good. Not to jinx myself, but personally, it's been an excellent season. Plus, me and DeeDee are official. Finally got her to admit she can't live without me, so I'm set for life, man." He smiled, glancing at Bingo's nephew. "You get any autographs yet, kiddo?"

"Naw, I didn't bring anything for them to sign." Tyler looked down at his lap, fiddling with plastic tubing taped to the back of one hand.

"Well, we can't have that. My friend going without autographs on what is arguably the easiest day to acquire said autographs? No freakin' way...because me? I gotcha covered, my man. We hockey players might not have all our teeth, but we got things to sign." He lifted a hand, getting Lee's attention, miming holding up something between his two hands, pinching fingers and thumbs together. Lee nodded and turned to one of the team's media assistants. When he spoke to her, she reached into a bag and pulled out a bundle of fabric. He argued with her a minute and she reached into another bag, pulling out a mini-hockey stick and another bundle of cloth. He made his way to where Jase sat next to Tyler, uncapping a marker on his way. Tossing one of the bundles to Jase, he nodded at Bingo, but focused on the young man.

"Hey, kid, what's your name?" he asked, standing casually in front of them.

"Tyler." The boy breathed his own name and said more loudly, "You're Duke It Out Dugger. Oh, my God. Next to Jase, you're my favorite player!"

"Ouch," Lee pretended to grab his heart, "that stings, Tyler. I guess I should be honored I made runner-up to Mr. Popular here?"

Clearly afraid he had hurt the hockey player's feelings, Tyler attempted to backpedal, "I didn't mean it like that, Mr. Dugger. I like you a lot. Like...not a-little-lot, but a-lot-a-lot. I just know Jase."

Lee finished signing the mini-stick and handed it to another player striding past. "Sign this and circulate it. Make sure it gets back to Tyler here, okay?" The player nodded with a smile for the boy, pulling his own marker out of his pocket and scribbling on the wood as he walked away.

"Now, for the big guns." Lee scrawled his signature on the back of the item he held in his hand, then he flipped it with great showmanship, revealing a jersey with the team's logo and a 'C' on the front. He turned the garment, showing Tyler his signature, name, and number on the back. "Boom! There you go, kid. Wear it and wish me luck, okay?"

"Oh, my God. A signed Leeland Dugger jersey? Are you serious right now? Are you serious? You're fu—messing with me, right? Don't be messin', man. That ain't cool." Tyler's eyes were dancing, and Jase grinned. He didn't think the boy even realized he corrected himself barely before dropping an f-bomb in the hospital waiting room.

Tossing it to Tyler, Lee put his head back, laughing. "I'm not messin' kid, but am I your favorite player now?"

"Yessir, Mr. Dugger." Tyler's head was nodding so fast Jase thought he could feel the breeze from where he was sitting. He reached out and jerked the marker from Lee's hand, turning the jersey in his lap over and signing on the back, next to his number.

"You gotta wish me luck too, Tyler." He handed the jersey over and laughed at the wide eyes the boy turned on him. "I've known you longer, so I think it's only fair I call dibs on being your favorite. I don't care how pretty the Duke is; I got dibs." Tyler was speechless, looking from one man to the other, then down to the two jerseys in his hands.

Glancing at Bingo, Jase caught a look of such sadness washing over the man's face that it killed his next breath in his chest. Turning his face away, Bingo's jaw tightened and clenched, his lips pressing into a hard, thin line as he struggled to retain his composure.

Lee noticed and asked the boy, "Tyler, are you mobile? Ya wanna meet the Lady Tridents?" He turned and pointed to the team's cheerleaders, dressed in their team-matching short dresses and leg warmers, leaning against the far wall.

Looking up at him with a broad grin, Tyler nodded and stood, taking a small shuffling step forward, clutching the two jerseys to his chest. “I’m mobile, just not fast.”

“Dat’s okay; we can go as slow as you need, my man. These beautiful ladies aren’t going anywhere.” Lee wrapped an arm around Tyler’s shoulders, steadying him under the guise of pulling him close for a whispered secret about the cheerleaders.

“Bingo, want to go get some coffee?” Jase stood, reaching out a hand. “Lee’s got your boy. He’s in good hands.”

With a sigh, the grizzled, older biker reached up, accepting the wrist clasp offered to pull himself to his feet. “Coffee’d be good,” he muttered, raising a hand to wave at Tyler, receiving an older-than-his-years chin lift in response.

Seated across from each other in the cafeteria, Jase looked at Bingo, seeing a weariness and exhaustion written on him that was so profound it seemed to seep from the man’s pores. Taking a page from Mason’s playbook, Jase simply said, “Tell me.”

They sat in silence for a minute, but then Bingo jerked as if kicked and settled back into his chair. Looking up, he fastened his gaze on Jase and nodded.

"Boys ain't supposed to have titties, ya know? We didn't know what was going wrong when he started growing titties. First doc said his T-levels were low and they didn’t know why. Fuck, I didn’t know what a ‘T-level’ was until then. That doc sent us to another doc, who then sent us to another doc. Fucking round robin of referrals. Last doc sent us here for tests. Brought Tyler for the tests, and they say it's cancer. Did you know his mama died from cancer? I hear the word, and all I can think is *Dammit, we don't need this, too*. After all those kids have been through, they don’t need this shit." Bingo sighed.

"What kind of cancer does he have?" Jase didn't know what else to ask. This was uncharted territory for him. Sharon's beating was the first time he ever saw a family member brought low by an accident or illness.

"Testicular. He had surgery yesterday; should have already been home, but they wanted to keep an eye on him a little longer." Bingo blew out a hard breath. "Kid's a rock, man. He's fucking solid, worried more about his sisters and brothers than anything to do with himself. Doc told him he had a tumor on his ball, and the only questions he had was if they had to take both nuts and if he could still have kids of his own. Not about how painful it would be, what kind of follow-up poison will they pump into his veins, not about fucking dying from it. He only wanted to be able to have kids."

Jase shook his head. "Tough guy, or a smart one, focusing on what's important to him. Sounds a lot like his uncle. What'd Goose say, eh? And what in the hell are you doing here by yourself, Bingo?"

"I didn't tell Goose. I haven't told anybody. Don't want anybody here. He's my family and I got everything covered." Picking up the paper cup, he sipped at his coffee and winced. "Damn, this shit is raunchy," he said, making a face as he took another sip. "Club's been busy with other stuff. They don't need me bringing this down on them, too."

Jase frowned. He knew DeeDee had been tense recently, but she claimed club business to blame, saying it had been dealt with. "What stuff? DeeDee said everything was good."

"Yeah," the man answered glibly, "everything's good. There's always shit stirring around the club; you know that, man." He sipped from his cup again, lifting his gaze to Jase's face. "Hey, I wanted to thank you for taking part in the poker run a while back. I know you ain't club, but it meant a lot to me, you taking it up like you did. So, thanks."

"Was my pleasure, Bingo. We raised quite a bit for the hospital, so it seemed like a success. Thank goodness Mason and Tug made sure I minded my Ps and Qs so I didn't embarrass the Rebels." He laughed. "I spent the next two days walking funny. Was sore all over. I don't ride as much as you guys. Weekend warrior, I guess. Birdy called me a waxer once. At least I'm not that bad, eh?"

"Could be more, if you wanted. Just sayin'." Bingo stood. "I'm headed back upstairs. Tyler'll be coming home soon. Gotta get my boy healed up." He turned to look at Jase again. "Thanks for what you did up there today, too. He wanted to go to the waiting room to see you guys come in, but, man...the smile you slapped on that kid's face? It looked good on him, Jase. I appreciate it."

Jase clapped a hand on his shoulder as they walked the halls. "My pleasure. Let me know when he feels better and I'll get you guys some game tickets if we're still playing. We'll see how effective Tyler's good luck wishes are, eh?"

17 - You let me keep you

She pressed her forehead against his, eyes closed, breathing hard. *Chasing Cars* by Snow Patrol played in the background, the words echoing her feelings; she could definitely spend all her days like this, lying in his arms. "Jase, baby, I love you," she whispered, glorying in how his arms tightened possessively around her in response.

"That's just the sexing talking, isn't it?" he joked, out of breath himself. "I'll admit it was good sexing, the best. Superlative sexing. I totally loved it, too. Best sexing of my life, totally enough to get you to whisper sweet nothings in my ear, eh?"

She shook her head, laughing. "You know, you could give me a complex, mister. If I were a less secure person, less confident of your love, saying things like that to me could make me nervous. It's a good thing I know what love looks like, and it's lying right here in bed on top of me." She tipped her chin up, kissing his lips, and then tightened her legs around his hips as he made to shift off her. "No, don't move. Don't leave me. That wasn't me complaining. Not a complaint at all, I love being this close to you. Don't leave me."

His head dropped forward as he rubbed his cheek against hers, lips nibbling on her earlobe. He shifted, moving one arm so he could cup the back of her head. Using that grip to tip her head backwards, he slowly kissed down her neck. He left behind a trail of tongue touches and lip presses that burned her skin with arousal even now, after he had just taken her with wild abandon. He whispered, "I'm not leaving you ever, DeeDee."

Her hips tilted in response, back arching as she felt his cock hardening inside her again, and she found his passion for her still had the capacity to amaze. "I love you. *Mon amour, ma belle. Je t'aime,* DeeDee. So much, baby." His mouth moved across the skin of her shoulder. "So much. My life. My lover. Mine."

His body bowed as he shifted to one elbow, cupping her breast with his hand, lifting it to his mouth. She drew in a short breath, panting as his lips and tongue worked and rolled her nipple, his long fingers kneading the flesh. She took another inhalation as the sharp sting of his teeth registered, followed quickly by the comforting warmth of his tongue sliding across the puckered peak.

Rolling his hips, he pressed his length deeper inside her, grinding his pelvis against her clit, dragging a low moan from her lips. Pressing his upper body up and away from her, propped on one elbow, he used his free hand to cup her face, thumb dragging across her lips. Her eyelids slipped open partway and she watched his face as his gaze moved from her eyes down their bodies to where they were still joined. With a sense of satisfaction, she saw a look clearly filled with love cross his features before his eyes met hers again. Then, when his eyes darkened, gazing into hers, it was with lust, which brought its own happiness, knowing she aroused this feeling in the man.

Reaching up, she dragged the backs of her fingers across his cheek, saying wonderingly, "Out of all the world, you picked me."

He leaned in to kiss her lips, murmuring as he moved his mouth across hers. "No, baby. That's backwards." He set a slow, deep, rolling rhythm with his hips, thrusting in and out, and the tantalizing drag against her inner walls and clit had her gasping. "I found you. You shone so brightly. Amazingly dazzling, standing out from all the world had to offer as distractions…I found you. Then, oh, God…then you let me keep you. *Je t'aime*, baby."

18 - Babies

DeeDee stood in the kitchen, leaning one hip against the cabinet, lifting a mug of coffee to her lips. She was worried, turning things over in her mind, because so many things were in flux in the club right now.

Bear had been MIA for weeks, and no one seemed to know why, or at least they wouldn't tell her. She had become close friends with his mother when they were all working together on Ruby's wedding, and she had been calling and checking daily to see what she could do to help. He adopted four kids a few months ago, the children of a former Rebel member, and now Maggie was trying hard to keep everything together for them. DeeDee smiled, thinking, *Thank God, she has Tug to lean on. That man has a knack for being in the right place at the right time to help.*

Then they found out Eddie Morgan, Bear's girlfriend, and daughter of a rival club out in California, had been kidnapped. Mason got the word from Willa, and he called DeeDee right away after setting a response in motion, ensuring she would show at the apartment to help. Thank God, her presence hadn't been needed, but with what had happened to Ruby barely a year ago, the eerily empty rooms were as frightening as anything she had ever experienced.

The front door had been unlatched and open when they arrived, and the members moved through the apartment with caution, but no one was there. The only indication of a struggle was evidence of blood on a broken glass in the kitchen floor, but even that wasn't proof of anything. She prayed the Rebels would find and rescue Eddie as they had Ruby; sometimes the life could be cruel and frightening, nothing more so than winding up in the middle of a club war.

Eddie's father, Shooter, was president of a club in California, and the club found out he had her taken home to use her as leverage in order to broker a deal with another club. From what DeeDee had heard, the girl's brother, Judge, was the one who had taken her. He had been in Fort Wayne for years, sentenced to watch over his sister and keep her safe. DeeDee shuddered, thinking, *Even though the boy is kin, he always made my skin crawl.*

Maggie called last night to say Bear had finally returned to town, but he had gone straight to the clubhouse, not even swinging by the house to see the kids. Now, he and Tug had left this morning with several other members, all heading to California to bring Eddie home. DeeDee hadn't heard anything since then and prayed this would be a case of no news is good news.

She caught the roar of bike motors from the parking lot and shifted to watch her front door. Her house had practically become club central in the past few weeks, even after Gunny moved himself and Sharon out. She tilted her head, thinking with a smile, *Kind of like it was when Winger was alive.*

There was a rap of knuckles against the doorframe as the knob turned, the door pushing open to show her five men all vying to be the first through the doorway. Hoss' shout of her name died on his lips as soon as he saw her standing there, and his booted feet quickly carried him across the room to her. Cupping his hands around her upper arms, he bent his knees to put his eyes level with hers, searching her face, but still not speaking. The silence of the men was uncanny, fear raising the fine hairs on the back of her neck in waves.

Her phone rang from her jeans pocket and she automatically reached to pull it out. Before she could answer it, Hoss plucked it from her fingers, checking the display before tapping the screen to connect the call. He put the phone to the side of his head and said, "Yeah."

Eyes wide, she looked around at the men, saying in a whisper, "Someone say something, please. What's going on?"

Hoss ended the call without speaking again, slipping her phone into his pocket before putting his hands back on her arms, holding her steady. Softly, he said, "Ruby's gone into labor. She and Slate are at the hospital, Dee."

She nodded, concern pulling the corners of her mouth down a little. She knew it was early, but not as soon as it might have been, given the fact she was carrying twins. "Okay, take me to her. I'll call Jase." She twisted to grab her purse, and Hoss pulled her back to face him, his hold tightening on her arms.

Hoss' gaze searched her face and he nodded at whatever he saw there. "Something's wrong, Dee. Ruby ain't talking to Slate, but he said something's not right. Said it don't feel right." He took a breath. "Ride with me, babe. We'll head over now, okay?"

In sudden terror, she reached out and grabbed the shirt under his cut, pulling him closer. "Are the babies okay? Please tell me the babies are fine." She was having a hard time finding enough air to support conversation. Ruby was with Slate now, body and soul, assured of his love for her. But DeeDee knew the baby Ruby lost from Demon's abuse haunted the girl. And because she had trouble catching pregnant when she and Slate were first trying, Ruby's worst nightmare would be for something to happen to their babies. "Is Ruby okay? My girl? She's okay?"

"Let's get to the hospital, okay? We'll find out how our girl is doing. Slate's there with her; that was him on the phone. He said the doctor went in with Ruby, but she kicked him out of the room. He was going back in to find out what was going on." Hoss paused, then tilted his head, looking down at her and drawing a breath as what she said finally registered, slowly repeating, "Babies?"

She held out her hand imperiously. "Give me my damn phone." When he placed it in her hand, she quickly dialed Slate's number. He answered, and she said, "Slate, son, listen to me. It's gonna be okay. She didn't want you to worry."

Somewhat predictably, he blew up in her ear. "What the hell are you talking about, DeeDee? What didn't she want me to worry about? She's not telling me something, so what the fuck is it?"

"Take a breath, baby. Just slow down, son. It's going to be okay. Take a breath." She asked, calmly, "Are you doing okay?"

"Fucking great. Now will you goddamn well tell me what the fuck is going on with my goddamned woman?" He shouted the question into the phone.

"Ruby's pregnant with twins. She knew she might go early. Son, we aren't far away from her due date, so unless the doctor is telling you something is wrong, then he's probably trying to keep her secret. After her last appointment, she said that everything looked fine, Slate. She's going to be fine. Hoss is bringing me to you, but you take care of my girl until I get there, okay?" She listened for anything coming from the phone, hearing only silence. "Slate, honey, you're going to take care of my girl, okay?"

He whispered, "Twins?" A hollow thumping noise came through the phone and his voice stuttered. She imagined him pounding his chest with his fist as he shouted, "I'm having twins?"

"Yes, Slate. Ruby is having twins. Now get in there and stay with my girl. I'll be there fast as I can, okay? We're nearly in the wind now." There was silence and then a somewhat muffled woosh of a door opening, and then Slate's voice again, soft and distant.

"Baby? Ruby? Twins? We're having twins? Everything's okay, right? Our babies are healthy? Everything's good, right, baby?" There were murmurs and then the clear sound of kissing before he yelled, "Twins! Oh, baby, why in the hell didn't you tell me we were having twins? We need more of everything; we'll need two of all of it. Woman, we aren't set up for two babies. Whose fault is that, hmm?" DeeDee shook her head with a grin. He had put the phone in his pocket without hanging up. Pressing the disconnect button, she put her phone in her own pocket, giving Hoss a pointed look that said, *My phone, thank you very much*.

He and the other Rebels in the room were all smiling widely, and she grinned along with them. Hoss said with admiration, "Prez didn't know. Mother*fucker*, our Ruby can keep a deep secret."

Jase was at practice, so when she called, she left a quick voicemail about Ruby, asking he meet them at the hospital. She looked up at Hoss, smiling as he stood there holding her leather jacket, and said, "Take me to my girl."

***

"Yeap, the baby seats are in the car, Slate. It's all covered. Your boys got everything taken care of at home that you wanted, too. DeeDee checked up on them this morning and reported everything is in order and ready to go. It's okay, man. Breathe. The babies are beautiful. Ruby is glorious as a mom, and you are the best daddy I've ever seen." Jase stood in the hospital hallway, hand on Slate's shoulder encouragingly.

"Allen and Danielle are both doing better than fine. DeeDee told me the doctor said that in a couple of weeks, you would never know they were born early. Said he never had twinsies go home so soon, but they are healthy and sassy, exactly like their pretty mama, eh?" He couldn't puzzle out the mood Slate was in. The man should be ecstatic about the babies, but he had a growing cloud of angst around him. He looked around at the club members hovering nearby, noting several missing faces. "Is something else up, man?"

"Club business." With two words, Slate shut down the line of inquiry. Jase sighed. He always tried to respect Slate's desire to keep Rebel business close to the chest, and as much as he would have rather known what was going on, he wouldn't push and ask anything else. DeeDee would likely know, because she was club, but he wouldn't be looped in. Sometimes that stung, especially when she would have to say those same words to him, underscoring his position on the outside.

Hell, Bear's mother probably knew more than he did, since she was dating Tug. *Bear*, he thought, remembering a snatch of conversation he overheard in the hallway earlier. Bear was here in the hospital. Something had happened out in California, and he had seen Eddie walking up the hospital corridor, leaning on Duck and crying.

He looked around again, pressing his lips together and nodding his head. "Okay. No worries." Rolling his neck, he said, "Hey, man. I'll bring the car around, be waiting downstairs." Turning to go, he was surprised when Slate's hand gripped his arm. Looking back, Jase saw what looked like an apology on his face before he closed his mouth and shook his head, releasing his hold.

Waiting curbside, he was surprised when several of the club members showed, stationing themselves around the vehicle and keeping a close eye on bystanders. He looked over at Hoss and asked, "Anything in particular going on I need to know about?"

"Nah, we got it covered, man. It's all good." The words were uttered without Hoss actually looking at him, the man's gaze continually sweeping the area around them. He gestured at the vehicle, asking Jase, "Slate know you did this?"

"Nope. It's gonna be a splendid surprise. Can't wait to see his face. He's nearly my son-in-law, ya know? That makes his kids, *my* grandkids, and I'm allowed to make sure my grandkids are safe." He shared a grin with Hoss then paused, asking, "You seen Bingo lately?"

He tried to phrase the question casually, but he was actually fishing for knowledge. It had weighed on him for days whether he should keep the man's confidence about his nephew's illness, knowing without a doubt that Bingo could use the support of the club. If he got any indication at all they knew what was going on, he would feel better about sharing what he knew. He hated for the man to be going through such a terrible time alone, when he had so much support waiting in the wings. There was also the troubling feeling that something else was going on. Bingo had not looked good.

"Nope. Man's been absent more than present in the past few months. Guess the kiddos keep him busy." Hoss' roving eyes latched onto him and he frowned. *Shit*. "Why? Something up?"

I suck at lying. Okay, stick to the truth. Truisms only. "Nope, nothing's up." *True, nothing is elevated off the ground.* "Just a curiosity. He's a good guy to talk to, and I know he's been a good friend for DeeDee." *This is also true; no falsity registered, because it was all true.* "Everything's good." *Shit, shit, shit. Shoulda stopped my mouth when I had a chance*.

Tilting his head, Hoss' gaze sharpened. "No, it's not all good, is it?" He shook his head. "I don't have time to suss this out right now, man, but we will have words later." He pulled his phone out and looked at it, calling out, "They're on their way down. Look sharp."

The circle of men expanded around the vehicle, encompassing a greater perimeter than before. Backs to the front of the hospital, they looked outward, searching the environment for...something. The only time he had seen this level of tension in club members was when Ruby had been taken. During those hours before her rescue, the men had exuded a combat-ready attitude, and Jase was feeling those same vibes again now.

"Hoss, what's going on? Are Ruby and Slate in danger?" He sucked in a harsh breath, clenching his fist tightly around the keys. "Is DeeDee? Is everything okay?"

"Not my news to deliver, man. If there is danger, you know we have her back. Like I've told you before, she's always going to be ours, Jase." His eyes didn't stop sweeping the area, gaze returning to Jase only after he completed his evaluation. "We got her, and because she's with you, we got you, too."

The doors behind them opened and Jase turned to see a smiling DeeDee walking beside Ruby's wheelchair. Each woman was holding a baby, the one in Ruby's arms wrapped in a delicate pink blanket, and the one in DeeDee's swaddled in blue. He hooted and held up a palm for Slate to high-five, his other hand clicking the fob to slide the van's side door open. Slate slapped his hand then grasped it, holding on as he looked over at the vehicle sitting beside the curb. "What the fuck's this?"

"Our present to you, man. You are such an overachiever, because…two kids, seriously? Are your swimmers doing cross-training? Crazy ninja swimmers. That boy's gonna be a beast, and your girl? She's already a princess. DeeDee mentioned you needed a vehicle for the kiddos. I did my research and found out this one is way plenty big, and it's safe. Hella safe. Ratings are off the charts safe, like really good." He looked over where the women were standing, matching smiles on their faces.

"I know it's actually a present for you, Ruby, because you'll be driving it mostly. But this is our present…it's from me and DeeDee to you and your not-so-little family." *Let me shut my jabber mouth,* he thought and grinned broadly. He loved being able to give these kinds of gifts. Not the bigness of it, but the unexpected part of the surprise.

Loved seeing the stupefied look on someone's face when they realized he thought about them and had cared enough to figure out something that would make a difference.

"Jase." Slate's mouth hung open and he snorted a laugh. "Man, please. It's a mini-van. I'm a motherfucking biker. President of the Fort Wayne chapter of the Rebel fucking Wayfarers. I cannot be seen in a mini-van. Ain't happening. I appreciate the gesture and everything, but a mini-van? Dude, what were you thinking?"

Jase leaned close, stage whispering, "Don't 'dude' me. It's not a mini-van; it's an SUV. Now, just listen, because here's the most important part. Slate, the backseats fold down into a bed."

Immediately, Slate said, "And a fine SUV it is, too. I'll be right proud to be seen driving this lovely fuck-mobile. Thank you, brother." Slate threw back his head and laughed loudly, his attitude of ease belying the tension Jase sensed from the men standing nearby. "Help me get my woman and babies home, would ya? Babies, as in two of them. Hey, didja hear about my swimmers?"

19 - Winding down

"Dammit, get back in it," Jase shouted to his line. "Help him, dammit. Push. Push." Lee had fluffed a give-and-go pass, and a Kalamazoo player was trying to capitalize on the mistake. There were only four minutes until the final buzzer, and they were ahead one to nothing. Skating backwards, he swept his stick back and forth over the ice, creating an obstacle screen against the opposing forward barreling up the sheet towards him. As long as he kept this guy from... Jase read the player's movements and reached forward, stripping the puck from him with a smooth poke check, redirecting the puck towards Lee.

Racing down ice alongside Lee, he broke off to skate into position and whirled in time to deflect a rebound off a defenseman's skate. He heard a blade insistently tapping the ice behind him and slapped the puck back to Lee who took a shot, angling the puck over the goalie's shoulder and into the net for a goal. Arms up, Jase watched Lee take a sliding knee in celebration, coming up to be surrounded by their teammates, slapping each other's helmets in excitement.

Headed back to the bench, Jase heard one of the players begin to say something about the game being a shutout and he yelled at him, slapping the back of his helmet. "Don't jinx us. Don't you fucking jinx us," he said with a scowl, hearing agreement from several other players. "Doncha know it's a jinx to talk about what you almost talked about? So don't say anything about that thing you almost talked about until after the buzzer sounds, eh? Long as our man's between the posts, we don't speak about that." The kid looked at him with wide eyes, nodding.

Sitting, Jase watched while the faceoff played out, then as the third-line players put up a successful defense against a rush and breakaway. He stepped back onto the ice for the shift change, digging in and transitioning into full speed skating as quickly as he could drive his tired legs. Skating around the opponent's net, he only halfway paid attention to the obnoxious level of chirping and taunting that Kalamazoo's Biannac was maintaining. His focus was on the puck, slapped down ice and away, so it took him by surprise when the Tridents' play fell apart. He registered the sound of a soft grunt from behind him and saw players yelling and skating towards him, the sound level in the arena rising in a swell.

Spinning around, he saw a clearly unconscious Lee dangling from Biannac's hand. As if in slow motion, he saw the man's other fist pulling back, ready to land another giant blow, the linesmen circling like black and white pigeons tentatively looking for a place to land. Launching himself at the man, Jase hit him hard, knocking Lee from his grip. Inertia was in his favor, and the momentum knocked both Biannac and himself away from where Lee was awkwardly sprawled on the ice. From his prone position, he watched the skates of his teammates glinting in the lights, saw the blades rising and lowering around him as he scrambled on hands and knees towards Lee.

Hunched on his knees over Lee's helmetless head, Jase took a blow across his back, then another. Twisting around, he saw Biannac had picked up a stick and was swinging it wildly, first connecting with Lee's lower body, and then coming down hard on Jase's shoulder. "Goddammit," Jase shouted, "knock it the fuck off. Somebody get that motherfucker under control."

Two of the Kalamazoo players hooked hands under Biannac's arms, dragging him backwards toward the boards. With an enormous effort, he pulled away from them and turned, lunging towards the glass, hitting it several times with both fists. He was screaming wordlessly at a woman standing inches away, on the other side of the obstacle. Her head jerked back every time he pounded on the barrier, the expression on her face horrified. His teammates hooked him again, skating him towards their bench, this time with less resistance from the man.

Looking back down at Lee, he saw his friend was coming to, squinting up against the lights, blinking. He had a hell of a mouse under his eye already, but Jase was glad to see him becoming aware even before the team staff had reached the cluster of players surrounding them. Lee grimaced, struggled to sit up, and asked, "What the fuck happened?"

"Biannac happened," Jase said as he stood, skating backwards to give the medical staff room. He turned to where the Kalamazoo team had retreated to their bench, noting with relief that the crazy man wasn't anywhere to be seen. There was a pounding on the glass behind him and he twisted to see the woman that had drawn Biannac's focus was now looking worriedly across at Lee, one fist still pressed against the glass. She was pretty but pale, her gaze darting back and forth between Lee and the staff on the ice beside him. Looking at her, everything clicked, and with a shock, he realized this had to be Biannac's sister. Lee's 'one that got away' was standing not five feet away from him, and from the look on her face, the woman hadn't moved on either.

He got in her line of sight, drawing her eyes to him, and moving his mouth slowly, asked, "Are you Mareena Biannac?" She nodded and he grinned, calling in a singsong over his shoulder, "Hey, Lee, I think I found you a Ree." The staff had begun helping Lee to his feet, and he turned so quickly he nearly tumbled out of their hands and back to the ice, asking with astonishment, "She came?" Looking at the stunned expression on his face, Jase laughed as he followed the group off the rink, watching the trainer assist Lee down the tunnel into the locker room.

***

Fuck, he thought, looking around the locker room. Everyone was looking at him, waiting for the standard, rousing captain's speech to the team after the win. Lee was at the local hospital getting a scan, and right now, it looked like he would be out for the rest of the season with a concussion, which left Jase a not-so-*co*-captain. *Daniel,* he thought, *I've seen Daniel do this enough times. Stand up and talk already.*

He stood, drawing the gazes of the few players who weren't already watching him. "Anybody get the number of that truck that hit Cap'n? Damn, that was Zamboni-sized, eh? Coach called; he said Lee'll be headed home when the hospital turns him loose. Us lucky saps, however—we have another four away games this trip before we get to see the inside of our homes again, so maybe he's the lucky motherfucker here, right?" This drew laughter as he intended, and he watched the men slowly begin to ease into their post-game rituals.

"We have an early practice skate tomorrow in Waukesha, so plan on getting plenty of bunk time tonight so we're all fresh as can be. Coach'll have to change our lines a little with both Lee and McCormick on the injured list. Take note, because you motherfuckers better practice your short straw-drawing skills or you'll wind up having to skate a shift with me." There was good-natured laughter from the players and he grinned.

"This was a good win tonight, boys. We left it all on the ice. Our fans are behind us, which helps. Didja see all the jerseys and colors in the arena tonight? Those people drove more than two hours to watch us play and we gave 'em a hell of a show. Now, let's keep it going, yeah? Good skating, good game, good team." He knew it wasn't as good as Daniel would have done, but it was passable. He took off his jersey, dropping it into the bottom of his gear bag, praying the equipment managers were going to have time to do laundry before tomorrow's game.

"Let's get rolling, guys." He chivvied them along without looking. "I'm fucking hungry."

His head came up when the first man slapped his shoulder on their way past and said with respect, "Cap'n." His first thought was denial, because that was Daniel and Lee's title, but he realized he was what these men now had. He was their Captain.

Wedged into the front seat of the bus later that evening, he video-called DeeDee to chat. It wasn't until she gasped through his earbuds that he remembered the half-dozen stitches in his eyebrow, gained not even courtesy of Biannac's wild swings with that damn stick, but due to his own stupidity. "Shhhh, baby. It looks worse than it is," he smiled at her image on the phone, "and you look so good it should be illegal. God, baby." His call had woken her, and he loved the way her hair was tousled, curling around her face in soft ringlets.

"Silly man," she said with a sleepy grin. "We listened to the game, me and the twins. Y'all won; that's great." She yawned, covering her mouth with one slim hand. His view of her moved and changed then went away entirely, and he saw the lampshade for a moment before her face came back into view. She had stretched out on the bed, propping her phone on the pillow next to her. He groaned silently. This would be his view if he were home right now. Curling one hand underneath her cheek, she smiled at him. "Is Lee okay? When did the face thing happen?" She quickly had to get used to seeing bruises and stitches because of the physical side of the game, and fortunately, she was not easily thrown.

"Second frame, I got a little too friendly with the opposing goalie, slid into the post with my head." He sighed. "How are my babies tonight? Is everything good?"

She smiled broadly. "Babies are better than good. They're sleeping down the hall. Slate had some business for the club and Ruby decided to go with him, so I get to play GeeGee for two days. These babies are perfect."

"God, I wish I was there," he said, and was immediately sorry, because he watched as her sleepy-happy face became sleepy-sad.

"Me too, Jase. I miss you when you aren't here." Her hand reached beyond the frame of the video and he heard a gentle patting sound. "Wish you were right here beside me, within reach." She sighed, "Or wrapped around me." Giving a slow, sleepy blink, she said, "I miss you holding me."

He looked around. Coach would be renting a car and coming later, and most of the team was sleeping, so no one was listening in on his conversation. It was time to ask. "Baby," he said slowly, "I've been thinking about that thing Mason wants, him offering me a job in Fort Wayne. I have three more semesters before I'm done with my degree, but I get the feeling that wouldn't matter. I know you told me to think about it, but how would you feel about me being there all the time?"

The video jerked and moved, then the call disconnected. It sometimes happened, so he stared at the screen, waiting for her to call him back as she normally did. After a couple of minutes of waiting, he hit redial and got a message she wasn't available, then got a text that said, ***Sec baby***. *What the hell*? he thought. *Is she upset over the possibility of a closer connection between me and the club?*

He waited impatiently, and when she finally called him back, he answered before the first ring completed sounding. "Why did you do that? Why did you hang up?" He was halfway to being pissed and knew his tone showed it.

"I didn't hang up, doofus; my ass did. You startled me and I sat up, and then the phone slid under my ass and we got disconnected. And then I had to pee." She laughed and smiled. "If it were just a call, I would have risked sitting on the can and talking to you, but not on video."

"Ah," he said, watching her face intently. "Okay, you're forgiven, but are you gonna answer my question?"

"Not yet." She bit her bottom lip, thinking, then said, "The questions I had about the job are still valid. First, are you sure that's the job Mason is offering? We need to know exactly what it would entail before you can tell him yea or nay. Second, would you still be able to complete your degree if you're working fulltime for the club? I know that piece of paper is something you've been putting a lot of time and effort into, and I want to see you succeed."

"Baby," he said softly, and she tilted her head, looking at him. "I like you saying that 'we' stuff. It sounds all couple-ish and I like being coupled with you."

Tilting her head down, she said, "I know. Me, too."

She shook her head and looked up, taking a breath. "I'm serious here, though. Let's talk it through, okay? So, third and really most importantly, how would you actually feel about not playing hockey? You've played the game for nearly your whole life. If you weren't playing, you were preparing to play, or conditioning...but everything has revolved around the game, so what would that even look like for you?" With a smile and downward glance, she said, "Having you here all the time would be so good, but only if you'd be truly happy, Jase." She frowned and looked back at the camera, sitting cross-legged on the bed, cupping her chin in one hand.

"From what he said, the job would be taking on a large part of your load, in one sense. He asked me to manage all the Fort Wayne businesses," he said then laughed, because before he could finish the sentence, she interrupted with a loud, "Yes."

"Tell me how you really feel, baby," he joked and watched her bite her lip again. *If I were there, I'd be biting other places on that woman.*

"Business manager would be an above-board position. You wouldn't get pulled into any sketchy club business, so you'd be safe. If you could take on the extra work I've been doing, trying to help Myron out as much as I can, that would be phenomenal, baby. And...you would be home. I'd get to sleep with you every night? Yes. Hell yes." She shook her head and laughed. "When I say it like that, it sounds selfish, but I still say hell yes. So let's talk about finishing that degree, and what life without hockey looks like. I've listened to you talk about when you were hurt, and how you couldn't wait to get back onto the ice. Why would this be any different? How can you manage that kind of loss?"

He nodded; this was the piece he struggled with the most when contemplating Mason's offer. Hockey was all he had known his entire adult life. He enjoyed the physicality of the game, the excitement of executing complex strategies, and the adrenaline rush of competing against other top athletes and winning. The camaraderie of the team, everyone working together towards a common goal. The excitement and ego stroking from the fans and media. But in his mind, none of that mattered. When he compared that to the woman in his bed and in his life, it came down to one important thing: DeeDee.

Slowly, he said, "It would be different, because of us. Before, when I was hurt, I didn't have you. I had a bare taste of you before Ruby got hurt, and to have that taken away left a huge hole. Then I got injured, and losing hockey too? It turned that hole into a gaping crater." He saw a look of pain cross her face and she turned away from the camera. "Baby, I'm not saying that to hurt you, but to make sure you understand the difference. Some people get lost in drugs or drinking when they are hurting emotionally; I played hockey until I couldn't see straight.

"Now, I have you, not a simple taste, but all of you. You've seen how I have to force myself to drag ass to practice, because I don't want to leave you. I'm not showing up an hour or two early like I used to. Not doing non-mandatory two-a-days in the gym to exhaust myself. I'm home with you whenever I can be. However I can. Between the sheets, or in the wind, if I can be with you...I am.

"Between you and the twins, now I hate to leave for road trips. I hate to be away. I resent the need to sleep in a bed not shared with you. I want to be there every night. With you. Hockey's becoming the obligation, and you, my refuge. If I want to stay involved with hockey, there are other ways that won't have the same travel requirements. I already have an idea about something, because I want to set up a foundation to help disadvantaged kids discover hockey, a way to pay my love of the game forward. But if the job offer from Mason works out, I think I'll be busy enough to not miss it too much. Plus, to be honest, I'm tired, baby. I'm sore, beat up, and just plain tired." As he spoke, she turned to face the camera again, watching his face as he explained himself. By the time he finished, she was nodding her head.

"Why don't you think on it a little longer? You have a few more weeks before the season plays out, then a couple months before you have to worry about signing, right?" She paused, waiting for his nod. Once it came, she continued, "Call Mason and talk to him. Make sure this is what you want, okay?"

"Okay, baby," he said with a smile. "He wanted a month, but I'm sure he'll understand. Honey, you need to go back to sleep; it's late. I need to get some shuteye, too. I love you, *mon amour. Je t'aime*, DeeDee."

"No more than I love you, crazy man. Come home soon, okay?" She smiled and disconnected the call.

Jase leaned his head back against the window, staring up at the ceiling of the bus as they traveled up the Dan Ryan. *Chicago*, he thought, *Mason is in Chicago*. Without pausing to give it too much thought, he lifted the phone and dialed the number for Jackson's and left a message with the bartender.

***

"Ma, I told you. I'm on the road for another week. Right now isn't a good time to come down." Jase scrubbed his hand across the top of his head, cursing the one-hour time zone difference that made his mother forget he might already be asleep. “Before you ask, I don’t know what DeeDee’s schedule is either. I’m on the bus right now.” He yawned noisily.

“Well, I can hear that, can’t I? When will you be home, Jase?” Her voice carried that thread of steel he knew so well.

“Week from Friday, we play in Indy, then head home. I’ll be back in the condo early Saturday morning.” He had a feeling he would be losing this battle, but still needed to fight it for both his and Sharon’s sakes. Things were too tenuous right now with her and Gunny, and even between him and DeeDee. It might be selfish, but he didn’t want to bring his family into the mix yet.

“Then I can be there Sunday,” she said without hesitation.

“No, Ma. This isn’t a good time to come down. Don’t make this hard, woman.” He yawned again, leaning his head against the bus’ window.

“Why don’t you want me to come visit, son? Have you gotten too old to enjoy a visit with your mom and dad?” There was a quavering tone to her question, but it sounded forced, so he wasn’t fooled.

“Not bamboozling me, woman. You know things are busy this time of year. The season is winding down, but I have to focus. Dugger got hurt—”

“Lee? What happened?” She was genuinely concerned, knowing and liking Lee from Jase’s descriptions of the man.

“A fight gone wrong, you know the risks. It’s always a chance every time we glide out.” He sighed and closed his eyes.

“He’s okay though, eh?” He could tell she was backing down from the trip idea, thankfully.

“Yeah, he’ll be okay. Probably sitting at home right now, feet up, with a book in hand.” He laughed. “Makes me effectively the captain, though.”

"You'll do fine, son. Do him proud, eh?" There was a smile in her voice, and he responded to it.

"Will do. Tell you what, Ma. I'll call you when this away trip is done and we'll sort out a time for me to head up." He yawned again, rubbing his eyes, then sat up straight when he heard the sudden whip crack of her voice.

"Jason Wade Spencer, you're not going to put me off forever. I will be coming to see you, your woman, your sister...everyone in your life there in the States. Don't think you'll get away with this, and don't think I don't know what you're doing."

Smiling, he said, "I know, Ma. We'll sort something out, eh?" He sighed, ready for sleep. "Love you."

"*Je t'aime*, Jase. Be well, son." She smacked a kiss into the telephone and hung up.

Jase leaned back against the window and settled his shoulders onto the hard surface. Even if he wanted to, he couldn't protect Sharon from their family forever.

20 - Take the deal

They won the game in Waukesha handily. It was irritating that the team was playing so well now, because it was late in the season, to make up for all the missed points from earlier in the year. Now, there was barely a chance of making the playoffs, given the limited number of games left, paired with their current point position in the division. If they had tightened up like this earlier, they would be sitting pretty, but it didn't matter now, except how it played into the players' individual contract prospects.

Prepping for their next game, he was sitting in his hotel room in Rockford reviewing tapes from the last time they met this team. Three games in three nights with a half-dozen key players on the injured reserve left them a whole lot of missing talent to make up for. He worked with Daniel enough over the years to know a large part of the game was strategy and preparation. Being able to read an opposing team's play and call it out to the players was part of what made a good captain.

A knock sounded at the door and he looked up in irritation. "Fuckin' rookies. Better not be a practical goddamn joke," he grumbled, walking to the door. Looking through the peephole, he pulled his head back in surprise, quickly fumbling to open the lock.

"Mason," he said in greeting, holding out a hand. "Whatcha doin' here?"

"Merry said you called the bar. Thought I'd come watch the game, have a talk," Mason said, pulling Jase into a one-shouldered clench.

"Come on in, man." Jase closed the door. "Want a bottle of water?" He laughed nervously. "It's all I keep in the room." He shrugged and gestured towards the chairs near the window when Mason shook his head. Grabbing his tee from the bed, he pulled it over his head, glancing around the room nervously, but everything looked pretty much in order. He realized what he was doing and thought, *Why do you feel the need to clean up for Mason?*

"I'm not going to beat around the bush. I'm hoping you called to accept the deal I made you, but if not, then no hard feelings. You'll still be a friend of the club, welcome at all the neutral bars, and into our clubhouses by invitation." Mason grabbed a chair, turning it around and sitting, folding his arms across the back. "And DeeDee's position is independent of you and any decisions you make, so you don't have to worry about any blowback her way. Just throwing that out there; don't want any misunderstandings."

"It never occurred to me to worry that you'd hold her job hostage." Jase pulled a chair out and sat, crossing one ankle over the other knee. "And, I did want to talk to you about the offer." He laughed. "Didn't expect you to come all the way to Rockford to have a chat."

"Some things are better done in person." Mason shrugged.

"Yeah, I can see that," Jase said and sighed. "I'm interested. Very interested, but I have some questions. At the rate I've been taking classes, I have less than two years left to finish my degree, three semesters. I want to finish it, and I plan on it, but is this offer contingent upon me finishing, or could I begin working sooner if I wanted? That's the first question. Second is what exactly would my relationship be with the club? An employee? A member? Do I have to do a probation period, kinda like a rookie hockey season?"

Mason looked at him and nodded. "Good questions. Easiest one first. You could start tomorrow and never finish your degree. I don't actually give a shit about that, except if you do. You're one smart motherfucker, and I don't doubt you'd do fine as-is. But, the offer to pay for the classes stands, whether you keep going and start work now, keep going and start work later, or keep going and never start work. That's the easy shit, because I know you, man.

"Okay, now for the harder question, because, for this, you need a little history lesson." Mason laughed. "This course credit is free, and there aren't any prerequisites here. School of hard knocks. The club, we...me...I need men like you, just as I need members with the diverse and specialized skill sets of brothers like Gunny and Tats. Every member of the club, every person associated with it, serves a purpose. There aren't any free rides, and we all pull our own weight. For me, it's a matter of matching up pegs and holes.

"With you, fuck...man, you're more than halfway into the life already. Look at you and DeeDee being together, and her long history with the club. You go on runs with my men, even help raise money to make us look good. We've all seen you protecting members when you can. Hell, a lot more than halfway into the life, I'd say. As far as I'm concerned, you quit being a hangaround the day you borrowed my scoot in Chicago. At that point, you became a friend of the club.

"But, that said, I don't want to sidestep our prospect period, because it's important for a whole lot of reasons. We'll both need to make sure of the fit, and it gives members time to get to know you...but for you, that period would be different. It will look different from how most of our guys spend their probation. You'll be learning from Myron more than anyone.

"Want you to know that even being a prospect doesn't mean your position in Fort Wayne is contingent upon anything other than doing your fucking job. Think of the club like any other employer. But you need to fucking know what else you're going to be exposed to, the darker side of our business. These are things most men looking to patch in would already know, but you're coming at it from a sideways angle. You ready for this part of the conversation?" Mason looked at him steadily, unmoving.

Jase thought for a moment, then agreed with a nod. "Yeah, I need to make an informed decision. I feel like I know some of what you're going to say. I've seen bits and pieces over the past couple of years, with Mica and Daniel, then since I've been with DeeDee." He shrugged. "Go ahead. I'm ready."

"Okay, man, listen up. Rebels have three rules. Three key rules that carry the weight of everything we are on their backs. The first one is no whores. We don't run hookers, don't allow hooking out of our businesses. Girls can be trouble, and hookers are a magnet for even more. You'll hear women referred to as club whores, but that's a different thing. Those'll be hangarounds looking for a good time so they fuck members, or women looking to hook up with a good old man. Fucking is their preference, and if a brother becomes a problem, I deal. So that's the first thing." His gaze never wavered and Jase sat still, soaking it in.

"Second rule is no hard drugs, and is non-negotiable. No heroin, no meth, no hard shit. Do we sell blow and pot? Fuck yeah. It's a chapter-by-chapter decision, but there's a lotta money available in the trade, and helps keep my brothers' cash flowing in like magic. Some of our guys come to us from other clubs where they are used to that kind of easy money, and it is fucking hard to clear out.

"Putting a lid on the hard stuff gets us a step farther in what I think is the right direction, even if it's a slow fucking trip. I've slammed the door on chapters for crossing the line, though, so every fucking member understands the risk if they stray." He stared hard at Jase, nodding, satisfied with whatever he saw in his face.

"Third rule is no military-grade weapons. Handguns, sawed-off, and some semi-A, yeah. Again, not every chapter wants in on the trade, but some of them pull in most of their non-channel money through resells." He rolled his shoulders, leaning back and stretching his arms, crossing his wrists on the back of the chair for a moment before he sat upright again.

"And that's it, three rules. Everything else is on the table. Brothers wanna line up new shit, they go through me. With every chapter I charter, we're working our way more into the legal businesses, what I call channels. Bars, strip joints, the bike shops and garages, parts stores, restaurants, motels, clubs...the legal side of things is where I need your help. We need things to be squeaky, so when the feds come calling, we got good books to show them. And that's it, man. Pretty simple, yeah?" Mason laughed.

Jase had struggled to keep his face impassive as Mason talked, but by the time he was done, Jase was wrung out from listening. He knew Mason had skipped over some parts, and that was okay; what he laid out was enough to try to wrap his mind around. There were a lot of gray areas to digest. "You must be pretty confident of me to tell me all that," he said, nervously uncrossing his legs.

"Not sure of you, no. But I've known you long enough to understand you like things straight up, no bullshit. I won't get a year down the road and have you feeling blindsided because you didn't know the lay of the land." Mason shrugged. "Easier to get it all out there now, give you a feel for the size and scope of everything. You know about the businesses in the Fort; this is added volume, but it's shit that you wouldn't be responsible for." He paused for a moment, then asked, "You got any other questions?"

"What happened in Texas?" The second it was out of his mouth, Jase could have slapped himself for blurting the question. Daniel had talked about the attack on Mica that Mason had stopped, and had speculated as to what the bikers had done with her ex-boyfriend. He watched Mason's face settle into harsh lines and knew the no-bullshit rule was still in effect.

"Motherfucker doesn't breathe her air anymore," Mason said, clenching his jaw and nodding sharply once.

"That's good," Jase said, surprising himself. He liked Mica a lot, and being witness to how she had blossomed since marrying Daniel was gratifying, because she deserved good in her life. He also liked that it made his friend blissfully content for her to be healthy, happy, and whole. The answer Mason had given him settled comfortably on his shoulders, because it was the right one. It was the answer he most wanted regarding Sharon and her ex, so he understood where Mason was coming from. He got it.

"So with all that said, you still feeling like you're on the fence, or did I tip you onto one side or the other?" Mason had settled into stillness again, waiting for an answer.

"I've definitely tipped, but I think we're both going to be pleased with the direction. I want to finish playing out this season, fulfill my current contract with the Tridents. After that, Mason, I'm all yours. I've already talked to DeeDee, and she's on board with the idea, as I understood it a day ago. But, so we don't have any crossed wires, here's what I get from everything we've talked about—why don't you listen and tell me if I'm right or wrong, eh?"

Mason nodded, so Jase continued, "It sounds like I'd basically be the business manager and CFO for the companies in Fort Wayne. Those properties include Slinky's, Marie's, the storage place, Tamari restaurant, that other food place I can't remember, the two motels, apartment buildings, the bike shop, and the parts place, plus anything

I've missed knowing about. That's the extent of my responsibility, to ensure the profitability of the businesses and to manage the documentation and records associated with that cost effectiveness.

"I want to keep working on my degree, but I can take that slow while I get on track with Myron. I suspect there will be some travel at first, back and forth to Chicago, but my hope would be that could be limited, because I want to stay home with DeeDee and the babies as much as I can. I'll keep coming to club events with DeeDee as I have been, and there may be additional responsibilities there. We'll call that TBD, yeah?" He sat back then leaned forward, resting his forearms on the table between them. "Whew, Jesus Murphy, that's a lot!"

"Yeah, and DeeDee and Myron have been keeping up with all that on top of everything else. You forgot the gun range and the two pawn shops. Barring playoffs, the season ends in April, right? We get you immediately afterwards, or we could wait until the end of that semester. A couple weeks either way won't make a difference." Mason stood, extending his hand.

Jase unfolded from his chair, reaching for Mason's hand to shake, and found himself caught in a forearm grip, pulled into a one-armed hug. "Fucking awesome, man," Mason said and pulled out his phone to make a call. He spoke briefly into the phone, saying, "Yeah, bring it in," then hung up. He slid the phone into his jeans as he walked towards the entryway, getting there just as there was a knock on the door. Mason opened it while Jase looked on bemused, seeing Slate, Tug, Hoss, Bear, and Gunny walking into the room.

"Hey," he said, and stopped talking as Slate stalked across the room towards him, a piece of black leather in his hand.

Thrusting it into Jase's hand, he pulled him into a one-armed clinch similar to Mason's, but he spoke quietly into Jase's ear. "You're my prospect, Jase. Make me proud, man." Slate pulled back and looked into his face. "Put on the colors, brother. Welcome."

Stupefied, Jase looked down at the vest in his hand, feeling the weight of the supple leather. He shrugged it on over his long-sleeved shirt, settling the fabric across his shoulders, feeling the heat from his body immediately begin to seep into the garment. "Looks good, brother," said Slate, reaching out to thump him on the back.

Jase nodded and grinned, saying, "It feels good." He pointed at Slate first, then the men in turn. "So my son-in-law, my brother-in-law, and my brothers? I've got an awesome fucking family, man."

Mason laughed as the rest of the men greeted Jase, each taking a moment to speak to him and remind him of the strength of their existing ties, of his long-time involvement in their lives. Jase shook his head. This had been a long time coming, and he wasn't kidding; it did feel good.

***

"Lee, I wanted to tell you in person. I'll be talking to Coach before the season is over, but you deserve to hear it from me," Jase said, looking straight ahead. They were sitting on a couch along the back wall in the team's lounge area in the offices, watching as several players reviewed game tapes on the eighty-inch flat screen. There were a couple of tough teams coming up in the next few days, and it paid to be prepared.

He knew Lee's eyes were on him, but he kept his face resolutely forward. They had mended their friendship over the past weeks, but with Ree entering the picture again, the two men didn't spend as much time together as before Lee's season-ending injury. "Okay, what's up?" Lee asked, and Jase saw him shift, putting elbows to knees as he leaned forward on the couch.

"I'm not re-signing with the Tridents. This season is my last as a professional hockey player." There, he had said it aloud for the first time to someone who would know the immensity of what he was giving up. Not the money, because he would make twice his current salary working for the Rebels, but what it meant to be quitting hockey. Sure enough, Lee took in a harsh breath then blew it out slowly.

"Not signing? Why the hell not?" His voice rose as he spoke, and across the room, a few of the players looked over at them in confusion.

"Keep it down, asshole," Jase shot at him, turning his head to pin him with a stare. "I'm not signing; that's right. But I want to control when I tell the owners. They've been far better than decent to me, and deserve for me to do this the right way."

"What the hell?" Lee said, modulating his voice and glancing around the room. "Why would you quit? You're at the top of your game, worked your fucking ass off to come back from an injury. You couldn't wait to get back on the ice; I've never seen a man push himself harder to recover. Why would you quit?"

Jase looked down at his feet, then up at Lee. "Because of the injury. It brought home the fact that we never know from week to week if we'll be playing. Look at you, man. Another couple of hits from Biannac and you'd be wearing a bib, your lunches spoon-fed by a cute candy-striper. I heard Coach talking to Adam. Is it even certain that you'll be back next year?"

"No, it's not," Lee said easily, lifting one shoulder in a shrug. "Even if I'm healthy though, I'm considering retiring. Not that Coach knows anything yet, but getting my bell rung like that wasn't fun. Now that I've found Ree again, I can't imagine being hurt badly." He paused and sighed, asking, "What will you do?"

"I have a job lined up," Jase said quickly. "I'm going to finish my degree, make DeeDee smile, play with the babies, and maybe work with kids as a coach. I've been skating with Tyler, the kid from the hospital, and he has a hell of a slap for someone that didn't come to hockey until after his voice changed. Kid played football, if you can imagine. Travesty."

“Sounds like you’re getting everything lined out,” Lee said, reaching a hand over to punch Jase’s shoulder lightly. “More than me, at least. I finished my degree a couple years ago, but don’t know what I’ll use it for yet.”

“I’ll keep my eyes open for you; if anything comes my way, I’ll let you know,” Jase said, resolving to mention it to Mason.

***

Mason looked around the bar, seeing the mix of citizens, Rebels, and Tridents players that filled Marie’s. He twisted to look at the stage and shook his head. Slate’s little brother, Ben Jones, was supposed to play tonight, and it looked like he recruited some help. Along with the standard gear for Benny’s band, Occupy Yourself, he recognized two of Bear’s guitars on stands near the side of the stage. That would be good, because anything that helped continue to pull Bear out of himself was welcome as far as he was concerned.

“Hey, Gypsy,” he called down the bar, drawing the attention of the member who managed the business for the club. “You know who Ben has playing with him tonight?”

Shaking his head, the Rebel walked towards Mason. “Not sure, Prez. I saw Bear come in and set up some stuff earlier, but I think Benny is babysitting so Slate and Ruby could go to Jase’s last game. Sorry, I’m not sure.” He shrugged, wiping at the bar top with a rag.

“No big deal, man.” Nodding, Mason turned to face the room again. Quite a few of his Chicago Rebels had come down for the game, and the bar was filling up quickly. He saw Tug come in, Maggie at his side, and Mason sighed. He liked the fact the man had found some companionship and was pleased, because Tug deserved it after so many years alone, focusing on the club. Mason was all about being happy for him at that level, but goddamn if the man hadn’t picked a citizen to get entangled with. There were few damn ways that would end with everyone happy, even if she was the mother of one of his members.

He was about to head over to speak to the couple, when there was shouting from the front of the bar, followed by a slow, building applause. The clapping grew louder and spread throughout the room, members and players both turning as they watched someone walking through the crowd. The corner of Mason's mouth lifted in a half-smile when he saw Jase's face burning red from the honor. His arm was wrapped around DeeDee's shoulders, and hers was behind his back. Mason knew from past experience she would have her hand tucked into the back pocket of his jeans. He was glad she finally decided to find her way to a comfortable place with the man, especially after they had such a rocky start.

As they approached where he stood, some of the Tridents' players were calling out something, but before he could decipher the phrase, laughter came from beside him. "There you go, Jase. That's your club name: Captain," Slate said, and the members who stood nearby laughed.

Mason nodded and reached out a hand, clasping Jase's shoulder in his grip. He greeted him, seeing the man's eyes widen at his immediate adoption of the road name. "Cap'n, you played a good game tonight. Congratulations on the win in the final game. On to the playoffs now, right?"

"Thanks, Prez," he said with a grin. "Yeah, that was my last regular game as a Trident, last game as team captain, last game as a carefree, travelin' man." DeeDee lightly punched his shoulder and he gasped in pretended surprise. "Sweetheart, where did you come from? Hey, did you know you look a lot like my girlfriend? You remind me of her in all the best ways. Wanna find an empty room and get busy?" She shook her head, leaning against him as he loudly kissed the side of her head.

A discordant noise from the stage drew his attention from the couple and he turned to see Ben Jones and Bear making their way across the stage, followed by...his son, Chase. *What the hell is my boy doing up there with the musicians?* Mason frowned, watching Chase pick up one of Bear's guitars, parking his ass on a stool set along the edge of the stage. He turned to Slate, standing behind him. "You know anything about this, fucktard?"

Ruby laughed from where she stood next to Slate, tucking her face against his chest. He had slipped an arm around her before he answered, "I might, Prez. I might. But you ain't gonna find out anything by calling me names. Hell, that shit cuts deep, man." He was grinning widely as he spoke, and Mason glared at him for a moment, then turned back to watch.

On the stage, Bear stood near Chase, talking him through something, and then he turned to look across the room, catching Mason's eye and giving him a chin lift. Returning the gesture, Mason's gaze swept the room, noting Bear's adopted daughter sitting near the stage. She was watching Benny, but Chase was watching her. *That could be a cluster*, he thought, shaking his head. *Triangles suck ass; I should know. Might need to say something to Bear.*

Within a couple of minutes, guitars in hand, the three people on the stage began playing, and Mason was startled at how good they sounded. Chase didn't look comfortable at first, but both Ben and Bear appeared confident in his abilities, and as Mason watched, he slowly relaxed, settling into his playing. They started out with one of Occupy Yourself's songs, *Feeling You*, and even after they finished and moved on to the next song, all he could think about was Willa. The words from the last stanza of the chorus kept repeating in Mason's head. *'Loving you is possible, Giving you my heart. Love, it bears repeating, Our lives together start.'*

21 - Rude awakening

Slate asked curtly, "Have you seen Birdy lately?"

Jase frowned at the odd question, pausing for a beat to sit down before responding. He had come in to tell Slate something, but the man had hit him with the question before he could even begin. "Before tonight?" He shrugged. "Until tonight? Not for a while, certainly not since Bear's been back. What's up, man?"

Slate sighed, reaching out to slap the door separating the office from the main room of the clubhouse closed. "Shit's not right, man. You say you saw him tonight?"

Jase frowned at the closed door, nodded, and waited a minute for him to continue, and when he didn't, asked, "What kind of shit?"

"Shit that doesn't wash off, man. I've heard rumblings that he's been tucking his boots under Manzino's sister's bed." Jase sucked in a shocked breath. Manzino was a drug dealer the club had problems with off and on again for a couple years. If Birdy were sleeping with the man's sister, that could be bad for him. "I was going to talk to Mason last night after church, but then Gunny gave him the Vincent, sidetracked me."

“I thought the dealer had left town. Didn’t he go out west to try his luck there?” Jase hadn’t been part of the club when that all went down, but he heard about it afterwards as part of the story about how Slate’s brother had come to Fort Wayne. “What the hell is Birdy thinking?”

“Thinking with his dick, most likely,” Slate said, pulling at the back of his neck with a rough hand. “If he’s fucking her, he’s fucking himself. Brother has to know that.”

"What will you do if it's true, if he's tangled up in something like that?" Jase wasn’t sure what the reaction of the club would be, but he knew there had to be one. Birdy’s association with drug dealers would be breaking one of Mason’s key rules.

"If he's lucky, we'll cut his patches...drum him out of the club, cut his rockers." Slate ran his hand across his jaw, clenching his teeth so tightly Jase could hear them gritting together. "If he's lucky."

Hesitantly, Jase said, "I came here...I needed to talk to you anyway, Prez. I...uh...I saw him earlier tonight out back of Marie's. He was whaling on someone pretty good. I figured it’s not my business, so I got what I was after in my bags and headed back inside. But he looked up, saw me, and booked it." He looked up at Slate, taking the measure of his mood. "It made me wonder why he ran, so I walked over to see who he had been smacking on. Prez, it was one of DeeDee's girls, and she was high as a kite."

"Fuuuck," Slate ground out the word. "How long ago?"

"About thirty minutes," he said. "I tried calling, but when you didn't answer, I talked to Goose and DeeDee. They're taking care of her now. I took a chance you'd be here, came on over."

Slate stood still and silent for a long time, and Jase thought that this was more nerve-racking than the final two minutes of any game. He had to get everything out there, though. "There's more, Prez." Slate was moving towards the door, but Jase's words stopped him in his tracks.

"Gunny was supposed to work at Slinky's, but he didn't show. He wasn't picking up his phone either, so Hoss went to the house and found it buttoned up tight. He said the dogs didn't raise a ruckus, and you know how loud those dogs are when someone's around, so he made his way inside. He found several bodies in the bedroom, all shot at close range. Brother...one was Elkins, Sharon's ex. It looks like Gunny and Shar are gone."

"Are you fucking kidding me?" Slate snarled, whirling and stalking back to the desk. He stood for another moment, and Jase could nearly hear the gears turning in his mind. "Lockdown. Get ahold of DeeDee; tell her to bring the girl here." He pulled out his phone at the same time Slate did, and as he called DeeDee, he heard him tell Ruby to bring the babies to the clubhouse.

Pulling the office door open, Slate yelled out into the room as he made another call, "Church, right the fuck now, brothers... Yeah, Mason," this was said into the phone, "got some kind of shit going down. I'm putting the Fort on fucking lockdown. Yeah, we're going to need some trash taken out at Gunny's. I'm getting some brothers on that right now. Looks like Manzino's lifted his head, gonna find out... Yeah, he's right here." Slate looked at him as Mason spoke on the phone. "Yeah...I'll call. You too, Prez."

Turning to look at Jase, Slate's gaze was considering, eyes narrowing in response to some emotion Jase didn't recognize. "You've had an easy run, brother. Now's when the grit hits the grindstone and we get to figure out what kind of men we are. Right now, you have one priority: find Birdy."

He stood, already shaking his head. "No way, Prez. My baby sister—"

"That's exactly why you aren't gonna be the one looking for her and Gunny. I need you to be the planner and plotter I know you can be, not an emotional fuckup. Find Birdy and bring him in, but we assume the best until shit lands on his head. Need you to explain to the club what's going down. Birdy, Gunny and Sharon, Gunny's house—that's three fucking fronts we have to clear, and you're point on the Birdy/Manzino one." He motioned to the door. "Let's sit for church. Then we'll sort what's needed."

Yelling into the main room as he walked out of the office, Slate pulled the eyes of every man to him. "We got shit, motherfuckers. Captain has the floor." Backing up a step, he nodded at Jase once, encouraging him.

Nodding back, he looked around the room at the faces of the men he had grown to know and trust. He knew every one of these men would have his back, would help him through anything...would die for him. This was what he had been looking for, this brotherhood. For them, he could do the captain's speech, but it meant so much more here. Taking a deep breath, he began.

"Gunny's in the wind. His old lady, my sister, is with him. He left some bodies behind." At this announcement, there was a shifting in the room as the men turned and looked at each other, then back at him. "Right now, we think it's not voluntary, that they've been taken. One of the bodies was Elkins."

At this, the prospect who'd been blindsided by the man uttered a low, hate-filled, "Fucker."

Jase nodded at Piebald. "Yeah, exactly. We don't know much more than that." The men's voices rose as they talked among themselves, and he had to raise his voice to be heard over the swelling sound. "Hey. Listen up brothers, there's more. Birdy's in the wind too, but for a different reason. I caught him fucking up one of the girls from Slinky's earlier tonight, and there's rumor he's been bagging Manzino's sister. Our brother ran—that's not good—and we need to find him and figure out what's going down. Prez talked to Mason; he's put the club on lockdown. Call your families and get them in here. There's too much we don't know, brothers. Let's keep the folks we love safe."

Turning to look at Slate, he said, "Manzino and Birdy detail is led by me. I'll need four or five brothers who know Birdy well, know his hidey-holes. Slate, did you decide who you want to head over to Gunny's and meet Hoss there?"

Nodding, Slate said, "Tequila, PBJ—you boys pick four more, we'll do six plus Hoss. Take a cage; you'll need to take the trash out while you're there."

Captain turned back to the room of men, nodding. "Get your families moving. Talk to me about Birdy. I want us off the lot in fifteen."

***

Mason rubbed his forehead with the fingers of one hand, the other thumping out an irregular rhythm against the desktop. His cell rang and he picked it up immediately, answering with a flip of his thumb across the screen. "Talk to me."

"Prez," Slate said, "got you on speaker. Cap'n and Bear are here with me. We wanted to update you." Grunting noncommittally, he waited for them to continue. "Gunny's house is clean; we found the dogs locked in a crate in the basement, but still no sign of him or Sharon. None of his bikes are gone, and his truck is in the drive, so we're pretty sure they didn't go willingly." There was exhaustion in Slate's voice, and he hated how events like this turned the man deep inside himself. Shit like this was hard for everybody, but it seemed to hit brothers like Slate hardest.

"Myron can't get a fix on either of their phones. He said it looked like they were being jammed, which might mean LEO...or might mean something else. We had better luck with Birdy's phone, and Cap'n dispatched a cage. They picked him up about an hour ago. They're on the way here now, with both him and Manzino's sister. Fucker was sitting in her operation center, watching her toothless bitches cook that meth shit up. I can't see my way past anything he did, Prez. I'll hold my final word until I talk to the motherfucker, but as far as I can see right now, he's done." Slate took a deep breath before saying, "Not sure what we'll do with the woman."

Mason shook his head, knowing the men couldn't see him. *Shit was hard*. He sighed and asked, "If it was Manzino, what would you do?"

"End him. He's hung himself a dozen times over." Slate spoke immediately, saying exactly what Mason had been thinking, but before he could respond, Captain's voice filled the void.

"Slate...brother. There isn't any way she's innocent. She had to know coming into her brother's old, outlawed territory and pulling this shit would rile the club. It was a calculated move on her part, possibly driven by Manzino in some way. I say talk to her, but we have to be willing to turn the same judgment on her that we would her brother." He could tell saying this had a cost for Jase, but was pleased he didn't have to be the one to state the obvious.

"Cap'n has the right of it, Slate. You know it." Mason paused a minute before continuing. "Talk to Birdy; talk to the woman. I'm on my way down soon, brother. Wait for me if you need to, but Slate..." He paused again, waiting until an affirmative noise came through the phone. "You have full authority. Your voice is my voice."

***

"Fuck you." This was said in a voice thick with pain and filled with what had to be false bravado, because surely Birdy knew he was fucked six ways from Sunday. "I ain't talking to you. Fucking prospect's got no reason to ask me shit. Get a fucking officer in here. I might have a word or two to say."

Jase blew out an angry breath, grinding his teeth. They had been hearing the same kind of statements off and on all afternoon, wavering between threats of death and pleading. This hadn't been an easy interrogation to watch, knowing the man as he did. Harder still to take part in, but Slate had put him in as lead, so he had to step up.

He remembered the battered face of the dancer from last night and fury welled up inside him at the way Birdy had treated Mercy. Jase found himself enraged at the memory of how the man had left the unconscious woman vulnerable, running to save his own cowardly ass. In his mind, Sharon's face overlaid the woman's, and in a rage, he leaned over to cuff Birdy hard on the side of the head, splattering fresh blood up and across Jase's face and neck.

"Fucktard, if you don't talk to me, you don't get to talk, period. Don't you get it? There aren't any officers who care enough to try to make you see sense, man. I'm all you've got." He reached up to wipe his face, and seeing the blood covering his swollen knuckles, thought better of the motion. "Last chance, Birdy. What ambition does Manzino have in the Fort? Why did he send his sister in to fuck with us?"

Shaking his head, Birdy snarled at him again, "Fuck you."

Jase looked up at Hoss and Pinto as they stood leaning against the wall where they were out of sight from Birdy. He shook his head, acknowledging they wouldn't get anything else out of the man, and they both nodded in agreement. He watched as Hoss reached over and pounded softly on the door, muttering to the member who opened it, sending him back out. Three standing and one tied to a chair, the four men in the room waited in silence, each isolated in their own thoughts.

The door opened and Slate strode in, his gaze sweeping the room and taking in the scene before him. He held his position and nodded curtly at the floor by the chair, watching as Jase leaned over to pick up the dark cloth bag he dropped there earlier. Jase stared Birdy in the eyes as he pulled it over the man's head, holding his gaze until the blood-soaked material covered his face.

Lifting his head, he looked at Slate and glanced over to where Bear was standing in the doorway behind him. "It's gotta go down this way?" He startled at the question, sure for a moment it had come from his lips, but he saw Slate and Bear turn to look at Pinto, who was shaking his head. “Never mind, I know. It’s a fucking shame. Birdy coulda been a good brother.” With that, he and Hoss turned and walked out of the room, shutting the door behind them.

Struggling wildly, rocking the chair side-to-side on its legs, Birdy’s shaking voice came from underneath the hood. “Wait. Wait. I can tell you routes and schedules. Manzino has plans. I know his plans, his routines, who his lieutenants are. Hold on.”

“He tell you anything up to now?” Slate’s voice was flat and cold, and Jase shivered as it lashed through the air in the room directed at him.

“Nothing. I don’t think he has anything, Prez.” Jase shook his head, knowing he probably had sentenced the man to death.

“All right.” Bear stepped forward, pulling a gun from the back waistband of his pants. “Cutting isn’t enough, Prez.” His voice was as cold as Slate’s, and Jase watched his eyes as he stepped up behind Birdy, reaching out a hand to grasp the hood. “Betrayal of a brother, a chapter, is treachery that can’t be set aside.” He looked into Jase’s face searchingly. “He brought shit back to town, shit that cost us brothers in order to run it out the first time. Good men, Rebels all. That sets him against the club.”

Jase nodded and stepped to the side. Bear continued, eyes still on his face. “He knew the score.” Jase nodded again, but then took a single step closer.

“Let me try once more,” he said softly, leaning close to Bear. The big man looked at him carefully, then nodded slowly. Jase glanced down as his arm flexed, his hand tightening on the hood and pulling it up and off Birdy’s head, uncovering his face. There was a look of stark fear embedded there, but then he focused on Jase and it shifted quickly to fury and loathing. Jase shivered; he had never been the recipient of so much hatred, and he couldn’t figure out what he had done to earn it.

"Talk about Manzino," he prompted, and was surprised with the vehement shake of the head from Birdy that met his request.

"No, dammit. Just no. Fuck you. Fuck you and your goddamned club. Goddamn Mason lets bitches run his club now. I don't want no fucking part of it anyway. Knew that shit years ago when I met that motherfucker Slate for the first time, him and Tug. Fucking lesbo bitches were on the Rebel lot, and they protected them. Beat me and my brothers to protect fucking lesbo bitches." He drew in a ragged breath and laughed harshly.

"Ain't no mistaking you bought my fucking bike," he spat at Jase, who sidestepped the blood-flecked phlegm, staring at him in confusion.

"I didn't buy your bike, Birdy," he said, stopping when the man laughed again.

"Fucking bitch with her head all up in my business all the time. Hands off the fucking girls decreed by her, then she wouldn't sell me the fucking bike. Put it up for goddamn auction, where a fucking citizen bought it," he spat at Jase again. "Fucking waxer." He sneered. "Fucking weak-ass prospects, can't keep a fucking prisoner secure, never shoulda let me in the fucking room."

"Winger's bike?" There were a dozen revelations that needed attention, but Jase was focusing and slowly putting things together on just one of them, remembering conversations with Tug and Mason about DeeDee's position being somewhat precarious at times.

"Shoulda killed the fucking bitch when I had the chance. Had plenty of chances, you're always leaving her the fuck alone. Kill the bitch, take the bike, fucking go back home to Mor—my real brothers." Birdy tipped his head back, blood trailing down his cheek and neck. "If I killed the bitch, you wouldn't be standing here right fucking now."

Jase looked at the man now sitting silent, and his blood ran cold as he finally put a name to what he had been seeing all along. *Hatred.*

Birdy held an unmitigated hatred for the Rebel club, because his loyalties lay elsewhere. That hatred bled through from the club to DeeDee, and then to him. He was a threat to everything Jase held dear; there was no coming back for him. He never had ties with the club, with them. If they let Birdy go, there was no doubt in his mind that he would circle back around...come find him—*find DeeDee*—and take revenge for every slight, real or imagined. His stomach clenched as the realization of what had to happen here became apparent.

As he stared wordlessly at the man tied to the chair, face twisted into an ugly mask of impotent rage and disgust...in hatred, something Mason had told him once rose to the surface of his mind. Mason had said that as people, we are hardwired to protect the ones we love, our families. His family had expanded over the past few months to include DeeDee, and further, to pull the Rebel club into the circle that he wanted to protect. The club meant everything to him. He would die for them...he would kill to keep them safe.

Reaching out, he took the hood from Bear's hand, tossing it to the floor as he leaned down into Birdy's face. Locking their gazes, he got near enough to feel the heat radiating from the man. Speaking quietly, he said, "Just signed your own fucking death warrant, motherfucker. God forgives, Rebels don't." He held out his hand and accepted the burden of the cold metal willingly.

***

He held DeeDee in his arms, watching her sleep. He, Slate, and Bear had walked out of the basement room of the clubhouse to find out Gunny had called from a location downstate. He and Sharon had been released, and Jase shook his head, because the part of the story about what had happened to them was muddy.

Why had Elkins been in their house? How was he hooked up with the people who had taken them away? Why had they been taken, and why were they released? Was there a connection between the shit with

Birdy and Manzino, and what happened to them? So many questions and no answers; at least, not right now. Gunny had gone into the office with Mason, Slate, and Bear, coming out several hours later. He refused to talk, striding away with hardly a word to where Sharon waited, picking her up and cradling her gently to his chest as he walked up the staircase.

He and Sharon were in a room here, and Jase suspected he would see his sister at breakfast. He hoped he could get more out of her than he was able to find out from Gunny.

His mind turned back again to the scene with Birdy, rolling things over again and again in his head, trying to find a better solution. Why would Birdy have done it? Why would he voluntarily fuck up so badly? Why would he work to become part of a club that he so obviously hated?

It didn't matter which way he looked at it, what angle he came at it from, the outcome was always the same. If Birdy's actions didn't change, then things had to shake out the way they did. Because the club was a brotherhood, it depended on adherence to specific rules of conduct. Betrayal of your brothers was the worst thing you could do and, as a result, had the highest cost in response.

Look what had happened to Bear in Des Moines last year. He was working with Slate and Mason, uncovering issues with the chapter out there. When it was evident he found problems, several of the local members had taken him and beaten him nearly to death. Some members might feel badly about what happened to the men who'd done that to Bear, but Jase understood why, just like he understood what had to go down tonight. Didn't mean he liked it, but he had agreed to it.

DeeDee stirred in his arms, and he stroked down her back, feeling her naked skin slipping like silk beneath his palms. *I'd do anything to keep you safe. Pay the cost from tonight a dozen times,* he thought. He took a deep breath, nuzzling the side of her head and kissing her softly. "I love you, baby," he said. *"Je t'aime, bebe. Je t'aime."* Angling his body to pull her closer, he whispered, "Everything changed tonight. But for the first time in my life, I don't feel alone. You and me, baby, we're permanent; we're family. *Rester avec moi pour toujours*, baby. Stay with me forever."

***

Hoss looked up at her as she walked into the main room of the clubhouse. She knew his gaze held a question, because there had been some terrible club business last night, and she hadn't missed her man's part in everything that happened after the club went into lockdown. She walked over to him and he handed her a mug of hot coffee, which she accepted with a wry smile of thanks. Leaning against the bar, she waited for him to ask.

"Captain still in bed?" The tone was casual, but everything this man did was calculated.

"Yeah, he's snoozing. Was late when he came to bed. Later yet when he went to sleep." She blew across the top of the coffee in her mug, knowing the conversation wasn't yet over.

"He okay, DeeDee?" The question was quiet, and she doubted anyone else heard him. So, she took that to mean it was serious.

"He is." She lifted her chin when she answered him, attempting to convey the depth of her belief in Jase's wellbeing.

"Yesterday was a cluster." He sipped at his own coffee, watching her over the rim of the mug. "We'll be off lockdown by this afternoon, but there will be ripples for a long fucking time." He sighed, eyes shifting to the room, his gaze sweeping side-to-side, cataloging the members present. "Mason's gonna need us all, DeeDee. Birdy hadn't been a member long, but he came with a recommendation from someone Mason trusted."

She nodded, taking a drink of her own coffee. "You thinking someone wanted to sink a mole in the chapter? Wasn't he Chicago first? If he's snooping for another club, why would he leave the mother chapter to come to the Fort?"

"Good fucking questions, woman," a voice said from behind her, and she turned, seeing Tug standing there. "We're going to need you to see if you can get some answers from the dancer he fucked up. She is the most likely person to have any insight into his motives."

She had known from Jase's mood when he came to bed that things had gone badly sideways, and from Tug's statement, she knew Birdy hadn't survived the night.

Last night, she met Jase's demands with eagerness, giving as much back to him as he would accept, following his lead, knowing it was a life-affirming action for him at that moment. They had rocked against each other for long moments, his hands roaming her body, his mouth slanting across hers possessively. When he pulled out, reaching down to tug at her hip, she turned to her stomach, arching her back and lifting her ass into his hands as he took her from behind. Moving together like that, she met each thrust of his hips with her own, letting him control the pace of their lovemaking, allowing him to cover her protectively with his body.

Now she would wait to see how things stood when he awoke. The raw and hard side of club life could turn a man against things, and she prayed that wouldn't be the case with Jase.

***

Tug watched her walk away and he sighed without looking away. "Prez, last night was not a well-done thing." Turning, he looked up into Mason's face, expecting to see remorse, but instead was met with a steely, cold gaze.

"That's where you'd be wrong, Tugboat. It was very well done," Mason said assertively. "Our brother stepped up like we needed, and the club became what he's needed for a long time." Nodding at the prospect behind the bar for a mug of coffee, Mason looked back at Tug and Hoss. "He's been a team player all his life. All his fucking life, he gave everything he had to his team. Transient players, called up, pushed in and out, long-time team members, franchise players, there for the haul...they all got the best of what he had to offer. You saw him play; man gave a hundred and fifty percent, every fucking game. Not a damn thing to show for it in the end but a love of the game. Man's been looking for something that's worthy to be a part of for a long time. He found it in the club, and circled the edges looking for a way in, and now he's found that in, he ain't gonna be going back anytime soon."

Taking a drink of his coffee, he settled back into the bar, leaning one elbow on the top. "He came in when he accepted the colors, and he fucking knew the score that day. I made for-fucking-sure of it. I don't recruit many people, and you both goddamn well know that, but I pursued him, recruited him. We need him as much as he needs us."

He took another drink. "Last night, he closed the door on his past life, became a Rebel. We patch him today. He's found something worth fighting for now. We'll have the best of what he has to offer, from here on, brothers. Rebels forever," he said, Tug and Hoss echoing his next words. "Forever Rebels."

22 - Protect the club

Jase softly kissed her temple, struggling hard to catch his breath, hands smoothing up and down her back as she lay draped across his chest. Lifting DeeDee's hair off her shoulder, he twisted it into a loose knot and out of his way, wanting his hands on more of her.

They finished making love, slow and sweet, their bodies moving together in comfortable patterns as they focused on each other. He was addicted to the feel of her and could never get enough of her against him, under his hands, her taste in his mouth. His thumb brushed across the outer curve of her breast and he caught his breath at the softness of her skin. As his fingertips caressed her gently, desire was again coiling low in his belly, his cock twitching where it lay soft against the crease of his hip. She tipped her head and he kissed her temple again, dragging his fingertips deliberately along her side so his thumb stroked her breast more firmly. He smiled as her hips flexed in response, and he felt more than heard her soft sigh.

"Round two, lover mine?" Using his chin, he nudged her head back, dipping to capture her lips in a soft kiss.

"Mmmmm," she hummed against his lips. "I always want more of you. Always ready for you." She deepened the kiss, opening to him as he shifted them on the bed, easing her into a reclining position. He rose over her on an elbow, his cock growing hard and thick at her words, at the sight of her beside him in the bed.

He watched her face as he slid his hand down her belly, skirting her core except for the most glancing of touches, still enough to draw a low moan from her. Hand on the inside of her knee, he tugged, pulling her left leg up and over his hip, canting her body at a slight angle, opening her legs wide to give him full access to her pussy.

Dusting soft kisses along the slope of her shoulder to the arch of her neck, he slipped his fingers between her folds, slowly stroking and tugging, circling the entrance to her pussy teasingly. Shifting his hips, he thrust, the head of his cock sliding between her pussy lips from behind, the crown bumping against and over her clit, and she let out another throaty moan.

Thrusting steadily, moving in her slippery wetness, every time he pulled back, he circled her clit with his callous-roughened fingertips, feeling that nub firm and engorge as she became more aroused. Her hand reached up, cupping the back of his neck, and she twisted her head around, lips seeking his. Complying with her wordless request, he slanted his mouth over hers, tongue questing and dipping inside, smiling against her lips to hear another purring moan.

She surprised him with a shift in position, and suddenly he was buried deeply inside, her inner walls contracting around him in rhythm to the working of their mouths. "Ah, fuck, DeeDee," he ground out, thrusting faster as her heat and the tight feel of her pussy around him had control slipping from his grasp. "Too fucking good. You feel so good. Baby, are you close?" he asked, laying his head alongside hers, cheek-to-cheek, looking down her body at his hand still working her clit while her hips moved in time with him.

"Yes," she breathed, and as her grip on his neck tightened, he watched as muscles slid and moved underneath her skin while she chased her orgasm. She whispered, "Nearly, Cap'n. Almost."

"Thank fuck," he said, thrusting again, then again, and a third time before shoving himself deep inside her. His fingers were plucking and tugging at her clit, teeth nipping her earlobe, dragging her over the edge alongside him with that tiny bite of pain that drove her so crazy. He stayed that way, buried to the root, intimately connected with her while riding out her climax as well as his own. He loved this, feeling her tighten down on his pulsing cock, listening to her gasp out his name, fingernails biting into his skin. He kissed down her neck, his chest plastered against her back, sweat covering both of them, their rapid breathing loud and raspy in the quiet of the room.

"Jesus Murphy," he whispered minutes later, his softened cock still inside her. "Woman, you make me crazy for you. God, I love you, baby." He laughed and they both groaned as he slid out. Kissing her cheek and then her raised, demanding lips, he laughed again, repeating, "I love you."

"I love you, too." Her head dropped, resting on his bicep as he shifted them, arranging them side-by-side in the bed. His arm curled around her waist as he slid his hand up to cup her breast in his palm, relishing the weight and softness.

"Are you all packed?" As he knew it would, his question drew a sigh from her and she shifted uneasily next to him.

"I'm not sure this is a good idea." She tucked her head into the crook of his elbow, screening her face from view. "Why don't you get Sharon to go home with you instead?"

How could he make her understand what this meant to him without making her feel badly if she honestly didn't want to go? If it wasn't only fear holding her back? *You could talk to her, eh?* He snorted a laugh at his thoughts and then frowned when she reacted, pulling away from him. "Roll over," he said, tugging on her hip. "I need to see you, baby."

Propping himself up on one elbow, he looked down into her face with a soft smile. Gently tracing the edges of her jaw with the tip of his thumb, he dragged it across her bottom lip, then tapped the end of her nose. "Neither decision will anger me. It's up to you, baby. Come with me, or not, your choice. Sharon's got her own stuff going on, so that's a no-go. But," he held up a finger when she would have spoken, placing it across her lips in a shushing motion, "please know how much I want you with me.

"I want to show you my hometown, introduce you to my family and friends, and have a chance to show you off to the world." Leaning down, he kissed the corner of her mouth softly. "I want everyone to know how fucking lucky I am that you've let me keep you, that you are mine. I want people to see the love I have for you, the passion we share. I want you to know and meet other people in my life who are important to me. I want you to understand that everyone already approves of us...of you, crazy lady. My lady.

"If you decide to stay here—decide to not go, not come with me," he breathed out softly, "then do it because you're moving towards something, not because you're avoiding something. Don't *not* go because you're worried about what people will think or say. Mason's already spoken to the MC there in Red Deer and we have an open invitation, so there aren't any club conflicts to hold you back. Hoss can manage Slinky's for a week and you know it.

"Ruby will miss her babysitters, but even with that, she seems excited to hear about my family from you. And I have to go, for me it's the right thing to do. I owe Ma and Da explanations in person why I'm calling my career at this point." He leaned in and kissed across the freckles on her nose, then trailed his kisses down her cheek and nuzzled into the side of her neck before pulling back and looking at her. "Well, beautiful lady? What do you say?"

She was silent for a long minute, her gaze turned up at him, her focus shifting between his eyes to his mouth, back to his eyes. The muscles in her face tightened, her expression taking on a worried aspect, but still, she said nothing. He sighed and pressed his forehead into her shoulder to hide his disappointment. "I love you, baby. It's okay, no stress. It's okay. I didn't mean to pressure you."

Gathering her into his arms and holding her tightly against his chest, he kissed the top of her head. "I need a nap, woman. You wore me out," he laughed, feigning a lightheartedness he didn't feel. The condo was quiet, and he listened to the far-off sounds of traffic as he shifted restlessly beside her. *Damn*, he thought. *If I stay here, she's going to realize I can't relax*. "Gonna go clean up," he said, kissing her temple and rolling to the edge of the bed.

The season had ended and, surprising everyone, most especially him since it seemed the stars had miraculously aligned, the Tridents had made it into the first round of playoffs. They lost to Cincinnati, but made the other team work for it, taking the series to the full seven games. Now, officially in the off-season, Jase planned to head home to explain to his parents that he was quitting hockey while he was still young and healthy enough to prepare for and enjoy another career. There were some folks he wanted to see while in Red Deer about a few different future plans, but without DeeDee there, those ideas would have to be put on hold.

In the bathroom, he turned on the shower and then leaned both hands on the countertop, looking at his reflection, he watched as it slowly faded from view, obscured. He smiled; in the condensation on the mirror, he could see the faintest outline of something DeeDee had drawn weeks ago, a heart with his initials on one side, and hers on the other. "She loves you," he reminded his likeness, nodding and smiling to himself as he turned to climb into the shower.

***

"Hey, Ma." He smiled at her as he stepped out of the car. She grinned broadly and looked around him expectantly, scanning the front seat, her face falling when she realized he was alone.

"Where's DeeDee?" she asked, disappointment clear in her voice. Over the past week, she told him repeatedly how she was looking forward to meeting the woman who finally captured her rogue of a son's heart.

"She wasn't able to make the trip. We didn't know until the last minute." He wouldn't lie to his mother if she asked outright, but he would sure skirt the issue if he could.

Looking at him, she tilted her head and nodded, sighing. "Nerves get the best of her, did they?"

"You gotta admit you're kind of intimidating," he joked, not really confirming her suspicions.

"Did she not care to meet us?" The look on his mother's face held a world of hurt, and Jase shook his head, rushing to reassure her.

"No, Ma. It's not that. She's terrified you and Da won't like her. She can get so focused on what she sees as issues that she can't always get past them." He reached out and pulled his mother in for a hug. "She cares *too* much."

Resting her head against his chest for a moment, she took a deep breath and leaned back, pulling away. "Give me your phone."

"Ma, no. Let's go inside. I need to talk to you and Da." He shook his head, trying to lead her up the drive towards the house.

Digging in her heels, she scowled up at him. "Give me your farkin' phone, Jason Wade Spencer." She held out her hand and he sighed again.

"Ma—" he said, but she interrupted him.

"I want to tell her one thing. I won't badger her, I promise. Just the one thing to ease her mind, eh?" Her scowl softened, not quite into a smile, but nearly. "Just the one thing."

He handed over his phone, stepping back to the car and grabbing his bag out of the backseat as she found DeeDee's number and dialed it, putting it on speaker. He smiled when she spoke, his heart quickening in his chest; even from thousands of miles away, she had that effect on him. "Hey there, you. Did you make it to your folks' okay?"

"Baby, you're on speaker," he said, and his mother smiled up at him.

"Okay," DeeDee said, confusion evident in her tone, and then she went quiet.

"DeeDee, this is Jase's mom, Jacque." She paused and then frowned when there was no response. "I wanted you to know something. Are you listening?'

"Yes." He recognized this as the even tone she used with club members when she was afraid or worried about their response to something. This was her 'I'm freaking out, but you'll never know it' voice.

"I already love you," his mom said, warmth and affection apparent in her tone, and a quickly stifled gasp come through the phone. "I already love you, because you've made my son happy. I don't care if you are black, white, polka-dotted, or striped. I don't care. You matter to Jase, so you matter to my Kenny and me. We already love you, sweetie."

Silence hung in the air like a weighted blanket, and then finally, DeeDee said, "You don't know how much that means to me, Jacque." She took a deep breath, audible over the phone. "Thank you."

Jase took the phone from his mother's hand and smiled at her, mouthing the words 'Thank you'. He shifted the call off speaker and put the phone to his ear, walking away from his mother. "Baby," he said softly, hearing her unsteady breathing. "Talk to me, eh?"

"Alberta boy," she teased on an outrushing breath. "Was it your mom's idea to call me?" She sounded much better, calmer. Her voice was evening out, but hadn't shifted into that artificial calm he had so grown to dislike.

"Yeah, I didn't even hardly get a hug; she looked around me a dozen ways from Sunday before she realized you weren't in the car. Then she was all, 'Give me your phone'. Wasn't anything I could do, baby. I had to give it up." He laughed at himself. "You don't know Ma when she's got something in her head. She's like a terrier once she latches onto an idea."

"Well, I'm kinda glad she did." She laughed lightly.

"She had control, baby. There wasn't anything I could do!" He paused and smiled. "Did she make it better?" Reaching into the front pocket of his pants, he fingered the small velvet box, teasing at the seam between the hinges with his calloused fingertips.

"Much better, Jase. I should have trusted you. I should have known you'd never put me in a situation that was uncomfortable. I'm sorry." She sighed again, and he knew her gaze was unfocused, probably directed down at the toes of her shoes. "Tell her thank you again from me, okay? Come home safe. I love you."

"I love you, too. See you soon, baby." He hung up and turned to look at his mother, standing where he left her near the car. She pinned him with a sharp look and he shrugged at her. "She said to tell you thanks. You helped set her mind at ease."

She nodded and pursed her lips, staring at him. "Did you take the shot, Jase?"

"Several of 'em, Ma." He laughed soundlessly, pulling the ring box out and showing her. "I have another shot I'm lining up, though."

She clapped her hands delightedly and nodded, repeating, "Take the shot." Wrapping one palm around his upper arm, she turned him towards the house. "Now we hafta explain to your father why you're quitting, but aren't a quitter. Then, later," she looked up at him, "you're going to tell me about the patch I saw on the back of your vest, son. And then," she took a deep breath, "you're going to talk about Sharon. I want to know everything."

***

Back in Fort Wayne, Jase sat in the airport parking lot for a minute, his brain a muddle of thoughts and emotions. He had a good visit with his parents and believed his father had accepted his decision better than expected. Once he explained not only his reasoning, but also what he would be doing to pay back the sport that he loved, his dad was on board one-hundred percent. His mother was already a supporter of the decision, because she had nursed his injuries many times through the years, and knew that a career-ending one was always just a misstep away. This way he was going out while still healthy.

Sighing, he started the truck, leaning his head against the steering wheel. Coming to a decision, he pulled out of the lot and headed to the clubhouse, where he hoped he would find Slate. In Red Deer, he met with officers and members of a club with a chapter there, and he wanted to relay their well wishes to his president. He had been surprised at how quickly news of events in Fort Wayne had traveled, because after a couple beers, one of the men had expressed concern over what happened with Birdy. Seemed they knew the guy who recommended him to Mason, and had dealings with the Utah club before. *Just another mystery to chuck in the bucket*, he thought.

Pulling up in the lot, he was surprised to see a large number of bikes present, and he stood beside the truck for a moment, looking around and taking stock. He knew a bunch of the bikes, but not all, which meant visitors from another chapter. Smoothing his vest, he dangled his keychain from one finger, walking into the main room with a whistle and a shout. "Hey, man, did you know there's not a single bike on the lot?" Seeing Pinto standing behind the bar, he walked that way as some of the men got up to walk outside. Taking the seat of one of the men leaving, he leaned against the bar and said, "Wait for it...wait for it..."

Several of them came back inside, and one yelled over, "Thanks, asshole."

Jase turned on the stool, grinning widely. "You're welcome, dickhead."

There was a jolt as someone kicked the legs of the stool, and he turned to see Mason standing next to him. "Nice. Smooth move, fucktard."

Nodding at him, Jase said, "Gullible isn't pretty to watch, I know. I got a good seat outta the deal, though."

Giving him a half-grin and nodding, Mason said, "Come sit in the office with me and Slate. Wanna get your take on something we got going on."

Accepting a beer from Pinto, he followed Mason and narrowed his eyes when the door closed behind them. Greeting Slate, he waited for Mason to sit and then followed his example, choosing a seat that put him an equal distance from the two men. In silence, he waited for one of them to speak and clarify what the issue was.

After a couple of minutes, he couldn't stand it any longer and blurted, "What the fuck is going on?"

Slate and Mason both laughed, and Slate pulled out his wallet, handing a five-dollar bill to Mason with a quietly muttered, "Fuck me."

He laughed, leaning forward, and propped his elbows on knees, saying, "You bet on how long I could be quiet?"

"How long it would take you to want to know what was up," Mason corrected him. "I said less than five minutes; Slate thought you'd last longer." Mason shook his head. "I know you better." He took a drink of his beer and said, "Tell me about Red Deer."

Nodding, Jase related the events surrounding his visit back home. "The club there was welcoming. Thanks for that advance call; it seemed to make all the difference in the world." Mason inclined his head and made a 'go ahead' motion with his hand. "They already heard about Birdy and the issues we were having. Seems they've had dealings with Chief out in Utah before, said he was genuinely shocked at what went down. There's a lotta admiration for Rebels there. It was good to hear them speak so openly about their respect for our club."

He shifted in his seat. "The version of the Birdy outcome was pretty spot on to what happened. Does that mean we have someone who's talking out of school, Prez?" He looked at Slate when he spoke, but Mason answered.

"Naw, I outlined things when I made my call. They probably were testing you to see how forthcoming I'd been. It's all good." He looked at Jase for a minute. "How are you doin', Cap'n?"

"I'm good. Was good to see the family, get them behind my ideas." He lifted his beer for a drink, pausing when Mason spoke again.

"You know what the fuck I'm talking about. Don't dodge the question, motherfucker."

"No, really, I'm good, Mason. I was good with it when it all went down. You know...I heard you in my head that night, talking about how we protect the ones we love. I knew Birdy was threatening not only the club and my brothers, but DeeDee, too. He was there." He pointed at Slate. "He heard him. It wasn't something I could let back onto the street. Not and feel safe ever again."

Mason nodded. "You did good, Jason. You did a hard thing, but for the right reasons. You know the club has your back, and now the club knows you have theirs, too. No doubts on either side. Any man in that room," he pointed at the door, "or this one," he swept his hand in an arc, "would die for you."

He nodded and opened his mouth to speak, but Mason forged ahead. "You played hockey all your fucking life. Played in a bunch of different countries, on a bunch of different teams. All those people you played with on all those teams, how many are you still in touch with?"

"Two," Jase said without hesitation. "Daniel and Lee."

"When you played on those teams, did you give fifty percent effort or a hundred fifty every game?"

"Hundred fifty...or more." Jase tilted his head. "Where are you going with this, Mason?"

"Would you die for me? If needed, would you step up and save me at the cost of your own life?"

"Yes, Mason. You know I would, man." Sweat prickled on his back. This line of questioning was making him nervous.

"Is the club worthy of your respect? You were honored in Red Deer that they thought favorably about the club. Are you honored to be a member?"

He drew in a shaking breath. "Mason, yes. I am...it is. All my fucking life, I needed this. To find it now, when the club needed me...when I needed the club, that's fate at work. I'm honored. I'm proud, and I'm a fucking Rebel."

"Goddamn right you are," Mason said, leaning forward. "And because you are, you keep the club first. You protect the club against any threats, even from within. Because it's what we do." He reached out and slapped Jase's chest hard with the back of his hand. "Because we're fucking brothers...family, and we protect family. Don't let what happened with Birdy fester, man. It was needful. Un-fucking-comfortable and hard as fuck, but needful, because it protected your club, your brothers, your woman. Your family. You got me?"

Jase nodded, sinking backwards into the chair. "I got you, Prez."

23 - Supporting you

"Good, good." He called across the ice to where the gaggle of eight-year-old kids was slowly skating towards the goal, "Looking good." Bright laughter braided with a deeper, booming humor came from the stands behind him, and he glanced back to find Tyler sitting there with Bingo. One of the kids on the ice was one of his little brothers, Kane, and Jase grinned at the pair before turning back to the children.

His gaze swept across the untrained and awkward kids, automatically categorizing them into ranks, cataloging a few who looked to have raw skill, or at least the enthusiasm to take chances. Kane fell into that latter group, and he broke away from the pack as Jase watched. The boy fell to his knees and bounced up, stick swinging wildly as he chased the puck. Two other boys and a girl followed him, the rest of the kids looking on in surprise.

Jase called, "Stay on the puck, guys. Keep your stick blades flat and on the ice, the puck isn't up by your shoulders; it's by your toes. Good, Kane, that's really good. Now, turn and follow the puck." He looked up at the banner strung across the end of the rink in pride, Patterson-Spencer Hockey Foundation. When he talked to Anita Patterson about his idea to create a memorial for her father, she was touched and thrilled. He knew he wouldn't be the man he was today without Coach, and as he described it to DeeDee, it was a chance to pay the efforts of his mentor forward in a meaningful way.

He waved across ice for Lee to take over, waiting for his acknowledgment before he turned to walk up the stands. He had offered Lee the foundation manager's position once he knew his dream would become a reality, and his friend had gladly accepted. It was a way to both put his degree to use and keep hockey in his life, just like Jase had wanted...needed for himself. Taking the wide strides required to move from seat to seat up into the stands, he walked up to where Bingo and Tyler were sitting.

Turning to settle beside Tyler, he leaned back, propping his elbows on the bench behind them. "Didja come early to watch Kane? He's gonna be a monster; look at that swish. Falls down, he bounces right back up. Natural player. I noticed he favors left. We'll have to work on making him skate both directions; can't favor the dominant side." He was rambling, because he had been shocked when he got a good look at Bingo. Every time he saw him, the man looked worse than before.

"Brother," Bingo interrupted, and Jase went silent with a sucked in breath. He still wasn't used to the greeting from the Rebel members, but it gave him a thrill of pleasure every time he heard it spoken. Bingo continued talking, and at his words, Jase drew in another breath, but this one in dismay. "I'm sick. Kids need a place to crash for a few days while I get checked out. Think you and DeeDee could help out?"

"Yes," he said without hesitation. He knew all nine of the kids, had five of them signed up for skate classes. Tyler was the oldest, and there was a span between the kids, because the youngest was about four. Even though he knew he would be bringing home a huge distraction and disruption to their household, he also knew he didn't even have to check with DeeDee for her opinion. Bingo had been her husband's best friend, practically family in that right alone, and she would do anything for him. "When do you have to go in?"

"Tonight. I didn't know until a little bit ago," he said apologetically.

"No matter. We got you, brother," Jase answered, reaching out to ruffle Tyler's hair. The boy's face was set in somber lines, and he looked afraid. It was no wonder, because after losing his mother to cancer and dealing with his own illness, having his uncle get sick would be frightening. "Tyler, go see if Dugger needs some help. I think those kids are about to kick his ass."

Cutting him a grateful look, Tyler stood and made his way down the stands. Stepping onto the ice in his tennis shoes, he slipped a little, but then flatfooted it across the rink to where Lee was standing against the boards. Jase didn't say anything, figuring if Bingo wanted a chance to talk, he at least had created the opportunity.

The man cleared his throat, his voice hoarse with emotion. "Lung, before you ask. Doc thinks he caught it early. They're going to do a biopsy in the morning. I'll be out in a day unless something goes wrong. If it's what the doc expects, they'll cut out the one part, and I'll be back to normal in a few weeks." He shifted on the hard seat. "Thanks for this, man. The kids all like DeeDee, and most of them tolerate you pretty well."

Jase grinned over at him. "It'll be a hardship for her, I'm sure," he joked, and Bingo smiled back at him, both knowing she would love the hell out of having a full house of kids.

Leaning back on his elbows, matching Jase's pose, Bingo said, "Did she ever tell you she and Winger wanted a bunch of kids? The man wouldn't shut up about it for years until everyone realized they couldn't stay pregnant. Then you could tell he still wanted them, but quit talking about it to save her feelings." He shook his head. "I loved my sister, but it always chapped my ass that a poor excuse for a mother like her could keep popping out babies, but DeeDee—" He trailed off, clearing his throat again.

"She'll enjoy having kids in the house," Jase said. "I'll give her a call in a minute and we'll get everything sorted before you get there. I can bring Kane with me, but do you need some help packing up and transporting the rest of the little monsters?"

"Naw, Tyler and Megan, the two oldest, are a big help. We'll bring clothes and toys and shit, so they can amuse themselves as much as possible. Shouldn't be but a couple of days." Bingo stood, not looking at Jase as he spoke. "Not asking you to keep this to yourself anymore, brother. I gotta be man enough to admit when I need help, or I'm not a good example for the boy. I can't do this one alone."

He stepped carefully down the seats, the leather of his cut creaking with the movement. Reaching the mats that surrounded the boards, he motioned towards Tyler, and when the boy reached him, slung an arm around his shoulders as they walked out, lifting his hand in a two-fingered wave at Lee.

Jase dug into his pocket and brought out his phone. Taking a deep breath, he called DeeDee and filled her in on the fundamental logistics of the coming evening. He touched on what to expect over the next couple of days, promising he would explain everything once he got home with Kane. Then he dialed a number from memory, smiling at Mason's gruff response.

"Mason, need to bring you in the loop on something," he began, his calmness stemming from a sure confidence that the club would be there to support Bingo and the kids.

24 - Houseguests

"Baby, can you get the door?" Jase called from the kitchen, where he was in the middle of packing four school lunches. Hearing what he assumed was an affirmative response, he continued to focus on the baggies of raw vegetables and chips he was tucking into the chill and non-chill areas of the insulated lunch bags the kids liked.

Bingo's biopsy had gone well, and the results showed about what the doctors had expected. He had come to stay with them after that procedure, and when his surgery had been scheduled within a week, it only made sense for the kids to stay, so they had been installed with him and DeeDee since then. Still in the hospital, Bingo was on the recovery side of the operation, but still weak and grouchy. The plan was for him to be released within a couple of days, and Jase hoped he would be coming back to their house for a while.

"Okay, did you guys get socks on today before you put on the shoes?" He looked over his shoulder at the table full of kids eating breakfast. "I'm not even asking for matching socks, eh? Just socks before shoes. Gimme a positive confirmation now, sound off." He joked with the kids and received a few snickers of laughter from his method of garnering a response.

"Jase," DeeDee called from the living room, her voice raised over muted conversation from that direction.

"Yeah, babe?" he called, closing the lunch bags and lining them up on the floor next to the corresponding child's book bag. "Lunches are all done; I'll go online and add money to the high school account once the kids are out the door. We have a serious problem this morning, though. Baby, no one will tell me the state of their feet, whether socked or not. It's scandalous; I know kids need to wear socks. Hey, did you know that one kids' store sells socks in three-sock sets? They don't even try to go for pairs anymore. That's genius, based on what I've experienced over the past few days.

He sighed. "Socks and bunnies, who knew they could be so hard to find once lost? But I promise Duchess Penelope shall be found." He put his hand on his chest. "I do hereby pledge to go on a bunny hunt today. Duchess Penny of Notahamburger will be located." He squatted down, looking through the papers in the little kids' backpacks to make sure they had all their homework. Straightening, he recognized the voices raised in laughter at the front of the house, and he turned in surprise.

"Ma!" Striding across the room with arms out, he swept his mother up into a hug then turned to his father. "Da," he thumped his back and then pulled back, "what are you doing in the States?" He looked back at his mother. "When did you decide to come visit?"

Without giving her a chance to answer him, he frowned, shaking his head, asking, "Ma, did your phone break again? You need to stop watching those reality shows. They steal all your reason. Then you throw the phone, eh? Your phone musta broke, eh? Otherwise, why would you not have called?" He looked past them to where DeeDee was hovering close behind his mother. When he caught sight of her outstretched arm leading to their linked hands, he smiled, thinking with a silent laugh, *Trust Ma to make sure she got her hands on DeeDee right away.*

Stepping towards DeeDee, he deftly unwound their hands, taking both of hers in his. *Take the shot*, he thought, pulling her in for a soft brush of his lips against hers. Turning her in his arms to face his parents and the suddenly quiet table of kids, he wrapped himself around her, pulling her close and whispering, "Love you, babe. Breathe, okay? It's all right. It's only my folks, and according to Ma, they already love you."

Her hair teased the side of his face as she nodded, and he let his lips drift across her cheek to her ear. He whispered loudly, "If we run, we can get away. We don't even have to move fast; Da's knee is junk, so no way he can keep up with us. Hmm. Maybe he'll be valuable fodder to have around in a zombie apocalypse, though. Remember what we learned from that show? Keep the country kids around, and you don't have to be the fastest runner, just not the slowest. Maybe we should stick around, eh? Just in case? Zombies, eh?"

She laughed aloud at his teasing and he pulled back, pleased with the composure and joy he saw on her features. Between his mother and him, they somehow managed to reassure her enough, giving her confidence in his love for her...in them. He took a deep breath, feeling a tension he didn't even know he was carrying begin to fall away from him, leaving him feeling light and happy. In his normal voice, he introduced the two sides of his family for the first time. "DeeDee Moser, this is Jacque and Kenny Spencer. Ma and Da, meet the love of my life." At her inrush of breath, he tightened his arms and shook her lightly, reminding her, "Breathe, baby."

Lifting a hand, he pointed at the table. "Rugrats, these are my parents. You can call them...well...basically, anything. Especially Da, he'll answer to anything, as long as there's food involved." The kids laughed, and the littlest girl gave his mother a shy wave before picking up her cereal spoon studiously.

He gave a brief explanation, figuring they could go into more detail later if needed. "The kids belong to a friend who's in the hospital, so they're staying with us for a bit." He looked at the clock on the microwave. "And if they don't put a hustle on it, every one of the monsters is going to miss the bus." He released DeeDee, clapping his hands loudly. "Do not leave this house without socks on your feet. Teeth, hair, clean faces...all are optional. Socks are mandatory. It's a mandate. A mandatory mandate on tubes of material covering your appendages."

DeeDee pushed past him, holding out her hand to Jacque. "Let me show you where you can put your bags." His mother shook her head at DeeDee, deftly avoiding her hand in order to pull her into a tight embrace. "We'll stay at a hotel, sweetie, but I can promise you we'll be here early and late so you can get to know us well. These children are precious." At a glowering glance from Tyler, she amended her statement, "Precious *and* devastatingly handsome. Take care of your morning routine. I'm going to make myself at home and get some coffee." Jase held his breath, watching DeeDee's arms encircle his mother's waist passively at first. As she became more convinced the affection was real, her hands moved up Jacque's back and her shoulders rounded in as she visibly relaxed into his mother's hug.

Lips to her ear, his mother whispered something to DeeDee, and he could barely see her lips enough to read, "We already love you. I'm so glad to meet you, sweetheart."

***

"Oh, shut it, Jase," his mother said without compassion. He put on a fake-wounded expression.

"All I asked was if you thought through this plan of yours, Ma. First, you drop in on DeeDee and me without warning, not giving her a chance to think before reacting—"

His mother interrupted him. "And it's a good thing we did, isn't it? She was forced to meet us and accept that what she saw as an enormous barrier in your relationship is less than the smallest bump. If she hadn't seen it on our faces, she would have continued to wonder if we were paying lip service to liking and accepting her." She brought her hand up, cupping his jaw.

"Jase, I understand what you see in her, son. The two of you fit together in a way I never expected. I always wanted you to find someone to love, but didn't realize the extent of what you'd find, and I am so glad you did. The fit between the two of you is seamless and fine, and I'm happy for both of you." Her voice changed in tone. "But, I'm not going to let you distract me from my next mission. I haven't seen my daughter for too long, Jase. I will see her, either here if you call her to come over with her new man, or at his house. The map on my phone says I can be there in about 10 minutes, and I'll give you half that to help decide how this happens. But, son? I will see her."

He looked at his father, leaning against the cabinets on the far side of the kitchen, but the man shook his head. Jase knew he would get no help from that quarter. "Sharon's different, Ma. She's changed," he said, and she nodded.

"To be expected, she's grown up on her own, so she'll be her own person. But underneath that, she's always going to be my daughter. I'm not looking for the eighteen-year-old girl who struck out on her own, Jase. I'm not stupid. I'm looking to know the woman she's become, but I can't do that if I can't talk to her, see her...listen to her. So call her now, or I'll just be waiting in their driveway for them to come home." She placed her balled-up fists on her hips, elbows akimbo. With her head tilted impatiently, all that was missing was the tapping of her toe to complete the impression of anxious frustration.

"Okay," he capitulated, making a face, "but we do this my way, okay? I'll make a couple calls, get the ball rolling, and then Shar gets to say where." His mother nodded, and he saw his father relax minutely. Pulling out his phone, he called Slate first, explaining the situation and giving him a quick update on Bingo as of this morning. Likely Goose had already checked in, but he felt responsible for Bingo and the kids, especially since the man had come to him for help.

Slate agreed with his plan, so his next call was to Gunny. Since Sharon had healed enough to move, he had kept her with him nearly twenty-four/seven, especially after they were taken. His obsession with her didn't seem to be easing, but Jase and Slate had talked about it and they agreed that it looked more like a burgeoning relationship than anything else. It was clear to anyone who saw them together that Sharon was comfortable with the man in a way that couldn't be faked, especially given her recent experiences. Jase shook his head and dialed the phone.

"Yeah," came the gruff response, and Jase called the image of Gunny to mind. Tall, at well more than six feet, the man was thick and solid with muscle.

"Sharon's parents are in town. They would like to see her. I want to give her the chance to pick the locat—" The call disconnected and he pulled the phone away from his ear, looking down at it in surprise. His service was usually reliable on this side of town, and he never had a call drop in the condo before.

He dialed the number again and heard a roaring noise he recognized as a motorcycle engine before Gunny said, "We're on our way." The call disconnected again, but he grinned this time, turning to see his parents hovering in the kitchen doorway.

"She'll be here soon," he said and watched as his mother covered her mouth with a hand, holding in a sob of relief.

***

Later that night, as he lay in bed beside DeeDee, her head pillowed on his shoulder, there was a quiet stirring in the hallway and he lifted his head, seeing a silhouette in the door. "What is it, kiddo?" he asked, thinking it was one of the seven-year-old twins. When she spoke, he recognized Alicia's voice.

"Sissy had an accident." Her voice was sleepy, but not complaining. Gilda, the youngest, was still trying to stay dry at night, but she was only four.

"On my way, sweetheart. Do you need a dry nightgown?" he asked, knowing Gilda had probably crawled into bed with the twins when her own bed became uncomfortably cold and wet.

"Yessir," she said, yawning.

DeeDee shifted restlessly in the bed, and he quietly shooed the little girl out of the bedroom and down the hallway. "Let's get you taken care of. Is Patricia up, too?" He dragged on a shirt and scooped her up, letting her rest against his shoulder as he carried her back to the guest bedroom the girls all shared.

"Nope," she drawled, twisting her head to push into his neck trustingly in a way that made his heart stutter a little.

"Okay," he said, opening the linen closet and pulling out two sets of sheets. Grabbing the flashlight they left on the hallway table for this purpose, he turned it to the lowest setting before pushing the door wide. Crossing the room, he opened a drawer on the dresser and pulled out a clean nightgown for Alicia. Setting her on the floor, he handed it to her and pointed her in the direction of the Jack and Jill bathroom shared between these two guest bedrooms. "Clean up and change, baby. I'll have everything in here all fixed up before you know it."

"Yessir, Pappa Jase," she mumbled, and he had to swallow down the emotion that threatened to swamp him at the affectionate name the kids used for him. His nephews always called him Unka Jase, but Pappa Jase took things to an entirely new level.

He turned to see Gilda curled up on the edge of the twins' bed and smiled. Picking her up, he swaddled her in a blanket from the foot of the bed and settled her on the floor. Changing the sheet underneath Patricia was tricky without waking her, but he managed, and soon had

Alicia tucked back into bed alongside her sister, already beginning to drowse and nod off.

Changing the sheet on Gilda's bed, he silently thanked DeeDee for buying the mattress covers. He cleaned the child, changing her clothes and grinning to himself when she failed to wake, rolling limply back and forth as he tugged the nightclothes onto her body. Settling the little girl back into her bed, he had second thoughts and picked her up, carrying her into the bathroom. He set her on the toilet, gently waking her and waiting patiently until she had finished, before scooping her up and carrying her back to bed.

Sitting on the edge of the mattress, he slowly and gently stroked the child's back as she relaxed back into sleep, listening as her breathing grew deep and regular. A scuff on the carpeting came from behind him and he looked up, seeing DeeDee standing in the doorway with an odd expression. Tucking the covers around Gilda a little more tightly, he stood and walked to DeeDee, gathering up the soiled sheets and clothing as he went. Holding them in one hand, he reached out the other to wrap around her waist, but she was already moving back up the hallway away from him. *What the hell?* he thought, opening the closet and depositing the dirty laundry in the basket.

"Hey," he said, catching up to DeeDee as she crawled back into bed. She turned her back to him, and a shiver of trepidation crawled up his spine. Moving into place behind her, he reached out and wrapped his arms around her, tugging her backwards into him, feeling her shake with what he realized were silenced sobs. He whispered from beside her ear, "Baby, what's wrong?"

"You're so good with the kids," she said, her voice choked and under tight control.

"They're pretty easy to take care of. Unlike that damn bunny, but I promise I'm gonna find Penny. There can only be so many false poop trails." He was hoping to draw a laugh from her, but no luck. Her frame shook as she hiccupped and tried to sniff quietly. Rising on one elbow, he leaned over her, gripping her chin with his hand to bring her face to his. "Talk to me, baby. I can't know what's going on in that beautiful head of yours without your help."

Her voice was quiet and full of love when she said, "You are a perfect father, Jase. Patient, sweet, not squeamish, funny, loving," she laughed brokenly, "and tidy." He snorted, and she shook her head. "No, you are. I wish..." Her voice trailed off, but he wasn't going to let her get away with not completing that thought, because he knew where she was going with this and it was pissing him off.

"You wish...what, DeeDee?" His voice was firm and she stiffened. "What do you wish, baby?"

"I don't know," she whispered, but he shook his head.

"You do know, baby. Tell me," he urged. "Talk to me, beautiful; tell me what you're thinking...what you wish."

In a rush, she spoke, her words tumbling over each other, "What do I wish? Oh, baby, I wish I were thirty-two. I wish I could have children. Your children...our children. I don't understand how life could be so cruel, to position us with more than two decades between us. It's not the age difference that I hate; it's the fact I can't...couldn't..."

Her voice trailed off again, but it held the sound of the tears she was trying to hide, turning her head to the side to avoid his gaze. Jase felt a clenching in his chest, so incredibly sad for this woman who had so much love to give, but fate had stepped in to deny that love an adequate outlet.

"Baby," he said tenderly, hand cupping her jaw and turning her so he could look into her face. "How can I explain to you? If you want that, it's for you, not me. And if you want a baby, then we'll find a way. You're right. I enjoy being around the kids, and I'm glad we can be here for them, but wanting a baby is not me." He shook his head then grew still, struck by a thought.

"Do you love Ruby?" he asked, waiting for her answer.

"Yes, of course, I do," she said, frowning up at him.

"You love her? You're sure?" he asked again.

"Yes, Jase. You know I do." Her frown deepened.

"But she's not yours," he argued lightly, pleased when he saw a wave of anger cross her face.

"Just because I didn't birth her, doesn't mean she's not mine. She's my daughter in all the ways that matter, Jase." She said this tartly, not even realizing she had fallen into his plan.

"I know," he breathed, kissing her nose. "She *is* your daughter. Her babies are yours...ours. Because of love, not birth, sweetheart."

"It's not the same and you know it." Now she sounded pissed, and he wasn't sure what he had stepped in, but it looked to be painful and old, profound in a way that had caused hurt for a long time.

"If I said I love Tyler, would you tell me I didn't know what it was like to love a son?" He wasn't sure this was the question he wanted to ask, because it hinted at how much that kid had gotten under his skin. Hell, all the kids, but he wasn't yet ready to examine those emotions.

"But he isn't yours, Jase. He's not your blood. For men, it's different." She said this with so much authority that if he had been any less sure of how he felt, his faith in himself might have been shaken.

"Not for me," he said, shaking his head. "He's a good kid, sunny disposition, even in the face of overwhelming odds and problems. He's smart and funny, deeply loyal to his brothers and sisters. He's exactly what I would want in a son. It doesn't matter if he has my nose, looks like me, or shares my genes. What matters is the person I could help him become and how he could change me." He looked at her, raising one eyebrow in question. "Where did you hear that bullshit about 'for men, it's different'?"

There was a pained, guttural sound as her breath caught in her throat, and he suddenly realized what had happened. Before she could say anything, he dragged her against him, holding her close with his arms, legs twining between hers, comforting her with the close press of his entire body against her. "Oh, baby. My love, DeeDee. You wanted to adopt, didn't you? You wanted kids so badly, a child you could love and raise, a child you could watch grow. A little person. A child you could watch as they developed a sense of self and independence—and Winger didn't want to, right? He turned down the idea out of hand, because the child wouldn't be his blood, because he couldn't see that child as being his."

She nodded, arms tight around him and hands fisted in his hair and shirt, drawing him even closer as he continued speaking, "He had Lockee, the perfect combination of him and you, and for him, that was enough. So you made do, right? He probably had no idea how much it hurt you, and being who you are, you made do."

He had a sudden flash of memory from the party for Mica and Mason, how DeeDee had circled out and back all night long. She talked to so many people, encouraging them and loving on them in turn, gently chastising the ones who were stepping out of line, and lavishly praising the ones who weren't. "You loved the club instead, didn't you? You loved Melanie...Ruby, of course, because she and Lockee were joined at the hip, but you also love every member of the club like they are your own."

He marveled at the depths of love this woman had in her body and soul for so many people. "That's why you've stayed part of the club, because they truly are your family. You love to hear about their successes and you grieve for their losses, because they are yours. I get it, baby. You have so much love to give. We have Ruby's babies, Bear's kiddos, and now Bingo's tribe, and you can love on them. Oh, baby, I think they are going to be our tribe. I have an idea," he whispered the last against her neck, holding her and letting her cry against his chest. "Shhhhh. I love you, baby. I have an idea," he repeated, rubbing his jaw up along her cheek to drop soft kisses on her temple.

***

"Tell the truth," he said, a frown on his face as he looked down at DeeDee. He held her loosely in his arms as he leaned against the counter in the kitchen. It was the next morning, and the kids were already off to school. His parents hadn't yet shown up at the apartment, and he and DeeDee were slow to start the day. They talked for hours last night, turning and twisting his idea every way they could think of, finally coming to an agreement. Heady with their joint plan, he made love to her, worshiping every inch of her as he loved to do, drawing responses from her, even in her exhausted state. They fell asleep twisted around each other, sheets damp with sweat and the air in the room heavy with the scent of sex.

"Okay," she said easily, smiling up at him. "What's the question?"

"Do you prefer to ride your own bike, or behind me?"

She blinked and shook her head. "Sometimes on my own, but sometimes with you. Why are you asking?"

"I don't think I need two bikes," he said and watched as the mask he so hated settled into place on her face. "Dammit, don't do that," he scolded, leaning in to kiss her lips hard, slanting his mouth across hers again and again until they were both breathless.

"Don't do what?" she asked, biting her bottom lip softly.

"Don't give me your club face." He realized he said this in a grouchy tone and wrinkled his nose at himself. "Sometimes you work so hard to not show reactions it makes me crazy. I say, 'I don't think I need two bikes', and you freeze up. Why?"

Her gaze dropped to his chest and she licked her lips nervously. "If you get rid of one…which one? What one are you going to keep?"

"Do you have a preference, baby?" he asked, dragging his nose along her neck, nibbling his way down to her collarbone, kissing and licking along her skin.

"Mmmmm. Keep the Bobber," she said breathlessly, arching her neck.

"Okay, baby. Why the Bobber?" He bent his head, nipping at the top curve of her breast with his teeth.

"Just get rid of the other bike," she said, fingers threading through his hair.

"Keep the Bobber I bought from Road Runner?" he asked again, making sure, slipping one hand down to cup her ass, pulling her tightly against him.

"Yeah, Road Runner is a good guy. That bike has a lot of good memories." She pulled his head closer, urging him wordlessly to continue fondling her breasts.

"Get rid of Winger's bike?" He tugged at her nipple through her clothing, squeezing her ass tightly.

"Yeah, sell that motherfucker," she whispered, her head falling back, and he lifted her, setting her ass on the countertop.

"Okay," he said, fingers working to unbutton the waistband of her jeans and his other hand pushing her shirt over her head. He leaned forward to suckle her breast through the fabric of her bra, biting her nipple sharply then drawing it into the heat of his mouth again. He tugged her towards the edge of the counter, telling her, "Wrap your legs around me, baby." Picking her up, he cupped her ass in his hands and carried her to their bedroom. Having gotten the answer he was looking for, he went in search of a response of a different sort, eventually finding that one, too.

25 - Memories

"Dammit, Bingo, of course I knew. I also knew you didn't want anyone fucking around in your goddamn business, so I stayed out of it. I made sure we took care of the club, freeing you to take care of your family. Doesn't change the fact I'm pissed as hell that you didn't trust me with the information without me pulling it out of you like teeth. We're family too, brother." Mason stretched out his hand, gripping Bingo's shoulder.

Bingo reached up, wrapping his fingers around Mason's wrist. "I know, Prez. It just felt like I failed you. You trusted me with a chapter, and I fucked it up, let the trash in that nearly destroyed our brothers. Put you in a dangerous place with other clubs. Every way I could twist that bitch, I torqued it right over. But I had to take care of the kids."

Mason nodded. "I know, brother. There's no anger from me to you, and no disappointment, either. I know you hold the club close, and always have." He leaned in, cupping the side of Bingo's head, and pulled the man over so he could roughly kiss the top of his head. "Love you, man."

Bingo laughed, cuffing Mason's shoulder and pulling away. "No mushy shit, motherfucker. Save that for the ladies."

Jase was glad to see there was no anger on the old man's face. He had come to like Bingo, and if he was pissed because he talked to Mason, even if he had given permission in a roundabout way, there would be some guilt. But it looked like everything was going to be okay between them.

Bingo looked over at Jase and grinned, teeth shining in the middle of his thick, gray beard. "Cap'n, thank you, man. Appreciate what you're doing for my kids."

Jase made a face and nodded. "Want to talk to you about that." He saw Bingo's eyes narrow and a grin light Mason's face, the dichotomy of the expressions making him laugh aloud. Mason knew what was coming, but he had to sell Bingo on the idea.

"My parents are visiting from up north. They've decided they want to set up a home base here, since both Shar and I are sticking in the Fort. Myron found DeeDee and me a house that's both hella nice and a lot larger, so the club is moving us tomorrow and my folks are taking over the condo." He sighed, because that was the easy part.

"DeeDee and I want you and the kids to move in with us, brother. I know your prognosis, Bingo. You didn't send me out of the room when the doc came in this morning, so you know I know. You have more surgeries on the horizon, and this isn't going to be an easy road to ride. Let me help you. You're not only my friend, you are my brother, and I need to do this. Let me be there for the kids. For you.

He took a breath, because Bingo's expression was shuttered, unreadable. "Give this to DeeDee, man. She loves you like family, and you know the truth of that. She's already kicking herself that she didn't see what was going on with Tyler, that she wasn't there for you when that all went down. She loves you so much—let her love on you, brother."

Bingo held his gaze for a long moment, and then slowly nodded. A grin quirked up one corner of his mouth, lips curling in amusement. "Woman gets her baseball team this way, too, right?"

"Fuck yeah," Jase chortled. "She's already talking about how much fun it will be to have what amounts to a second clubhouse for family activities." The smile fell away. "She said it will remind her of how it was in the early days with Winger, when the club was over all the time. She liked that, feeling central to everything. I think she's missed it since she moved out of the clubhouse."

Mason lifted his chin. "The house got a big backyard? That's a requirement, so if Myron fucked that up, I'll have words with the man."

"Biggest backyard I've ever seen." Jase laughed. "I already have my eye on a grill, man. Kids get to mow, though. Fuck that shit."

They all laughed and Bingo reached out his hand. Gripping his forearm, Jase shook it once then leaned in as Bingo tugged on his arm. Wrapping his other around Jase's neck, he pulled him close, whispering in his ear, "Thank you, brother."

Jase hugged him back, saying, "You got it, man."

***

When she calmed, her sobs trailing off to softly hiccupped sounds that gradually diminished, he pulled back, looking down into her face. They were getting ready to go to a benefit for Bingo being held at Checkerz, when Jase had asked her again why she and Winger hadn't adopted. The question had been so unexpected it triggered an uncontrollable emotional response that he tried to comfort and soothe away. She attempted to cover her face with her hand, but he captured her wrist in one hand and pulled it away. "Baby, did he know how much it meant to you?" She shook her head, not answering aloud.

"What's getting you so wound up?" he asked, and she shook her head again, not yet trusting her voice. "DeeDee," he said, "if you don't want to donate the bike, we won't."

Rolling her eyes, she pulled free and used the back of her hand to wipe her nose in an unladylike fashion. "It's not the bike." Her voice squeaked a little to begin with, but evened out as she continued. "Any sentiment I had for that bike was tied up in being Winger's old lady. I told Slate a long time ago that I was ready to move on, and I am. I have been, with you."

"If someone from Fort Wayne buys it, you'll be okay seeing someone else riding the bike? That's the reason I bought it at the last auction, you know. I couldn't stand to see someone else riding what I thought of at the time as *your* bike." He smoothed her hair away from her face with his palms, gently rubbing their noses together. "I didn't want to see anyone straddling the seat that I'd seen your ass resting on for so many miles."

She murmured, "Jealous of a bike, Cap'n?"

"No, but buying the bike made me feel a little closer to you. You sure you're willing to give up this big a piece of Winger?" He tilted his head, looking at her, and she felt exposed, on display, afraid he would see the disillusionment on her face.

"I'm ready to move on," she repeated her words, hoping he would drop the topic. "Jase, are we nearly—"

"You're angry with Winger." He uttered the words like a statement, and she froze, unwilling to either deny or acknowledge the truth of what he said. He continued in a relaxed, conversational tone, "Furious with him. Baby, why would you be mad at him? You loved him."

"Past tense. Loved being the operative word." Her mouth was open with the sounds falling out of it before she realized what she had done. Shaking her head, she tried to step backwards, but Jase locked his arms around her, holding her into place. *In for a penny, in for a pound,* she thought. *Might as well get this all out into the open.* "I've come to realize that maybe things could have been different if he had been willing to bend a little. To give me just a little. He was older than me, and I was so young when we got together. It was natural for him to take on the role he did, and the club reinforced that position every day. I think I loved him because I didn't know anything else."

Jase made a brief raspberry noise, shaking his head. "You loved him because he loved you."

"I've begun to wonder about that, too." She laughed harshly, tipping her head to the side and leaning her forehead against his chest. "Did he really love me? If he had, wouldn't he have cared if he made me happy?"

He tensed his arms around her, pulling her tightly into his chest. She turned her head, pressing her ear against him, listening to the steady, calming beats of his heart. He sighed softly then asked her, "Didn't he make you happy?"

"In the moment, he did. But looking back..." She stopped when he tensed.

"Baby," he said softly, "in the moment is all we have. It's all we'll ever have. We go moment to moment, in love, out of love, together, apart...it's all in the moment. Even a love like what I have for you—so strong I know it exists beyond us standing here—is still me loving you moment to moment. He loved you, and you know it. Best as he could, he loved you. He didn't want to leave you, never meant to be gone so soon. Don't be angry with him. Don't second-guess his love for you. And baby, never, ever second-guess mine."

They stood like that for a long time as she rested there in his arms, considering everything he said. It made sense, and actually...what did her anger gain her? It wasn't as if she could run out and ask Winger why he had done this thing or that thing. What they had...was real. She had loved him. And she loved Jase, now. She remained silent, soaking up what he said, her tears renewing, because all the anger she had been cultivating against Winger was gone. Jase had swept it away.

After a few minutes, he stirred against her and said, "I can't take his place, baby. I wouldn't even know how to try. He made such an impression on so many people; I can see why you'd love him. How you grew to love him. And I have no doubts he loved you, too." He paused, leaning his forehead against hers. "Keep that feeling, baby. He loved you."

26 - Coach

Lee shook his head. "I think I'm a better fit for the more advanced kids."

Jase snorted a laugh. They were at the foundation office, trying to determine who would be responsible for teaching the different classes. It was apparent Lee had taken a liking to Tyler, so he was determined to be the one to teach the kid. It didn't surprise Jase, and he didn't entirely disagree with Lee, but if things went down the way he was afraid they were going to with Bingo, he needed every bit of advantage he could get with the boy.

"What if we switch out, Tuesdays and Thursdays? You teach one, I get the other. That means we swap the little bits too, but they're the most fun." Jase tried to find a flaw. "Would it be confusing to the kids who are attempting to learn specific skills to have them taught by a different instructor half the time?"

"Nope, it will make them a more flexible and intuitive player," Lee said decisively. "It won't hurt the little bits, either. Begin as we intend to continue, yeah?"

"Yeah," he agreed. Pausing for a minute, he shuffled through the applications in the pile on his desk. "Hey, look at this kid," he said, holding one of the papers out to Lee. "He's pretty impressive. The Norwell coach called me, because he saw the kid playing inline hockey and he was killing it. I don't know if he's ever had skates on, but it sounds like he's got the natural skills. His family background fits our profile, too. Eight years old, he's in foster care, because his mom OD'ed, his dad was never named, and his only sibling was killed in a car wreck three years ago.

"I called Eddie," he said, then saw Lee look a question at him, and he explained. "She's the wife of one of the Rebels. You know Bear, right?" At Lee's nod, he continued, "She works with special needs kids, and I asked her to use her contacts in the system to find out what she could about the kid. He's been bounced around from foster to foster, and been flagged as 'troubled', whatever that means to an eight-year-old kid. Hell, he's had the whole world set against him since he was born. I think I would be 'troubled' too if I were him." He was pissed off on behalf of the boy all over again.

Lee looked at him with a confused look on his face. "Okay, so we give him a scholarship and get him into classes. If he's aggressive, it will give him an acceptable avenue to burn off that shit. If it's trouble of a different sort, we'll have to see what else we can do."

Jase laughed again. "No, not what I meant. I think DeeDee and I could foster this kid, see what kind of difference we could make. He wouldn't need a scholarship that way, so we can save it for a kid who'll need the financial help."

Visibly taken aback, Lee looked at Jase. "Foster parents? Are you kidding?"

He shook his head, smiling confidently. "Nope, not kidding. I've done my homework. There is an enormous need for foster homes, especially for kids who need extra attention. We've already passed the background checks and home visits when we were getting the paperwork done for Bingo's kids. Now that we have the larger place, it's all good…well, because it's all good. I'll leave it at that." He grinned at the bemused look on his friend's face.

His cell rang and he looked down, seeing Mason's name on the screen. Standing, he walked out of the office and into the conference room, closing the door for privacy. "Prez," he said in greeting, "did you…were you able to find out anything?"

"Yeah, Myron was able to track down the info. They put the DNA shit out there in some fucking database, so he was able to nab it and had a lab match things up. You were right about who his dad was. You sure you want to do this, man? This is a twisted cluster beyond anything I've ever seen. Now that we know…hell, Jase, it's more my shit to clear than yours, so you just gotta say the word and I've got it covered." Mason's concern for his family and friends was evident in his tone.

"No. I got this, Prez. I think it's the right thing to do. So, unless you can convince me otherwise, I'm moving forward." Jase let his certainty ring in his voice, ensuring Mason understood his commitment to this decision.

"Will you tell DeeDee?" Mason's inquiry indicated agreement with his plan, even though the question was followed by a heavy sigh.

"Yeah. I'll talk to her tonight before anything else goes forward. This knowledge is just for you, me, and Myron right now, right?" Jase wanted to control this, because he didn't want DeeDee hurt in the disclosure.

"Yeah, we've kept this close to the vest so far. There are people other than DeeDee who'll need to know, though." There was a noise in the background, and Mason said something indistinct then came back to the phone. "Fucking goddamn Skeptics, I'm going to kill someone today. I swear to fucking God. Gotta go; let me know how she takes it."

He stood in the conference room for a moment, tilting his head up, hand pulling at the back of his neck. Unsure how best to approach DeeDee with the information, he decided to play dirty and called the social worker they were working with. Within five minutes, he had approval to do what he proposed, and he prayed it wouldn't come back to bite him in the ass.

***

"Jonny," DeeDee said, coaxingly, "what grade are you in?"

Jase tilted his head. So far, the kid had been quiet, only answering questions with a brief yes or no. She was changing tactics, trying to draw him out gently. Looking into the kid's face, he could tell the social workers and foster care folks probably used the same tactics on him, and DeeDee, for all her good intentions, wasn't going to get squat-ala-Jara out of the kid this way.

He interrupted her, drawing the kid's eyes his way with a brusque, "I hated school."

DeeDee's mouth fell open, but Jonny nodded and said, "Right? All they ever want me to do is memorize stuff."

"That was the worst," Jase agreed. "But I liked hockey, and I had to have good enough grades to play."

"I want to play hockey, but the fosters can't swing it." He shrugged, looking down and picking at his plate of food.

"Sucks to want something and not have the power to make it happen." Jase nodded at the kid, picking up his burger and taking a huge bite. DeeDee was watching their exchange with interest, gaze switching between the two of them with each addition to the conversation.

"Life sucks, pretty much," the kid said, eyeing Jase's burger with interest. He had ordered the cheapest thing on the kid's menu, but apparently didn't much care for the nuggets and fries.

Without a word, Jase set his burger down and cut it in half, putting the half without the bite marks on the kid's plate. He stole the nuggets and popped them into his mouth one at a time, grinning widely. Once he was sure he had the kid's attention, he did the biggest, grossest 'show me' with the half-chewed food in his mouth, sticking out his tongue and pulling a loud laugh from the boy, smiling to see his steel grey eyes sparkling. Propping one elbow on the back of the booth, he looked over at DeeDee and saw her trying and failing to hide a smile behind her sandwich.

After dinner, they went to the rink, and he had DeeDee help Jonny put on skates and lace them. He watched from the ice as she gave the boy her arms to grip when he stood, wobbling on his weak ankles as he watched Jase intently. Jase was speeding around the rink, weaving back and forth, flipping from forwards to backwards, skating with the ease born of long experience. Jonny shouted at Jase, "Why's it feel so different from inline?"

"The blade's narrower than wheels, so your balance is altered, uses different muscles," he shouted back, not slowing down.

Watching from the corner of his eye, he saw DeeDee step onto the ice with her boots and winced. She would be going down at some point; leather soles and ice were a dangerous combination. Walking backwards, she led Jonny onto the slippery surface gingerly while he tried tentative pushing movements that probably worked with wheels on pavement, but just slid the blades uselessly back and forth on the ice.

Slowing down, he slid to a near stop next to DeeDee and reached out a hand. "Grab the boards, Jonny," he said, and saw the boy do as he was told, a sure balance returning as his wobbly support was replaced by one that didn't move or give. He leaned over, wrapped his arms around DeeDee, and lifted, pulling a squeal from her as her feet left the ice. "Baby, you're gonna fall with those boots. Lemme get you back to safety."

He lifted his head, shouting to the empty rafters, "Safety crew coming through! Watch out. Make way. Got a safety violation to deal with. Violations of safety to deal with. Watch out." Making loud ooougah noises, he skated once around the rink with her in his arms then deposited her gently on her feet at the gate. Kissing her nose before skating away backwards, he made loud 'beep' noises, like he was a truck backing out of a parking space. She laughed, and he grinned at her, looking around to see Jonny was away from the boards, slowly finding his feet on the ice.

"Good job, kiddo. It's kinda the same, but different. Hard to describe, but easy to feel, yeah?" The boy nodded, concentrating on keeping his feet underneath him. "Keep doing just that, kiddo. We've got as much time here as we need. Take it slow, keep it safe, and have fun." Skating over to where DeeDee was sitting on the bench, he turned and sat next to her.

"I have a confession, baby," he said softly, without looking at her. He reached out and picked up her hand, threading his fingers through hers. "I have an ulterior motive with this kid."

She made a questioning noise and he nodded. "Yeah, I know, big surprise, right? So, bear with me, 'cause I've got a story to tell."

He cleared his throat and quietly said, "Eight years ago, a young man was sent to Fort Wayne so he could watch out for his sister. Being young and stupid, and probably angry, he didn't watch where he dipped his wick, and he had a hookup that wound up pregnant. She already had a daughter, about eleven years old. When he realized what had happened, he freaked out, because his father would kill him for what he had done. See, he was the result of an affair his old man had, and it had nearly destroyed his family." DeeDee took a breath, apparently recognizing who he was talking about, and he nodded.

"Yeah, I get you recognize the player, but let me tell you the whole story before you ask questions, okay?" She nodded, and he squeezed her hand, bringing it over to lay on his thigh.

"So no dad in the picture, a junkie mom, and a sister who tried to take care of too much, Jonny was born. When he was five, a neighbor saw him sitting outside on the apartment steps, crying. The weather wasn't bad, so she didn't think much of it, until several hours later, when she saw him still sitting in the same place. She went over and asked him what he was doing, and he told her that his mommy was sick. She took one look in the apartment and realized Mommy was much worse than sick." He cleared his throat, eyes tracking Jonny's progress around the rink. He smiled briefly when the boy nearly fell but recovered, then his expression sobered.

"She left him sitting there and went back to her house. She texted his sister, who was barely sixteen, had just gotten her license, and was driving home from work. The text said, ***I think your mom's dead. Come home***. No one knows if the sister read the text and reacted emotionally, or was trying to respond, but she lost control of her vehicle." He looked over to see tears rolling steadily down DeeDee's face. "Baby, I—"

She shook her head fiercely and took a breath. "Finish it. Tell me the rest, okay?"

He nodded, squeezing her hand. "She swerved into Winger's vehicle. It was hours before anyone sorted out that there was a little brother. By the time the cops got to the apartment, he had been outside for probably ten hours, sitting outside while Mommy was 'sick' inside." He paused, because DeeDee made a choked noise, but she waved him on.

"No father, dead mother, dead sister. Jonny hit the foster care system. He's been through eleven placements in three years. He can't go on like that. He's a good kid, but he needs stability and love, or he's going to be fucked up beyond all hope. DeeDee...baby, he's Judge's son, Mason's great-nephew. Your cousin. John Justice Morgan, your blood.

Baby, can we love him? Can we be his family?" His chest hitched with tightly held emotion. When he was putting all the puzzle pieces together, this had seemed like a good idea, but now his mind was whirling, questioning his actions. *What if it hurt her worse? What if she decides it's not—* He gasped as her arm wrapped around him, her head nestling underneath his chin.

"Yes." She whispered the word, then sniffed loudly and laughed. "Just...yes. I need a bathroom. Back in a minute." She moved to get up and then paused. "How much does he know?"

"Who you are to him? About what went down a few weeks ago? Zippo right now. We can tell him everything...or nothing. It's your call, baby. He knows his sister's accident hurt another family, and it bothers him a lot; his counselor made notes in his file about that. He's a good kid, but he's all alone and needs someone who gets him." He paused for a second, and then said, "I get him. I don't know why, but I get him. You saw that, right? At dinner? There's a connection, baby. He and I...we fit together in a way I never expected. I think I need this kid more than he needs us."

She reached up and put her palms on either side of his face, pulling his lips down to meet hers. "I did, Jase. And yes, there is a connection; it's not your imagination. He communicated to you with words, and then without them. You get him." She kissed him again. "Yes, make a call and get it done. I never want him to wonder if he's loved again. Just...yes." She sniffed and shook her head, smiling through her tears.

27 - Coming home

DeeDee looked around the lower floor of the house from where she stood in the kitchen, taking in the sweating bodies lifting and moving boxes and furniture. Most of the men had removed their shirts, and if she weren't a one-man woman, she would be drooling over the view right now. *Hell, I'm not dead*, she thought. *I can still enjoy the show, just won't be going back to the dressing room with any of the players.*

"Baby?" Jase's voice called her name from upstairs, and she stepped out into the living room to look up at the third-floor landing, where she saw his head sticking over the rail.

"Yeah?" He had Jonny next to him, and the little boy had something in his hands. The something was squirming...

"You allergic to cats?" Jase asked, and she knew what the dark bundle was.

"No, but if it pees in my shoes, it's out of here. And it has to leave Penny alone; bunny is not on the kitty's menu." He nodded and squatted down next to Jonny, talking earnestly to the boy. He reached out and ruffled his hair, and her heart stuttered a minute, seeing that intimate moment of affection. The man was made for this. Loving all these kids was instinctive for him, and she was amazed at how that touched her. "Jase," she called up, and he turned his head, looking at her between the banisters. "I love you," she said, and he grinned.

"Crazy lady, I love you, too." He shook his head and stood, walking back up the hallway and out of sight, one hand on Jonny's shoulder, that simple, loving touch bringing tears to her eyes.

"DeeDee, where you want this stuff, honey?" Tug asked from beside her, and she turned to see him holding a box that had 'Winger' written on it in black marker.

She reached out a hand, tracing a heart over the name, then stepped back and told Tug, "Attic. Everything from the storage building can just go straight up to the attic. Get the boys to sort them by labels though, so I can find things I need for the kitchen and stuff."

"Good enough, pretty lady." He leaned in and kissed her cheek, and she laughed as that damn mustache tickled her like always.

She walked back into the kitchen, taking in the platter of half-made sandwiches, and grinned. She had missed this, the hustle-bustle of having dozens of people to care for, the chance to catch up with her boys about their lives, wives, and kids. The connections that made the club a family may have slipped for a little while, but damned if she would ever let them go.

Sighing, she picked up the bread and was laying out slices in preparation for another layer of sandwiches when two arms bracketed her, bracing on the countertop on either side of her hips. She looked down, seeing the familiar tattoos, her gaze tracing the phoenix rising from the back of the left hand in flames to the glory of the mythical bird, raised from ashes. His other arm had a new tattoo, and she looked carefully at the inside of his wrist.

"New ink?" she asked, pulling his arm up so she could see it closely. There were two closely spaced lines of text, followed by three initials, and she smiled. "*Fear and Loathing*? Davy, I didn't know you were a Thompson fan."

He laughed. "I haven't been called that name in years, Dee. Yeah. Gunny gave me a present, and this seemed a good way to mark the occasion."

"I heard about the Vincent. Damn sweet ride. Wish the man loved me like that. I would get rid of my Sportster in a heartbeat if he had something lighter and easier to handle." She jumped when a voice came from behind them, and Mason's chest rumbled with laughter at her reaction.

"I think I have something in my cache, DeeDee. I'll look it over when I get home. Give Captain a call, okay?" She turned to see Gunny leaning against the archway between the kitchen and living room, Jase's sister Sharon nestled against his body, both his arms circling her shoulders where she stood in front of him.

"Goddammit, Gunny. Stop sneaking up on me," she scolded with a smile. Reaching out a hand to Sharon, she pulled her out of the man's arms and into a tight hug. "Shar, sweetheart, it's good to see you." Stepping back, she looked down. "I need some help getting food ready for this crew. Want to help?"

Seeing the look of relief that flashed across her features, she knew she had read things right. Sharon was nervous about being here, and DeeDee wanted Jase's sister to be comfortable around her, because even if DeeDee was the boss and de facto sister-in-law, she still wanted to be friends. Mason greeted Gunny, and she listened as the two men moved out into the house, looking for ways to assist in the move.

She handed the lunchmeat and cheese containers to Sharon, picking up the condiment dispensers she abandoned when Mason had come in. "Everyone eats anything, so just plunk a mix of meats and cheeses on the sandwiches. They'll care more about the quantity than the selection." She laughed. "Even the kids are easy. I swear Gilda, the littlest girl, would eat just the bread if you let her."

Shar ducked her head and DeeDee frowned slightly. "You're looking good, sweetie. Is Gunny taking good care of you?"

"Yeah," she said softly and bit her lip. "DeeDee, I have a question."

"Shoot." She reached up and pulled another platter from the top of the refrigerator, setting up for another assembly.

"Did your husband—" She bit her lip again, cutting her eyes over to DeeDee, interrupting herself when loud voices came from the front of the house.

"Sec, hon," DeeDee said, stepping out to look across the rooms. She smiled broadly, calling back to Sharon, "My babies are here."

Slate and Ruby were walking in, each with a child on their hip, bags in hand. Not moving, DeeDee just held out her arms, waiting as the couple brought her grandchildren to her. Scooping up first Dani then Allen for a snuggle and a kiss, she turned with both babies to Sharon. "Take one of these monsters, please."

With a smile, Shar took the rowdy little boy from her arms, dropping her face to his neck and blowing raspberries on his skin to draw a giggle from him. DeeDee raised her face for Slate's kiss on her cheek then leaned into Ruby's hug, laughing up at him when he pulled Ruby away from her with a softly growled, "Mine."

"She was mine first, Prez. Don't forget that." He grinned at her, kissing the side of Ruby's head.

"She's mine now, though. You can't have her back. She's my fuckbuddy now, mother of my kids. All three of them," he said, turning them to walk out as Ruby shot her a grin of acknowledgment. His voice rose then fell as he greeted his friends. "Mason, motherfucker, how the hell are ya? Didn't know you were in town, man. We gonna be treated to a repeat of the pussy, lovie-dovie shit between you and Gunny?"

DeeDee closed her eyes for a minute, standing in her new kitchen and holding a grandchild she never thought to see. Overwhelmed, filled with an emotion she couldn't name moving through her, bringing her close to tears as she listened to her huge, raunchy, loving, dangerous, protective...growing family. Pride, love, satisfaction, pleasure...while accurate, those weren't the right labels for everything she was feeling right now. Footsteps came rattling loudly down the stairs, and a mounting rumble of high-pitched children's voices swept through the house as Bingo's kids mixed with Bear's kids and with her and Jase's kid and ran into the backyard. Contentment. That was it. She was content.

***

Mason watched DeeDee throughout the day. He saw how quickly her wide smiles spread across her face, how the corners of her eyes stayed tilted up in pleasure, and he liked every bit of it. She had become a different woman with Jase in her life, more confident and open, and he was glad she found this for herself. Earlier in the afternoon, Jase had put on Ray Gelato's classic *Mambo Italiano* and danced with DeeDee, whirling and dipping her with panache and style, much to the amusement of everyone present.

He leaned against the back of the house, watching the pack of kids as they played in the yard. He made a note to thank Myron; the man had outdone himself with this house. He thought back to the scared, skinny kid he found in a shelter in Chicago years ago and shook his head. Who could have known that the boy, who amused himself by counting beans and buttons in jars, would turn into such a whiz kid for finances, with a serious knack for locating things?

His eyes fell on Bingo, released from the hospital that afternoon, parked for now in a recliner the brothers had carried outside so he could be comfortable and still be surrounded by his family at this celebration. Mason knew his eyes were hidden behind the sunglasses he wore, so he slowly swept his gaze from member to member, cataloging their experience and strengths, weaknesses and skills. This was what he did best, lining up his brothers and friends with things that needed doing, and identifying people who needed...something.

He saw Tug standing with Maggie, noting she still didn't have a rag. He frowned slightly, looking over at Shar and DeeDee; neither of them was wearing leather vests, either. He would talk to Jase. The man might not know the importance of the 'Property of' patch that the other women wore. He didn't think DeeDee would turn the man down, so that wouldn't be a factor. Gunny and Tug both knew what it meant, however. There was no reason for them to hold back if they were in these relationships for the long haul, and from the looks on their faces as they watched their women, he thought they were.

All his brothers were finding their one, their always. He wished Willa had shown tonight, but then he was also halfway glad she hadn't, because he needed to take care where she was concerned. He was not willing to get into another situation like he had been twisted up in with Mica, back in Chicago. He decided to never again love someone who could only accept half of him, who could only take part of who he was. He needed a woman who would be all-in with him, ready to love him in suits as well as leather, someone who could wrap their legs around his ass on a bike and their arms around his waist at a high-class function.

Shaking his head, he lifted his beer and took a long drink, scoffing at himself. The perfect woman just didn't fucking exist, and he goddamn well knew it. He looked around the backyard again, seeing Jase motioning from beside the grill. Walking over, he raised his chin, and Jase nodded. "First burger's for you, Prez. Thank you."

"Thank me for what, motherfucker?" Mason asked, bemused.

Jase shocked him by pulling him into a one-armed hug, hitting his back hard with a closed fist. "For giving me this life, man. Fucking honored."

Mason thumped his back twice, pulling back to grip his forearm. "Do me proud, brother. I've known for a long time that we would suit you. Now you just gotta find your place with us."

Jase nodded, handing him a plate, and Mason made his way over to a spot near Bingo, smiling his thanks at Sharon when she brought the man some food. It wasn't long before there was a gathering of his brothers around them, and the talk ranged from women to bikes and back again.

Smiling, Mason let the conversation flow around him, offering an occasional quip or insight that drew laughter. He looked up to see DeeDee watching him and he nodded at her, receiving a chin lift in response. He saw her draw in a deep breath, somehow not surprised when she raised her hands, cupping them around her mouth to call across the yard, "Slate. My son. Congrats on the new baby, man. I heard you had good swimmers. Guess the proof is in the pudding, yeah?"

The yard erupted in laughter and shouts of excitement as the women gathered around Ruby, who stood stock still with a look of shocked dismay on her face. Mason laughed, reaching out to thump Slate's shoulder with his fist, laughing harder as Slate rocked sideways, even though the blow wasn't hard. "Gratz, man. Another baby already? That's awesome, brother."

Slate grinned. "Yeah. Ruby wasn't too happy about it being so soon after the twins, but she's come around to the idea now. We'll find out in a few weeks what we're having. I told the woman she doesn't get to do any of the visits by herself this time, no fucking secrets." He scowled, still annoyed that she kept the fact of the twins from him for so long, but then his face lightened. "Maybe we'll have twins again." He leaned back with a broad smile, tucking his hands into the front pockets of his jeans.

Bear laughed and grinned, "Seems our kids will have built-in playmates, brother."

Mason stood for a second and then, deciding he'd sat on the information long enough, shouted, "Goddamn big families, you people ever do anything but fuck? Eddie? Tell me again. When are you due, darlin'?"

The women squealed again as Eddie yelled, "Mason, dammit, you weren't supposed to..."

***

Hoss walked over to where Jase stood and bumped knuckles with him. "You get it?" he asked, casually looking around to ensure DeeDee wasn't anywhere close.

"Yeah," the man said with a grin. "It looks good, too. I think I really understand for the first time, how much it matters."

"If you're serious, then it will always matter." Hoss clasped a hand on Jase's shoulder, shaking him gently back and forth. "Now you just gotta get your nerve up, but that's easy. You're a fucking biker, man. No worries."

"Yeah," he laughed a little. "No worries." There was silence between the two men for a minute, then Jase said, "I don't think I ever thanked you for everything. I know I was Slate's prospect, but it felt like I learned more from you than anyone. Love you, brother. From the bottom of, man."

"DeeDee's special to us, Cap'n, I had to make sure her old man was a good'un." Hoss grinned. "Couldn't have just any old hockey player taking our best gal, ya know?"

"Speaking of best gals, what's up with you and Mercy? I halfway expected you to bring her today." Jase elbowed him in the ribs. "Watch out for her shoes. They're registered as deadly weapons, eh?"

"Man, it ain't like that with me and Mercy. She just needs someone to unload on sometimes. She's a good woman, just had life deal her a shit hand, ya know?"

***

Standing in the kitchen, Mason leaned against the counter as he watched Jase and DeeDee put away the last of the clean dishes. He looked around. Nearly everyone was gone; there were just a few members sacked out on the floor and furniture, sleeping off a few too many beers before they hit the road to go home. The kids who lived in the house had all been sent off to bed hours ago. When Bear and Eddie left, he helped carry their sleeping little ones to the van, the exhausted boys not even waking as they were buckled and tucked into the vehicle.

He looked at the couple in front of him, noting again how comfortable they seemed with each other. "Y'all sure about this arrangement with Bingo?" He wanted to ask them this question while they were together. He had already had individual conversations with them, but liked seeing the two of them react as a duo so much he couldn't resist the question. It was a good lead-in to the conversation he wanted to have with his cousin, too.

"Yeah," Jase answered. "It's a good fit in a lot of ways, man. We can help him out, and be there for the kids."

DeeDee reached out a hand, stroking slowly down Jase's arm, threading her fingers through his and pulling his hand against her hip. "I already love the kids; this just makes it easier to love on them," she said with a smile, and Mason nodded.

"It's going to be hard," he warned them, watching as they looked at each other. "And you've just settled a new piece into your puzzle with Jonny."

Jase answered for them again, "We know. Bingo's prognosis is not the best. They found that second spot in the lower lobe, so he'll be back into surgery in a week or so, as long as he stays healthy enough. That means he'll have less lung capacity, probably have to go on oxygen, at least for a while. Even if this surgery is successful, he'll have radiation and chemo if he chooses to treat things. If he decides on the treatment, the doc said he could have ten...twelve years. If he doesn't, then it's less. We know, Mason. We're totally on board. And Jonny is already settled in here. He's doing a ton better in school, and he gets along with the tribe like they were raised together. He's bonded with every one of them. I think he needs them in his life. I know he needs us. But, the kids all need this, man." He looked at DeeDee. "I need this."

Mason looked at DeeDee too, taking in her too-bright eyes. "You okay with everything, darlin'? It's not too much to ask, just when you're finding yourself again?"

She frowned at him. "Finding myself again?"

"Yeah, after Winger died, we nearly lost you. Lost parts of you for a long time." He shrugged. "In the past year, you've come back to yourself. It feels like we have the old DeeDee back, but in a newer, improved model." He gestured to her body. "You aren't skin and bones anymore. I don't have to worry about breaking you when we hug. You smile and laugh like I haven't seen you do since we were kids, Dee. I can't tell you how great it is to see you like this. I just want to make sure taking on this for the club isn't too much."

She scoffed. "I wasn't that bad, Mason. And I'm not taking this on for the club. I'm doing it for my friend and my family. Bingo and I have been friends for a long time. He and Winger were tight...brothers, even before they were in the same club. I'm doing it for the kids...all of them...and for me. This isn't a burden, Mason. It's an honor."

"He and Winger were tight," he agreed, seeing the smile slip from her eyes. "Winger would be proud of you, babe."

"Thanks for that, Prez, but it doesn't matter so much what Winger would have thought," she said quickly, looping her arm around Jase's waist. "Jase's opinion is what I worry about. Jase and you."

"So Winger don't matter?" He narrowed his eyes. There was a dynamic here he didn't understand. He knew she had loved Winger, and she loved Jase now, but something was going on.

"Of course, Winger mattered," she said, lifting one shoulder in a shrug, putting the lie to her words. "He was my husband for a long time, my old man."

Yeah, I need to talk to Jase about getting her a rag, he thought, *because it's important to her*. "And Jase is...?"

"My old man," she said, leaning her head against Jase's shoulder as he looked down at her in wonder.

"Yeah?" Jase breathed the question, and Mason grinned, watching the man's hand go to the pocket of his jeans, fingers caressing a lump there like a talisman.

She lifted her head, rising onto her toes to press her lips against his. "Yeah."

***

Jase was breathless; with fear or anticipation, he wasn't quite certain which. She called him her old man, which meant in her mind, they were together in the way the club saw things...saw couples. God, he was glad Hoss had talked to him about this and he was prepared. He was ready.

He cut his gaze over to Mason, saw the man grinning at them like a loon.

"I'll be right back," he whispered, drawing away. He walked into the living room, going to the bag he had dropped in the coat closet earlier, and pulled out a box. Striding back to the kitchen, he held it out to DeeDee. "I was going to give this to you later, in private, baby, but I kinda like the spectator factor we have going on. I heard he's a fan, eh? Can't disappoint. Gotta put on a show." He waved his hand towards Mason. He had seen a couple of members' heads pop up when he walked into the living room and knew they would have a larger audience soon. He had to rush things if he was going to keep it to just the three of them.

Handing her the wrapped gift box, he waited for her to focus on it, knowing she would untie the bow first. Taking advantage of her distraction, he pulled the other box from his pocket, palming it and using his fingertips to open it while he leaned in and kissed her lips. "I love you, baby," he said, dropping to one knee as she opened the larger box.

"Be my old lady?" he asked, laughing as she lifted the leather from the box, letting the cardboard and paper fall to the floor. He loved the look of awe on her face as she took in the new patch on the back of her vest, the older pieces of fabric still in place, the grime of long-time association with the club an honor he would never take from her. What was new was the large rocker on the bottom, where he had replaced the old one. This one had his name on it, his club name, 'Captain', so the patches on the back of her vest read, from top to bottom, Rebel Wayfarers MC, Property of, Captain.

She was already saying, "Yes," when she looked down at him and gave a little scream as she saw the much smaller box balanced in his palm. "Be my wife?" he asked the second question and watched the tears overflowing onto her cheeks, holding his breath as he waited for her answer.

"Yes," she repeated, reaching down past his hand to draw her fingertips along his cheek, plucking at his lips with a smile. "I love you, Cap'n. Yes, to both."

Mason threw his head back and shouted, "Now that's the way you do it, motherfucker!" He began applauding and more hands joined in, the noise growing around them as the members jostled closer, hands reaching out to touch DeeDee even as Jase rose, pulling her in for a hard, demanding kiss. He knew the raucous well wishes would wake the kids, but didn't care. He wanted everyone to know that she finally had given him everything he ever wanted. All of her.

THE END (of this story)

THANK YOU FOR READING *JASE*!

This is Book #4 in a series. *Jase* is the result of a longtime love of hockey, and a rocking band's front man, combined with a burning desire to talk about the life of a professional athlete and how they enjoy giving back to the sport and communities they love. They embody the idea of paying it forward, because they willingly teach and train the next generations every chance they get. Along the way we had characters who tried to take over the story, which means we now have more books in our joint future. You can learn more about Mason, Gunny, and Sharon's stories in Book #5 of the Rebel Wayfarers MC book series, *Gunny*, available now.

JASE'S PLAYLIST

I put together YouTube playlists of music both mentioned in the book, and used during writing and editing. Want a peek into the mind of me? Be sure of your decision, it's not always normal here! Jase's playlist: bit.ly/jase-playlist

ABOUT THE AUTHOR

Raised in the south, MariaLisa learned about the magic of books at an early age. Every summer, she would spend hours in the local library, devouring books of every genre. Self-described as a book-a-holic, she says "I've always loved to read, but then I discovered writing, and found I adored that, too. For reading...if nothing else is available, I've been known to read the back of the cereal box."

Also by MariaLisa deMora

Alace Sweets

A dark thriller, this book is not a light read. Filled with edge-of-your-seat suspense, this intense story commands the reader's attention as it drives towards the explosive ending. Alace Sweets is a vigilante serial killer, with everything that implies and is sure to trip all your triggers. Be ready.

At seventeen, Alace Sweets turned a corner in her life, taking the wrong shortcut home from school.

Resisting the harsh knowledge her attackers will never be made to pay for their actions, Alace takes a stand. Justice must be served, and if fate's scales are out of balance, she's determined to set things right as best she can.

When the laws of men fail, the rules of Alace prevail.

5-Star Reviews for Alace Sweets

"deMora has a superb story-line and exceptional character development. All of her characters have such depth that will intrigue the reader..."
~Turning Another Page

"Hot, sweet, dark thriller."
~Beth D

"It will keep you on the edge of your seat and give you chills."
~Escape Reality Book Blog

"Disturbing, haunting, sickly; yet hot, sexy and heart racing!"
~Amanda L

“From the first page [deMora] pulls you into the world she has created and you do not even try to escape...”
~Little Shop of Readers Blog

“A must read for all those dark, gritty romance fans out there.”
~Sweet & Spicy Reads

“You will find yourself so drawn into the story that the outside world is blocked out and your locking the doors and turning on all the lights.”
~Danena F

“Don't judge me for bonding with a vigilante serial killer, she's more than what she does.”
~iScream Books

“Thrilling...chilling...full of suspense, nail biting edge of your seat excitement.”
~Tracey H

“Every time MariaLisa deMora picks up her pen (or opens her computer), she creates characters you want to believe in.”
~Gail S

“Intriguing dark storyline, beautiful love story and nail-biting conclusion, what more could a reader ask for?”
~Manda M

“This book takes you a dark and twisted ride that is gripping...”
~Renee Entress' Blog

“This book is dark and gritty and I literally had to take a day off from reading it because it's that intense.”
~My Girlfriend's Couch

“This is my favourite book so far from this author ... I recommend this book if you enjoy dark romantic thrillers.”
~Cheekypee Reads and Reviews

“There's not enough stars to give this book and 5 just doesn't really do it justice!”
~DeLane C

“I couldn't put this book down from page one! Tried to stop & go to bed but couldn't sleep thinking about Alace and got up & finished the book.”
~Debbie M

“MariaLisa DeMora, wordsmith that she is, made this a story of the enlightenment of a woman and finding love in a life where she has had none.”
~Kat W

“Whatever deep dark trench [deMora] pulled a character like Alace from should be revisited again and often.”
~Confessions of a Serial Reader

ADDITIONAL SERIES AND BOOKS

Please note that books in a series frequently feature characters from additional books within that series. If series books are read out of order, readers will twig to spoilers for the other books, so going back to read the skipped titles won’t have the same angsty reveals.

Rebel Wayfarers MC series:

Mica, #1
A Sweet & Merry Christmas, short story #1.5
Slate, #2
Bear, #3
Jase, #4
Gunny, #5
Mason, #6
Hoss, #7
Harddrive Holidays, short story #7.5
Duck, #8
Biker Chick Campout, short story #8.5
Watcher, #9

A Kiss to Keep You, novella #9.25
Gun Totin' Annie, short story #9.5
Secret Santa, short story #9.75
Bones, #10
Gunny's Pups, novella #10.25
Never Settle, short story #10.5
Not Even A Mouse, short story #10.75
Fury, #11
Christmas Doings, #11.25
Gypsy's Lady, #11.5
Cassie, #12
Road Runner's Ride, novella #12.5

Occupy Yourself band series:

Born Into Trouble, #1
Grace In Motion, #2 (TBD)
What They Say, #3 (TBD)

Neither This, Nor That series:

This Is the Route Of Twisted Pain, #1
Treading the Traitor's Path: Out Bad, #2
Trapped by Fate on Reckless Roads, #3 (TBD)

Other Books:

With My Whole Heart
Alace Sweets
Hard Focus

More information available at mldemora.com.